The Handler

www.davidtcady.com

The Handler

A Novel

To Rachael Best wishes David Cady

David Cady

Book Surge
2008

A Kindle Book

The Handler

ACKNOWLEDGEMENTS

I am indebted to a number of individuals who helped *The Handler* be more readable than it might otherwise have been. Hoyle Hyberger read every rewrite, and I lost count of them at twelve. My dear friend Bette Chesser read this three times and gave me wonderful and useful suggestions. Bette is also my greatest cheerleader. My colleague, Mary Anne Fogle, helped me finalize *The Handler* and is one great editor. Sye Williams designed the cover. Adolph Moranes, a great artist, drew the picture used on the cover.

AUTHOR'S NOTE

In writing the following pages, I understood that much of what I wrote would be unbelievable for the reader. Few understand how cruel and demented some spiritual cults can and did become. While researching the more famous religious groups, and long before I wrote one line of this story, I was staggered by the brutality encountered in the name of God. What leads people to follow these religious fanatics, and why do some of these leaders become so evil that they rape, mutilate, and destroy their followers? No one may ever understand this behavior, but I have tried to give some reason to their happenings. Even though this fictional story with its fictional characters may seem beyond belief at times, I assure you that in reality, it is worse, much, much worse.

To my wife Cindy, who put up with my mental and physical absences while writing and rewriting this book and her encouragement to get it published.

CHAPTER ONE

To keep from crying, Sarah Brindle concentrated on her breathing. Sarah knew better than to cry. If she cried, Emmanuel would punish her, especially now that he had found another for his bed.

Trapped. That word explained it all. Trapped in hell. A hell called "The Refuge of God." Did the other three hundred know they were trapped? She doubted it.

Outside the windowless wooden structure, Sarah heard thunder rumbling—a sign of the first spring storm that would open petals of new flowers and add color to these dark woods. For a moment Sarah smelled the rain through the stench of humans who had been in the hot building too long. On second thought, maybe she smelled fear that now spread across the room as the multitude waited on their self-proclaimed God to identify all the sinners. Emmanuel, their God and leader called it penance, but it was punishment—his penalty for transgressions. Sarah prayed he didn't bring the snakes out—not the snakes—not tonight.

Sarah looked at her hands, hands only twenty-nine-years-old, but they trembled like an old woman's. She could think of nothing that she had done to displease their savior. But that didn't matter, because if Emmanuel or one of his chosen disciples wanted to torment a member, they would. All they had to do was accuse someone of breaking one of Emmanuel's rules and the penitence from sin began.

Her back ached. She twisted her shoulders. Sarah had been sitting in the same position for almost three hours. Fluorescent light that spilled from the ceiling hurt her eyes. Without moving her head, Sarah glanced to her left at her husband, Chuck, who sat with the other men across the middle aisle that transected the packed sanctuary. It had been almost three months since Chuck's penitence. If they punished him again tonight his frail body wouldn't take it.

They had beaten Chuck with a piece of rubber hose until he'd passed out. He stayed bedridden for several weeks before he was able to walk. Because of damage to his neck, his head now tilted at almost 45 degrees to the left.

Only a week ago Sarah had sent Chuck a message asking to talk to him, but because the men and women lived in separate quarters, it took five nights before they could meet. After making Sarah wait for over an hour at the edge of the forest behind the women's dorm, he crept from behind a tree. She reached out to touch Chuck, but he backed away like she had leprosy. Because he couldn't move

I

his neck, he turned his body almost completely around looking in all directions to see if anyone saw them.

Finally, when he faced her, Sarah looked into his eyes and said with a quivering voice, "I can't live like this any more. We've got to get away. I want to see my mother." Tears filled her eyes.

Chuck shrunk back. "It's too late."

"Why?"

"He'd get mad. You know how he is when he gets mad."

"When can we?"

"Never. We can't." His voice drifted away. She could hardly hear him.

"Chuck, I'm going to run away. If you want to come with me, you can."

"Sarah," Chuck's eyes widened. "What if somebody hears you?" He turned his body again to look in all directions. "We shouldn't be here. I shouldn't be here. I'm going to act like I never heard this."

"But you heard me. You're part of it now."

"No. You tricked me." He backed away.

She reached for him. "Wait, Chuck." But he slid into the darkness.

She heard his last words. "You're going to hell, Sarah Brindle."

Now she sat in hell, Emmanuel's hell.

A sudden clap of thunder brought Sarah from her daydreams. She turned her gaze upon the pulpit to see her eighteen-month-old son, Tommy, asleep on Emmanuel's lap. The child's hair looked like cotton. It dropped in curls over his forehead. Tommy's ice-blue eyes remained hidden, but she knew they were there. He had blond hair like her, but her eyes were hazel, Chuck's brown, Emmanuel's were blue. Maybe that's why the preacher believed Tommy belonged to him.

Unlike the boy, Emmanuel had black hair—too black to be its true color. Emmanuel's hair appeared too big for his head, the way it puffed up and out over his forehead and swept back on the top and down both sides to meet in the back where it stuck out several inches over his collar.

If her son, Tommy, belonged to Emmanuel, it was Chuck's fault. He made her sleep with Emmanuel. He forced her to after Emmanuel selected her.

As soon as their group had moved from Georgia to this refuge, Emmanuel started picking young men and women from among them for his special "baptism of sex." Sarah wondered what he did with the men. She knew what he did to the women.

Sarah's mind drifted back to that night over two years ago when Emmanuel, who was crazed after handling several copperheads, had ended his sermon by telling them about the evils of sex.

"Sex is not that important to me," Emmanuel, body dripping sweat, had said in a whisper much like a breeze thrashing through fallen leaves. "I don't need it like other men...For one thing...All women are unworthy of me. I must close

2

my mind to sex and open the doors to God. My wife wants sex, needs sex, but we don't have it anymore. Some of you need sex, but…I know what you want…Men, you want me to sleep with your wives. Women you want me to sleep with you." He paused and stared at the crowd for almost a minute. No one moved. They knew better.

"God gave me something special," he said very quietly. Then he grew louder and more eager to explain himself. "I can satisfy any woman. God gave me something special—you women that have been with me know what I'm talking about—I know what you want…Yes, yes, yes, and the ecstasy continues all night. I know you God-fearing-women want to bed with me and not with your husbands. Yes! And that's only right, for I am the Chosen One. Part of my mission is to bring satisfaction to you…God has ordained it."

He paused and sucked in a deep breath. After several seconds, he thrust his hand up and pointed toward the ceiling. When everyone glanced up he said, "I talked to God last night. He told me I must pick one of my worthy subjects and glorify Him by having carnal knowledge with her."

Emmanuel stopped and lowered his finger so it pointed into the crowd. In a low voice he said, "Romantic love with another is selfishness, and that keeps Emmanuel from being first in your hearts. I know all women want me, but I must pick only the deserving one to bed with me."

Sarah was horrified that Emmanuel's finger pointed directly at her.

Later that night her fears surfaced when Irene Master, the queen of Emmanuel's harem, came to Sarah and informed her that God had chosen her to sleep with Emmanuel. Nobody argued with Irene for she stood almost six feet tall and weighed over two-hundred-and-fifty pounds. She had breasts like over-ripe melons that dropped to her waist. She had short, straight, brown hair outlining a moon-shaped face. Irene's three chins of fat hid her neck.

Sarah loathed going to Emmanuel's bed. She had refused to go in the beginning, but they brought Chuck in to persuade Sarah that it was her duty and privilege to bed with Emmanuel.

After a barrage of persecution from Emmanuel's chosen disciples Sarah had no other choice. Chuck took her to Emmanuel's apartment in the compound. There, Irene helped Sarah remove her clothing, and then she made Sarah look at herself in a full-length mirror.

"You are almost perfect," Irene said with a frown on her face. "You're not fat or skinny. You have beautiful breasts that have not yet fallen. Your blond hair and fair skin is proof of good white blood running through your veins. Emmanuel will appreciate you."

Sarah quivered when Irene ran a finger down the middle of her bare back. Irene laughed. Sarah started trembling like a frightened child.

Irene squeezed Sarah's arm and led her into Emmanuel's room. After Irene released her grasp and tiptoed out, Sarah's arm continued to ache. It took Sarah's eyes several seconds to adjust to the lack of light, but when she did there sprawled Emmanuel under a sheet in a king-size bed with those ice-blue eyes peeking out at her. Trying to cover her breasts and womanhood with her hands while he inspected her proved futile. She saw his erection lift the cover, and so she closed her eyes. In silence, Sarah stood shivering for several minutes waiting for his lechery to end.

At last, he said so low she could hardly hear, "Child, get in this bed."

She didn't move.

"I said get in this bed," he shouted.

She touched the sheets and he grabbed her by the wrist. She tried to pull away, but he yanked her so hard that she fell across his chest. He laughed and threw back the sheet. She rolled off of him, but Emmanuel still held her wrist. Her hand grew numb.

Trapped, she lay motionless. He released her arm. She didn't move. Sarah closed her eyes and listened to him breathe while he jerked about next to her. He turned to her and placed a cold hand on her breast. She stiffened. He began to rub her chest as if he were petting a cat. Without warning, pain exploded in her breast when he pinched her nipple. His breaths came in quicker bursts. His hand slid down across her navel to her crotch. There, his fingers intertwined with her pubic hair. She squeezed her legs together and stiffened. He pushed and prodded there but couldn't open her legs. Finally, he forced his fist between her thighs, and the pain caused her to open her legs. His hand cupped her genitals, and she couldn't close her legs. He tried to force a finger inside her.

Emmanuel, grunting like a boar, rose until he knelt over her. He took both of his hands and forced Sarah's legs farther apart and then pulled her forward until his hips rested between her spread thighs. He took his right hand and grabbed his stiffness. His breathing came in short bursts like a runner at the end of a race. Still holding her left leg with his right hand, he jerked her closer. She felt him jab at her with his manhood.

When he entered her, Sarah made a quick *oh*-sound deep in her chest like an injured child. Her initial dryness, not the size of his organ, created her pain. Emmanuel felt no different inside her than her husband. Emmanuel, with all his weight on top of her now, thrust his hips slowly at first, but in only seconds he grabbed the bed beside her shoulders and started shoving harder and faster inside Sarah like he wanted to drive her through the mattress.

"Oh, Mother of God," Emmanuel said. "Jesus Christ."

His body grew rigid. Then he quivered for a few seconds while moaning like a bull. Next, as if being clubbed in the head, Emmanuel went limp. His dead-weight crushed Sarah and she could hardly get a breath.

4

The sex was brutal and humiliating and continued for two weeks. Sarah and Emmanuel never spoke to one another, and she went back to her dorm immediately after he finished. There she washed herself over and over while she cried.

All during this time Chuck never asked Sarah about the 'baptism' she continued to receive from Emmanuel. Finally, one night Irene failed to come for her. It stopped as quickly as it had started. Her son Tommy came thirty-eight weeks later. Because he came early, Sarah thought Tommy may belong to Chuck. She prayed she had been pregnant before going to bed with Emmanuel. Nonetheless, she knew that Chuck, Emmanuel, and everyone in their assembly thought Tommy belonged to their leader. Chuck had avoided Sarah since her encounter with Emmanuel, and that was okay with her. She had no desire for him or his lovemaking anymore. It would be fine with her to never have sex again.

A sharp bolt of lightning struck something outside the sanctuary and the lights inside blinked off and then on. The people stirred in their hard seats. Sarah watched Tommy asleep in Emmanuel's lap and thought of ways she and her son could escape. She tried to understand why Chuck refused to leave with them. Sarah had thought of suicide, but then there was Tommy.

A few of Emmanuel's followers had already come forth to call up three members for breaking various rules. The accused, one young boy, and two women stood on the platform next to Emmanuel waiting for their castigation for sinning. Other than the accused boy, they had taken all the other children out of the sanctuary to wait in the cafeteria.

Out of the corner of her eye, Sarah saw someone moving from the audience toward the stage. When she recognized the man, her heart ceased beating. There, stealing up the three steps leading to the platform was Chuck. She had failed to hear anyone call his name. Thinking about what her husband might say to the crowd made Sarah quiver.

Chuck stopped in front of Emmanuel and bowed his head in reverence. Looking like a king on a throne, Emmanuel nodded his own head in approval and continued stroking the child's hair. Chuck turned to face the gathering. His balding and tilted head, covered with beads of sweat, glistened in the lights. Sarah's heart now raced.

When Chuck began to talk, his voice cracked. He stared at the floor in front of his feet. "I'm so sorry to have to report something to all of you."

Sarah's breath caught in her chest, and her vision blurred as moisture formed in her eyes. She fought against crying but failed. Salt-filled tears burned her cheeks while making their own course down her face to a quivering chin. She choked on dread, and it felt like someone was trying to pull a cloth from her throat. Breath only came in small gulps.

"Almost three years ago," said Chuck. He stared at the floor. "Several years ago my wife and I came to join you…We came to teach your children. We tell them to love Emmanuel above all else...We have tried to live like Emmanuel wants us to live...But..." Chuck moved his eyes up, looked at Sarah for a brief second, then, dropped his gaze again.

Tears rolled down her cheeks. She tasted the tears in her throat. Reaching inside her white blouse pocket, Sarah removed a paper Kleenex and wiped her nose.

Chuck said very quickly, "My wife came to me this week...She came two nights ago wanting to...She came to me wanting to..." He looked up.

Sarah's blood fell into her stomach. She tasted the bile.

Chuck said, "She wanted to flee."

"She what?" said Emmanuel, springing to his feet and moving next to Chuck. Tommy awoke, and one of Emmanuel's women took him out of his arms.

"Escape, run away," said Chuck. For a fleeting moment, Sarah saw the selfishness in her husband's face.

Sarah watched the woman take her son through a door near the back of the pulpit. She wanted to run after them. New tears ran down Sarah's throat almost choking her. She sensed someone moving beside her. Irene grabbed Sarah's arm and yanked her up. Pain shot through Sarah's shoulder, but she hardly noticed. Irene pushed her toward the platform where her persecutor, Chuck, stood staring at the floor.

Emmanuel, with a frown covering his face, shook his head. "Sarah, tell me this isn't so, It wounds me to think you, of all people, would want to leave me. I've let you teach our children. I've loved you for so long. You are my favorite one. You had my child." He turned his back on her.

Sarah moved next to the other three charged members. Facing the crowd, she lowered her eyes and stared at her own toes sticking out of brown sandals. She heard Chuck's footsteps as he lumbered to his seat. He had done his job for their leader.

"You know," said Emmanuel over the microphone. "This hurts me much more than it will them. When my people turn against me, they turn against God. And God can't allow this."

He faced the accused boy next to Sarah and said in a soft voice, "Paul, you've been skipping classes at school, and you won't listen to your teacher, Mr. Brindle, when he talks about me...about God. You have been asking too many questions. You should know better than that. Give Paul twenty licks with the board-of-education. That should help him remember to go to God's school and not question that my love for him stands above all."

Irene grabbed the eleven-year-old by the hands and pulled him forward. Before the boy could react, Irene jerked his jeans and jockey-shorts down exposing his bare bottom for all to see.

Sarah closed her eyes and started praying.

Irene placed her hand on the back of Paul's neck and pushed his upper torso forward making it parallel to the floor. The boy bent his knees and kept his backside pointed at the floor. Irene reached between the boy's legs and grabbed his testicles. He screamed. When she squeezed, he tried to pull away from the pain by standing on his toes.

"Don't move," said Irene. "Or I'll pull them little nuts off." After a few seconds, she released her grip and the boy remained motionless.

Luke Belcher, rumored to be Emmanuel's half-brother, moved forward. Sarah had always questioned if the gossip about them being siblings was true because the two men didn't look at all alike. Luke had brown eyes, Emmanuel had blue. Luke stood about five-seven and had broad shoulders and girth, while Emmanuel reached over six feet with narrow, sloping shoulders. Luke's face featured a short, blunt nose and a square chin, while Emmanuel's nose and chin were slender. Both men weighed about one-hundred-and-sixty pounds. Each one appeared to be in his mid-to-late-forties.

Luke held a three-foot paddle containing numerous dime-size holes over his right shoulder. He reminded Sarah of a baseball batter walking to the plate. She could tell he enjoyed taking his time and making the boy wait. Luke drew back. With the speed of a striking snake, he brought the board down across the boy's bottom with a smack. Paul screamed and tumbled forward over a group of folding chairs. He came up shrieking and jumped up and down. He rubbed his red buttocks with both hands and shuddered while moving from one foot to the other. Irene yanked him back into place and held him up as Luke commenced beating the boy. Each swat echoed through the hall. Irene held her hand over the boy's mouth trying to muffle his cries.

After twenty licks, Irene released Paul. His legs trembled like a newly born calf's for a moment before he pitched forward and back into Irene's grasp. His bottom had turned to ox-blood red. Irene shoved the weeping child toward his mother, Claudine, who led him through the back door.

Looking distraught, Emmanuel moved to the speaker's stand. "God be with that child that he might learn from his sins."

"Amen," said Luke.

"Amen," said Irene.

Emmanuel turned to stare at the three women charged with crimes against God. "See Julia and Crystal here? I allowed them the opportunity to work in town, and how did they repay me? I'll tell you how. They were seen riding around in a car with strange men smoking cigarettes and drinking beer." The crowd gasped. "Yes, they were. You know I love them so much, but that kind of behavior leads to whoring and sex and…and…and…you know…and, other things."

Tears formed in Emmanuel's eyes. He shook his head. "This devastates me to punish my people. What do you think we need to do?"

From the front row sixty-five-year-old Justin Martin stomped his foot. "Give'em the iron."

Bill Hubbard leaped to his feet. "Yes!"

"The iron," yelled several others in the crowd at the same time.

"No. No. Please, God, no." said Julia Perkins, the girl at Sarah's side. Julia was a petite woman of no more than twenty with fair skin and long blond hair tied into a pony's-tail. She had grown up in this church, since her parents had brought her here at an early age. Rumors circulated that Emmanuel had groomed her for himself. Now, with head in hands, Julia wept.

The other accused woman, Crystal Nelson, waited next to Julia. Crystal, an Afro-American woman in her early thirties, remained transfixed, staring over everyone's head at the back wall. Crystal had an athletic body. Standing at about five-eleven, she appeared slim with long legs and narrow hips. Sarah knew that behind Crystal's mahogany skin stood a proud woman.

No one moved as Luke Belcher exited the rear. Irene whispered something into each woman's ear. Julia only stared at Irene in astonishment, but Crystal reached under her denim skirt and jerked off her panties. Irene grabbed Julia's arm and snarled something else in her ear. In definite pain from Irene squeezing her arm, Julia unfastened her Levis. They dropped to the floor around her ankles, and she stood there facing the crowd only wearing her pink blouse and white cotton bikini briefs. Slowly, one leg at a time, she stepped out of the jeans.

When Luke entered the back door holding a smoldering branding iron aloft the crowd screamed "yes" as if on cue. The iron gave off its own red blaze as a trickle of smoke curled toward the ceiling. A coiled snake with a chicken's head glowed at the end of the metal. Once branded, Julia and Crystal would carry the sign of the cockatrice on their bodies for life.

Julia's wailing intensified until Irene smacked her across the face with an open palm and screamed, "Shut up."

Trying to quiet herself, Julia sobbed into her own fingers that she kept clamped across her mouth.

Crystal remained motionless. Her eyes stared straight ahead.

Luke turned toward Irene and said, "Crystal first, bend her over."

Irene hesitated in touching Crystal. She approached the woman with caution, as would a person moving toward a lion they feared.

However, Irene never had to touch Crystal for the black woman turned her back to the people and stooped forward. She pulled her dress to her waist without uttering a word. Nothing of her womanhood remained hidden from the hundreds of members that wanted to see. Irene motioned Luke to proceed with Crystal's punishment.

He brought the glowing branding iron down to Crystal's turned-up buttocks and held it there, only inches away, for a few seconds. Slowly, like a man that loved his work, he inched the branding iron toward the woman's flesh.

The sizzling made Sarah flinch.

A groan of agony came from Crystal the moment Luke touched the iron to her body. Crystal's hips shot forward, and she staggered into a group of empty chairs. Wincing in pain, she slapped at the back of a chair and knocked it over with a crash.

Sarah smelled the stench of burning skin.

Smoke collected at the ceiling.

Crystal staggered toward the back door. Irene placed a hand on Crystal's shoulder to hurry her on, but the woman shrugged from Irene's grip and strode out the door on her own with her head and back held straight.

A buzzing of whispers ran through the crowd when Luke hurried out to re-heat the branding iron. Emmanuel wept like a grief-stricken parent.

In only a few minute, Luke reentered the second time holding the glowing iron over his head. Julia tried to jerk free of Irene's grasp, but Irene held her tightly as Myra, another member of the elite group, came forward to help.

Unlike Irene, Myra was a short, skinny woman, but she looked as fiery. Once Sarah had told Chuck that Myra looked as mean as one of the Devil's disciples with her long, wavy red hair and hawk-billed nose. Like Irene, Myra was in her late fifties.

Irene and Myra wrestled with Julia until they had her lying on her side, curled-up into a fetal position on the floor. Irene sat on Julia's shoulders and head while Myra pinned down the girl's legs.

"Pull her panties down," said Luke, now standing over Julia and inching the weapon of torture closer. He stopped about a foot from her rear.

"We can't turn her loose," said Irene. "You pull 'em down."

Luke grabbed Julia's briefs and jerked. The cloth ripped, and he came up holding a piece of it in his free hand. The girl wrenched one leg free and inadvertently kicked Luke in the leg. He grunted and stepped back, waiting for Myra to secure Julia's free leg.

"Hold her," said Luke. He plunged the serpent of fire toward the victim's milky-white flesh.

Sarah turned away just before it touched the girl, but she heard the blistering of fire cooking meat a moment before the girl squealed out in agony. Julia's outcry reverberated off the walls and soaked into Sarah's bosom.

Still moaning in pain and nude from the waist down, Julia crawled across the floor and through the back door. The smoldering cockatrice on her buttocks beat with its own heart.

Emmanuel moved to face the crowd. He had to wait only a few seconds before the excited group grew quiet. Sarah's throat tightened in trepidation making it impossible for her to swallow.

Shaking his head, Emmanuel said, "Sarah Brindle, the teacher of your daughters, was once chosen by God to be the mother of my child. This was a great honor for any woman, for I chose her among all you beautiful women. Yes." He paused and turned to face Sarah. She tried to stop the hate from pouring through her eyes but failed. For a moment, Sarah thought she saw a frightened look cross Emmanuel's face. He had tears in his eyes.

Emmanuel turned back to face his people. "Now, she wants to leave us. She asked her husband to run away with her, but he saw Satan in her and came to me in time. Yes, this is not the Sarah that birthed the child of God. I know this, but I don't know what to do. You will. I will let you decide." He stepped back and flopped down in his chair.

The murmur spread through the crowd but no one came forward. Sarah's heart thumped an extra beat when Irene waddled to the microphone. Irene cleared her throat. "Sarah is full of the Devil and we must get Lucifer out of her before he destroys the children…and us all…We can't rid her of the Devil by using the iron or the paddle. No! No! No! We must use the rubber hose to dislodge the Monarch of Hell from this poor creature."

Sarah went numb. She had witnessed Chuck's beating with a piece of water hose, and it almost killed him. She knew she could die from this torture. Closing her eyes, she could still hear the dull thud made by the length of rubber squashing Chuck's flesh.

"Yes!" said Justin Martin. "Amen, praise the Lord!"

Bill Hubbard leapt to his feet. "Do it!"

The congregation grew louder until the murmur grew into an uproar of arguing voices.

"Don't do it," said a group of women sitting together near the front. Most of the people sat stunned.

"We must," said Irene. She turned on Sarah whose head stayed bowed.

With uncommon speed for such a big woman, Irene tore Sarah's white blouse from her back. Myra tugged at Sarah's skirt freeing it from a trembling body. In a matter of seconds Sarah stood before the crowd wearing only her white bra and nylon panties. Losing all strength, Sarah's legs gave way, and she fell to her knees. Irene snatched Sarah back to her feet.

Sarah sensed her body moving forward as Irene and Myra held her up by her arms. Sarah felt already dead. She felt helpless. At the edge of the platform, facing the congregation, the two women released Sarah. Her knees slammed into the wood floor as she slumped forward onto her hands. Her head hung forward and down between her shoulders, causing the tips of her blond hair to touch the planking.

Pain shot through her scalp when someone grabbed her hair and jerked her head upright. Tears of agony blurred Sarah's vision. A ripping sound startled

Sarah as she realized they were tearing her hair from its roots. Sarah tried to ease the suffering by getting back onto legs too weak to hold her off the floor.

She reached back for the person pulling her hair when Irene and Myra grabbed her wrist and pulled her arms in a horizontal position out by her side. Luke released her hair, and Sarah fell back on knees full of pain. Perspiration dripped down her forehead and ran off the end of her nose. The people sat in silence, listening to the moans of Sarah as they mixed with the grunts of her attackers.

With her arms outspread by the women, Sarah thought of Jesus' suffering at his crucifixion. Peacefulness surged through her body and the pain left. Silently, she prayed to die quickly. She held her head erect and tried to see the people before her, but her vision was blurred from all of her tears. In vain, she tried to shake the tangled hair out of her face.

Someone moved before Sarah casting a shadow over her eyes. She recognized a man's odor. She recognized the scent.

Someone's fingers pushed her sweat-soaked hair back. Only inches from Sarah's nose appeared Emmanuel's ice-blue eyes.

He said in a whisper, "Sarah, Sarah, what have you done? You've disappointed me so much, lately." Gently, with one finger he wiped the sweat off her nose then licked it from his finger. "I loved you so much, this hurts me. I'm gonna make a deal with you. I'm not gonna let them use the hose. That would probably kill you. Anyway, if it didn't kill you, you wouldn't be very attractive any more once the wounds turned into scars." He whimpered a cry of distress that only the three women could hear.

Irene squeezed Sarah's arms until they throbbed.

Emmanuel continued to talk in a whisper. "Here's the deal. You come live with me and my women for awhile—say—a month or two. Chuck's not much of a man, anyway, you know that. Besides, I'd forgotten how lovely you are, Sarah...And Tommy needs a brother...Yes, that's what we'll do."

Irene and Myra wrenched Sarah's arms and the suffering intensified.

Emmanuel slid his mouth next to Sarah's ear. His cheeks felt like sandpaper against her face. "Sarah, you are the best, you know. I wish this wasn't about to happen, but I can't stop it now. My people have demanded it. Maybe it won't be that bad or leave scars. I'll pray for you."

He stood before her and her sight fell on his erection that jumped under his pants. She wanted to lunge forward and rip off his obnoxious manhood.

"Use the leather strap," Emmanuel said, just before someone tore off Sarah's bra.

Emmanuel moved out of her sight. With eyes filled with tears, Sarah saw Chuck staring up at her. He cried. Confused, Sarah's hate subsided.

The first blow, landing mid way up her back, took Sarah's breath away. The stinging sensation blazed across her shoulders. A shriek came from deep in her lungs when the breath came back. She began to quiver with the agony. The women stretched her arms wider, still. Sarah rolled her head back trying to relieve the pain.

The next blow wrapped around her chest and fire exploded from her right breast where the end of the strap landed. Her head flew forward. Sarah wanted to lick away the pain like an injured dog, but the two women held her arms tightly keeping her from reaching the pain that burned into her ribs. Instead, Sarah blew on the whelp that now blistered across her bosom.

The third impact struck Sarah across the hips with such a force that she lunged forward while pulling her buttocks in and pushing her pelvis outward. A moan that sounded more animal than human replaced her screams. Sarah no longer controlled her muscles that quivered unchecked. She couldn't get air to enter her lungs, but she tried. Irene and Myra jerked her arms wider, causing Sarah's head to slump forward.

When the fourth blow struck the back of her neck, everything went dark. A roar raced in Sarah's ears. Bright lights twinkled in a field of black. She saw lightning bugs dancing as on a summer's night. It turned twilight. Then everything started spinning. She tried to open her eyes but failed. She had lost all direction. A dull ache crept up the back of her neck and settled within her brain. The twinkling lights spun and spun. She heard someone weeping. It sounded like a child in trouble. *O! God! It's me*. Circling faster and faster, she fell through a tunnel. A new pain shot across her side and chest. Air rushed from her lungs. *God! Help me*. A cloak of blackness enveloped Sarah.

Tennessee River

SIX MONTHS LATER

Chapter Two

Matt noticed how she walked along the marina's wharf, and the way she carried herself like royalty, a long time before he realized she wanted his services. *The Dance*, a ballad by Garth Brooks spilled out of a portable CD player onto the dock's planking beside him making Matt feel great for a man speeding past fifty.

He had taken this mild November afternoon off to work on his boat, a boat that had turned into his home since the divorce. Matt had awakened early, changed into a pair of *Wrangler* jeans, and slipped into a pair of *Tony Lama* cowboy boots that were almond, ostrich quill, and old. He loved the way they wore. At one time it bothered Matt that the boots made him look two inches taller than his normal six-one, but that was back then when a lot of things bothered him.

When he looked up at the deep blue sky and felt the wind brushing across his face, Matt felt so good about himself. In fact, Matt felt so right with the world that he had forgotten about his old friend the pain—a pain that kept reminding him of his companion, the scar—a scar no wider than a pencil. It meandered out of his hair, down the right side of the forehead, through the eyebrow, and across his right eye. Midway down his cheek it made a ninety-degree turn before traveling to a spot just below the right earlobe. Long healed on the outside, the pain and the wound had lingered with Matt for over thirty years.

Unexpectedly, a wave of pride swept through his body, which made Matt pull his shoulders back and stand a little taller. Few men could recover from the dreadful things that had happened to this unlucky bastard, or was he a lucky bastard. Matt guessed he was a bastard, because he never knew a mother or a father. He only knew the old man who raised him, an old man who always reminded Matt that they were not related, that Matt wasn't related to anyone.

And, Matt felt special this moment because he knew that few men his age could turn their life around after loosing everything. It had taken him awhile to come back, but mentally and physically Matt felt better now than he did when he was in his twenties. Of course, back then no one was allowed to feel too good about himself after returning from the ass end of the world, Vietnam.

With a head swelling too big with pride, Matt continued watching the ash-blond move toward his end of the Brown's Ferry Marina, home for fifty-six houseboats, cabin cruisers, and one or two yachts.

Matt took great pleasure in looking at beautiful women, even if thirteen years ago he stopped trusting them. He'd decided then to never get married again. He didn't want anyone to misunderstand, he went out with women, but, so far, he'd avoided becoming romantically involved with anyone since she had left him. His friends, the few he had, said he was paranoid about getting involved with any female. Matt figured they were right.

From a distance, Matt thought the woman approaching might be in her late twenties or early thirties, but as the span between them diminished he noticed she was nearer his age, or possibly even older. Age, like a bad attitude, is hard to conceal for long.

Young or middle-aged, she appeared stunning in her royal blue, wool blazer that draped over a black, mock-neck sweater. Her black-and-white, hounds-tooth, wool skirt swayed at mid-knee—a fine looking knee. Matt's gaze moved down to her black stockings and black, medium-heeled shoes as she placed one foot ahead of the other like a model in a fashion show. A black purse on a long, narrow strap swung over her right shoulder. She realized she looked good; he could tell that by the way she carried herself.

As she drew closer, Matt saw that she wore small gold earrings and a gold watch that dangled at the end of her narrow wrist. He looked for a wedding band—not there.

Matt continued gawking as she pranced like a Tennessee walking horse over the wooden planking—heels making that same clicking sound like a thorough-bred. He observed, with something close to lust, her slender nose framed by an oval face, and her strong but elegant jaw.

The second their eyes met Matt did something all southern gentlemen do when being approached by any woman: he smiled. She failed to return it. His prideful mood evaporated and the air lost its sweet fragrance.

She stopped five feet in front of him and pulled her shoulders back. "Can you possibly tell me how I might find a man by the name of Matt Fagan?" Her accent showed a hint of the Irish, maybe something between South Georgian and Irish.

Matt looked into a pair of hazel eyes and, before he could stop himself, smiled and said, "I sure can. May I ask what you need him for?"

"That's my business," she replied without returning his smile. "Are you going to tell me where I might find this man, or do I need to ask someone else?"

"Hold on, now," he said trying to hide his flared up antagonism. "I am Matt Fagan. What can I do for you?"

"If you're Mister Fagan, then I may have need of your services."

Trying to project an unemotional persona, he said, "I am Matt Fagan. So, what can I do for you?"

"Do you have a place where we could talk?"

Sensing that this was a paying job, Matt dropped the orange electrical cord and wiped his already clean right hand on his jeans. He took two steps toward the woman, took off his bark-brown western hat, and extended his right arm in a gesture to shake hands. When she took a step backward, Matt felt that old wound—rejection. He forgot about being mannerly and placed his Stetson back on. He frowned and, in his best business voice, told a big lie. "I usually meet clients at my downtown office, but if you don't mind climbing those stairs into my boat, we'll meet there." He didn't have an office down town. Hell, he didn't have an office.

"That'll be fine," she said. "Is it safe? It looks real old." When she hurried past him and toward the back of his cabin cruiser, Matt caught the aroma of her perfume causing him to linger a moment.

Then he comprehended what she said about his boat being old. "Of course, we got about an hour before she sinks."

She turned and gave Matt a look of disgust that reminded him of a teacher he'd once had in the third grade. Old wounds put on his heart by an unfaithful wife flashed through his mind. She moved to the bottom of the landing and stopped. Finally Matt moved to assist her up the five steps to the platform leading to his V-hulled home on water.

Matt kept his boat backed into a rented slip. Its rear door was four feet above the surface of the water at the same level with the raised landing where she now stood waiting on him.

He climbed the stairs, pulled open the glass door, and hopped into the pilothouse. He held it open waiting on her entry. She hesitated while looking down at the water below her feet. She appeared apprehensive about crossing the open six inches between the platform and the cruiser, so Matt reluctantly extended his hand to her. She had no choice but to accept his aid, because she was like most of his visitors who wanted to leap the short distance into the door as if sharks swam in the river below.

Her hand felt cold in his as she squeezed it while crossing the threshold. Once inside the seven-by-eleven-foot room she pulled her fingers from his grasp like she had held something unclean or even dangerous.

Fire streaked across his face. The scar smoldered. Matt took a shallow breath and pointed toward a leather-covered sofa along the wall. "You want to talk here?"

"This'll be fine," she said, moving to the edge of the sofa and taking a seat like she was unsure of its hygiene. She crossed her right leg over her left, laced her fingers together, and laid them over her exposed knee. Keeping her back stiff, she stared up at Matt, waiting for his response.

Without taking his eyes from her, Matt removed his hat and threw it onto the flat dashboard behind him. Then he moved to the raised Captain's stool that stood next to the flywheel. He shoved the back of the chair causing the top half to spin around. Slightly bending his knees, Matt slipped into the seat, crossed his arms, and stared down at this woman. "Can I get you anything from the galley?"

"From where?" she said.

"The galley. That's the kitchen. Do you need coffee, tea, coke, anything to eat, or drink?"

"No, thank you."

"What can I do for you, then?" He slid back in the seat and locked his heels behind the bottom brace of the stool.

"I need you to find someone for me. Can you do that?" She looked intently at his boots.

"Maybe." Matt waited a moment until she looked up. "It all depends."

"On what?"

"On a lot of things." He noticed how white her teeth appeared beneath her mauve lipstick. Matt wanted to pinch himself. He'd never met a woman her age put together like a teenager. He forced his mind into its serious, business mode.

"To start with," he said, "it depends on who you're looking for, and why you need to find them."

She looked at him without a glint of desperation on her face. "I need you to find my daughter and her son."

"And why do you want me to find them?"

"I don't understand. What difference does it make?"

"It means everything to me."

"That sure didn't answer my question. But, never mind, I'm willing to pay you good money, so all I want you to do is find them and bring them home."

"Wait just a minute," he said, holding up both hands and showing her his palms. "First, if I decide to do this work for you, it makes a lot of difference why you want to find 'em. And second, you said nothing about me bringing them home. And third, if I decide to help you, yes, it will cost you some of your money, but never more than it's worth. I'm not out to steal from people."

"I'm sorry," she said, but her lips drew up like somebody who had just gotten a whiff of dog shit. "I didn't mean to say you were a thief or anything. I don't understand why you need to know so much."

Matt glanced over her head toward the row of boats and yachts tied up at the marina. He had a habit of continually checking his surroundings, because a man in his business made many enemies, and paranoia was just part of his weird psyche.

After he'd calmed, Matt looked back at her. "Let's start over. You know my name, but you haven't told me yours."

"Medora Meehan," she said. "From Atlanta."

"Atlanta? Ma'am, why'd you come all the way to Chattanooga? Doesn't Atlanta have someone to help you?"

"Does this mean you'll help me?"

"Let me slow down, just a little," He said realizing he'd moved too fast. "Why do you need to find your daughter?"

"She's lost. What difference does it make, anyway?"

"It makes a lot of difference to me."

"Like, how?" Her eyes glared hard into his. This woman wasn't as soft as she looked.

"To be frank with you, Ma'am, do you plan to harm your daughter or grandson if I find them?"

"What a stupid question! Of course I don't plan to hurt them. Why would you ask such a dumb question like that? How could a mother hurt her child...or her grandchild?"

"It happens." He fought to conceal the anger boiling up inside his gut for her insinuation that he was stupid and dumb. Calmly Matt began again, "I realize why you don't understand my questions, but you gotta comprehend this fact. In my business, if I track down a person for a client, and they hurt this person, kill 'em, or even try to kill 'em...well, I'd be in a world of trouble. I'd be an accessory to a crime. I've got to ask these questions to protect myself. I've had parents ask me to find their children, and later they try to kill their children, so this is just a routine question however dumb it sounds."

"Then, you'll help me?" She started to sound slightly desperate.

"Mrs. Meehan," he said, reaching in a cabinet door beside the flywheel and taking out a yellow legal pad. He fumbled around on the flat, wooden dash until he found a ballpoint pen.

"I am Miss Meehan," she said. "I am no longer married. I was once Missus Williams, but I took my maiden name back after the divorce."

"Oh." Matt wondered if Medora Meehan had cheated on her husband, too. "I'm going to ask you a few questions, and you have to tell me all you know. Then, we'll determine if I can help you find your family."

"Thank you," she said. "I could never harm them. I just want to save my family."

"Understand," he said, holding the pad in his lap. "Do not ask me to do anything illegal, because if you do, I'll have to report this to the local district attorney's office. Do you understand this?"

"Yes, I would never do that, intentionally."

"Fair enough," he said writing Medora Meehan across the top of the page. "What is your daughter's full name, and has she ever gone by any other name?"

"My daughter was christened, Sarah Meehan Williams. When she married, she became Sarah Williams Brindle."

"Birth date?" he asked scribbling on the pad as quickly as he could.

"April 10, 1976. She's twenty-nine."

He looked up and said, "Married to who, and when?"

"To whom," she said.

"Yes," he said; then Matt realized she had corrected his grammar. He looked back at the yellow pad, recoiled, and said as calmly as possible, "Give me her husband's name."

"I'm sorry?" she said, "I didn't understand you."

"Your daughter's; her husband's name is what?" He said a little louder.

"Charles Eugene Brindle, but everyone calls him Chuck." Medora reached into her purse and took out a notebook no bigger than her palm. "They were married...Let me see...Here it is...June 29, 2001."

"Keep that out," he said, motioning with a nod of his head toward the book. "You have social security numbers, driver's license numbers, or any other numbers for Sarah, her husband, or her son?"

"I have Sarah's social security number, but that's all." She read the nine numbers very slowly.

"That's good," he said. "That helps. Unless she's changed it, along with her name or everything else."

"She hadn't changed anything, as of two months ago."

"Is that when she disappeared?"

"No, yes, well, yes and no. It has been over three years since I've seen her."

Confused, he stopped writing and looked up. "Then, how'd you know she was using her legal name and numbers two months ago?"

"Timothy Broadway discovered that for me."

"Wait a minute, who's this Broadway?"

"The private detective I hired to find her."

"Hold on now," he said about to ask her to leave. "I work alone or with my part-time assistant, not with someone I don't know."

"He doesn't work for me anymore," she said. Medora slid against the back of the sofa. "Mister Broadway discovered that Sarah had applied for a driver's license in Hamilton County, Tennessee."

"Did she get the license?" He wanted her to leave, but he couldn't stop asking questions.

"I don't know."

"Did Mister Broadway happen to give you a number?"

"No."

"Do you know if he got a copy of it?"

"No...I don't know...He may have."

"Excuse me, but this Mister Broadway should've done that if he's in this business."

"If he got it, I don't know about it."

Matt tried to breathe slowly, even though air became hard to find. "What do you mean?"

"Mister Broadway died before giving me all his information."

"He did what?" When Matt realized his mouth stood open, he shut it.

"He was killed in a car accident. Day-before-yesterday."

Matt stared back at his pad trying to comprehend all of what she had told him.

She sat quietly. Waves started slapping against the wooden hull of his boat and the fishy smell of the river moved into the room.

Matt glanced over the stern to see a 25-footer churning out of the dock. "I'm trying to get all this straight. Now, you can't find out all Mister Broadway learned. Is that true?"

"Yes."

"Tell me what you know, then."

"He told me over the phone Wednesday morning, just before he was killed, about locating my daughter and grandson. That was the first I'd heard about Sarah having a child. I don't even know his name. That's when Mister Broadway told me about her applying for the driver's license here in Hamilton County. He was on his way to meet me at my home, to give me more information, when the accident occurred."

"Was there information found in his car?"

"I don't know. Nobody wants to help me."

He looked back up at her. "Didn't you talk to the Police or the State Patrol?"

"Yes...Well, I talked to somebody."

"And did you tell 'em about him working for you?"

"No. I mean, yes," she said. "They called me because he still had my number on his cell phone."

"The Atlanta police, or the Georgia State Patrol, which one called you?"

"He wasn't killed in Atlanta. He was killed only a few miles from here, near Chattanooga, on Interstate 24."

With his brain racing at top speed, Matt turned to the second page of the legal pad and continued to write. New waves slapped the side of the boat interrupting the silence. Matt tried to relax, but when he looked up, their eyes met. He took a gulp of air and said, "But you said he was on his way to see you in Atlanta."

"Yes, I did…I mean, he was…He told me he was in his car, a few miles on the west side of Chattanooga, and would be at my house in about two hours. He told me to wait there, because he had some vital information to give me." She stopped to clear her throat. "Would it be too much trouble for me to have that cup of coffee now?"

"Of course not." he jumped out of the Captain's chair and bounded down a set of narrow stairs leading to the rooms below while being careful to duck his head before hitting it on the low ceiling. Matt turned left, took two steps into the galley, and pushed the start button on the Mister Coffee. He always kept coffee ready to brew.

The galley only had space for one person at a time. A bar separated the galley from a ten-by-eleven-foot stateroom. Like the outside of the boat, the bar was made of white oak that he kept polished like glass.

Matt moved to the other side of the galley and through a door leading down one step to the bedroom, which was located in the stern, below the pilothouse where he'd left Miss Meehan. In the bedroom, was a queen-size bed, but there was little room for much else. Matt turned on a nine-inch television, positioned on a built-in dresser across from the bed. In a few seconds, a black-and-white picture of the dock appeared on the TV's screen. He checked and saw that no one moved on the landing directly behind the boat. He pressed a button on the remote, and a color picture flashed on the screen. It was from another camera pointed down the jetty toward the entrance. The only living thing in the surveillance picture was Mrs. Barton's calico cat.

When Matt went back into the galley, Miss Meehan stood in the center of the stateroom. He wondered how she had moved down the stairs without alerting him. Then, he remembered laying carpet on the steps just last weekend. The aroma of coffee filled the room.

Standing in the bedroom doorway, Matt watched her as she waited with her back to him. She stood motionless studying a picture of his two sons that sat on an end table next to a recliner.

Afraid of startling her, Matt cleared his throat.

She turned.

Matt said, "The coffee's almost ready."

"Your children?" she said, glancing back over her shoulder at the picture.

"My boys, yes." He reached in a cabinet over the sink to find two black mugs. "The older one is twenty-one, and the younger is nineteen. That picture was taken two summers ago when they came up for the River Bend Festival." He poured the coffee into the mugs. Steam rose from them. "What'll you have in your coffee?"

"Nothing," she said, reaching for it. "The boys are really nice looking." She took a sip of the coffee. "I can tell they are yours."

Stunned, Matt stood transfixed. He could think of nothing to say. Matt never took compliments easily—if she really meant it as a compliment.

While standing in the middle of the room holding her coffee cup in two hands, she continued to stare at the picture of his boys. "The one with the beautiful blue eyes like yours; is he the older?"

"No, the taller one on the right; he's the older." That was definitely a complement. Matt frowned and touched the scar.

"I don't see any pictures of their mother."

"No, and you won't."

"Divorced?"

"Yes."

"Do you spend a lot of time on your boat?"

He wondered why she wanted to change the subject. Smart woman he thought.

"I live on it." Matt felt restless. He wanted to ask the questions. "You want to go back upstairs, or you want to continue the interview down here?"

"It doesn't matter. Down here is fine."

"Have a seat," He said before flying up the steps. When he came back down with his notes, she had moved to one of the barstools still cradling her coffee in two hands.

"What kind of yacht is this?" she asked.

"It's not a yacht," Matt said, moving to the green sofa. "It's one foot short of being a legal yacht, so it's a cabin cruiser. It's called a Trojan."

New waves rocked the boat.

Matt said. "Do you have any information about your grandson?" Gloom spread across her face making her appear much older.

"No," she said. "I thought I told you earlier that I didn't know Sarah had a son until Mister Broadway informed me. Did you not write that down?"

"What else did Mister Broadway say?" Matt controlled his urge to throw the pad at her.

"Not much," she said. She placed her mug on the bar. "Just what I told you earlier."

"Okay," he said. "Let's head in another direction. Tell me about the last time you talked with Sarah?"

"She calls me every year around Christmas and on my birthday in August, but she didn't call me this year on my birthday. So I last talked to her about 10 months ago."

"What do you talk about when she calls?"

"Not much. She says she loves me, and asks how I'm doing. I ask her how she is, and she says she's doing great. But I can tell she's not. Last year was the worst. She sounded upset. A mother can sense those things. I tried to get her to

21

tell me where she was, but she wouldn't. I've tried to talk her into coming home, but she won't."

Matt thought he noticed a tear rolling down the woman's cheek. Then, she looked hard into his eyes. "What else do you need to know?"

Matt looked down at his pad. "When was the last time you actually saw Sarah?"

"Saturday, January 20, 2003," she said without having to check her notebook. "She and Chuck came to my house that day about two or three in the afternoon. They acted a little strange. Well, Sarah acted weird; Chuck was always a strange type of oddball, if you really want to know."

"What you mean, she acted weird?"

"She knew she was leaving Marietta," Medora said, and then her gaze traveled to the wall behind Matt, but she appeared not to see it. "She was so sweet and nice...Anyway; she didn't mention that they would be leaving. I just never saw my only daughter again."

"Did they have jobs?"

"Yes. They didn't show up one Monday at school."

"I thought you said they worked?"

"They did. They were both teachers at West Cobb High School. That's in Marietta...Georgia."

"I guess the school system doesn't know where they'd gone?"

"No."

"I'll need the latest pictures of them that you may have, and I'll need you to fill out this form. It has other routine questions on it concerning your daughter."

"Thank you," she said. The muscles relaxed in her face and her beauty reappeared.

"One other thing," Matt said. "I'll expect to be paid before I begin my search...I work by the day plus expenses, and I expect this to take four or five days. If it takes less you'll get a refund. If it takes more, you'll be billed. And, when I locate your daughter, I'll let you know exactly where you can find her. I may take you there, but I won't go get her and bring her to you. Do you understand these conditions?"

"I don't mind paying you now, but what if you don't find them?"

"Oh, I'll find them. But if for some strange reason I don't find your daughter and grandson, I keep half the money."

"You sound very sure of yourself."

"I'm good at what I do," Matt said handing her the papers for her to fill out. "Take your time and, if you can, answer all of these questions. I'm going upstairs to make a few calls."

She reached into her purse, pulled out a pen, and started filling out the form.

Matt climbed back up to the pilothouse and dialed the Hamilton County Police Station. In less than a minute he had an old friend on the phone.

"What's up, Matt?" asked Joe Johnson, a homicide detective for Hamilton County Sheriff's Department.

"Joe," Matt said. "I need a favor. It'll be the same payment as always."

"Fagan, you don't have to pay for my help."

"I'm not. My client will."

"Maybe I need to quit this police business and be a Private Dick, too."

"You'd starve, Joe. You couldn't stop at every greasy spoon and eat if you had my job. And by the way, you're already a dick."

Joe laughed until he choked. After he stopped coughing Joe said, "What you need, Fagan?"

"I need a copy of an automobile accident report."

"Sure, which one?"

"It happened two days ago, on I-24. The driver was killed. His name was Timothy Broadway. When you find it, can you fax it to me?"

He didn't reply. Matt waited, wondering where Joe had gone.

"Fagan," Joe finally said. "What the hell you got yourself into this time?"

"What you mean?"

"Timothy Broadway was in a car accident, all right," Joe said. "But that ain't exactly what killed him."

Matt took a deep breath. "What the hell killed him, then?"

"Fagan, we ain't suppose to give this information out, 'cause we think this could be a murder case...In fact, we're treating it as a homicide."

Matt's heart picked up a few paces causing his entire body to stiffen. "What can you give me, Joe?"

"You can't say where this comes from. Promise me that?"

"Of course, Joe. You know you can trust me. Now, what killed the man?"

"This is the strangest damn thing I've seen in a long time, Fagan."

Matt waited.

But when Joe Johnson finished his next statement, Matt almost dropped the phone. "We can't figure out exactly how it happened, but that Broadway man was bitten by a damn rattlesnake. The slimy bastard was still in the wrecked car when our boys arrived. That rattler almost bit Sammy Snider before one of them 'state boys' shot that no-shoulder sumbitch—had nine rattlers and a button."

CHAPTER THREE

Physically, Sarah had almost recovered from the summer's beating, but mentally, the humiliation lingered. The only scar that remained ran along the lateral side of her right breast. It was about five inches long and crimson. At times pain would swell up in her nipple and extend across the length of her bosom. She often thought of cancer. Two lumps had appeared along the outside of her breast just under the skin and the other in her armpit. One of the nurses at the infirmary said she only had swollen lymph nodes from an infection.

In the sanctuary, she sat on the right side with the other women. Tommy slept in her lap. Looking across the aisle at Chuck proved impossible now. He had given up trying to contact her. She would never speak to him again even if he sent word that he wanted to escape. She could never trust her husband again.

Because Tommy's weight pressed down on her legs for the past three hours, she no longer had feeling in them. She just hoped Emmanuel would forget about her tonight. It was only two nights ago when he last violated her, but she knew how he got himself worked up after a particularly long sermon. She was nauseated just thinking about him crawling on top of her again.

When Emmanuel stopped preaching and sat down in his chair behind the rostrum, Sarah took the opportunity to shift Tommy in her lap. In only a few more minutes now she could get up and stretch her legs. Tommy stirred but never awoke when she again tried to move him into another position. She waited on one of Emmanuel's deacons to say a prayer and send everyone back to their dorms.

The clamor of boots marching in behind Sarah interrupted her trance. She turned and saw the guards spilling through the doors in the front of the building. About twenty of them marched along the walls, and the others moved down the middle aisle. They all wore navy blue jumpsuits and held shotguns across their chests. They reminded Sarah of army soldiers with their short-cropped hair, clean-shaven faces, and solemn expressions. When the guards had the assemblage surrounded, they halted and turned to face inward.

The people stirred in their seats.

Tommy awoke and started whimpering. Sarah kissed him on the forehead and rubbed his tummy. He pulled himself up beside her, wiped his eyes, and looked around the room.

Bert Taylor, one of the deacons, picked up the microphone. "Let's pray."

Everything grew quiet, except for a couple of spasmodic coughs bouncing among the gathering.

Sarah wondered if they'd have punishment again tonight. Last Sunday they had brought Stephen Walker, a boy of seventeen, before Emmanuel. Someone had caught Stephen masturbating in the men's bathroom. Emmanuel's chosen group beat the boy's buttocks until they turned blood-red.

Bert began to pray, "Father, bless this gathering of Thy followers that they may serve Thee better. Let not one person deny that Emmanuel knows best and will deliver us to Thee when he is ready. Have everyone do as they are told tonight by Thy son and our savior, Emmanuel. Don't let anybody doubt his judgment, for he talks with Thee, Lord God. We should never question that his word is Thy word. For it is in His gracious name, I pray. Amen."

Out of the back door and across the pulpit, came all eight of the affiliation's nurses. Each clutched an oxford-brown bottle the size of a quart jar as they walked down the stairs to face the group. Irene, Myra, and Daniel brought in two water coolers like the ones used by athletes at sporting events. One of the guards called Oscar carried a cardboard box of Dixie Cups and placed them on the altar.

A low mumbling spread around the room. Sarah tried to think of anything she may have done recently that would merit punishment.

Emmanuel stood again and moved to face his people. He appeared tired. He placed each hand along the outer edge of the rostrum and looked out into the crowd with the whites of his eyes the color of blood. In only seconds all hushed.

Emmanuel started in a low pleading tone, "Brothers and sisters, my love for you is great. That's why I'll ask you to do something for me...and yourself." He stopped for at least half a minute and tried to look into all three hundred pair of eyes there.

Sarah held Tommy too tightly, and he started squirming and pushing away from her clutches. "Shhhh," she said in his ear. He slapped at her hand.

Emmanuel said, "Everyone is against me...except you, my beloved sheep. The government is corrupt, as I have told you so many times before. Now, they are snooping around, asking questions about me and trying to bring me down. They are afraid of me. Yes, they think we are going to hurt someone, but we're not. No, we just want to be left alone. They don't understand us. They don't understand our family. All of you and me, we're a family, stronger than your birth family. We love one another like no one can understand. Did Jesus not say that true enlightenment was only achieved when a person is separated from his loved ones? Jesus asked his disciples to forsake their families and follow him, and they did. When you came into my family, you left your old family and friends. Is this not true?"

Sarah felt confused. She had heard Emmanuel preach this message many times, but why now with all the guards holding shotguns and nurses carrying bottles? A feeling of doom spread over Sarah. Her body quivered once from head to foot. She took a deep breath and tried to quiet a heart that raced in her chest.

Emmanuel continued, "Just last week an attempt was made on my life." The crowd buzzed. He held a hand up. "The outside world wants to get rid of me as they did Jesus. A man from Atlanta was asking questions about us...about me. The guy was sent here to kill me by a woman from Georgia. The woman is the mother of one of our very own. That's why we must be armed."

Emmanuel eyes fell on Sarah.

Sarah sat upright. Adrenaline shot through her veins, creating momentarily blurred vision. Her mother lived in Atlanta, and she would be the kind to send someone searching for her.

Emmanuel said, "They are coming for us as I speak."

Sarah flinched.

His gaze glued to Sarah. "We are departing this place. You and me. All of us now, we are leaving together." He took a deep breath.

Sarah felt a wave of relief rush through her body. Emmanuel and his people had kept her from leaving the compound since the beating. This might be an opportunity for her to escape. She thought about her son. She had to take Tommy with her.

Emmanuel said, "You must show your loyalty to me. We must stand together. We cannot show weakness, now, or ever. I'll lead you to a better place. Praise God Almighty." His upper body began to quiver. He dropped his head between his shoulders, and his hair dangled in front of his eyes. After a long few seconds, he raised his head and pointed at the men surrounding the congregation. "Guards, watch and see who's faithful to me. Make sure they all go when it's time." He waved the back of his hands at the nurses. "Hurry, women, do your job. It's time to go to the next level. Hurry." He walked backwards a few steps, crossed his arms over his chest, stood with legs spread, and nodded his head at Irene and her group of women.

The nurses hurried down the aisles handing everyone something from the brown bottles. Irene and her crew worked frantically pouring water into paper cups and handing them out to the members in the front row. They worked so fast some of the water spilled on the people. A buzz of conversation started in the middle of the room and grew outward. Nurse Sanchez started screaming at eighty-seven-year-old Gladys Varnell to hurry and take her pills.

What was happening hit Sarah like a train running her down. Her heart stuck in her throat, and a breath failed to enter her lungs. She squeezed Tommy too hard, and he began to cry. No one noticed the child's whimpering among all the chaos and confusion.

Sarah stood and looked around the room for a way to break out. Armed guards blocked all the exits. Three young men hurried down the outside aisles, but guards grabbed them and threw them back into their seats.

Emmanuel moved back to the rostrum and leaned toward the microphone. "Calm down. We must be orderly. Sit down, be calm, everything will be all right."

The panic continued to spread.

"Calm down," Emmanuel said very slowly. He raised his hands over his head and looked up toward the ceiling. "God...God be with my brethren and lead them to your home in the sky. Let it be in their hearts that You love them, and I love them. God calm their hearts and let them follow me, Your servant."

Slowly the group began to calm. Emmanuel smiled. He knew he had tremendous power over his people.

"We must take our time," he said. "It will not last long. I will be with you all the way. I will meet you at our home in the sky. It'll be so great to be together again—with no pain—no one to ridicule us—love for one another—I will take care of you there."

Sarah rubbed Tommy's hair. The room grew quiet and, the nurses started handing out the pills again.

"Sing a song, choir," ordered Emmanuel.

The chorus director, Zachary Self, jumped out of his chair, waved his arms at the choir and started singing,

"Softly and tenderly, Jesus is calling, calling for you and for me."

The choir caught up with Zachary and started half singing and half mumbling the tune.

"Here," said Betty, a white-headed nurse who looked like a bulldog. She pushed three yellow pills into Sarah's hand. "Two are for you, and one is for the kid. Don't take'm now, wait on the ones with the water. It's easier that way. Besides, they've got to see you swallow them." Betty moved on to someone behind Sarah, handing out her doses of death like one would distribute candy.

Sarah glared down into her palm at the tablets that would kill her and Tommy. Her hand trembled. Her mind raced trying to think of a way out of this. She took a deep breath and told herself to slow down and concentrate on an escape from this madness. She shook her head to clear the confusion that spread through her thoughts. The people continued to sing, about going to meet Jesus, as if dying was something that happened to them daily.

Tears started to run from Sarah's eyes. Her breath came in short gasps. Daniel Crider and Irene worked like machines filling cups with water and passing them down the row of people in front of Sarah. Guards stood over each person, forcing them to place the tablets in their mouths and swallow. Then, they inspected the insides of each person's throat.

Sarah looked up and saw that the people on the first couple of rows were already slumping in their seats. Heads fell over like cut trees in the forest.

"God, help me," she said to herself. Then, she had an idea. She reached in her pocketbook, trying to find a bottle of aspirin she always kept there. She felt of everything except the aspirins. Irene and those with the cups of water approached. Sarah couldn't get a good breath. Her vision blurred. Then her fingers touched the plastic.

"Hurry," Sarah said to no one. Her hands trembled. Sarah moved the bottle out of her purse and placed it between her legs. She continued to clutch the poison pills in her left hand. The top off the aspirin bottle held tight. She wanted to smash it open. She shook it.

Irene handed a cup of water toward Sarah and Tommy. "Hold this."

Sarah shoved the aspirin bottle between her knees and reached over her son for the water. Her hands shook so violently that the liquid splashed out on her dress.

Irene squinted her eyes. "Pass it down, Clumsy."

Sarah flinched and dropped the cup. Water spread over the floor. Sarah reached down and tried to scoop the liquid up with her bare hand. The aspirin bottle fell from between her knees. The top flew off and tiny white aspirins scattered in all directions like they were alive with minds of their own. Sarah tried to hide her mistake by kicking the pills under the pew in front of her, but that proved impossible.

"Sarah," said Irene. "What in the world you doing? Get your head out from between your legs and get another cup. Can't you do anything right?"

Without hesitation, Sarah looked up and took the cup. Tommy started to cry.

"Shut that brat up," said Irene, "and pass that water down."

The cups of water moved from hand to hand until everyone on their row had one.

"Give me those pills," said Irene, snatching them out of Sarah's grasp. "I'll do this myself." She took one of the tablets and pushed it into Tommy's mouth. "Drink this, honey."

Sarah reached for her son, but Irene slapped her hand away and poured water down the boy's throat. It was too late to save him.

Irene bent over and snarled in Sarah's ear, "Here, you bitch!"

Sarah took the pills of death from the woman, and, without remorse, placed them on her tongue. A bitter taste spread through her mouth. Indifferently, she brought the cup to her lips. All of this felt like a dream. She closed her eyes, sipped the water and let the tablets glide down her throat.

Tommy slipped into his seat and slumped his head over onto his mother. She looked down at the child's blond hair. He closed his eyes and went limp.

"Open your mouth," said the guard.

Sarah spread her jaws wide for inspection. Irene and the guards moved on down the row, checking others.

Sarah glanced toward Emmanuel who had moved back to his big chair and now watched only her with a look of delight on his face. Hate boiled from Sarah like hot lava from a volcano.

Sarah's fingers, then toes, began to lose feeling. The paralysis advanced up her legs and arms, and everything in the room began to spin. Her neck became so weak that her head fell forward, and peace diffused through her body as the numbness spread. A ringing developed in her ears. She laid her head on the back of the bench and closed her eyes. She fell through a tunnel the color of night and lost all feeling. Then, darkness covered her.

CHAPTER FOUR

Matt turned on his computer and typed in his password, Desperado, which was also the name of his boat. The new Dell Computer made its usual clicking and buzzing noises as its super-fast processor switched gears. He had always used Hewlett Packard or Compaq but traded for a Dell several weeks ago, because Steve Dial, his hacker friend, advised him to.

Once on line, Matt moved to FAVORITES and highlighted www.gemco.com, then hit return. He sat back in his seat, pushed his hair back, and waited on the technology to connect him to one of his data sources. The Internet had made Matt's business much easier, especially the waiting and the running around he once did, trying to check each fragmented piece of information. He rarely did legwork these days, but the downside was that he stayed in front of a computer all day. Since this inactivity had made Matt gain a few pounds in the beginning, he had started a weight lifting and a running program over a year ago.

Medora Meehan had gone back to her room at the Choo Choo Hotel in downtown Chattanooga where they planned to meet tomorrow for lunch. It didn't bother Matt that she had decided to wait in town until he found her daughter; in fact, he'd probably do the same if one of his boys were lost. Besides, Matt hoped to have everything finished in two or three days and get the rest of his fee from her.

Matt jumped when the cell phone started playing "Rocky Top," the University of Tennessee's fight song. He hit the send button and said, "Matt Fagan, here."

"Catch you sleeping," said Officer Joe Johnson.

"I'm on the Internet," Matt said. "What'd you find out?"

"One of these days, I'm gonna get me a computer. Hear they got some fine looking chicks on the Internet."

"I wouldn't know."

"Bullshit, you wouldn't."

"What'd you find out about Broadway."

"You won't believe this bullshit, 'cause I don't believe it myself, but they weren't no papers, briefcase or anything similar to that in his car. Cell phone and wallet in his pocket is all they was. You believe that shit?"

"Snake probably ate it."

"Where the hell is somebody gonna get a damn snake in November, anyways? Them sumbitches don't come out in the winter, do they?"

31

"If it's warm enough, it don't matter," Matt said still clicking buttons on the computer and talking at the same time. "It all depends on temperature, and it's been warm enough lately, you know."

"That still doesn't explain where somebody got one, and why the sumbitch put the slimy bastard in Broadway's car."

"Somebody wanted to make a statement, I guess."

Johnson whistled then said, "They made a damn statement all right. I can't believe that…"

The computer screen changed and a multicolored homepage appeared. While Johnson rambled, Matt moved the arrow to the SS category and double clicked the left button. Quickly a blue page appeared with a white box in the middle of the screen. Below the box it read: ENTER SOCIAL SECURITY NUMBER. Matt typed in Sarah Brindle's nine numbers and pressed return. The screen turned black and the computer started humming.

Matt picked up Johnson's last words, "…damn trucker said so."

"What?" Matt said. "What'd the trucker say?"

"Ain't you been listenin'? The damn trucker said when he passed by Broadway, doing 'bout sixty-five or seventy miles an hour, he saw him slapping at something in the passenger's floorboard. Had to be that rattlesnake, 'cause next thing you know, Broadway drove up under this man's eighteen-wheeler. Course, I figured the truck driver was a damned liar cause he was going lots faster than seventy, but I believed the rest of his story."

"Johnson, what would you do if you were driving along and a rattler crawled out from under your seat?"

"I'd bail outta the fucker and let the damn snake have the car. I ain't as big a idiot as I look." Johnson paused. "That didn't come out right—screw you, Fagan."

Matt laughed.

"Go to hell, Fagan." Johnson hung the phone up without saying another word.

Matt couldn't get his mind off the rattlesnake in Broadway's car. He hated snakes—was terrified of snakes, but he didn't know exactly why.

Suddenly, the monitor's screen changed and a name appeared. SARAH MEEHAN BRINDLE, born 10 April 1976, De Kalb County, Georgia. Below this information, it showed a long list of items to use as a cross-reference-check on the latest use of Sarah Brindle's SS number.

Matt double clicked the pointer on Driver's License. In seconds the screen changed. Two listings came on screen. One showed Georgia license, and beside it was the word _expired_. The other listing showed Tennessee license with nothing beside it. He clicked the latter. Up came a Tennessee driver's license with a picture. A woman of about forty-five or fifty stared back at him from the screen.

She had brown, straight hair, black eyes, and a face like a pig, double chin, and all. Matt reached for the picture of Sarah that Medora had given him earlier. He didn't have to, but he placed the small snap shot next to the picture on the computer screen just to make sure he was seeing things correctly. They were definitely not of the same woman. Medora Meehan had given Matt a picture of a woman in her late twenties or early thirties that looked like a model—she looked good. She had shoulder length blond hair and hazel eyes. The eyes struck him first for she had those moist eyes; eyes that made a woman look like she had just finished crying. She was definitely a beauty and looked a lot like her mother.

Checking the Tennessee licenses on the screen again, it clearly read Sarah M. Brindle beside Miss Piggy's picture.

"Same name, same number," he said to no one, and then he looking at the birth date on the license again. "No way."

He printed several copies of the driver's license. This was not going to be as simple as Matt had once thought. Either someone had stolen Sarah's identity, or there were two women with the same social security number and name. He continued talking to himself, "Damn. Identity theft."

Matt went back to the main screen on the computer. He clicked on the Georgia license and immediately saw the younger, blond woman's picture appear on screen. He clicked more buttons; that got the computer busy tracing credit cards issued to Sarah Brindle. In seconds, across the screen, flashed NONE FOUND. He typed in the SS number and asked them to try again. NONE FOUND appeared on the screen.

"Ah, crap!" He said aloud and picked up a copy of the printout of Miss Piggy and her license. He looked at the address on Miss Piggy's licenses: 2209 Cash Canyon Road in Lookout Valley, Tennessee. "I'll be damn." The community of Lookout Valley was only across the road from his boat dock where Matt presently sat. Cash Canyon Road was a narrow road that ran along the foot of Raccoon Mountain. If he went outside and looked southwest, Matt could see the top of Raccoon Mountain. The license was issued in March of this year; consequently, there was a good chance the woman, calling herself Sarah Brindle, still lived at that residence. Of course, she could have used a fake address.

Matt checked his notes from the conversation with Medora Meehan. He was right; Timothy Broadway had called Medora from somewhere on this side of Chattanooga. He was killed soon after calling her on I-24, east of the city. Lookout Valley, Cash Canyon Road, and Raccoon Mountain were all west of Chattanooga.

By sliding the mouse, Matt moved the pointing finger to a box labeled LAST TRANSACTIONS and clicked the left button. The Dell Computer started humming. In seconds, the computer told him the answer. The Sarah Brindle with the pig face had paid income taxes of $254 on $1,987 last month from Erlanger Hospital. She had paid $2,034 in taxes this year as a registered nurse. Medora had said her Sarah taught school.

Matt moved the computer screen back to the driver's licenses, copied Miss Piggy's picture, and transferred it to another program. There, he enlarged and enhanced the image. Knowing this would take more than several minutes, Matt sat back closed his eyes and let the computer work. His thoughts drifted back to the old man that took Matt in and raised him, but his thoughts could not go back past that time no matter how hard he tried.

CHAPTER FIVE

Matt had to get away from the computer, so he grabbed a Diet Coke and went up to the pilothouse. Out of habit, or because he was a paranoid bastard, Matt searched for anything unusual in all directions through the glass windows that wrapped around the room. Originally the only window on the bridge was the windshield, but he had enclosed the area making it almost airtight. Now, when he took the boat out in the winter Matt stayed warm and comfortable. Another set of controls could be found on the roof above.

The day had little light left with the sun already behind Raccoon Mountain. An orange hue spread across the western sky. "Red sky at night, sailor's delight," Matt said while moving off the boat and onto the dock.

He thought about taking the _Desperado_ out on a short run. It had been almost two weeks since he'd cranked its engines and gone down to Nickajack Dam. The fall leaves looked beautiful then, having just reached their full showing. Presently, the red leaves of the oaks, red buds, and dogwoods, along with the yellow ones of the maples and sweet gums, had turned brown and now fell from the trees. It had only taken two weeks, and the leaves were about gone. If it rained, they'd all disappear leaving the trees' branches to stand bare all winter until spring. The area needed some rain. They'd seen very little this summer and fall. In fact, they'd stayed below average on rainfall for several years.

A slight twinge of pain shot across his facial scar, signaling Matt that the weather would soon change. He figured that a cold front would drop out of Canada soon. He didn't mind; Matt liked all seasons.

As expected, a candy-apple-red, 1967 Mustang convertible pulled onto the marina's parking lot spinning gravel under its wheels. It sped straight toward Matt. He had been expecting its driver for almost thirty minutes now. The Ford, riding low to the ground, threw up more rocks as it fish-tailed into a parking spot next to Matt's car—a black Ford Explorer XLT.

Matt took a sip of Diet Coke and watched as Leaky Waters, his associate, leaped out of his Mustang. As the young man swaggered toward the gangplank that led down to the docks, Matt thought of his friend's father, Frank Waters. Matt had promised Frank twenty-eight years ago when Leaky was born that he'd look after his son. And that he had almost done. Leaky had taken care of Matt once about thirteen years ago when Matt was hospitalized from a bullet wound to the head—a self inflicted bullet wound—a grazing bullet wound. Matt had been stupid and weak then, but who wouldn't be right after his wife ran off with another man—a friend at that—another policeman.

Nearly a year later, when Matt finally stopped feeling sorry for himself and rejoined the real world, Leaky had quit high school. Matt badgered him until he went back. During his senior year, Leaky became an all-state football player and received a scholarship to Middle Tennessee State where he played defensive back for four years. After his football-playing days had ended, he had tried to move back home without getting his Bachelor's degree, but Matt talked him into staying at MTSU another six months until he received his degree in Physical Education. Leaky then taught and coached for two years at Central High School, but quit when he started making more money doing odd jobs for Matt's new information gathering business. Presently, Leaky worked for himself doing surveillance work for lawyers and jealous spouses. Matt gathered most of his information from the Internet or the phone. He didn't like spying on other people, especially someone's cheating spouse. When he needed this done, Matt called on Leaky.

The six-foot, 180-pound Leaky Waters, with hands in his pocket, sauntered down the wooden dock by swinging the upper half of his body back and forth like an upside-down pendulum. An Atlanta Brave's cap sat sideways on his head, and he wore a red and yellow plaid, flannel shirt over his wide shoulders. He also wore baggy jeans—waist riding below his ass—pants legs doubled over a pair of blue and white Nike shoes—spotless Nikes with no strings. His teeth showed through a wide grin. Matt knew he'd just gotten off an assignment, because he usually dressed well and didn't walk like a pimp or a dope dealer.

Leaky slapped Matt's arm. "How's it hanging, bro?"

Matt looked directly into his friend's dark eyes set in his light, mahogany face. "What the hell you doing?"

The marina's lights, hanging under the metal roof, blinked and flickered until they came on. They cast a yellow tint on everything under their domain. A moist breeze whipped out of the southwest and blew across Matt's face. He smelled the rain, but he figured it was still hundreds of miles away.

Grinning, Leaky pulled his pants back up to his waist. "I been taking pictures of a client's husband going in and out of a Motel 6 door with his personal trainer. I guess when I show his wife them pictures, she's gonna hit him so hard with a lawsuit he's gonna stagger around like a duck that done been hit in the head with a stick."

Matt took the last sip of the Diet Coke. "You gonna make much money out of this one?"

"Hell, yeah," said Leaky, turning the bill of his Brave's cap forward like a baseball player. "The old man's got a backyard full of money. I got all I need on that horny bastard now, but I'm gonna wait a few days before I lay it all out in front of the wife.

"Really."

"Even though she's been expecting this news, she's gonna shit bullets when she sees what I got. What you need with me, good buddy?"

Matt turned back toward the boat. "Come inside a minute, I'll tell you what I got. I still say you should have been a professional comedian."

"Hell, I might do that, when I grow up."

Once they made it down to the stateroom, Matt handed Leaky the real picture of Sarah Brindle, given to him by her mother and the computer-enhanced picture of Miss Piggy from the driver's license.

Leaky took both pictures to the light at the bar. "Jesus H. Christ, what an ugly white woman—that face could stop a clock—even set it backwards—she looks mean as hell, too. Damn, I'd hate to meet that she-devil in a dark alley."

He studied the other picture. "That other one looks gooooood."

Matt picked his notes up off the bar and went over all the details of the case as they had developed. When he got to the part about the rattlesnake in Broadway's car, Leaky started shaking his head in disbelief.

"Have you looked up this address on the computer, yet?" said Leaky.

"Not yet." Matt turned back to the computer and in few minutes a map of Hamilton County appeared. He typed in _2209 Cash Canyon Road_ and in only seconds, the layout of Lookout Valley came into view. He waited for the familiar red arrow to point to a spot on Cash Canyon Road that would be 2209. Nothing happened. Matt typed in the address again, and in less than five seconds a message blinked in the upper right corner of the screen that read: _NO ADDRESS FOUND_.

"Bull shit," Matt said. From the toolbar at the top of the screen, Matt used the touch pad to pick up a representation of a magnifying lens and slid it over Cash Canyon Road. He double clicked, and the image changed to a closer view of the area. He clicked an icon that gave more detail, and the map changed again. Along the road appeared a few small black squares that represented homes or buildings. Some of the squares could even be barns. He picked a square at the beginning of the street as it turned off Pan Gap Road and asked for the address. An address appeared above the black square, 101 Cash Cannon Road. Matt clicked on the last dot as the road ran out of Hamilton and into Sequatchie County. The address was 2433 Cash Canyon Road.

"Okay, looking good," Matt said feeling Leaky lean over his shoulder. Next, Matt clicked each square going back toward town. The next one was 2431, the next 2420, the next 2410—odd numbers on the left side of Cash Canyon Road and even on the right. Finally, he got to a small square next to a large wooded area. Its address was 2301. He passed over a large uninhabited area on the map and clicked the next square. The number 1905 came up. He saw no building on the map to go along with the address of 2209.

"Fake address," said Leaky. "You know where she works?"

"Yeah, Erlanger Hospital."

"What shift?"

"Don't know."

"I'll find out," said Leaky. He pulled a small, black cellular phone from his front pocket, flipped it open and punched in some numbers. Little beeping sounds came with each number he touched.

Matt switched to another program while waiting on Leaky to make his call. He then switched to another source he'd not tried before but had paid his hacker friend Steve Dial heavy dues to use. It allowed Matt entry into the U.S. Army's satellite system that continually took aerial photographs of North America. It was the same system that was used in Afghanistan and Iraq. Matt had heard that a person could read a postage stamp on the ground using these satellites, but he didn't believe anything could be that good. His computer started making clicking noises as it worked. Matt drummed his fingers on the desk.

"Is Roy Lee there?" said Leaky over his cell phone. "Well, put his black ass on."

Leaky tapped his left foot on the floor as he waited.

"Lee Roy," said Leaky in a different voice than the one he used to talk to Matt. "Is your black ass drunk?" He waited a few seconds and continued, "I can't believe you, Lee Roy Beck. Your tongue's about three times thicker than normal. Don't lie to me...your ass is drunk. You're so drunk youse plumb whomper-jawed." Leaky listened and grinned. "Well, you're always gonna be Lee Roy to me, 'cause that's what we called your black ass when we's grown up. Shit man, don't try to fool me, youse is Lee Roy, and not no mudder-fuck'n Roy Lee."

Leaky changed to his serious voice. "You still working at Erlanger, ain't you?"

Matt couldn't help but grin listening to Leaky. He thought Leaky could talk Japanese if he had to. A blue screen appeared on Matt's computer's monitor. It wasn't long before a green screen emerged, which quickly changed to a yellow before going back to blue. The program came online. It asked for an area and gave a long list from which to pick. Matt pointed to _SOUTHEAST UNITED STATES_ and clicked the mouse. Another list of locations came on screen. He pointed to _TENNESSEE_. In seconds, another index of cities came into sight, and he pointed to _CHATTANOOGA-AREA_. The computer started clicking and humming again like it was full of crickets.

"I got something you gotta do for me," said Leaky into his phone. He opened his mouth to say something else but halted to listen to what Lee Roy had to say. Leaky grimaced. "How's about a pint of Vodka?" He listened again. "Hell no, I ain't getten you no mudder-fuck'n half gallon. Shit. I'll get youse a fifth, and that's all. Shit, I ain't askin' youse to kill the President of the United States or nothin'."

On the computer screen came a satellite view of what Matt recognized as the Chattanooga area. The images were different shades of red, black and white. It took a moment before he realized he was seeing infrared image. These night shots could actually see through thin clouds. He easily found the Tennessee River winding through the picture. He also saw hundreds of lines crossing each other and millions of lights where downtown Chattanooga was located. It amazed Matt how geometrically perfect manmade structures appeared from a hundred miles in the sky.

Off the tool bar at the top of the screen, Matt let the arrow pick up an icon that represented a magnifying glass. He located the sharp _U-turn_ in the Tennessee River, the Moccasin Bend area, and moved the magnifying icon just to its left where Cash Canyon Road should be located. He clicked and the image started to change from top to bottom very slowly as the new picture worked its way down the screen.

With phone still at his ear, Leaky moved to the sofa next to the computer. "I'll bring a fifth of vodka over in a few minutes. If you know anything about a nurse at Erlanger by the name of Sarah Brindle, that is?"

Leaky looked at me and rolled his eyes as he listened to the drunk. "Dammit, Lee Roy, I said I'd bring the bottle over in a minute, but your black ass best have some mudder-fuck'n answers for me, or you ain't getten shit. Understand…Okay…Let's start over. Her damn name is Sarah Brindle, and she's a mudder-fuck'n nurse."

Matt watched Leaky's face change from anger to concern, as he became the listener. Leaky pulled a small notepad from his shirt pocket and an ink pen from his pants. He started to write, and say _Yeah_, and _Go on_, every few seconds.

Glancing back at the computer's monitor, Matt noticed that the close-up picture of Lookout Valley had finished. He bent at the waist and peered into the screen from about seven or eight inches away. It took a second but Matt found Cash Canyon Road that disappeared periodically, drifting in and out of vegetation. It ran parallel to the Tennessee River, but he couldn't see it as clearly on this real image. He followed its northern route past Williams Island until it made a forty-five degree turn toward the northwest. Just there, something bizarre caught his eye. Something not on the map he had just seen a few minutes ago. He placed the computer's magnifying icon over this area and clicked. The screen started changing as it proceeded to enlarge the sector. Matt started tapping his foot along with his drumming fingers.

"I'll be there in a few minutes," Leaky said folding his phone once and placing it in his jean pocket.

Matt leaned back in his chair. "You got anything?"

Leaky didn't say anything for a moment as he wrote in his notebook. "Yeah, Lee Roy says he knows that white woman. Of course, he could be lying to me, but I don't think he could make up a story like this one."

Matt didn't say anything but just listened, tapping, and drumming.

"Two days ago, security at Erlanger discovered they were missing some drugs—a lot of drugs. And they think this Sarah Brindle, along with some other nurses, may have had something to do with their disappearance."

"What kind of drugs?"

Leaky looked at his notebook. "Quaaludes, for one...That's the big one... four 100-tablet bottles. Then, sodium something. It starts with a _W_, but Lee Roy can't remember what it is. He says the drug thins blood, and if someone takes too much, they'll bleed to death on the insides."

"Warfarin," Matt said. "Sodium warfarin is what's used in rat poisoning. It may be used as a blood thinner, too. I think the drug is called Cummidun or something like that."

"One more thing," said Leaky. "They pilfered some cyanide."

"Everybody knows what that does. How much?"

"Lee Roy didn't know, but I'm going over there and snoop around after taking Lee Roy his vodka."

Matt turned back to the monitor. "Call me when you find out something."

"Yeah," said Leaky, already walking up the narrow steps to the pilothouse.

Matt hollered back toward the empty steps, "One more thing."

Leaky walked half way back down, bent at the waist and looked at Matt. "Yeah."

"Did you learn anything else about this woman calling herself Sarah Brindle? What shift she works or anything?"

"Yeah, she works the day shift—six to three."

"Have they questioned her yet?"

"No, can't find her. She and two other nurses didn't come in today. All three of them called in sick."

Matt watched Leaky disappear up the steps before he turned back to the computer. There on the screen, Matt saw a huge, cleared area. The resolution was not as good with this magnification, but it surprised him at how distinct everything appeared. Even spying this close to the earth, he could see the area contained three large buildings and several small ones. It looked like tiny lanes connected all the structures. It took him a few seconds to realize the bright red specks dotting the lanes were the tops of people's heads. He grinned. A small, very winding road led several hundred yards from Cash Canyon Road to the clearing. Matt remembered that this was on a very hilly area of Raccoon Mountain. Matt thought he noticed a fence around the sector. It looked like a compound. It looked like a prison.

Matt picked up the phone and dialed Joe Johnson's number to let the authorities know where they may find their stolen drugs. And it might just help him find Sarah Brindle.

CHAPTER SIX

The splattering drizzle of rain that washed across the tin roof of the women's dorm awoke Sarah. Tommy slept in her blood-starved arms. For a few seconds, she forgot where she was, or what had happened to her and the others last night. It felt like a curtain of fog had washed across her brain concealing the nightmare that had taken place. Unwillingly, the horror of it all began oozing through the folds, twists, and turns of her memory. Closing her eyes, she tried to return to the land of sleep but couldn't, so she rubbed her fingers through Tommy's hair; it comforted her.

Emmanuel had called last night's ordeal a test to see if his people were willing to die for him. He had announced to the gathering that they should not worry for he was proud of almost everyone for following his orders, passing his test, and that he would always do what was best for them.

"Trust me," he had said after they awoke from their drug-induced slumber. "Follow me, and you will never die." Sarah remembered hearing vomiting throughout the sanctuary. She remembered the smell but barely remembered returning to the dorm or getting in her bed. This was a nightmare, and she had to escape.

Without awakening her son, she slid out of the lower berth of her bunk bed, and on her tiptoes, slipped toward the communal bathroom at the far end of the long room that housed over a hundred women. The walls echoed the rhythmic slapping of her bare-feet on the tile floor. Although her bladder ached, she slowed her pace in fear of waking her companions and walked the last few feet into the bathroom.

Relieved, she exited the lavatory and hurried back to her cot. From the bed above Sarah's came the breathing sounds of a sleeping Zuly Martinez. Sarah had taught the sixteen-year-old Zuly to speak English, and Zuly had taught Sarah a little Spanish. Zuly's black hair draped over the side of the mattress. Standing on her toes, Sarah covered the girl's shoulders with the sheet. Zuly Martinez didn't awake but turned onto her other side.

Sarah sat on her bed, feeling the springs through the mattress and placed her hand on Tommy's hot cheeks. He didn't move. She knew she needed to change the child's diaper, but she didn't want to disturb him or any of the other women this early.

Sarah felt a flood of heat spread across her face when she thought of last night. She folded her arms across her chest, crossed one leg over the other, and stared at the wall only feet away. She tried to think of a way to fight back and keep this madman from destroying her. Her muscles tightened.

Someone's coughing brought Sarah out of her trance. Clad only in a white, cotton T-shirt, and panties, she felt a sudden chill brush across her bare arms. She started to shake. She thought about getting back into bed. Someone coughed. Then she thought of escape. Since she couldn't live this enslaved life any longer, she decided to do something drastic if necessary. She'd die or even kill to get out of this hell. At times, she felt like she was outside looking in, watching a horror show that never ended.

Sarah was convinced that Emmanuel had gone totally insane. In the beginning when they first met Emmanuel, he was a different person. He was as kind as a loving father. Now, he thought of himself as God, but he had become the devil. That was not the major problem, however. All those who believed Emmanuel really was God created the anarchy. Sarah should have seen his deception, but like everyone else, she had failed. Now it was too late.

Sarah couldn't believe that only three years ago she and Chuck had ridden with two of their Atlanta friends into the North Georgia Mountains to hear this different kind of preacher. The minister had captivated Chuck that very day. Emmanuel was not Emmanuel then; he was simply Reverend Mark Belcher, a man that offered many answers to the world's problems.

In the future, if she had a future, someone might ask Sarah why she joined his group, this cult. Never before this day had she thought of their assemblage as a cult, but that was exactly what it was, a cult. They were a religious sect that most people would consider extremist, a cult. They lived in an unconventional manner compared to most people in the world, and they followed an authoritarian, charismatic leader. A crazy man. It was a cult, wasn't it?

There were no simple answers to why she and Chuck had joined this cult. No one had used force. In fact, at first, they had to win acceptance into the group. It was a privilege to belong. Of course, at first Reverend Belcher only called it The Holiness Church of Refuge. It grew into a cult and its numbers tripled. Sarah wondered why others had joined. She assumed some had joined in moments of weakness, others when angry about something in their personal lives like a meddling parent, a lost boy friend or girl friend, divorce. Some felt angry about the state of the world. However, for most, Sarah saw, life had just become empty, and Emmanuel gave them hope, a reason to live. The "Refuge of God" had become an instant family, the answer to all those who entered.

In these quiet, early morning hours, with the tapping of rain peppering the metal roof, she thought of Chuck before Emmanuel had entered their lives, and the way her husband had changed after they started teaching school. His life's dream had always been to teach, but he had failed. Communication with the teenagers proved impossible for Chuck and that destroyed his confidence. Some students made fun of him, challenged his authority, tried to take over, and he began to lose control of his classroom—a death sentence for a teacher.

Sarah even worried then, that Chuck would lose his teaching position. She tried to help him face his mounting problems, but she couldn't. He wasn't flexible. He became stubborn and rejected his wife in every way. They were on the verge of separating when Chuck discovered Mark Belcher who welcomed him, made him feel good about himself, and brought him into his fold. Sarah, still in love with her husband, followed. Funny, Sarah thought, but it had all started with Chuck's need for simplicity, a life without problems. She laughed to herself. Now, she no longer hated Chuck. She didn't love him—she pitied him. She hated Mark Belcher, Emmanuel, their self-proclaimed God.

Closing her eyes, Sarah inhaled the dampness encircling her body. She thought about letting herself fall back into the bed next to Tommy. His rhythmic breathing along with the rain soothed her mind. Her body swayed.

"Sarah," someone whispered from a dark corner next to the exit door. "Sarah, it's me. Over here."

For a moment, Sarah thought she had dreamed a nightmare but quickly realized the truth. Opening her eyes, she searched toward the voice and saw the shadow of a person, man or woman, she couldn't determine, standing along the wall only ten feet from her. Sarah squinted her eyes but still couldn't see who stood in the shadows.

"Come here a minute, honey." The voice was barely audible.

There, standing in the early-morning dimness like a thief stood Chuck. Without saying a word she slipped into her robe and found her house shoes under the bed, and then she tiptoed in his direction. He had taken a risk entering the women's dorm. Emmanuel didn't permit such things from his subjects.

"Sarah," Chuck said then coughed.

"Yes," she said coldly. She stopped two feet from where he stood.

"Come outside," he said. "I need to talk to you."

Soon they stood outside in the cold on a small landing facing each other. The early morning twilight made it difficult for Sarah to see Chuck's face clearly. Rain splattered on the metal canopy over their heads. Sarah pulled her robe closer around her. It was too thin, and she began to shiver.

Facing each other, the man and wife were able to stare directly into each other's eyes. He stood only three inches taller than Sarah's five-five. When her eyes adjusted, she was shocked at how much he'd aged. His light-brown hair had begun to recede and was now extremely thin across the entire top. He wore it short around the sides. His eyes bulged from their sockets. Like his thin, pointed nose, his chin was very small. In fact, Sarah had heard people say that Chuck didn't have a chin—that his face ended at his lower lip. All of this, along with his skinny neck and rounded shoulders, made his forehead seem huge and out of proportion.

"Do you still want to get out of here?" he said, and then coughed.

Sarah said nothing and tried to stand as still as possible, but her body continued to shiver. She didn't know what to say. She didn't trust him.

"Talk to me, Sarah," said Chuck.

"You, talk to me," she finally said, trying to make her voice sound like a robot. "I don't know what you're talking about."

He sighed and looked away. The rain tapped the canopy.

He brought his face back toward her. "I know you don't trust me…And, I can't blame you, but…I'm dying, and I've got to find a real doctor. These nurses can't help me…And Emmanuel can't help, either."

Like the unnoticed movement of an hour hand on a clock, the light of day crept across them, illuminating Chuck's face. His eyes looked different, but there wasn't enough light yet for her to see in what way.

"Sarah, I know you still want to get out of here, so don't try and hide that from me. I've got to get out of here, and in a big hurry. So, if you want to go, too, I'm ready." He coughed again for what seemed like a minute.

Sarah took a step backward. "What's wrong with you?"

"I thought I had the flu, but it's more than that. They've been giving me medicine and telling me I'd be okay, but I'm getting worse. It took all my strength to get from my dorm to yours." He stopped talking to catch his breath.

She felt pity for him and almost reached out to pull him to her, but she caught herself in time and didn't. A light came on in her building, and she heard the murmur of women talking. She thought of Tommy.

"I'll come tonight," he said. Then he started to cough uncontrollably. Covering his mouth with his hand to muffle the sound, he turned away from her and bent over gagging. A fluid exploding from his gapping mouth. He choked again. Then, she saw that he vomited a dark liquid. A putrid odor reached Sarah, causing her to cover her mouth and nose with the palm of her hand. She stepped back and turned away from him. There, standing in the shadows of the slightly open door, was Sarah's bunkmate, Zuly.

Sarah jerked. "What do you want, Zuly? What'd you just hear?"

Zuly shook her head, backed into the building, and slowly closed the door.

"What was that?" Chuck said from behind Sarah.

"Nothing," said Sarah turning to face her husband. "The wind must have blown the door open. It was nothing…What…what's wrong with you, Chuck?"

"I don't know," he said, shaking his head. The sky grew much lighter, and, for the first time, Sarah noticed what was strange about Chuck's eye. The whites of them were red, blood red.

"Your eyes," said Sarah.

"I know. They get worse everyday…But that isn't all…I have these awful headaches…I can't eat…And, when I do everything comes back up…Blood

44

comes, too…Lots of blood pours through both ends of my body…What's wrong with me, Sarah?"

The smell of his rotten breath washed over her. She gagged.

"Sarah, you gotta help me."

"What are the nurses giving you, Chuck?"

"I don't know…They've been giving me these big brown vitamin pills…But they gave me those before I got sick. They make me keep taking these pills, and this liquid medicine, but it isn't helping…I'm getting worse."

As it got brighter outside, it got noisier inside.

Sarah glanced behind her, then back at Chuck. "Is that why you want to escape?"

"There's more," he said before a coughing spell quieted him. Finally, Chuck looked up. "And those snakes. Wait till you see those snakes."

"What?" said Sarah although she had heard him.

"Rattlesnakes, and copperheads," he said. Then, he started coughing again.

She stood there, tapping her foot on the wood, waiting on him to control his hacking. She knew he'd lost his mind, now.

At length, he regained his composure. "They keep a bunch of them in little cages in the storage building." He forced the words from his mouth, like he wanted to get everything said before he started coughing again. "Somebody told me Emmanuel was going to start having us handle snakes at some of the services. Can you believe that?"

Sarah saw Chuck glance over her shoulder and toward the door. She turned, and there stood Crystal Nelson looking down on Sarah.

"You okay?" asked Crystal.

"Yeah," said Sarah.

"That sonofabitch ain't bothering you, is he?"

"It's okay, Crystal. But don't tell…"

"I ain't telling nobody, nothing," said Crystal. "Your son was crying…"

"Oh, no," Sarah said trying to move past Crystal.

Crystal put a hand on Sarah's shoulder. "I've already taken care of it. I was just looking for you."

"Thanks," said Sarah. "I'm coming in, just a minute."

"Take your time, Zuly has him hushed up. But be careful of that little sonofabitch."

"You don't have to use that word."

"Sorry," said Crystal going back inside.

Sarah turned back toward her husband. "Finish it, Chuck."

He said, "We gotta get out of here, now. She'll tell on us, and Emmanuel will kill me."

"Maybe. Maybe not," said Sarah looking deep into his bloody eyes. "Meet me tonight an hour after the services."

"Where?"

"Not here, but behind this building, next to the fence in the pine-thicket."

"Okay," he said and turned to leave.

"Chuck," she called back to him.

At the bottom of the landing, he stopped and turned to face her.

"So help me, Chuck, if you turn against me again, I'll kill you myself. And that's a promise."

"I won't," he said. Then, he turned and ambled like an old man down the winding trail strewn with leaves.

She watched until he disappeared beneath the shadows of a large red oak. Just as Sarah started to turn and go back inside, she noticed the lights of a car moving up the hill toward their compound. She watched as it crept around the curves of the path leading from the river road. Sarah checked her watch. It was only six-thirty. Some of the ones that worked in and around Chattanooga would leave soon, but none came in at this time. Emmanuel allowed no one to work at night. He only permitted his people to have day jobs, so they could hear his evening services.

As the slow moving vehicle approached the gate, it turned off its lights. When she lost sight of it, she went back inside.

Many of the women shuffled toward the bathroom and only a few turned to see Sarah entering. Quickly, she moved to her son who sat in Crystal's lap rubbing his sleepy eyes. A soiled diaper sat at the foot of the bed.

"Thanks," said Sarah.

Tommy jerked his head up and extended his arms to their limit as he wiggled his fingers toward Sarah, signaling her to take him.

Crystal, handing the child to his mother said, "You don't have to thank me, Sarah. All I know is you best be careful. You know what that sonofabitch already done to you."

"He's sick, that's all," replied Sarah.

"He's sick, alright. Sick in the damn head," said Crystal, getting to her feet and moving away.

Sarah watched her friend glide toward the bathroom door. Tommy reached up and turned his mother's face toward his. Squeezing him gently, she started rocking back and forth and thinking about Chuck's proposition to escape. She closed her eyes.

"You not leave," said Zuly. Sarah's eyes shot open. The young Hispanic slipped onto the bed next to mother and child.

"What...what are you talking about?" said Sarah. "I don't know what you're talking about."

"Sarah, you can't leave...Emmanuel...he love us," said Zuly. "Please, Sarah, stay."

"I'm not leaving," said Sarah, lowering her head closer to Zuly's face. Sarah's body started to quiver. "You mustn't say anything to anyone, or I'll be punished."

"Yes...yes," said Zuly in tears. "I not."

"Promise me," said Sarah, reaching for the young Hispanic's chin and lifting it. "I won't leave you. Don't say a word to anyone about this, promise me."

Zuly nodded her head as tears streamed down her cheeks.

"I won't leave you," said Sarah, pulling Zuly next to her bosom. Noticing someone move toward the door, Sarah glanced up to see Crystal. The woman, fully dressed and wearing a yellow rain jacket had a large purse dangling across her shoulder. Sarah remembered that Emmanuel had not allowed Crystal to work or even leave the compound since her punishment.

"Crystal," said Sarah. "Wait."

Crystal stopped, turned slowly, and tiptoed back toward her friend. Reaching Sarah, Crystal knelt before her. "I'm leaving, and I ain't coming back." Instinctively, both women glanced about the room to see if anyone listened.

Crystal continued, "I'm gettin' out of here, and I don't care what you or anybody else says. Emmanuel's going to kill all of us anyway, so why not take a chance, and make a run for it? They'll have to kill me this time, 'cause I ain't letting that bastard or any of his whores touch me again. You best be careful, 'cause a lot of these women are jealous of your relationship with Emmanuel. They don't understand. Anyway, don't trust anybody, okay, sugar?" Crystal placed her hand on Sarah's shoulder.

"You be careful, yourself," said Sarah with tears forming in her eyes. Surprised she noticed that Crystal was attractive. Freedom radiated from her chestnut brown face transforming her into a lovely young woman.

"Sarah," said Crystal. "You gotta get out of here, you know...Like I said a minute ago, it won't be long before he kills everybody...Including himself. There's a place on the southeast corner of the fence next to a big cedar tree that you can get under if you ever take a mind to."

Sarah made a motion with her eyes toward Zuly trying to warn Crystal about not saying such things in front of the girl.

Crystal made a grimace with her face and waved an indifferent hand in the air. Then Crystal got to her feet and turned to walk away. She took two steps, turned back to Sarah, and blew her a kiss. "See ya, sweet-white-woman." Opening the door, Crystal didn't look back but walked out into the rain.

Zuly raised her head off Sarah's chest and glanced toward the closed double door. "Where...she...go?"

"Shhhh," said Sarah by puckering her lips and blowing air through her bottom teeth. "I'm not going to leave you."

Feeling Zuly relax in her arms, Sarah closed her eyes. They already felt tired and the day was young.

BOOM! Both women jerked when gunfire erupted outside. Half-naked women ran toward the door. Sarah sat on the bed, with Zuly in one arm and a whimpering Tommy in the other, thinking about the strange car, Crystal, Chuck, and herself.

CHAPTER SEVEN

Thump—swish—thump—swish—thump—swish, sang the wiper blades
on the Ford Explorer. Ahead, the low-beam headlamps reflected across the asphalt of narrow Cash Canyon Road, now covered with puddles of rainwater
that made a splashing sound every time the car ran through one even at this
slow speed. Glancing at the Explorer's illuminating digital clock over the mirror,
Matt saw it was six-twelve, quite early for him to be up, much less out on a Saturday morning. He tried to keep straight in his sleep-deprived brain what he had to
do today before meeting Medora around noon at the Choo Choo Restaurant.

Thanks to this weather his two scars, the one running down the right side
of his face, and the chunk of meat the size of a golf ball gone from his right
shoulder, continued aching, even though he had taken three Extra Strength Ty-
lenol tablets thirty minutes ago. To take his mind off the pain, Matt thought
of his two sons, but then a new pain appeared—pain that would never go away.
Desertion.

With his window cracked several inches at the top, Matt took in a deep
breath of air. He relished in the musty smell of a damp forest. It was getting
lighter already, and, off to his right beyond a slight embankment, Matt thought
he could make out the black water of the Tennessee River rushing toward the
Gulf of Mexico. The land between the river and the road was thick with oak,
hickory, sweetgum, maple, and other hardwood trees whose bare branches intertwined over dogwoods, azaleas, and small red cedars.

To his left, just on the other side of the road from the river, the terrain rose
dramatically up Raccoon Mountain. The same vegetation grew there. As the early morning light spread through the woods, Matt could see the green fronds of
ferns and the tiny moss plants covering the rock outcropping that jutted through
a thick carpet of brown leaves. Trumpet creepers, poison ivy, and other vine-type
plants had already gone dormant for the winter. Matt liked and appreciated all
seasons of the year, but he already missed the green of summer with its many
fragrances and its busy sounds. Winter had its own odor of burning wood from
fireplaces and the mildew of moist ground, but its sound was no sound at all. Except on days when it rained, winter stayed drastically silent through the woods.

Pulling off the side of the two-lane road, Matt stopped the Explorer and
reached across the seat for a copy of the aerial photograph taken from his computer. He placed it across the steering wheel and took out a pencil-shaped flashlight. Turning it on, he pointed it across the paper showing the fenced-in com-

pound. He glanced forward out the front windshield and predicted that just around the next curve would be the graveled path leading up Raccoon Mountain and to the compound's entrance.

From behind Matt another car's lights appeared and grew closer until it illuminated his photograph. Always cautious, Matt didn't turn around to see who came, but instead he looked into his rearview mirror. He slid his left hand along the outside of the leather seat and laced his fingers around the carbon-steel butt of a model 457 Smith & Wesson revolver. Blinding lights from the vehicle pulled to within several feet of his back bumper and stopped. Matt placed his thumb on the pistol's bobbed hammer and pulled it back until it clicked. He didn't turn his head, but sat still, waiting.

With the car's lights still glaring in the Explorer's review mirror, Matt heard someone behind open the door and step onto the asphalt. Matt looked in the side mirror and saw the shadow of a large man striding toward him. The pistol felt cold in Matt's hand. He pulled it close to the side of his leg.

Matt listened to the sound of heavy footsteps splashing and moving toward his half-open window. Without turning his head, Matt could hear the person's heavy breathing as the man looked inside. Matt slid the pistol higher until it was only an inch from the top of the window.

Then, in a deep, gruff, but familiar voice, the man said, "What the hell you doing out here this time of morning, Matt?"

Matt slid the weapon under the seat, and turned to stare into the round, fat, and smiling face of Detective Joe Johnson. At only five-foot-seven, Johnson was way out of proportion, weighing in at a little over two hundred and fifty pounds. He didn't have a double chin, but a triple chin hung across his buttoned shirt collar. Matt often told him he looked like he'd been put together by a drunk committee. Water drained off Johnson's wide-brimmed hat through the Explorer's window and onto Matt's shoulder. He knew this was one way Johnson liked to aggravate some of his friends. Johnson played rough and loved it when his friends played even rougher.

"What you trying to do, drown me?" Matt said, pulling back away from the window.

"What the hell you think I'm doing out here in this damn rain?" Joe Johnson said. "I want your dry ass to get wet today, and maybe it'll get a little chapped like mine is. What the fuck you doing out here? I told you I'd look into this shit. Let me see that damn aerial thing-a-ma-gig you told me about."

"Aerial photo," Matt said turning the paper so Johnson could get a look. "Why don't you get in?"

"Hell, no!" said Johnson, blowing his cigar breath on Matt. "You know, after fifteen years as a deputy, I ain't never been this far out on this road. Really, I don't know anybody that has. But I'm gonna find that damn place you was telling me about last night." He took the photo out of Matt's hand without warning. "Where the hell is that camp you told me about, anyway? Damn if this don't all look the same to me."

"I think it's around that curve and off to the left," Matt said pointing across the dash. "You wanna follow me?"

"Hell, no!" said Johnson. He threw the photo back in Matt's lap. "You stay right here and don't follow me. Okay? You keep your ass down here, and I'll tell you all about it when I get back." Joe turned to go back to his patrol car.

"Wait," Matt said, opening the door. The November rain engulfed him. Matt reached back inside, got his bark-brown, wide-brimmed hat, and slipped it on. He walked up to Johnson's car and said, "What you gonna do with Sarah Brindle? You taking her down town, or what?"

"I like that damn hat." said Johnson pointing at Matt's head. "What kind of Stetson is that? I like that little, narrow leather strap it's got."

"Catera. What you gonna do with Sarah Brindle?"

"Can't you ever say 'thank you'? I told you I like your damn hat?"

"Thank you, asshole," Matt said. "Can't you answer a damn question?"

"I don't know. Why the hell you gettin' mad?"

"Who the hell is getting mad?" Matt growled. He thought about his rain jacket in the Ford.

"I like that damn hat." Johnson grinned and turned to get inside his car. After opening the door, he turned back toward Matt and peered over the half open window. "I like them damn boots you got on, too. Them are Tony Lama Boots, ain't they?"

"Yeah," Matt said, walking up to his friend and looking down into his beady eyes. Johnson even had a small mouth that appeared even smaller on such a big moon-shaped puss. Matt glanced down at Johnson's black, flat-heeled boots.

Johnson's voice turned serious. "If that's where this Sarah Bridle is, I'm gonna ask her some questions. And if I don't like the way she answers the ones about them drugs taken from Erlanger, then she's going down town."

Once getting his question answered, Matt turned to walk away without a reply.

Johnson continued, "You can wait here, or go back to your place, and I'll call you. Whatever you wanna do. Hell, I doubt if she's even at this god-forsaken place. Hell, I don't even know if there is a damn place, yet. I don't trust them damn computers, anyway."

"Thanks, Joe," Matt hollered back from beside the Explorer's door.

It wasn't long before Johnson's brown Plymouth rolled past Matt and around the curve. After its taillights went out of sight, Matt looked up the rocky hill toward the top of the mountain. Because the trees had lost their leaves, he could see a long way up the slope. He didn't notice a sign of the compound, but he knew it should be up there.

Matt walked off the left side of the road, stepped over a small drainage ditch, and moved several feet up the steep slope into the woods. The incline was so steep he had to dig his heels into the loose soil to keep from slipping back down into the water-filled ditch. Holding onto a small oak sapling, Matt moved several more feet up the slope. He stopped and watched. Rainwater thumped on his Stetson, ran off the back of its brim, and onto his shirt making him shiver. When Matt started to turn back toward the car, he saw a glimpse of what looked like a person moving horizontally a hundred yards up the hill.

Matt grabbed a small sapling and pulled himself two additional strides farther up the hill where he propped his rear end against the trunk of a large white oak tree. Water oozed down his back and under his leather belt. Shaking from the chill now, Matt wrapped his arms around his chest trying to keep body heat inside his clothing. Matt jumped when something darted across a small clearing about two hundred feet above him and then disappeared behind a clump of cedars. He felt it had to be some kind of animal.

Matt pushed away from the tree and prepared to climb deeper into the woods when gunfire boomed off to his right. He flinched and fell against the tree. There were three quick blasts. It came from the same direction Johnson had just traveled.

On pure survival instinct, Matt ran out of the woods, hurtled the ditch, hopped across the narrow road, and stood beside the Ford. Two additional blasts of what sounded like a high powered rifle, thundered from around the curve. The sound of tires spinning in gravel and a car's racing engine reached Matt a few seconds later. He opened the Explorer's door, grabbed his pistol, and jumped inside.

In seconds, Joe Johnson's Plymouth rounded the curve and almost slammed into Matt before stopping just past the Explorer. Matt twisted the keys cranking the car's engine. He prepared to turn around in the middle of the road to follow Johnson, but Joe backed the Plymouth next to his window. That's when Matt saw the missing windshield in the deputy's car.

"What the hell?" Matt said, and then Johnson started yelling at him.

"Get the shit outta here, now. There's some crazy sumbitches up there, and I'm gonna get some fuck'n back-up. Look what them bastards did to my car. Shit, shit, shit."

"Did you ask about the woman?"

"Dammit. I ain't got time to talk to your ass. Get the fuck outta here you crazy sumbitch."

Matt watched Detective Johnson reach for his two-way radio, but before he could hear what Joe said, the Plymouth, minus its windshield, shot down the pavement leaving Matt alone along the side of Cash Canyon Road.

Matt knew he'd better turn the Ford around, but rebelled against his better judgment and started inching forward toward the curve. He had to find some answers before Joe returned with half of Hamilton County's law enforcement and about a hundred nosey reporters.

When he rounded the curve, Matt saw a small graveled path leading up the hill into the woods. He swung the Explorer's nose up onto the trail and stopped. Quickly glancing out each window, he saw nothing, so he turned on the headlight but still couldn't see very deep into the forest. The path made a sharp turn to the left only ten feet ahead.

SNAP! Tree limbs cracked above his car and a fraction of a second later the explosion from a rifle came piercing down the hill. Matt jumped when pieces of the tree's branches banged onto the Explorer's hood as the shot echoed past him and down the valley. He didn't wait for another report from the weapon. He threw it into reverse, slammed a Tony Lama boot into the accelerator, which caused the Ford to jerk backward onto Cash Canyon Road. Gravel banged against the car's undercarriage. Matt stomped on the breaks, which stopped the car just before it careened down an embankment that stopped at the Tennessee River.

He threw the gearshift into drive as another gun blast reverberated across the canyon. Matt pressed the toe of his boot hard into the rubber accelerator, and the Explorer jolted forward and around the curve.

Before he had reached any speed, a person moved out into the path of the car. Using reflexes Matt thought he had lost; he slammed on the Ford's brakes and spun the steering wheel to his left. Wet tires on rain soaked asphalt screeched. Slowing but out of control, the Ford slipped off the road and bumped into a huge shagbark hickory tree.

When his forehead smacked into the steering wheel, Matt remembered not putting on his seat belt. For a moment, bright lights flashed before his eyes, and a taste of blood settled in his mouth. Without opening his eyes, Matt fell backward against the rear of the seat causing his hat to fall off and onto his lap.

"You okay?" asked a woman after opening the passenger's door. "I'm so sorry."

"What?" Matt said, trying to focus his vision on the voice. A liquid trickled down Matt's forehead, so he reached up trying to wipe it away. There was no blood, only water, but a small bump grew in his hairline. The woman slid inside, sat down, and closed the door.

"I'm really sorry," she said talking frantically. "Can you drive? If you can't, I can. Your car's okay. You just barely hit that tree. All you got to do is back-up, and we can get out of here."

"I'm fine," Matt said backing the Explorer from the tree. Once on Cash Canyon Road, he sped the Ford forward and sensed the woman settling into the seat beside him. Matt felt the bump continuing to form on his head and reached in the edge of his hairline again to check for blood but found none.

After fishtailing around a curve in the road, Matt slowed. Finally he glanced her way. In spite of the rainwater dripping from a few strands of black, curly hair hanging over her face, she was beautiful. She had light brown skin, and her appearance reminded Matt of the singer, Natalie Cole. She was a rain drenched woman—not too tall or too short but all female, and he liked the way she looked. "Who are you?"

"Crystal," she said turning to face him.

Matt checked the wet road ahead, slowed the Ford more, looked back at this young woman, and said, "And where'd you come from?"

She dropped her head and whispered, "I just came from hell."

Thump—swish—thump—swish—thump—swish.

CHAPTER EIGHT

"Come to the sanctuary," said Irene over the outside speakers situated on poles at each corner and center of the compound. "Everyone come to the sanctuary, now."

Sarah slipped into her hunter-green, cotton dress and reached for Tommy's one-piece blue jumpsuit. The other women had moved away from the door soon after the gunfire. One of them said it happened at the entrance gate, but no one knew what had really taken place. Women now hurried in and out of the bathroom, trying to get their clothes on.

"Everyone come to the sanctuary, now!" said Irene in her heavy voice. "Emmanuel will save us all, so hurry!"

After getting Tommy dressed, Sarah found her brown, flat-heeled, penny loafers and put them on. She got into her yellow rain jacket and threw a handful of diapers in the diaper bag. Picking up Tommy, she fell in line with several other women going out the barrack door into the drizzling rain. Daylight had crept upon the mountain with the sun hidden somewhere behind the clouds. Sarah pulled Tommy's hood tightly around his face and marched off with everyone else toward the sanctuary. Someone grabbed her rain slicker from behind, and when she turned and looked down, there was Zuly's wet face looking up at her.

Sarah put her free arm around Zuly. "Stay with me, child." As they turned to follow the moving herd of humans, Sarah noticed a group of guards at the compound's entrance. Two men held long binoculars to their eyes and peered off into the woods toward the distant river road below. Standing on her toes, Sarah thought she saw a black car of some kind through the trees. Another of the guards wrote something down, probably license numbers, on a yellow pad as he stood next to the ones with binoculars.

Before Tommy, Zuly, and Sarah reached the entrance to the church, a group of men walking in the same direction joined them. Sarah looked for Chuck but didn't see him.

After they had moved several hundred feet, she noticed that a man in the group kept watching her. She couldn't decide if she should ask him about Chuck, or not. Finally, she made eye contact with the man who kept glancing her way.

"Willard," she yelled at him. The man stopped as Sarah approached. "Have you seen my husband, Chuck?"

"He's in bed," said Willard.

Sarah looked past Willard toward the men's dorm. "He's in bed?"

"Yeah," said Willard. He turned and scurried away.

Sarah didn't want Tommy to see his father sick, so she handed him to Zuly and told her to take him inside the sanctuary. In seconds, Zuly and Tommy disappeared in the crowd, all moving in the same direction toward the meeting room. Sarah felt relief that Tommy didn't cause a fuss about leaving her.

Over the loudspeaker boomed the voice of Irene, "All move to the sanctuary, now! Emmanuel will inform everyone of what's happening! Please move quickly and quietly into the sanctuary and have a seat!"

Sarah listened and almost turned to follow the crowd into the church before catching herself.

She had trouble moving against the flow of people, but she pushed her way ahead until she reached the side entrance to the men's dorm. She stood there a few minutes waiting for anyone to come out of the door, but no one did.

Sarah ran to the door and hurried inside. There were no lights on, but she could tell it looked exactly like the women's quarters. She noticed the different smell, a man's smell. For a moment, the man's scent relaxed her, but then it quickly turned to terror when the odor turned to that of Emmanuel and death.

All the beds were empty except one near the back corner. She tiptoed to it. There, under a bloodstained sheet lay Chuck trying to get a breath. With half open eyes the color of blood, he glanced up at her. She wanted to turn and run but couldn't move. It had only been thirty or forty minutes since they had last talked, and he looked much, much worse now.

"Oh, Chuck," she said looking into his eyes that looked past her as if she wasn't there. "It's me, Sarah. Oh, Chuck."

"Sarah, help me," he whispered. His rotten breath made Sarah gag.

She moved closer to hear what he said and stepped in something slick along the side of his bed. She looked down and saw a large pool of blood on the floor. She placed her hand over her mouth to keep from throwing up.

"What, Chuck?"

His mouth moved but she couldn't hear what he said. She put her ear next to his mouth.

"I...don't want to...die," Chuck said. He kept moving his lips, but nothing, not even air, came out.

"Oh, Chuck," she said, standing up and looking down on her husband.

Chuck's whole body jerked, and a rasping sound came from his throat. Then he started shaking so hard the sweat-soaked covers slid off the bed and into the pool of blood. He gasped for another breath of air but none came—only a gurgling sound. When blood spewed from his mouth and nose, Sarah jumped back and watched as her husband died. With one final quiver, his chest flew upward stiffening into an arch, and then, like letting air out of a blown up doll, his body settled deep into the mattress. His half-open blank eyes stared at nothing as the last bit of air escaped his drowning lungs.

CHAPTER NINE

Instead of stopping at his boat with the woman who had just jumped into his vehicle only minutes ago, Matt drove the extra mile onto I-24 and now sped along the base of Lookout Mountain three-and-a-half miles from downtown Chattanooga. Here the eastbound lanes of the interstate highway ran for almost a mile next to the rock-walled cliffs of the famous mountain, site of a great Civil War battle. There, only a railroad track separated the highway from this jagged, lichen-covered outcrop of granite.

Opposite the mountain, and on their left beyond the narrow grass median, ran the westbound lanes of traffic going in the opposite direction. Beyond these busy lanes and the shoulder of the road was a six-foot high wire fence. Just past the fence, a graveled bank dropped several feet to the imposing Tennessee River. Here, at Moccasin Bend the river made a gigantic U-turn. The greenish-gray waterway was almost a quarter of a mile wide here, and across on the far embankment stood the Moccasin Bend Mental Hospital, and the Swallowed Re-Education Center. When a tourist looked down from the top of Lookout Mountain, this part of the River looked like a giant nipple, and the city of Chattanooga was the breast.

When Matt reached the part of the highway that made a sharp turn to the north toward the city of Chattanooga, he reached up, for the tenth or eleventh time, to rub the small bump on his forehead. He expected to have a headache, but the pain had not yet visited him.

His passenger sat silently, staring out the windshield at the rain-covered world. Matt planned to take her to the police station, but he hadn't asked her where she wanted to go, yet. He just presumed that was where she needed to go.

Ahead, Matt saw the flashing lights of approaching patrol cars in the west bound lane headed in the opposite direction. Matt assumed they were going to the compound where someone had fired at Joe Johnson, knocking out his car's windshield. Matt wanted to follow, but because he needed to talk to his passenger, he stayed on course back to the city. As the train of emergency vehicles passed by him, Matt counted four cars from the sheriff's office, one State Patrol car, and one unmarked black Dodge with a portable emergency light on its top. He wondered if the FBI had already arrived. A white van with *TV 12* printed on its side paneling followed close behind these cars.

His passenger, Crystal Nelson, turned in her seat to watch the cars with their flashing lights speed by and out of sight around the curve behind them.

Once they had disappeared she said, "Where you taking me?"

"To the police station," He finally identified her odor as that of Ivory soap.

She failed to respond but stared out her side window.

Matt waited until they passed a transfer truck. Then he turned to her. "Is that where you want to go?" He saw that she wore Nike tennis shoes, faded jeans, and a yellow rain jacket.

"No. No, I don't know," she said calmly. "Why should I want to go there? Don't take me there...You a policeman?"

"Oh, no, I'm not the law."

"Then why were you out there, trying to get in the gate?"

"Looking for somebody," he said.

"Who?" She rotated her lower torso in the seat to face Matt and sat on her left leg, making that knee point at him. Her hands lay folded in her lap.

"Do you live in the compound?" Matt said

"Yes, and I'm never going back."

"What's that place, anyway?"

"*The Refuge of God,*" she said. "Except, God hadn't visited there in a long time. It should be *The Refuge of the Devil,* but it's not. It's Emmanuel's place."

"Who?"

"Emmanuel," she said turning only her head forward as the road ahead curved to the right and went over another highway that would have taken them to downtown Chattanooga. Their present course would take them toward the airport and the Georgia State line. She turned back to Matt. "His followers call him 'The Blessed,' but he's really Satan."

"How many followers?"

"About three hundred, I guess. I can't tell about those things."

Matt was filled with curiosity. "How'd he get all those followers?"

"I don't know," she said with a distant expression on her face. "My mama, she took me to him. I was young, very young. I had just had a baby and the father—a married man in the projects—he wouldn't claim it. In fact, he ran away from his family and me. Mama gave the baby away."

Her voice cracked. Tears formed in her eyes. Matt didn't comment, so they rode listening to the wiper blades beat their rhythm. He thought about babies being given away and the old man that had raised him.

Finally, she said, "I didn't know what she'd done with my baby until it was too late...until the baby was gone. I tried to kill myself, but..." She blew out a long breath of air before continuing, "Emmanuel took me in—loved me—told me God loved me. He was so kind...He made me feel so good about myself."

Matt interrupted, "I thought God or Jesus was called Emmanuel in the Bible, but I don't know much about religion."

"Emmanuel's gone crazy, now," she said, turning back to face Matt. Her face turned hard. "Last night we had a mock suicide..."

"A what?" He said before realizing what she'd said.

"A fake suicide except we didn't know it was fake, and he was testing our faith. He gave us something that made us feel like we were dying. Some of the people went to sleep. I think we had one old man that had a heart attack. Anyway, it's not gonna be long before it'll be a real mass suicide, just like at Jonestown. He's crazy as a loon. Why, he's as bad as that bunch in Texas that burned themselves up instead of coming out of that compound."

"Waco," Matt said.

"What?"

"Waco," he said. "That bunch in Texas was at Waco, and the leader was David Koresh. Is that the one you're talking about?" What she said made his face feel hot even though his body shivered from the damp.

"Yeah," she said, "and there was another bunch out in California that killed themselves so they could ride some dang comet."

"Hale-Bopp."

"No," said Crystal, "it was Heaven's Gate, or something like that."

"I mean the comet was Hale-Bopp," Matt said.

"Whatever." She pulled her legs out of the seat and crossed her arms over her chest.

Matt needed more detail. "Back to this place on Raccoon Mountain. Do all those three hundred believe in this Emmanuel? I mean, will all of them do what he says?"

"Yeah, I'm afraid so. There are a few that's lost faith and would love to get away, but most are either blind followers or so scared of him they would kill even themselves if he ask them to...Where we going?"

"I really don't know," Matt said. "Just riding around until we decide what to do. If you don't wantta go to the authorities, where you want to go?"

"I'm getting as far away from here as I can. He and his people must never find me...They'd kill me this time."

"You've left before?"

"Not really," she said, staring ahead of them as they traveled east up Missionary Ridge. "He punished me a few months ago."

"What do you mean, punished you? For what?"

"He don't need much of a reason. Somebody told him I was talking to a strange man while at work."

"What'd he do?" The windshield wipers continued to thump out their rhythm in tune with the rainwater splashing under the Explorer's tires.

"To me?"

"Yeah."

"He branded me."

"He what?" Again, what she said took a moment to register.

"He branded me with a red-hot iron, and it hurt like the devil."

"Where?"

"On the cheeks."

Matt turned and looked at her face. "I don't see it."

"I'm sitting on it," she said, without the slightest hint of a grin.

"What?" Matt's brain still lagged about two seconds behind his mouth.

"On my ass. It hadn't been healed long. Very hard to set down for a long time, as you might guess. I'll have the mark of the serpent for the rest of my life."

"What you mean?" Matt tried to form what she said into a mental picture, but it wouldn't appear.

"A snake," she said.

Matt sensed her anger, so he decided not to ask more about her particular infliction.

"Does he brand everybody?"

"He whips people, or paddles 'em without their clothes on."

"You're kidding." Matt suddenly doubted her.

"No."

"In front of the congregation?" He couldn't believe this.

"Yeah," she said. "He gets his rocks off watching women get beat in the nude."

"That doesn't sound like any church I've ever been to." Matt hadn't entered many churches.

"He takes some of the women he likes to bed."

"He does what?" Matt shook my head.

"I've heard he'll take young boys to his bed."

"Oh, don't tell me that," Matt said. Bile rose in his throat. "Damn. He's a sick bastard."

"That's why I had to get the hell out of there. There's going to be a lot of good people die. Especially now that the world is about to learn about him."

"There are good people there?" He couldn't imagine.

"Yeah, a few," said Crystal. "You never said who you're looking for, anyway."

Matt reached in his shirt pocket and pulled out several pieces of folded paper. While trying to drive with one hand and keeping his eyes on the road, Matt unfolded the sheets and handed both pieces of paper to Crystal. One showed the picture of the older Sarah Brindle from the Tennessee drivers' licenses and the other a younger woman by the same name from the Georgia licenses.

"Dang," said Crystal. "Where'd you get these?"

"You know 'em?"

"I sure do," said Crystal while holding up the picture of the older woman. "This one's the biggest bitch ever. She's mean as hell."

"What's her name?"

"Irene Master," Crystal said. "Queen of the harem."

"The what?" Matt did it again. He heard, but it didn't register.

"Emmanuel's got a harem of women. He's got a real wife, but she stays either drunk or drugged up. Irene goes out and gets him women he wants to have sex with, like Sarah here."

Matt pointed to the picture of the young blond woman. "That's Sarah Brindle?"

"Yeah," said Crystal. "How you know her name?"

"That's who I'm looking for. Is she in his harem?"

"She was, in the past...She even had a child with Emmanuel."

"Wait a minute," Matt said as we started descending the east side of Missionary Ridge. In five minutes, he'd have to decide to go north or south on I-75, or get off the Interstate completely.

"She has a baby," Matt continued, "and it belongs to this Emmanuel, not her husband?"

"Yeah," said Crystal. "At least everybody thinks so. It's got Emmanuel's blue eyes."

"Really?"

"It's a shame, too," said Crystal. "Sarah's a beautiful woman, inside and out. She got punished the same night I did."

"She got branded, too?"

"No," said Crystal. "He had her whipped with a leather strap, a belt. I don't think he wanted to scar her."

"Jesus!" Matt said as he started to believe what this stranger told him. Ahead loomed a large green sign that announced they neared the I-75 connection. On the left of the huge sign, printed in large white letters was the word KNOXVILLE with an arrow pointing down to indicate which lane one needed to drive in to go north. On the right of the same sign was printed ATLANTA with an arrow under it. Matt pulled the Ford into the far-left lane under the Knoxville sign.

After maneuvering into position, he said, "Why'd he whip her?"

"Her husband told on her for wanting to escape."

"Her husband?" Matt said shaking his head. "What kind of people are these?"

"Sick," said Crystal, staring out her window at a long line of northbound cars merging with them as they entered the junction of the two Interstates. "Really sick people."

They rode without speaking for almost a minute, until a white van came soaring by them blowing its horn. Startled, Matt reached for the 457 Smith & Wesson beside my seat but released it when he noticed the orange flags flapping violently above each front window of the weaving van. And, on its spare tire cover was a big UT sticker. He remembered that he'd planned to watch the Tennessee Vols play Vanderbilt in football this afternoon on TV. He'd lost all interest in the game.

Matt had only driven a few minutes north on I-75 when he took the Highway 153 exit west toward Chickamauga Dam. This would take them around the north end of Chattanooga.

After a long silence, Crystal turned to him. "Why you looking for Sarah?"

"I'm a procurer of information, and..."

"A what?" she said. What's a pro...cure...a...of information?"

"I obtain information for money."

"You're a private eye; a private detective?"

"Some people call us that," Matt said. "But we're not like what you see on TV or in the movies. That's not the way it really works. Actually, it's quite boring most of the time. I do a lot of my work over the Internet or over a phone."

"Oh," she said. "What about Sarah? Why you looking for her and that wicked bitch of the south, Irene?"

"Someone has acquired my services to find Sarah. And this Irene just happened to be using Sarah's name on her driver's license and at work."

"At work?" said Crystal. "I can't believe this. Why's she using Sarah's name?"

"I don't know, yet."

"Who hired you?"

"I can't tell you."

"I know who it was."

"Really, who?"

"Sarah's mother, she's looking for her, right?"

"What makes you say that?" Matt said wondering if this beauty was clairvoyant.

"You're from Atlanta, and you've been sent here to find Sarah, right?"

"Go on," Matt said, not correcting why she might think he was from Atlanta.

"Last night, before the mock suicide, Emmanuel told us someone from Atlanta was snooping around asking questions about him. He said they were sent here by one of our member's mother; then, he looked right at Sarah for a long time."

"What else did he say?" Matt kept asking questions although he'd found Medora Meehan's daughter, and she was clearly in danger.

"I don't remember all of what he said about that, but he knows everything. He's got a security system like you've never seen. It's scary, because if he knows about you and her mother, then, neither one of us is safe. Like I said, he's crazy, and I really think he'd kill someone, if he had to."

"How would he kill them?" Matt said trying to appear calm for Crystal's sake.

"I don't know. He'd probably have one of his disciples do the dirty work, though."

Matt thought about Broadway and realized why she'd said he was from Atlanta. "How about snakes?"

"Snakes!" said Crystal. "Oh my God. I've tried to forget about the snakes."

"Have you ever seen live snakes there in cages or anything like that?" The rain had slacked, but cars in front and beside them still sent water onto the Explorer's windshield. The wind had increased, and the clouds began to break up, showing patches of blue overhead. The air inside the Ford became noticeably cooler; signaling it had grown colder outside.

"He handles snakes, or he once did," she said, "until he was bitten on the arm by a copperhead about seven or eight months ago. I wish he'd died, but he didn't. His arm swelled to about twice its normal size. He didn't miss a sermon though, but he hasn't handled any since then. But I've heard he has plenty of them still around, and I heard..." She didn't finish her sentence but stared out the passenger's window into the rain.

"What'd you hear?"

"One of our members got bit by a poisonous snake about a month ago."

"Was it in church?"

"No," said Crystal. "I don't know where he was when the snake got him. Nobody ever said. Anyway, I thought it was strange, because they let the poor man die. The congregation laid hands on the man and prayed for his healing, but Emmanuel didn't. It took the man about a half a day to die. Poor man really suffered."

"Was anything strange about the guy?" Matt said. "What I mean is, was he causing any trouble for the cult, or anything that might make this Emmanuel want to kill him?"

"Oh, God!" said Crystal, looking at Matt with big eyes. "I don't know why I didn't think about that before, but his wife was the cause of his death."

"What do you mean?"

"See," said Crystal, placing her hand on the Ford's dash and leaning over to look into his face. "Emmanuel had the man's wife move into his harem. Emmanuel was having sex with the man's wife, and the husband was causing a big stink about it."

"I can't blame the husband for that." Matt's ex-wife's face flashed across his mind.

Crystal ignored his interruption and continued, "I heard that the man had tried to get his wife, beautiful little girl of about eighteen, to leave with him, but like a fool, she wanted to stay with Emmanuel. It wasn't long, maybe two days, until the husband got snake-bit and died. It's so obvious, now that I'm outside looking in. That snake-bite was no accident."

She leaned back against her seat and glared out her side window. She stayed quiet. Matt did too.

After riding in silence for several minutes, they came upon Chickamauga Lake, which was actually the Tennessee River, but the name had changed when the government dammed it here during the time of President Roosevelt's _New Deal_. Because of the dam, the river tripled its width here, and people thought of it as a lake. The work was all part of the Tennessee Valley Authority or TVA.

As they approached the bridge leading over the dam, Matt watched the whitecaps forming across the wide body of water as the wind raced across it. He would love to have his boat, the _Desperado_, out on the lake riding up river. The strong gale would make steering tough, but that was what he loved about cruising on the water. A lone, white and blue, thirty-eight foot Bayliner motor yacht pitched from side to side as it ran at slow speed along the far shore. During the summer months, hundreds of craft would cover the water, but now, only the bold ventured from shore.

Slowing down to fifty-five, they started across the Thrasher Bridge. On their right spread the spacious lake, while on their left ran the narrower part of the Tennessee River in Tennessee. Here it dropped about a hundred feet, and they called it Nickajack Lake. Thirty miles west and down river was another dam. All construction took place during the depression to control floods along the river and give men jobs at a time when jobs were nonexistent. Before the building of these dams, the Tennessee River often flooded Chattanooga as well as other communities along its banks.

Matt reached for his cellular phone and punched in Leaky Water's cellular phone number. After only four rings, Leaky answered. Matt placed him on speakerphone.

"Yeah," Leaky said in one of his homeboy voices.

"How long will it take you to get to my boat?"

"Not long, say—fifteen minutes. You there now?"

"No," Matt said. "Just crossed Chickamauga Dam, and I'm about to turn-off onto Highway 319 and head back there."

"What you need, man?" said Leaky.

"I'll tell you when we get there."

"What's this 'we' shit?"

"I'll tell you when we get there. You learn anything from your trip to Erlanger?"

"Whole backyard full of shit," said Leaky talking like a redneck. "Some of it's hotter than the hinges on the gates of hell."

Crystal laughed and quickly put her hand over her mouth to muffle the sound.

"Who that be with you?" Leaky said.

"I'll introduce you when we get there—bye," Matt said pushing the red button on the phone that read: "*end*."

"He sounds crazy," she said.

"He's something else, all right."

"So," said Crystal. "You're not from Atlanta, and you're taking me to your boat that's somewhere close, right?"

"Yeah, if you don't mind? I'll take you wherever you want to go after we talk to Leaky, but right now, I got a few more questions and one thing to ask of you."

"Like what?" she said.

"Would you mind letting me make a videotape of you talking about Sarah, Emmanuel and *The Refuge of God*, so I can show it to her mother?"

"For her mother?"

"No one else will see it. I promise. I'm only going to let her see it, then I'll destroy it—okay?"

"I guess," she said. "You sure nobody'll see it?"

"After we finish, I'll take you to get a bus ticket to anywhere in the States you want to go—okay?" He begged, now, and Matt didn't like himself for doing it. Since his divorce, he'd made a promise to never beg a woman for another thing in his life. Maybe this didn't count, he told himself. This was business.

They turned left off Highway 153 and onto 319 south. Heading back toward downtown Chattanooga meant that soon they'd have traveled a complete circle around the outskirts of the city.

"Tell me about this Emmanuel." Matt said. "How old is he? What's he look like?"

"He's in his mid-forties or early fifties. He was born somewhere north of Cleveland, Tennessee. He has a half-brother called Luke Belcher that..."

"Half-brother?" Matt interrupted. "Then, they have the same daddy, because they both have the same last name, right?"

"I don't know," she said. "He talks about himself a lot these days when he should be telling us about Jesus and God, so I think I remember him saying he was adopted. I believe his dad died before he was born. I'm not sure on that, but I think I remember him telling us about that once. Of course, he could be lying about everything."

"What's he look like?"

"He's about six feet tall, and about a hundred-and-sixty pounds. About your size, except you're built better than he is." Crystal suppressed a giggle. "He's got blue eyes...like yours. In fact, this is weird, but you look like him. Now that

I think about it, you could pass for brothers, except for your...I hope you ain't crazy like him."

"Really?" Matt said knowing she wanted to say except for the scar on his face. Matt had a powerful urge to reach up and feel the old wound again but fought against it.

"Hair's different, too."

"How?" Matt said.

"His hair is dyed jet-black—yours is brown, and his isn't short like yours, his is long and puffed up on top with a big pompadour. Sometimes it doesn't even look real."

"Lot's of hair." Matt said grabbing his Stetson and putting it on over his thinning hair.

She leaned forward, looked into Matt's face. "Yeah, you and him look enough alike to be relatives. You know about me, how 'bout you? You from around here?"

"I don't know where I'm from." Matt depressed the accelerator, causing the Explorer to explode down the highway. He couldn't put his finger on it yet, but he knew this assignment was far from the end.

CHAPTER TEN

From the stage, Emmanuel pounded his fist on the podium. He had yelled so much his voice broke like a rasping saw. "I'll never give in to their demands. We'll die first before I let them enter my camp."

Pausing for at least a minute, he glared out at his subjects through narrow-sliced eyes. The eerie silence boomed through the thick air and blared in Sarah's ears. She had never noticed such an utter stillness as they now experienced. Breath caught in throats, everyone was afraid to breathe. Sarah was afraid to close her eyes for even a flicker of a second.

After leaving her dead husband and entering the sanctuary, Sarah had failed to find Tommy and Zuly. She hoped they sat near the front and prayed everything would be fine. Emmanuel had made everyone wait ten minutes after all took a seat, before he came into the room wearing his purple velvet robe—the one he wore only on Sunday, never on Saturday.

Twenty-four male guards stood around the sanctuary with their backs pressed against the wall, watching the mass of humanity like the congregation was their prisoner. Each guard carried a shotgun suspended beside his leg. For the first time, Sarah noticed that several of these men had holstered pistols hanging from leather belts.

"Now you know why we had to take up arms," said Emmanuel. "I will protect you. Yes, I can do that. Believe in me, and you shall live forever."

Finally daring to breathe air again, Sarah had no doubts that Emmanuel had gone totally crazy. She wondered if the others knew it yet. She prayed that they did, before it was too late.

"We've lost another loved one, today," said Emmanuel dropping his head. Then slowly, he raised his eyes until he stared at the people through his eyebrows.

"Crystal has run away," Emmanuel said sadly as if he talked about someone already dead. "But we will find her, and bring her back. See, once you're under my protection, I can never let you stray from the flock." His voice began to increase in volume with each word. "We saw her get into a car with a man, and we'll find out who he is. See, with the power I have, I can see who she went off with..."

Sarah remembered the men who were looking through binoculars and writing something onto a piece of paper and wondered if they had gotten someone's license plate number.

"Yes!" he continued screaming. "It won't be long till we find her for my men are tracking her down as we speak...It won't be long till she's back with us."

He stopped yelling, paused for a moment, and when he began to speak again his voice stayed at normal volume but rasping. "But I hope nothing unfortunate happens to her while she's gone. That would be disastrous. I can't protect her while she's away from my side."

Sarah's head hurt from the screaming Emmanuel had done this morning. A fire she had never seen before radiated from his blue eyes. He looked inhuman, even savage-like, with that gaze projecting over the congregation. Sarah shivered, but she wasn't cold.

"Enough about Crystal," Emmanuel said, shaking his head and trying to clear his mind. "What about us?"

A siren wailed in the distance, causing Emmanuel's head to jerk upward from between his shoulders and his body to stand erect. His present expression reminded Sarah of jackals she had once seen on a National Geographic Special. The gray dogs had been eating the remains of a slain carcass when the photographer's bright light unexpectedly caught them. They brought their heads high and stared with wide-eyes, toward the camera. As with the jackals, Sarah saw the defiance spread across Emmanuel's face.

Outside the compound, the siren grew louder. Then, like a wind-up toy losing power, it wound down to nothing. It was somewhere near the entrance gate. Emmanuel waved the back of his left hand toward the guards, and four in the rear left the building. When the door opened for them to depart, Sarah heard the wind rushing through the dead leaves and pushing the fallen ones across the ground. A chill rushed across the back of Sarah's head, causing her to pull her neck into her shoulders.

Behind Emmanuel and through the back door, strode Irene. Her breast bounced as she approached her savior. When she stopped to whisper something into Emmanuel's ear, a smirk crossed his face as he nodded his head. Irene walked slowly this time out the rear door.

Emmanuel's gaze fell directly onto Sarah, and he held it steadfast. The short hairs on the back of her neck stood erect and her heart pounded its way up through her throat. Sarah wanted to crawl under the bench in front of her, but she couldn't move—she couldn't even blink.

"Sarah Brindle," said Emmanuel. "Come forth."

Her drumming heart stopped, and her head spun. Quickly, she glanced among the women looking for Tommy. Sarah couldn't find him. She felt all eyes on her.

"Sarah," screamed Emmanuel. Sarah jumped. "I said to come up here, now."

Leaping to her feet, she stumbled between the seats, stepping on a woman's toes as she made her way to the aisle. Her feet of lead and an addled brain caused her to stagger as she moved forward. She climbed the steps and approached Emmanuel. He stood facing her with a smile that twisted and distorted his face. Placing a hand on her shoulder, he brought his mouth next to her cheek and blew whiskey breath across her face. Her knees grew weak, and she almost fell backward as fear consumed her body.

"Sarah, Sarah," Emmanuel said in a whisper. "My beautiful little Sarah. You're mine to do with as I please, now." A low chuckle crossed his lips, and with his fingers on her shoulder, he squeezed until she winced in pain.

CHAPTER ELEVEN

When they got back, Matt was surprised to find the parking lot at the Marina full of cars. It wasn't unusual for many of his neighbors to be here on the weekend, but he'd assumed, because of the bad weather, most of the part-time mariners would stay in their land homes and away from the river today.

The sound of loose gravel under the tires of the Explorer comforted him, because it signaled that he had made it home again. Matt's body relaxed for just a minute as he drove past BMWs, Mercedes, Porches, and a few American-made cars. Only one other man besides Matt lived on his boat full time. With all the slips filled, the marina could harbor thirty-three variously sized crafts, and most of them were yachts.

Since his boat stayed at the far end of the pier away from the entrance, Matt drove the Ford to its regular parking slot near the *Desperado*. The earlier rain, and now the cold wind, kept everyone inside their crafts and their boats in their slips.

"Damn," Matt said, not to anyone, when he saw Leaky's fire-engine-red Mustang in the space where his Explorer should go. Looking in all directions, Matt didn't see another place to park. Like a child not getting his way, Matt hit the steering wheel with the palm of his hand, turned around, and sped toward the entrance.

"What's wrong?" Crystal said. It was the first words she had spoken in almost ten minutes. Realizing he needed to bombard her with questions soon, he'd decided to leave her alone for now. He knew a rested mind could think more clearly; consequently, he had stopped talking and put *Patsy Cline's Greatest Hits'* CD on. Crystal had hummed along with most of the old songs and even had sung along with "Crazy." She wasn't bad.

"Nothing's wrong," Matt said pulling the Explorer into an empty spot one space from the entrance road. "I'd rather not have to park this far from my boat, because…" He paused in mid-sentence after seeing a group of vehicles speeding north on Browns Ferry Road.

"It's about to hit the fan," she said in a regretful voice.

"Yeah," he said, opening the door and stepping out to feel the cold north wind bite into his face. Matt had to put his hand on the Stetson to keep it from blowing off. He jogged around to open her door.

She opened the door and stepped out before he could get there. She said, "I don't think he'll give himself up, or let anyone leave without a fight. He's crazy, you know."

"No, I didn't know, but I'm learning...Really this man, Emmanuel, doesn't look like me, does he?" Matt shut the car's door, and they moved down a ten-foot narrow ramp to the docks. They had to walk slowly because of the rain-slick wood.

"Yeah, you do favor a little, but you don't act much alike. Does that bother you that you look alike?"

Not wanting to answer her question, Matt hurried Crystal along to his boat, up the dock steps leading to the pilothouse, and inside. Once there, Matt reached down and turned on a small electric space heater to help eliminate the chill.

"Hell-LOW," said Leaky Waters, coming up the steps from the stateroom below. He held a steaming cup of coffee in his right hand. "What we got here?"

Startled, Crystal stepped back bumping into Matt's side.

"This is Crystal Nelson," Matt said. "And, Crystal, I'd like you to meet my best friend and sometimes partner, and all the time crazy, Leaky Waters."

She extended her hand. "Nice to meet you, Mister Waters."

He took her hand and bowed before her crisply like an actor on stage trying to be debonair, but he almost spilled his coffee in the process. "At your service, Missus Nelson, would you like some coffee?" Standing up straight again, he stared into her eyes without dropping her hand. He wore an indigo denim shirt over a russet red turtleneck. With faded jeans fitting snuggly over muscular legs and a scuffed pair of camel-colored Tony Lama boots on his feet, Leaky looked much like a black cowboy missing only a wide brimmed hat.

She pulled her hand free and grinned. "It's not missus. I'm not married, and please, I would enjoy a cup of coffee."

"At your service," said Leaky. He turned to go back down to the galley but stopped at the top landing to look back at her. "Your boyfriend must be worried sick about you."

"He may be," she said with a grin. The broad smile left Leaky's face.

"Leaky," Matt said, helping Crystal take off her yellow rain jacket. "While you're down there turn the TV to channel twelve."

"Already done that, and..." he said. Leaky stopped midway in his statement to stare at Crystal, now that she stood before him in a red turtleneck sweater that was so tight it accentuated the fullness of her breast. He swallowed hard and continued, "...and a lot has already happened at this _Refuge_ place. We got us a Waco stand-off going on with this Emmanuel fellow."

"They already know the name of the place?" Crystal said. "And they know about Emmanuel?"

"Yeah," said Leaky. "And he sounds like he's half a bubble out of plumb, too."

"A what?" she asked.

"He sounds crazy," Leaky said, "and how you know so much about this place and that Emmanuel fellow?"

She failed to answer Leaky's question.

Matt took Crystal's arm. "Let's go downstairs, or you'll never get that cup of coffee."

Leaky, still standing on the stairs, blocked their way. "Is anybody gonna tell me anything, or are you gonna keep this black man in the dark?"

Matt stared at Leaky and motioned with his hand for Leaky to move down the steps. "I'll fill you in later, Leaky. But first, what else are they saying on TV?"

Leaky, leaping down the steps ahead of them, said, "It started out the sheriff's men were looking for a woman that works at Erlanger Hospital. I think she's the same one we're looking for, too...Anyway, the law went to this compound this morning looking for her and tried to go inside, but shots were fired, and now the law has camped outside the locked gate. They're afraid to storm the place, so everybody's just standing around with hands in their pockets waiting on somebody to jerk all the slack out of the rope."

"You'll have to excuse Leaky," Matt said to Crystal, deciding to forgo telling Leaky about Sarah Brindle just yet. "He's all the time using some kind of colorful language, which makes him hard to understand."

"Wait just a second, Mister Matthew Fagan," said Leaky smiling again and handing Crystal a white mug filled to the brim. "My cow died, and I don't need none of your bull."

She giggled, and Matt ignored Leaky's last words. They all turned to stare at the television screen that showed an announcer talking while standing on Cash Canyon Road. Behind him sheriff's and state patrol's cars lined the road all the way to the end of a curve. Uniformed men, and some in plain clothes, hurried back and forth behind the reporter. Matt wondered if some of them might be FBI agents.

Picking up the remote, Matt increased the volume and caught the commentator in mid-sentence. "...Also, we've learned that they moved here from the mountains of North Georgia a year ago when..."

Crystal stopped sipping her coffee and interrupted, "It was almost two years ago."

Matt noticed Leaky staring at her with an expression on his sorrel face that was somewhere between bewilderment and longing.

The reporter continued, "We've also heard rumors that _The Refuge of God_ is vastly armed with automatic weapons, and we know they're not afraid to use them." He turned and moved to the side permitting the camera to show a larger view of the scene. From the TV the sound of someone's voice blared over a bullhorn somewhere around the curve ahead of the reporter, but Matt couldn't understand what was said.

The reporter turned back to the camera and said, "An officer in plain clothes,

73

whom we haven't identified as of yet, is calling for them to unlock the gate, throw down their weapons, and let the law enforcement enter, so they can…"

The reporter halted in mid-sentence, stood on his toes to see over the camera and stared hard at something beyond it. After only a few seconds, he pushed his face closer to the lens and said enthusiastically, "Two, no, three black vans have just pulled up, and men dressed in dark blue are exiting them. They have FBI in yellow letters across their backs."

"Oh, no!" said Crystal moving to a stool and sitting on its edge. "He won't give in to those people. He'll kill everybody before letting any outsiders in. They're all gonna die. Lord, Lord, Lord."

Leaky turned to her with a concerned expression replacing his mischievous one. "How you know so much about this place?"

Before she could answer him, Matt said, "Crystal, why don't you tell Leaky about yourself and this place, while I look up something on the computer."

Crystal agreed. Leaky moved to a stool beside her, while she began telling him about her involvement with the compound and Emmanuel. She did most of the talking, but he stopped her periodically to ask a question. Matt moved to the computer and quickly hooked in with the Internet. He went to Yahoo's search engine and typed in (Refuge of God). In seconds, he had a long list of Web sites with the word Refuge in it and many with the word God, but none for the listing of _Refuge of God_.

Next, he typed in _Cleveland TN_ and waited only a moment until a listing of Web sites in that town appeared. Seeing the one he wanted, Matt opened Cleveland's _white pages_ and typed in the name Fagan. He saw none by that name. He typed in Belcher and saw sixteen names, but none named Mark Belcher. He called up a town about ten miles northeast of Cleveland called Benton, Tennessee, and went into their white pages—no Fagan, or Belcher there. He did the same for the Tennessee towns of Athens, Madisonville, and Dunlap but found no Fagan. He found three by the name of Belcher in Dunlap. Matt saw none by the name of Mark Belcher, however.

Turning to Crystal, who was answering Leaky's questions, Matt said, "Excuse me a minute. Did this Emmanuel ever give you a town near Cleveland where he came from?"

"Yeah," she said, "but I don't remember, now."

Matt called up the site Map Quest on the computer, typed in Cleveland, Tennessee, and in seconds, a colorful map appeared on the screen. He moved the arrow to the _OUT 1_ icon and double clicked the mouse button. A new map of Southeast Tennessee and North Georgia appeared.

"Look at this," Matt said to Crystal, motioning for her to come next to him and examine the computer's screen. "How about Calhoun?"

"Don't sound familiar," she replied.

"Dunlap? Pikeville?"

"I don't think that's it," she said. "Which town had a monkey trial, or something like that? It was a famous trial back in the twenty's or thirty's. I heard him talk about that once. It had something to do with evolution. Emmanuel likes to preach against the sins of Darwin. Once, he said he grew up near a town where they had a big trial about evolution."

Matt said, "Oh, yeah! I saw a movie about that. I think it was called _Inherit the Wind_ or something like that. But I don't remember what town it was in."

Leaky leaned back on his stool. "Are y'all talking about the Scope's Trial? If you are, it happened in Dayton, Tennessee."

"That could be it," said Crystal. "I'm sorry, but I don't know for sure."

"That's okay," Matt said, already typing Dayton and Tennessee into Yahoo's search engine. Going to the _white pages_, he typed in Fagan and got two names. Luther Fagan lived at 508 Cedar Bluff Road—Carl Fagan next door at 510. He wrote the information in a small five by three-inch notebook. He typed in Belcher and got only three listings. Going over them, the name Rebecca Belcher caught his eye for a second. For some unexplained reason, the name Rebecca sounded familiar to Matt. Rebecca Belcher lived on White Hollow Road. He looked up the other two Belcher names and found that they also lived on White Hollow Road.

Matt went to Dayton's locate-file and typed in Carl Fagan plus the address. A map of Dayton appeared on the screen with a small red X in the upper left corner. Matt zoomed in on the red X, Carl Fagan's residence, which was in a community called Morgantown. It was about a mile from Dayton. He printed this map and quickly typed in Rebecca Belcher plus her address. Another red X appeared, but this one was a little over a mile north of Dayton at a community called Bryan Hill. Printing this map leading to her address, Matt went off line and turned to face the two people still watching over his shoulder.

Matt looked a Crystal. "Have you ever heard Emmanuel mention his mother's or father's names?"

"Let me see," she said, rolling her eyes to the room's ceiling and putting her fingers to her chin. After a long fifteen seconds she tightened her lips and shook her head. "I'm not thinking right at the moment; you'll have to forgive me. Since last night I've been through so much, and it's hard to think when..." She didn't finish her sentence but only crossed her arms over her stomach.

Matt thought he knew what she intended to say, so he stood up to face her. "Have you had anything to eat this morning?"

She shook her head, no.

Hunger was far away in Matt's mind, but he pulled the Explorer's keys out of his pocket and turned to his friend. "Leaky, let's take this beautiful woman and get her something to eat."

In only a few minutes, they were outside walking down the dock. Using his hand to hold the Stetson on his head, Matt hurried them along trying to avoid wasting any more time before meeting Medora Meehan in less than three hours.

While going up the ramp to the parking lot, Matt stopped when he heard a car accelerating through gravel near the marine's entrance. He hurried the rest of the way up the slick ramp but was too late. Only empty parked cars stretched across the lot.

"Did anybody hear that car?" He said leading them toward the Explorer.

"Yeah," said Leaky. "Why you so jumpy?"

"I don't know," Matt said, shaking his head and reaching for the Explorer's door handle. When he pulled on the handle, it didn't move. It surprised Matt that he had locked it. Too much had happened this morning, and he couldn't be sure of what he'd done.

Matt pushed the remote button and all the door locks clicked open. Crystal got into the front seat with him, while Leaky crawled into the back. Leaving the parking lot, they turned south down Brown's Ferry Road.

Before they reached the Waffle House, only three miles from the marina, Leaky screamed, "Holy mother of God." And then he jumped out the back door of the moving Ford.

CHAPTER TWELVE

After Sarah had reached the pulpit because Emanuel had ordered her to, she stood behind him while he commanded the congregation to pray in silence for thirty minutes and then go back to their dorms. Emmanuel and Irene then hurried Sarah to the men's dorm. Now Sarah stared down at her dead husband's glassy eyes while her entire body quivered. Tears formed in her eyes, blurring her vision to the point of near blindness, and she used both hands to wipe away the flood flowing down her chapped cheeks. She had loved him once, but that was in the past. Why did she weep for this once weak human being? He had deceived her, used her, hurt her and almost killed her by telling Emmanuel about her longing to escape. Slowly at first, like a spark igniting a small flame that builds and grows until it roars into life, it came to Sarah, and she realized why she now wept; it was for herself. In her mind, she cried out for God's help, to keep her sanity, to make it through the day and coming night. She cried for God to send her something, anything to keep her sanity, and allow her to survive for her son Tommy.

"Sarah, Sarah," said Emmanuel in a mocking manner. "I didn't know you cared for this little, sawed-off dickless-wonder. After all, he about got you killed." Emmanuel laughed. The hate and tears spilling from Sarah made her feel guilty.

"It's better this way," said Emmanuel, putting his fingers around her left biceps and squeezing so hard that pain shot to her shoulder as her lower arm and hand grew numb. She knew there would be a blue bruise there tomorrow. "I'm your family, now, not this piece of crap lying there. Didn't Jesus tell His apostles to forsake their families and follow Him? Yeah, He did, and I'm telling you, that not only is your husband dead, but so are your mother and father. Your child is dead and..."

Sarah yanked her arm free from his grasp, turned to face this lunatic, and screamed, "What have you done to Tommy?"

She didn't see the blow from his open left hand coming. It sent flashes of bright lights soaring through her distorted vision as she fell back into Irene's arms. The right side of her face was afire and a throbbing pain spread around her skull as she tried to regain her balance, and at the same time, free herself from Irene's grasp. She reached deep in her gut to speak to him, but only a growling whisper emerged. "Where's my son?"

"You bitch," said Emmanuel. "Don't you ever raise your voice to me if you want to live. Do you understand me?" He grabbed for Sarah's arms and jerked her to him until only a hair separated his nose from Sarah's nose. "Answer me."

She could only nod her head that she understood. His putrefied breath of rotten meat and alcohol made her want to vomit.

"My son is fine," Emmanuel said. "Come to think of it, he's not your son at all. You were only a vessel for carrying him and bringing him into this world. For that, you should be proud. But you're not. You're an obstinate, ungrateful whore that needs to be put in her place." His spittle speckled her face mingling with her tears.

The pain in both of her arms as he held her in mid-air almost caused her to forget the ache spreading across the right side of her face. The skin of her nose, cheek, and temple along that side grew tighter as it started to swell. In spite of all this, relief filled Sarah's body with the news that Tommy was alive and well.

"You'll come live with me," Emmanuel said. "If you're good, I'll let you take care of my son until Armageddon, anyway. And that won't be long, now that the government has come trying to destroy us." He dropped her, and she fell to the concrete floor, twisting her ankle. New pain exploded across the top of her foot and up her Achilles tendon.

"Bitch." said Irene. She snarled and jerked Sarah to her feet then pushed her back into Emmanuel's arms. Sarah's weak ankle almost caused her to fall again.

"Their government has gone too far," said Emmanuel to his congregation of only two. "The Branch Davidians in Waco showed them what can happen if they meddle with God's people, but I won't be like them or Jim Jones' group. No, I'll take them with me. Anybody that enters this haven of mine uninvited will die...That I promise...There'll be so much blood that the river will run red all the way to the sea...You don't mess with God without getting destroyed."

He turned and walked toward the door, then, stopped halfway there and spun back toward his two women. "Take her to my room and make sure you lock the door. Then, get someone in here to get that stinking sonofabitch and plant him in the ground with the others. I'm going to check the weapons and get everyone ready for this war."

Irene pushed Sarah in the back forcing her to stumble forward toward the door.

Irene pushed Sarah again. "You don't deserve to live." Sarah could hear Irene's feet stomping behind her. When they got to the exit, Irene shoved Sarah hard against the door framing. "I don't know what he sees in you, anyway. If it was up to me..."

Sarah wondered why Irene stopped in mid-sentence. The two of them remained silent for a long minute. They had come almost two hundred feet from the dorm where Chuck lay dead, when Irene grabbed Sarah's shoulder, and guided her in another direction. The sharp pain in her ankle turned into a dull ache as the cold wind swept through Sarah's hair driving it across a swelling face. It dried her tears. Sarah glanced in three directions but saw no one. The grounds remained deserted of people, and this told Sarah that they were still in the assembly hall.

Stumbling along, Sarah began thinking of Tommy, Chuck, and her mother. She longed to see her mother one more time and crawl into her arms. New tears began to form, but the wind blew them away. She wondered how many tears she had left. Her right eye, almost shut now, blurred, but she didn't care; Sarah didn't think she could hurt anymore. With a numbing body, she marched along the path toward the infirmary.

Once inside the building that reeked with the smell of alcohol, Irene made Sarah undress down to her underwear. Then she took her to an inspection room and placed her on a padded examining table. Irene left Sarah half-clothed and alone to shiver. In only a few seconds, Irene reentered carrying several brown bottles of what looked like medicine on a tray. Sarah wondered if this intimidating nurse was about to treat her swollen eye. But why did Irene make her take off her clothing?

"Get that little bra off," ordered Irene.

Sarah did as instructed, until she sat unrobed except for the thin, white cotton panties she tried to pull higher on her hips. When Irene reached for Sarah's right breast, Sarah flinched and pulled away.

"Sit still, you big sissy," said Irene. "I'm checking that lump you got there, you stupid cunt, I need to see if it's grown any bigger."

Slowly, Sarah removed her arms from around her chest. With lightning speed, Irene grabbed Sarah's breast with her cold hands and began to mash and palpate the old injury so hard Sarah almost lost her breath. Grunting in pain and closing her eyes, Sarah fought against screaming out and showing weakness to this woman.

"It's bigger," said Irene, squeezing Sarah's nipple and pulling it toward the ceiling. What little breath remaining inside Sarah soared out, and her eyes popped open to see Irene's smirk. As quickly as Irene had grabbed Sarah, she released her grip and reached for the tray of medicine.

When air returned to her lungs, Sarah pointed to the tray. "What's that?"

"Vitamins," said Irene, opening the dark brown jar and pouring two large, orange pills into a tiny, white cup. "And you're going to have to start some chemotherapy." She poured a dark, almost black liquid into another white cup. Irene visually searched the room, found a larger, blue plastic cup, filled it with water from the sink, and extended it, along with the pills, toward Sarah. "Take this."

The large capsule felt like they went down Sarah's throat sideways then lodged halfway between her mouth and stomach. When she had finished drinking all the water in the cup, Irene handed her the liquid. The aroma of the chemicals reminded Sarah of tar, and the bitter taste made her eyes squint and her face wrinkle.

"That's a good girl," said Irene, grinning. "You'll have to take this every day until that lump goes away. Now, get dressed, we've got to get out of here." Irene stood against the wall watching Sarah dress herself. When Sarah finished putting on her clothes, she marched toward the front door with Irene following close behind.

Sarah opened the infirmary's door and limped outside. Then she remembered that Chuck had been taking vitamins, and they had failed to help him. They'd killed him. Sarah saw Myra bring Tommy to her, and she smiled and forgot her thoughts.

CHAPTER THIRTEEN

By the time Matt stopped the Ford Explorer, Leaky had jumped from the car and now lay in a ditch beside the two-lane road. With the car's left back door still gapping open, Matt bounced out of his door and sprinted back toward his friend who was already getting upon his feet. Crystal watched from the front seat of the car.

When Leaky had first started screaming, Matt started braking the Explorer hard. But he was unable to stop them before Leaky leaped out onto the asphalt and rolled headfirst into a ditch.

"What the hell you doing?" Matt said out of fright for the terror-struck man that stood trembling before him. Leaky looked like a person that had just escaped a pack of wolves. The right sleeve of his navy-blue rain-parka, ripped from shoulder to elbow, dangled at his wrist, and the left knee of his trousers, split open, revealed bright red blood oozing from flesh that looked more like ground hamburger.

"Get her out of the car," yelled Leaky, running with a slight limp toward the Explorer.

"Wait up," Matt shouted while chasing after Leaky. He saw that the back of Leaky's parka, torn in a jagged line from right shoulder across and down to his left buttocks, dangled freely across the back of his legs.

"Get out of there," shouted Leaky as he opened Crystal's door. She only sat staring at this insane man with her surprised eyes. Leaky grabbed her arm and started jerking her from the Explorer's high seats. "Get your black ass out of there, now...There's a damn snake under the front seat."

He didn't have to repeat himself, because she sprinted from the car and went halfway up a grassy knoll before stopping to look back. On her face, an expression of trepidation replaced one of puzzlement as she craned her neck to peer into the car. Leaky, who hadn't yet noticed his injuries, stood beside her.

Matt looked up toward them. "You say a snake?"

"Yeah," said Leaky. "A big one, too. You better get away from there. It stuck its big, fat ugly head out and looked me right in the eye. And I decided it could have my seat, and the whole damn car, too, if that's what it wanted. You better get your white ass back, Matt."

A late model red Mazda pickup truck, going in the opposite direction of the Explorer, stopped on the other side of the road. An old man of about seventy wearing an Atlanta Braves baseball cap that looked every bit as old as he, stuck his head out the window. "What's wrong? You folks okay?"

"Everything's fine," Matt said waving at the old man. "Thanks, but we can handle it." The old man sat there for a few seconds before rolling up his truck's window and continuing down the road.

From a safe distance, several feet from the Explorer, Matt glanced through the open back door, searched the back seat and floor, but he didn't see a snake.

"You best get you some yonder, Matt," said Leaky, who had backed up several more yards and now stood twenty feet from the car beside a huge white oak tree. "That thing will swallow you whole."

When Matt moved to a position so he could see into the front seat and floor, his breath caught in his throat. There it was, sticking out from under the driver's seat, the yellow-brown body of a snake that was as big as a man's forearm. Matt couldn't see the head or tail, but it was definitely a living snake. As he stared at the creature, Matt saw its sides moving very slightly as it breathed.

Matt looked up at Leaky. "Find me a stick. I'm not giving him my car...And get your ass down here and help me."

"Hell no," said Leaky. "And I don't care if you are pissed off, either."

"Well, I'm about to get that way if you don't give me some help."

"You know what they say, don't you," Leaky said. "It's better to be pissed off than pissed on."

About that time, a muddy white Suburban carrying four men rolled up behind the Explorer. Before the vehicle could come to a complete stop, it shot around them and accelerated down the road. Matt noticed that all the men wore the same type blue tops.

"Oh, God!" said Crystal. She turned to run into the woods, but Leaky grabbed her arm and held her with him.

"Where the hell you going?" Leaky said.

Matt figured those guys were from the compound, and all this was beginning to make sense. He walked around to the back of the Explorer and looked up at Crystal. "Those were Emmanuel's men, weren't they?"

She nodded her head, yes.

"I bet I know where this snake came from," Matt said opening the Explorer's rear door behind the back seat. He took a three-iron from the golf bag he always kept there and went around to the driver's door. The snake had not moved from its position. Matt slipped the head of the golf club under the body of the serpent and started pulling it toward him. Its weight surprised Matt.

"You're crazy as hell," said Leaky, but he now stood only three feet from the passenger's door watching. Crystal stayed behind him at the edge of the road.

"When I get hold of it, I'm bringing it out this way," Matt said. "So you better watch where it goes."

Leaky backed up a step when Matt pulled the fat body of the snake from under the seat. When he got most of it out onto the car's floor, it started to crawl across the club's head and back under the seat. Matt thrust the club inside for a better grip on the snake nearer its head and gave it a jerk. For the first time, Matt saw its enormous, diamond-shaped, flat head and knew it was a poisonous pit viper, because of the heat-detecting pits situated half way between its elliptical eyes, and flared nostrils. It turned its head to crawl back under the seat. Matt realized it didn't want to come out from its warm hiding place and into the cold, but that was too damn bad. Giving one more cautious tug, Matt pulled the viper onto the road, where its body slapped the asphalt with a thud. Then Matt saw the rattlers. Two cars had stopped to watch the action. Several inquisitive people who had gotten out of their vehicles now sprinted to get back inside.

The serpent crawled under the Explorer, but before it got away, Matt pulled it back onto the pavement where it coiled, rattling its tail, ready to strike. Matt couldn't believe he'd stayed this close to such a deadly snake. For some strange unexplainable reason, it excited him to be so near this creature. This was as close as he had ever been to a poisonous snake, and he didn't feel threatened. In fact, Matt felt sorry for the damn thing. It didn't want to be here with him any more than Matt wanted to be with it. "Kill it now," said Leaky who had walked in a wide circle to stand several feet behind Matt. "Hurry! Hit it with your club!"

"I don't want to bend my three-iron," Matt said.

"Well, do something," said Leaky. "Cause I got to piss like a Russian race horse."

"How long you think this snake is?" Matt said.

"Who gives a shit!" said Leaky. "It looks like a hundred yards long...Jesus H. Christ, kill it!"

"You think it's over six feet?"

"Yeah, whatever you say," said Leaky. "Do something with it, or I'm gonna piss my pants."

When Matt noticed someone moving toward him out of the corner of his eye, he glanced up. Twenty feet away stood a tall, fleshy man in denim overalls worn over a red flannel shirt. The man walked toward them, while hauling a double-barreled shotgun across his chest.

"Move back," the farmer carrying the shotgun growled. He spat a long stream of brown tobacco juice to his side, and it made a splattering sound like someone had thrown a handful of mud onto the pavement. The chubby-faced man with the bulging cheek cocked the weapon's hammer, brought it to his shoulder and closed his left eye.

"Hold on," Matt said, but stepped back anyway. "You might hit a car or somebody. Let me get the snake off the road, first."

The farmer lowered the double-barreled shotgun, spat again and nodded his head. Matt took a deep breath and placed the club's head before the coiled snake, which now was producing a steady hum with its seven rattlers. Without hesitating, Matt pushed the club head beneath the thickest part of the snake. A few people that had gathered behind them began to *ooh and aah*. Matt couldn't believe that his hands didn't shake, or that the snake didn't strike at the metal club now under the midsection of its body.

Matt tried to lift it but couldn't. Again, the slithering creature tried to escape by crawling under the Explorer. Because Matt was about to lose the viper, he did something that shocked everyone that saw it, including Matt. He couldn't explain why or where he found the courage, but Matt grabbed the creature's tail and pulled it from under the car. He wasn't totally fearless because Matt kept the golf club over the snake's head ready to pin the creature down if it decided to strike. Its skin felt cool and dry. The creature's massive head turned and twisted trying to see what had its tail as Matt dragged it off the asphalt and onto the graveled shoulder of the road. He continued to pull it up the grassy knoll and beside the large white oak. They had traveled more than fifty feet into the forest. Matt glanced around to see that no one followed.

When Matt released the rattler, it crawled away and slid under a fallen tree that lay half decayed on the ground.

"Go, feared one," Matt whispered. He watched until the snake slithered from view, then, Matt turned and marched back toward his car. The farmer with his shotgun across his chest stood at the base of the knoll with his mouth hanging open showing teeth the color of mud. About ten people gathered in the middle of the road with Leaky and Crystal, and all of them stood staring at Matt with gaping mouths.

As if this was an everyday experience, Matt walked around to the driver's side of the Explorer and got in.

Looking back at Leaky and Crystal, Matt said, "Are y'all going with me, or you going to stand there looking like you've seen a ghost?"

It took several seconds for his words to register with Leaky and Crystal because it took that long before they started hurrying toward the Explorer. Once everyone was inside, Matt pulled the car back on the road. No one in the Explorer said a word for several long minutes as they hurried toward the Interstate.

Finally, Matt turned to Leaky. "You need to go to the hospital?"

"No," said Leaky. "I got to piss real bad. Hurry!"

Seeing I-24 looming ahead, Matt accelerated until they reached a combination Texaco Gas Station and convenience store, where he shot into its spacious lot. Leaky was out the door and running toward the side entrance to the bathroom before Matt could bring the Explorer to a complete stop. When Matt removed his hands from the steering wheel, he noticed they quivered. He already dreaded going to sleep tonight and facing his dreams.

"I can't believe you did that," said Crystal, staring at Matt with wide-open eyes.

"Me either," he said. "I've always been terrified of snakes."

"I'm not even hungry anymore," she said. "That's the bravest thing I ever seen in my life. I can't believe you did that."

"Me either. You want something to drink?"

They sat staring at one another for a long moment before she said, "Can I have some coffee?"

"Sure," he said, opening the door and bouncing outside. He got halfway to the store, then, suddenly turned back toward Crystal. On the way back, he half noticed a dirty white Suburban slowly pull into the station and drive next to a set of gas pumps. It didn't register in his racing mind that there might be anything unusual about it. Opening her door, Matt looked into Crystal's light brown eyes. "How you want your coffee?"

"A little cream," she said and smiled.

"Be right back," Matt said and closed the door.

CHAPTER FOURTEEN

The aroma of coffee was refreshing on a cool morning when a man was trying to forget an encounter with a rattlesnake the size of a football linebacker's forearm. Matt looked at his hands. The shaking had finally stopped.

"One sixty-seven," said the middle aged, bleached blond that looked like she'd just awakened from a three-day drunk. From behind a glassed-in cubicle, she extended a chubby hand, palm up, toward Matt.

He gave her two dollars, didn't acknowledge her by speaking, and walked out without his change. He took a deep breath of cooling air, trying to relax his already calming mind. His watch showed twenty-five minutes until ten, which made Matt think about the meeting soon with Medora Meehan. Leaky was already in the back seat when he got to the Explore, but Crystal wasn't there in the front. Matt figured she'd gone to the lady's room, so he slowed and looked around. An old man of at least eighty pumped gas in a green late model Dodge Ram. When Matt reached for the Explorer's door handle, he thought about the white Suburban that had been there earlier. The adrenaline that shot through his circulatory system caused Matt to almost jerk the door off its hinge.

"Where's Crystal?" He shouted. Blood rushed to his head.

Pressing a towel on his injured knee, Leaky jerked his head up. "I though she was with you."

"Dammit," Matt said, running to the lady's bathroom and slinging open the door. There squatted over the commode without touching the seat was a woman of at least eighty-years-old. When she looked up at Matt, her eyes grew wide like she'd seen a monster. Matt slammed the door the moment she started to scream. Matt sprinted to the man pumping gas into the truck, frightening the old codger to the point of collapse.

Matt tried to keep from yelling, but couldn't. "You see a white Suburban leave here a few minutes ago?"

Between his stooped-shoulders, the old man nodded his head that he had, and then he glanced in alarm at Leaky limping up behind.

"Did a black woman get in with them?" Matt said trying to appear calm.

Again, the old codger nodded yes. Gas spilled on the concrete when the gentleman, with violently shaking hands jerked the hose from the truck and tried to insert the nozzle in its housing on the pump.

"Dammit," Matt said between clenched teeth. "Which way'd they go?"

Again, the old man didn't speak but pointed a quivering finger toward the Interstate ramp, then he tried to open the Dodge's door.

"Wait, just a minute," Matt said, grabbing the old man's shoulder and spinning him around. "I'm not going to hurt you, so just wait a minute. Which ramp did they take, the one on this side or the other?"

About that time the old lady Matt had surprised while she was in the restroom, scurried up to the Dodge truck and got inside. She looked at Matt with the same wide eyes.

"The…other," said the old man. "They're going…toward…Chattanooga."

"How long ago?"

"About two…or…three…"

Matt spun toward the Explorer and ran headfirst into Leaky, almost knocking him to the ground. He grabbed Leaky's arm and yanked him in the direction of the Explorer.

"Where'd she go?" said Leaky trying to stay on his feet.

Matt pushed Leaky toward the Explorer. "Hurry. They got her."

Jumping inside, Matt cranked the Explorer, threw it into gear, and exploded forward, throwing his friend's head against the rear of the seat.

"Who's got her?" said Leaky.

Tires squalled as the Explorer shot across the access road, fishtailed sideways, straightened up, and raced up the ramp leading to I-24 east.

Without slowing but still accelerating, Matt got the vehicle under control and entered the flow of traffic on I-24. He shot to the far left lane. Horns and screeching tires blared behind them. "The men in the white Suburban got her. The ones from the cult."

Matt pressed the accelerator so hard his leg started trembling. The Explorer's engine whined, sounding like a hundred mountain lions were fighting under its hood. They roared by a line of vehicles so fast the panorama blurred around them.

"Oh, hell!" was all Leaky could get out of his mouth, while trying to snatch the seat belt from over his right shoulder and buckle it.

In seconds, they reached the section of Interstate that sandwiched between Lookout Mountain on the right and the Tennessee River on the left. Matt's anger renewed when he remembered that only a few hours ago Crystal sat along side him when they passed these rock ledges. He pushed his right foot harder, but it wouldn't go through the floor. Racing from one lane to another and dodging slower vehicles, Matt kept his speed but was unable to see very far ahead. He realized they had to find the Suburban, before it reached the next intersection that was now only two miles ahead.

"Help me find them," Matt said above the roaring engine.

"Watch out," said Leaky pointing ahead of them. "A wreck. Slow down."

Removing his boot from the accelerator, Matt felt the Explorer slow, but he still couldn't see the car wreck.

"Where?" Matt said, but as the words left his mouth, he saw dust and smoke billowing skyward only seconds ahead. The thought of Crystal being dead or mangled splashed across his brain.

"It's in the left lane," said Leaky. "Get over. To the right."

When Matt jerked the steering wheel hard right, he felt the Explorer's back-end began to slide. Matt's fingers clinched, and his back stiffened; but the Ford came under control as they shot past a dark car lying on its side. Its wheels where still turning. It wasn't the Suburban.

Without glanced at Leaky, Matt said, "Was that the only car involved?"

"Yeah," Leaky said trying to catch his breath.

A large green road sign loomed ahead. Matt would have to decide which route to take and fast. The left lane would take them to I-124 that ran almost downtown to Chattanooga and across the River. The right lane was a continuation of I-24 that led to I-75 where he'd gone with Crystal earlier this morning.

"Go left." said Leaky.

"You see them?" Matt steered left onto I-124.

"No."

"Dammit, why'd you make me go this way?"

"Trust me," said Leaky.

"I got no damn choice, now."

Leaky cleared his throat. "They must have caused that wreck, right?"

"Okay, I'll buy that, but…"

"It happened in the left lane, and all the skid marks showed that wrecked car had been forced to the left."

"Okay," Matt said.

"So, the Suburban was trying to get in the I-124 lane, and it ran that poor devil off the road."

Matt didn't answer but stomped his foot to the floor sending the Explorer exploding forward. Weaving in and out of cars at a high rate of speed sent additional adrenaline surging through Matt's veins to the point that he began to feel light-headed.

"There they are," said Leaky as the Explorer rocketed over Martin Luther King Boulevard that ran under I-124. The tall buildings of downtown Chattanooga loomed to their right.

Matt slapped the steering wheel. "Where?"

"They're about to cross the river."

"You sure?"

Leaky pointed ahead of them. "I knew it. Dammit, I'm a brilliant mother…"

Matt almost lost control when an early model Buick Park Avenue changed lanes ahead of them. He swerved into the middle lane and checked the Explorer by tapping the breaks lightly, so they didn't plow into the slower moving Buick.

As they entered the concrete bridge leading across the Tennessee River, the Interstate narrowed to two lanes. A hundred feet below the Tennessee River surged toward the sea.

"Where are they?" Matt said.

"Ahead, in the right lane," said Leaky. "I think they're about to get off. Slow down, dammit."

"Why?" Matt screamed. Then, he saw the white Suburban fifty yards ahead, its brake lights glowing. Matt took his boot off the accelerator and tapped the brake. They slipped into the right lane behind a red Volvo that was the only thing separating them from the Suburban.

Leaky said. "What are we going to do when we catch'em?"

"We're going to get Crystal back; if we can...some way...We got to get her back."

"Why'd you leave her in the car alone, anyway? At least why didn't you lock the damn door?"

Shocked but not surprised at the boldness of his friend, Matt didn't answer. He wasn't sure why he'd failed to take precautions. He knew better.

"You think they know we're following?" Matt said slamming the palms of his hands down hard on the top of the steering wheel.

"No, not yet, cause they're not going that fast now."

"Maybe they want us to catch them," Matt said.

"Never thought of that. But why?"

Matt didn't have time to answer for the Suburban swerved right off I-124 and onto highway 127, the Red Bank exit.

Matt took the same exit as the Suburban, and the Explorer shot down the long ramp. There were no cars separating the two vehicles now. Matt knew it was only a matter of time until the men in the Suburban detected them. Crystal and her captors turned west at the bottom of the ramp, heading in the direction that could take them up Signal Mountain or along the Tennessee River. Matt stomped the Explorer's accelerator, and they exploded toward the intersection as the Suburban disappeared from view under the interstate bridge. Matt reached for the 457 pistol with his left hand and placed it on the seat between his legs.

The caution light ahead was red, but Matt didn't stop. He slowed only long enough to find an opening in the opposing traffic.

"Oh hell!" said Leaky. "Watch out for that..." Tires squealed and horns boomed. Then Matt turned left, almost slamming into a new black BMW. The Explorer's engine screamed as they passed under the Interstate bridge seventy-five yards behind the Suburban.

"Never mind," said Leaky. "I was going to say watch out for that BMW, but hell...I can't talk as fast as you're driving."

"Then, I must be driving fast."

"Damn straight," said Leaky.

Seeing the white Suburban fifty yards ahead and passing through the next intersection, Matt tried to push the accelerator through the floor. Various types of convenience stores and small businesses dotted both sides of this busy four-lane street.

Leaky pulled his Smith and Wesson pistol from its holster that he wore behind his back. "What you going to do, now?" He pulled back on the weapon's shiny, stainless steel slide, and that placed a 45-caliber bullet in its chamber. That also cocked the hammer. Leaky put the safety on and the hammer slammed shut. Then, he placed the firearm in his lap and glared at Matt for an answer to his question.

"We're gonna catch'em," Matt said. "Then, we're gonna get Crystal back. Then I'd say some ass kicking is going to happen."

Seconds later, when they reached Fire Station Seventeen, Matt had closed to within fifty feet of the Suburban. Still, there were no cars between them. Matt slowed when he saw Crystal, sitting in the rear of the Suburban, trying to turn and look out the back window. One of the men slapped her with the back of his hand and pushed her head down out of view. In seconds she came up swinging her arms, hitting the blond-headed man on her left with the palm of her hand. Matt flinched when the man recovered and slammed his fist toward Crystal's face. Her head recoiled backwards like her neck was made of rubber. She dropped behind the seat.

"Son-of-a-bitch," Matt said between clinched teeth. He grabbed the 457. "Did you see that bastard?"

"Mudderfucker," said Leaky. "Catch 'em."

Matt screamed, "Hold on," just before they smashed into the back bumper of the Suburban. The seat belt pulled tight across Matt's chest as his body jolted forward. Tires screamed and the Suburban rebounded forward. Matt saw the caution light a hundred-feet ahead at a busy intersection. It was red with cars crossing in front of them, but the Suburban wasn't slowing to stop. Both cars burst through the intersection, missing other cars by only millimeters. Car horns and squealing tires faded behind them.

Leaky breathed in short quick bursts. "Where the hell they going?"

"Looks like up Signal Mountain," Matt said, just before the Suburban slowed enough to make a sharp turn to the left off highway 127 and onto a narrow two-lane road. The rear of the Suburban fish-tailed from one side of the small road to the other before its driver regained control and sent them flying in this new direction.

"Dammit," said Leaky. "That rules out the mountain. Looks like they're going to the river."

The two vehicles bounced, swerved, and skidded down Suck Creek Road that after a quarter of a mile ran parallel with the Tennessee River. Matt checked to the left and saw the river's gray water flowing beside a grassy embankment.

In a moment's time a mere ten feet separated the two cars now reaching speeds of seventy miles per hour on a road meant for only fifty at tops. Both cars had to use all of the paved area and part of the shoulder to stay out of the ditches running beside the road.

It wasn't long before what Matt thought might happen, happened. The back window of the Suburban exploded when someone fired a shotgun at the Explorer. Fortunately, the first blast didn't strike his car, but when the glass from the Suburban cleared, Matt saw that one of the shooters had the weapon's sight trained on him for a second shot.

Slamming on the brakes caused the Explorer to skid sideways. Matt released the pedal and worked the steering wheel like mad to keep them out of the deep ditch on the left. A blast erupted from the Suburban, and pellets skidded across the top of the Explorer. The gap between the two vehicles had widened to a hundred feet.

"Hell fire," screamed Leaky, holding his 45 in both hands. "Mudderfucker, what the hell we following?"

"Holy hell," Matt said, letting the Suburban get farther ahead. "They got to stop somewhere."

"Then what we going to do?"

"I'll think of something."

The Suburban, now two hundred feet ahead, went over a small rise and disappeared on the other side. When Matt topped the same little hill and looked down the road on the other side, the Suburban had disappeared. Smashing the brakes hard brought the Explorer to a complete stop, but not before they skidded over a hundred feet.

Matt could see almost a quarter of a mile ahead, and the Suburban could not have gone that far in the time allowed. It had to have left the road somewhere behind them. Matt put the Explorer in reverse and eased backward toward the mound they had just crossed. There was a densely wooded section on their left, and they hadn't seen the river in the last mile of the chase. Matt had backed only a short distance when he saw an unpaved trail cutting through the woods in the direction of the river.

He eased the Explorer onto the path. After going only fifty feet, the trail opened into a clearing that stretched all the way to the river seventy-five feet down a grassy slope. The Suburban was parked next to a brown unpainted dock that jutted out into the river. Before Matt could locate Crystal a shotgun blast roared, peppering the Explorer and causing Leaky to dive under the dash. Matt jerked the car into reverse and spun backward. The grass, mud, and rocks bouncing against the undercarriage sounded like a machine-gun. Matt flinched when the shotgun thundered again, but nothing struck the Explorer.

When he backed into Suck Creek Road, Matt slammed on the brakes and jumped outside gripping his 457 in his left hand.

Leaky opened his door and leaped out onto the asphalt next to the Explorer. "Shit, I'm about to get pissed-off."

Matt ran through a stand of oak timber toward the river. Reaching the edge of the clearing, he eased behind a large red oak and located Leaky who was already hiding behind a small sweetgum tree. Matt crouched low, got to his knees, and crawled forward in the tall, brown wheat grass. The wet ground soaked through his jeans and muddied the palms of his hands. He heard Leaky moving beside him.

Before Matt could see what was happening at the dock, he caught the familiar sound of someone trying to crank an outboard engine. It coughed and burped a couple of times before it roared to a start. In only seconds it settled into a constant purr that sounded like a well-fed tomcat. Matt craned his neck above the wheat grass and saw an open pontoon boat churning into the river. A man held a shotgun to Crystal's head.

Leaky and Matt stood watching the boat that was only a deck mounted atop long, silver buoys, make its way out into the greenish-gray river. Crystal, with surrendering eyes, stared at them across the great distance. Matt kicked the ground and screamed in rage like a wild animal. For a long minute, his breathing came in short bursts through his nose.

"I'll be damned," he finally said walking toward the river's bank with his 457 suspended from a ridged left hand. To go straight across the water, the pontoon boat had to turn against the strong current that flowed down river. After five minutes of hard laboring the craft landed on the far bank. As the group disembarked, Crystal looked back at them, and then she and the four men disappeared into the woods.

In the low tone of disgust, Leaky said, "Where you think they're taking her?"

"Back to the compound," Matt said in a voice that cracked. "They're taking her back to that bastard, Emmanuel."

"We'll get her back, if they don't..."

Leaky didn't finish the sentence, but Matt knew what part he left out—*kill her.*

Matt said, "This is getting to be one of the shittiest days I've had in a long time."

"Hell," said Leaky, shivering in the cold wind with half his clothes torn off. "We'll find them bastards."

With Leaky's final words still lingering in the air, Matt swung the Smith and Wesson toward the mud-covered Suburban, situated twenty feet behind them. As quickly as he could pull the trigger, Matt pumped all seven 45 slugs into it. When he lowered the pistol, air rushed from the vehicle's tires and steam spewed from under its hood.

"Feel better?" Leaky said.

"Not yet."

CHAPTER FIFTEEN

Sarah had never experienced a headache like the one that throbbed in her head. Furthermore, she couldn't keep her eyes open without the pain intensifying. Two aspirins had failed to help the agony; in fact, they had made it worse, because now she wanted to vomit every time she moved.

Lying on the large brown leather sofa in Emmanuel's apartment with Tommy asleep beside her was all Sarah cared to do at present. She was afraid to move, because if she stayed still the pain hid somewhere deep and out of the way. She prayed that Tommy continued sleeping until the physical agony subsided.

Without thought, she reached up with her fingers to wipe her running nose. She didn't feel like opening her purse to find a tissue, but the moisture trickling onto her upper lip had begun oozing down her cheek. She opened her eyes, pulled herself to a sitting position, and glanced at her wet right fingers.

Blood.

She felt a steady stream of the warm, sticky fluid spilling from her nose. She looked down and saw it dripping onto the front of her dress. With shaking hands, she reached for her pocketbook, dug inside and came out with a package of Kleenex. She pressed one of the tissues to her nostril, but had to replace it almost immediately when it filled with arterial blood.

Staggering to her feet, Sarah stumbled to a small bathroom off the main room. She turned on warm water in the sink, and using her hand, washed the blood from her face and dress. Sarah grabbed a towel and pressed it hard against her nostrils trying to stop the bleeding. Slowly, she brought her eyes up and was shocked to see her reflection in the mirror. How frightful she looked! Her face was ashen, and both eyes were so bloodshot they appeared filled with blood except for the hazel irises floating in their center. Who was that person staring back at her with one side of her face swollen where Emmanuel had smacked her? An ox-blood color had formed around one eye that was beginning to swell closed.

Sarah lowered the hand towel and watched as a small drop of blood ran out of the left nostril onto her lip. She wet the towel, pressed it back to the bridge of her nose, and pinched. Breathing only through her mouth was uncomfortable, and the headache was still raging. She turned off the light and struggled back to the sofa where Tommy slept.

She had just laid her head down and shut her eyes when the front door to Emmanuel's apartment burst open. Sarah didn't move a muscle. She didn't care to see or talk to whomever it was, so Sarah pretended to be asleep. She prayed Tommy didn't awake.

"The bitch is asleep," said Irene trying to whisper but not doing a good job of it.

"And the little bastard is, too," said Myra.

Sarah felt the two women move next to her. She stayed motionless for fear of confronting them in her present condition.

"Is she dead, yet?" Myra said.

Sarah wondered what she meant.

"No," said Irene. "It'll take several days and a couple more doses of warfarin to kill her."

"How much you giving her?"

"A hundred and twenty-five milligrams per dose. That'll make her get sicker every day. Soon Emmanuel'll want to know what's wrong with her. I'll tell him she's got a virus, and he'll want her out of here. Then we can do whatever we want with the bitch and her little brat."

Sarah's heart raced so fast she felt the sofa shaking. With all her power, she concentrated on her rhythmic breathing so they wouldn't discover her pretending to be asleep.

"Emmanuel loves that little stuff," said Myra. "He thinks it's his son. If he finds out, he'll—"

"He's not gonna find out," said Irene. "That is unless you tell him. Then I'll kill you if he doesn't. You best keep your mouth shut!"

Sarah felt Tommy stir. Additional panic engulfed Sarah's body when she thought of facing these two women. She opened her eyes but ever so slightly.

Sarah jumped when Emmanuel flung open the apartment door. Now awake, Tommy started to whimper. To protect him, Sarah squeezed him to her chest. When she sat up and opened her eyes, Irene and Myra had turned their backs on her and faced Emmanuel who stood with his hands on his hips glaring at them.

"They got her," said Emmanuel clapping his hands together. He glanced over Irene's shoulder at Tommy who was still whining in Sarah's arms.

"Who they got?" said Irene.

"That black bitch, Crystal," said Emmanuel. "The boys are bring her here now. I want to talk to her first, then I'll decide what to do with the bitch."

"Kill her," said Irene.

"I'll be the one deciding what to do with her," said Emmanuel. "I don't need you telling me what to do with what belongs to me. You just do what I tell you. You understand?"

"Yes, sir," said Irene. Her teeth stayed clinched.

"Get the hell out of here," said Emmanuel pushing by Irene and Myra to reach for Tommy, who was still whimpering.

"Now, now, son," said Emmanuel in a calming voice while holding Tommy in his arms and looking into the boys face. "Stop this crying or Daddy'll have to spank you." He handed the child back to Sarah. "Stop his crying."

The door closed with a bang when Irene and Myra stormed out of the room. Emmanuel turned and glared at the closed door.

Clutching the warm body of her son, Sarah stroked his back and started humming "Jesus Loves Me." The boy hushed and rested a sleepy head on his mother's chest.

"You look like a whore," said Emmanuel frowning at Sarah. "Go take a bath and fix yourself up, and give him one, too. I've sent for you some more clothes. Hurry up." He waved her to move toward the bedroom door with the back of his hand.

In a rush, Sarah turned and carried Tommy into the bedroom. Feeling Emmanuel following close behind, she hurriedly placed Tommy on the bed and started removing his clothes. When she finished, Sarah took him into Emmanuel's bathroom and tried to close the door.

"Don't shut that door," said Emmanuel. "I'm going to watch."

Sarah was beyond the point of caring if he saw her nude; after all, she was dying from some type of poison. That must be why she had the headaches, bloodshot eyes, and nose bleed. It must have been poison that killed Chuck, too. Having no place to turn, Sarah wanted to scream, but instead she directed all her hate toward the man now standing in the bathroom door gawking at her.

Sarah thanked God that it only took a minute to get the bath water warm. Tommy stood next to her shivering and whimpering to get back in her arms, but she forced him away and into the steaming bath. He quickly forgot her and started slapping at the water with his hands. Hurrying, in a race to end this nightmare, Sarah threw off her dress and reached behind her back to unclasp her bra. Purposely, she averted her eyes away from Emmanuel who stood blocking the door and watching her every move, but she could feel his presence and hear his chortling.

After removing her panties, Sarah lifted her foot to enter the tub, but Emmanuel grabbed her arm and yanked her back into the middle of the room. She tripped, almost falling to the floor, but he caught her around the chest and let one of his hands fall across her bare breast.

"What's the big rush?" said Emmanuel. He toyed with her as a cat would a mouse. "I've missed seeing that luscious body of yours." He spun her completely around, looking at her from all sides until they stood facing one another again. The rotten smell of his breath made Sarah want to vomit.

He reached for her left breast to cup it in his hand. She tried to pull away, but she was too slow. He palpated her flesh between his fingers and laughed. Defeated, Sarah closed her eyes and listened to his heavy breathing. She tried to will her mind to another place away from this hell but couldn't. Then, in an instant, she came up with an idea.

Trying to be sexy, Sarah dropped her chin, looked through upturned eyebrows and tilted her head to the side. "I feel so dirty. I sure would love to take a bath first, please can I?"

"Sure," he said. "Of course, take your time. I've got to deal with Crystal first, and then we'll have some fun. I knew you still wanted me." He laughed.

"What you going to do with Crystal?"

"I'm gonna make her wish she'd never been born."

"She's such a beautiful woman, and sexy," said Sarah. She heard Tommy splashing in the tub and giggling. This slightly calmed Sarah. "You know she likes you, don't you?"

"No, does she really?" he said. He failed to hide the surprise in his voice. "What you mean?"

"Crystal's got the most beautiful body," said Sarah looking at the floor like a shy child. Then she glanced at Emmanuel through fluttering eyelashes trying to appear as sensual as possible. "You should have her live with us. We would have the best time."

"I don't know about that," he said, rubbing his chin and smirking like a tomcat that had just devoured its mouse. "What would you two do with each other?" He started chuckling under his breath.

"Oh, nothing, just serve you," she said. The pain of a renewed headache started its push from deep inside her head. Sarah tried to force it away.

"I'll think about it," he said. "But she's got to be punished first."

A nauseated feeling started low in Sarah's abdomen and worked its way to her throat. She jumped when someone banged at the apartment door. Emmanuel hurried from the bathroom.

Sarah gagged into the commode, but nothing came up. Her stomach was empty of food or liquid. Checking on Tommy first and seeing that he was enjoying his play, Sarah crept out into the bedroom. There, she moved against the far wall, the wall that was next to the door leading into the main room. Emmanuel had left the door open, and Sarah knew that if he came back to find her snooping, she would be in even more trouble. She almost ran back into the bathroom, but something made her stay there with her naked back to the cool wall.

Looking around the room, Sarah checked for a place to hide if he should reenter the bedroom. To her right as she faced the room was the door to the bathroom where Tommy played and next to the door was a large, reddish-brown chifforobe. All the oak furniture in the bedroom was mahogany in color. Sarah knew it was very expensive, because Emmanuel lived extravagantly, while his people lived the simple life. To her left and across from the door to the main living room where she now stood was the large walk-in closet. Next to it was the bed with a large painting of Jesus—halo and all—knocking on an old ivy framed door. It surprised Sarah that Emmanuel allowed anyone's picture except his to be here, including that of Jesus.

In this room, with the only light coming from the bathroom, Sarah glanced straight across from where she stood and saw her bare reflection in the dresser mirror. She appeared too slim, and her skin was so pale it almost glowed against the dark wall to her back. She wondered how much weight she had lost since summer. She felt very small and helpless.

Sarah heard the apartment's outside door open.

"Bring her in here," said Emmanuel.

Sarah listened to the footsteps entering the room. She assumed from the sounds made that there were several men with Crystal. The door slammed shut causing Sarah to shrink back. She almost bolted back to the bathroom but stayed fast against the wall.

"Leave us alone," said Emmanuel. "Go outside but stay just by the door."

The door opened and closed.

"Set down," said Emmanuel in a calm voice. "Over there, on the sofa."

Sarah listened to the soft sounds of a woman moving across the room.

"Crystal, what am I going to do with you?" Emmanuel giggled. "I can't let you leave me. You mean so much to me."

Sarah heard the sounds of him sitting down on the sofa, too.

"Now," he continued. "Where have you been?"

There was silence for almost fifteen seconds.

Finally, he said, "I'm trying to be nice. Don't get me mad; talk to me while you've got a chance."

"Looking for a job," she said.

"Don't start that nonsense with me, woman. I'm gonna ask you the question one more time, and if I don't like your answer—well—I hope you like big, hungry snakes. Now, you ready? 'Cause here goes! Who was the man that picked you up?"

"I don't remember his name," she said, but even Sarah could tell Crystal's voice had a hint of panic in it.

"Now, now, my little brown beauty, don't play games with me. The man chased you all the way through Chattanooga, so don't tell me you don't know who he is."

"Matt or Matthew, or something like that," said Crystal so low Sarah had trouble hearing her from the other room. "You probably know more about him than I do. I just met him this morning."

"Why did Matt pick you up this morning? And where'd you first meet this Matthew with that big scar on his face? The boys said he's mean looking."

"I didn't know him until this morning," said Crystal. "His car ran off the road and I jumped in with him. That's all, I promise."

"Let's cut the crap, Crystal," said Emmanuel. "He lives at Brown's Ferry Marina on a boat, right?"

"Sure," Crystal said. "You know that anyway. You had the boys put a rattlesnake in his car. But I don't know which boat is his."

Sarah heard a hand slapping skin, then Crystal grunting in pain.

"Stop lying to me," screamed Emmanuel. "Which boat is his, that's all I want to know? What's the name of his boat?"

"I don't remember."

"The name of his boat, you stupid black bitch. What's the damn name of his boat? He's gonna have a little fire on it real soon!" Emmanuel's started screaming. "Tell—me—the—damn—name—of his boat!"

"Okay, it's, the," started Crystal just as Tommy screamed for his mother.

Crystal hushed. They only heard the child's shrieks.

Sarah froze.

"Mama." Tommy cried harder now.

A heavy footstep hit the floor in the other room. It moved fast toward the bedroom door.

Sarah sprinted toward the bathroom door just as Emmanuel tore into the bedroom behind her.

"What the hell you doing?" said Emmanuel.

She didn't make it into the bathtub. He grabbed the back of Sarah's hair and yanked her off her feet. Sarah's back and head hit the floor in an instant, causing flashes of light to shoot through her vision like streaks of lightning through a black sky. There was very little time to feel the pain before darkness overtook this nude and helpless woman sprawled on a spinning floor.

CHAPTER SIXTEEN

The appointment with Medora Meehan had been for noon at the Gardens Restaurant, which was in the main building of the old renovated train station, but Matt was twenty minutes late, and that agitated the hell out of him. As he hurried under the extended platform's covering, Matt glanced to his left and saw the long rows of wiry rose bushes waving in the breeze. Numerous blossoms of reds, yellows, pinks, lavenders and whites raised their heads in defiance for having to retreat from the long southern summer now coming to a close with these invading winds slicing out of the north.

To his right on a rise of several feet was the Gardens Restaurant. Because this side of the Choo Choo's Terminal Station was almost totally glass and the restaurant was five times longer that it was wide, Matt could see nearly everyone as they ate or waited to eat. He slowed his pace and scanned the crowded room looking for Medora but didn't see her. Matt thought he might have overlooked her and on that account stopped and checked the scene again. She was nowhere in sight.

He felt underdressed for the occasion, although he'd rushed home to change out of jeans and boots and into a black crew neck sweater, a charcoal Herringbone Tweed sport coat, khaki pants, and black suede oxfords.

After he'd gone back to his boat to change clothes, Matt sent Leaky to talk with the police at the compound. He wanted Leaky to learn all he could about this _Refuge of God_ cult blockaded on Raccoon Mountain. And, if he could, Leaky needed to find how Emmanuel's people were getting in and out of their retreat so easily. Leaky and Matt were to meet on the boat later in the evening.

The aroma of yeast bread overwhelmed Matt when he entered the restaurant's second set of glass doors. Before he could take two steps inside a heavyset man in a white tuxedo and holding long green menus blocked Matt's way. In a feminine voice the prissy maitre'd said, "Mister Fagan?"

"Yes," Matt said, surprised by the man's unmanly nature, as well as his knowing Matt's identity.

"Follow me," said the man, turning and strutting through the crowded room toward a large archway opening in the back of the restaurant. Matt wondered how Medora must have described his appearance to this headwaiter, but then Matt touched the right side of his face and understood. The scar felt almost numb at times, especially when cold weather arrived.

Matt tried to avoid staring at the effeminate way the maitre'd walked. The added aroma of fried chicken triggered Matt's senses and made his stomach growl. He'd forgotten how hunger felt. Because the restaurant was brightly lit by the many uncovered windows, the bar ahead appeared much dimmer and cozier. The man led Matt into the Victorian Salon, stopped to search for someone, and then marched to a small round table in the back of the long but narrow room. Other than the balding bartender there was only one other person present—her.

There, at a table in the shaded back corner sat Medora Meehan reading a book. Matt tried unsuccessfully to see the book's title. Just as he approached, she looked up at him. Her beauty overwhelmed him again. Matt felt insignificant in her presence, and that made him angry. Gently, she closed the book and placed it beside her black purse on the floor next to where she sat. She appeared dwarfed in the high-back chair with its plush red velvet covering. The red shade of the chair matched the dominant color in the wallpaper and the comparable pattern of the carpet. Four dimly lit chandeliers dangled from the fifteen-foot ceiling, and on each table burned candles in red containers giving the place a cozy ambiance.

"Madam," said the maitre'd. "Here is Mister Fagan. Do you wish to have lunch here or in the main dinning room?"

"Here, please," Medora said in a very businesslike tone. Matt figured she was upset that he was late.

"Yes, madam," the maitre'd said and bowed. He pulled a seat back and offered it to Matt, but Matt jerked it out of his hand and slid into the chair. The effeminate man opened a menu in front of them both.

"Here," she said handing the maitre'd a five dollar bill which he slipped into his pocket with a smile.

"A waiter will be right with you," said the man. Then he left with his prissy strut.

Matt opened his mouth to explain why he was late, but she said, "Please excuse me, I'll be back in just a minute."

Matt stood when she stood, and as she moved away he watched her, wondering why she had waited until he arrived to go to the lady's room, or wherever she intended going. When Matt sat down, her image wouldn't leave his mind. She had appeared graceful, although comfortable, in her light-gray cashmere cardigan, unbuttoned in front to reveal a matching jewelneck sweater of the same color and material beneath. Each of the sweaters had a neatly finished tubular trim at its neck, which helped emphasize a thin silver necklace. The cardigan had rib-knit cuffs and a bottom band that draped across her black, wool pants. The black leather belt with polished silver hardware embellished her waistline, which Matt knew a woman her age had to fight to keep trim. The tapered pants, with a wide cuff, were just long enough to brush against a pair of black leather loafers with silver buckles.

The waiter came, and Matt sent him away to return in five minutes. It was only a couple of minutes, however, before Medora reentered the room. Her short ash-blond hair, brushed back from the left front side of her head, exposed a small ear. Slightly wavy, lighter colored hair fell across the right side of her head, giving her half bangs that swept back and down over the top one-third of her right ear. Matt remembered that these golden strands continued to flow around and behind her head. As she approached him, her hair bounced with each quick step she took.

Matt grew apprehensive, and he dreaded their upcoming encounter.

"I'm sorry to be so late," Matt said standing until she slid into her seat. He didn't want to offer an excuse.

She smiled but with a forced expression. "If you have found my daughter, then I'll excuse you."

"I have information about your daughter," Matt said.

The young waiter approached, stood beside Matt, looked at Medora, and asked, "May I get you anything from the bar?"

"No thank you." Medora said.

Matt was surprised that she'd answered for him. Her eyes moved from the waiter to me. "I'm sorry. Do you want anything from the bar?"

"No," Matt fought to keep this woman from making him feel intimidated.

She turned back to the waiter. "I would like to order lunch then."

She asked for a house salad, and Matt ordered a club sandwich. When the waiter left, she didn't say anything but looked across the table at him, evidently expecting his report about her daughter.

"What were you reading?" Matt said. He didn't want to talk business just yet. Or he was being stubborn. He couldn't even tell.

"_Lamb in His Bosom_."

"Never heard of it. Who's it by."

"Caroline Miller. It was first published in 1933, won the Pulitzer Prize in '38, but it was re-released several years ago by the publishing house for which I edit. Now, what about my daughter?"

"It's a lot of information," Matt said realizing more about this woman. "A lot's happened this morning, and I was gonna wait until we finished eating."

"Why?"

"Have you turned on your TV this morning?"

"No, why?"

The waiter brought the food before Matt could answer, and they ate in silence. He didn't want to tell her anything until he'd finished eating, but Matt sensed her apprehension about asking more questions. She picked at her food, evidently trying to keep her thin waistline, but Matt was famished and ate his sandwich quickly. Afterwards, each had coffee but no dessert. When the waiter finally brought the check, Matt laid his Visa check card on the tray with the bill and sent the young man on his way before Medora had an opportunity to take control of the situation by paying for his lunch.

After the tab was paid and the waiter had left, Matt turned to Medora. "First, I think I've located your daughter, but I can't confirm my information, yet."

"Where is she?"

Matt raised the palm of his right hand between them to stop her from interrupting his story. "Second, I haven't figured out how I'm going to confirm it at present. Everything has happened too fast this morning." He told her about the data relating to her daughter, Sarah, on the computer. He recapped everything about finding the cult; the deputy getting his car's windshield shot out, picking up Crystal and part of Crystal's story of Sarah. There was one thing Crystal had told him about Sarah that he couldn't mention yet—the part about Sarah's involvement with Emmanuel. Matt saw no reason to worry this mother until he could confirm the account or, if it were true, do something about it.

Medora sat motionless intently watching Matt without interrupting his narrative, especially when he told of Emmanuel's bizarre behavior. When Matt recounted the story about Crystal's capture and their car chase from the interstate to the river, Medora's expression turned to anger. He didn't tell her about him blasting the Suburban with his pistol. When he finished, Matt sat back waiting for her comments.

"What's next?" she said. "Are you going to do anything else, or are you finished helping me look for my daughter? Do you want more money? What's next?"

"I'm not finished, and I don't need any more of your money, because I haven't finished my job, yet." Matt fought back his rage. "But first, I need to know your plans while I'm working. Where you going to be located?"

"Well," she said leaning over the table and looking him in the eyes. "I don't plan to leave until I find my daughter. In fact, I'm going with you, and I won't take no for an answer. So don't try and get rid of me. It's my daughter; it's my money; and I'm going."

"I don't know about you going with me," Matt said rubbing a finger along the side of his scar. "I don't need..."

"Don't worry," she interrupted. "I won't get in your way, and I know about men and their need to be in control. So relax, I'm sure you know your business. I'll stay back out of your way."

"But it's your money," Matt said mocking her earlier words.

"And it's my daughter," she shot back.

"Okay, whatever."

"What's next?"

"I've got to make a little trip about forty miles up the road this afternoon."

"Where?"

"Dayton," Matt said already irritated at her questions. "If you want to go along with me that's fine, but I've got to check something out, before I meet Emmanuel."

"Then, you plan to get into the compound and find my daughter?"

"Yes, I do," Matt said. "And do you plan to go with me?"

"How are we getting inside?"

"I haven't figured that out yet, but I will. Are you still with me?"

"You're not going to scare me off," she said leaning on one elbow and glaring into his eyes. "In fact, I've already checked out of my room and packed my bags."

"Where you planning on staying 'til this is over?"

"I've got a rented car that I'm leaving here. My bags are already in the trunk, and if you'll follow me there, I'll put them in your car."

"Where you going to stay?" Matt said this time more slowly.

"With you until we find Sarah."

"But…"

"Don't worry," she interrupted. "I'm not a dangerous woman, and I'm not interested in sex. At least with you."

"Thanks," Matt said getting to his feet. He couldn't help but grin. "I'm glad to know that, because I'm surely not interested in sex with an older woman. So get you bags and let's go. We've lots to do before dark."

She stood and glared at him before they both turned and marched out of the bar, elbowing one another to be first through the restaurant.

CHAPTER SEVENTEEN

"Sarah...Sarah...Wake up, darling."

Her name came rolling out of the depths of her mind like it was someone else they called. But she was aware of the name, Sarah—the name her mother gave her, called her.

"Please, wake up, darling," said her mother.

Sarah wanted to awake, but how? Maybe she was dead. _Mother, help me_, she screamed, but only in her mind, her lips didn't move. Sarah had to see her mother, needed to hear her mother calling her name.

"Sarah, wake up, child."

A light formed at the end of a tunnel and tumbled toward Sarah. Her body shook. Someone jostled her shoulder. She heard her name again, but it was not her mother calling. Whose voice called? The light grew stronger, brighter and suddenly it exploded before her, darting around her head. Breath rushed into her lungs, and her eyes popped open. Before her was someone's face, but whom? It was a brown face and a distorted face. On this face was a swollen and dark right eye—an eye almost shut. The face staring at Sarah had a Mona Lisa-smile—a mother's smile that says all is well.

"Sarah, you poor child," said the face in a familiar female's voice. "What's that bastard done to you?" She held Sarah in her arms and rocked her back and forth much like a mother cuddles her infant.

"Tommy," Sarah tried to scream, but only whispered. "Where is Tommy?"

"Shhhh," calmed the woman. "Emmanuel took him, but he's okay. Don't worry. Emmanuel would never hurt Tommy."

"Crystal, is that you?"

"Yeah, it's me." She rubbed Sarah's eye. "I guess we both got a shiner."

"A what?"

"We both got black eyes," said Crystal helping Sarah to a sitting position. "Who hit you?"

Sarah touched her own eye and felt the swelling. "Irene...no, it was him... Yeah, it was him." She couldn't bring herself to say his name. "Did he hit you, too?"

"No, but one of his goons gave me this shiner. I'll get even, though. We're gonna get out of here soon. You know?"

"We got to," said Sarah.

"Your mother's hired this man to find you, and I know he'll come looking for us."

"Mother." said Sarah grabbing Crystal's arm. "You saw Mother?"

"No, no, child," said Crystal. "But I've talked to the man she's hired to find you. And let me tell you, this man means business. I've never really seen anybody like him."

"Who?"

"His name is Matt," said Crystal. "He's not what you'd call handsome, you know, like the private eyes are in the movies, but he is attractive in some strange way. He's the manliest man I ever seen. You know what I mean?"

Sarah shook her head that she didn't.

"He's old, though. He's about fifty or older, but I know he can take care of himself. I just hope he and Emmanuel meet up with each other. This man means business."

Sarah watched Crystal's face—a dreaming face as she talked about this man that Sarah's mother had hired.

"He's got a scar," continued Crystal. "But that only makes him more attractive to me. It starts here." Crystal pointed to the top of her own forehead and traced her finger across her right eye, down her cheek; then, she turned it toward her right earlobe where she stopped. "And it ends here, but it's not a bad scar. It makes him more manly—a tough look—a man I wouldn't mind getting lost in the woods with. If you know what I mean, child."

"Is he a big man?" said Sarah. She had become fascinated with the man Crystal was describing. She had never known a man like this. Neither her husband nor her father had been this rugged type of man Crystal portrayed.

"Yes. No." said Crystal. "He's a little over six-feet tall, like Emmanuel, but he's got muscles where Emmanuel wishes he had 'em. For an older man, you can tell he works out and keeps himself in shape. He's hard. I mean I ain't ever touched him, but I can tell."

"When's he coming?"

"Soon, but I don't know when. He's got a friend, too—a partner—a black man—a good-looking black man, too. He's young, maybe my age. Now, he's built like a stud horse. I mean this man looks like a football player if I ever seen one."

Sarah saw a look spread across Crystal's face likened to a rainbow when it adorns the sky. Her friend needed a man of her own. For a brief moment, Sarah thought of her own situation, man-less. But she never wanted to be with another man. She didn't think she could ever care for another man.

"Where'd Emmanuel go?" said Sarah.

"I think it scared him when you fell and knocked yourself out. He thought he'd killed you. Not that I think he's got a conscience. No, I don't think he cares if you live or die, because he doesn't mind telling other people to do his killing.

But I can tell he doesn't want to kill anybody himself. Anyway, one of his men came and got him. It seems the law enforcers out front tried to break inside with their cars, but Emmanuel had women and children lay down across the middle of the gate to keep them out. Can you believe that egotistical bastard? Personally, I can't believe those fools still think he's God. But anyway, it's a stand-off right now between Emmanuel and the authorities."

"And Tommy?"

"He'll be okay," said Crystal. "We just got to stay alive until Matt and Leaky get here."

"Leaky?"

"That's the black friend of Matt's."

"How they going to get in?"

"I don't know," said Crystal. "But Matt will find a way." Crystal paused for a moment. "You know, we could break out of here. I bet they haven't found out about that hole in the fence up by the cedar trees where I got out this morning. If we could get out of this room, find Tommy, we could make a run for it. You with me, girl?"

"Sure," said Sarah. "How we going to get Tommy away from Emmanuel?"

"I don't know, but we'll find a way," said Crystal checking Sarah's eyes. "Why both your eyes so blood shot?"

"Irene's giving me rat poison."

"What? That bitch! One of these days I'm gonna take care of her in a way she ain't gonna like."

Sarah loved this woman.

As fast as lightning explodes from the sky, the front door to the apartment burst open, and, before the two women could react, heavy footsteps, booming like thunder, stomped into the bedroom. Stopping in the doorway and placing his arms on his hips stood Emmanuel, looking like an angry bulldog. In a panic, Sarah noticed that Tommy was not with him.

Emmanuel pointed his finger at them. "What you girls talking about? You're talking about escaping, aren't you?"

Sarah wondered how he knew. She began to shake.

He came over to the bed, jerked Crystal up by the arm, and flung her to the floor. "You'll have to show us that hole in the fence you escaped from." He laughed and glared into Sarah's eyes.

He had been listening to them, but how?

"You're wondering how I know so much, aren't you?" he said and laughed. "You know I can read your mind. I can hear through walls. Emmanuel knows all."

Sarah glanced around the room looking for a hidden camera or some type of microphone. She knew there had to be a microphone or some type of bug in this room. He had heard all they had said.

"This man named Matt," said Emmanuel glancing down toward Crystal who still sat in the floor staring up at him. "You think he's so much bigger and stronger than me. And you say he's coming to save you. Well, he's about to have some big problems tonight. I hope he don't mind having a little explosion on that boat. You know, the one you told me about." Emmanuel started laughing until he started coughing.

CHAPTER EIGHTEEN

By the time Medora and Matt reached the city limits of Dayton—a quiet town in the Cumberland Mountains—the sun had traveled so far to the west that the majestic oaks lining the side of the two-lane highway cast long, autumn shadows across the asphalt. As they entered town, there was an orange hue reflecting off the buildings and surrounding vegetation. Evening came so quickly these last few days of fall. Matt sensed, to his dismay, that winter was fighting its way back into their lives.

For the first time in over an hour Matt let the serenity of the landscape relax the knotting muscles in his shoulders and neck. The dull headache he had developed soon after leaving the Choo Choo persisted, but at last, it was decreasing in strength.

Neither Medora nor Matt had spoken to one another during the one-hour trip. He wasn't angry; he just didn't have anything to say to her. She had spent most of the time during the journey staring out her window at the farmland they passed. Matt wondered if she was upset with him for what he said to her as they left the restaurant. She would get over it, he thought.

During most of their trek north, he'd worried about what had happened or was happening to Crystal. If they killed her, he'd have trouble facing himself for a long while. Matt thought about the young Sarah and what she must be going through at the compound. Several times, he started to tell Medora about her daughter's involvement with the leader of the religious cult, but each time Matt opened his mouth to speak something inside his subconscious told him to stay quiet and wait. In due time he knew Medora would learn everything about her daughter. Maybe on the way home, he would tell her more. Matt was beginning to feel guilty for insulting her. But not very.

Presently, as they drove beside the old Rhea County Courthouse with its tall belfry of red brick, Matt contemplated the entire situation. First, he needed to learn all he could about Emmanuel before they met. Second, Matt had to find a way to gain entry to the compound without someone killing him. And third, he had to find Crystal, Sarah, and her family and get them out safely. He'd find a way. Now, time was his most pressing enemy. Matt questioned if he should've foregone this trip to Dayton, but something, he didn't know what, was drawing him to this place like a child to its mother's breast.

Medora brought his thoughts back. "Isn't that the courthouse where they had the Scopes Trial?" She lowered her head to peer out the window at the old brick building. The belfry clocks, one on each of its four sides, showed three-fifty-five.

"I guess," he said. "I don't know much about this place."

"Do you believe in evolution, Mister Fagan?" Her tone was cold and impersonal, but he thought it a beginning to their truce. Like it or not, it looked like they were going to have to be together, and this silly feuding needed to cease.

"I never thought about it a lot," he said. "Do you?" They were already leaving the downtown area and heading for the home of Rebecca Belcher whom Matt hoped could lead him to Emmanuel's family.

"Yes, of course. You do know what evolution is, don't you, Mister Fagan?"

He wanted to scream, BITCH! But he bit his lip and said, "Yes. Do you think I'm an idiot, or just plain stupid?"

"I want you to think about it, Mister Fagan," she said without telling him what she thought. "Everyone who knows what it means either believes in evolution or doesn't. How about you?"

"You say you believe in evolution," Matt said as they turned right off Highway-27 and onto White Hollow Road. "Well, do you believe in God?"

"No. Do you?"

"Yes," he said, creeping along the narrow asphalt road and looking for numbers on the strewed mailboxes—mailboxes that stood between a shallow ditch and the pavement. As they drove farther from town, the dwellings were farther apart and further off the road. "I believe in God, but I don't attend church."

"Then, you don't believe in evolution, right?"

"No, that's not what I said. I believe in evolution. Why not? Can't a person believe in God and evolution?" Matt fought to keep from showing any signs of anger.

"I don't see how anyone can believe that," she said. "In the Bible there's the story of Adam and Eve, and that doesn't agree with the theory of evolution."

"Who wrote the book of _Genesis_, the first chapter in the Bible that talks about Adam and Eve?"

"I don't know. Why?" she said staring a hole through the side of his head.

"Scholars of the Bible say Moses wrote it."

"So?" she said no longer smiling and no longer looking like a teacher that was enjoying correcting her pupils.

"They—I'm talking about real Bible scholars—say God inspired Moses to write the Bible, and..."

"What are you getting at?" she interrupted. "I don't understand where this is headed."

"Listen, and let me finish," he said letting the Explorer almost come to a stop alongside the road. "Do you think if God had told Moses about chromosomes or genes that Moses and the Jewish people would have known what He was talking about? Or, if He told Moses about natural selection of organisms over eons of time, he would have understood? And, oh yes, how about the laws of genetics or even mutations? The only thing about evolution I think Moses and the Jews of that time would have understood was survival of the fittest."

Medora, staring with wide eyes at him, opened her mouth to speak but after a long moment said nothing and gazed back out the front window.

"So," Matt said. "To answer your question—yes I believe in evolution. And yes—I believe in God."

As they sat in awkward silence again, he brought the Explorer up to normal speed. Matt kept checking each mailbox for numbers or names. It amazed him that so many of the boxes had nothing on them to distinguish their ownership. They had traveled about a mile since leaving the city limits, and the number of dwellings had become increasingly scattered and farther apart. In some places along the road he saw a mobile home parked next door to a big, brick home.

Finally, they reached the address Matt thought belonged to Rebecca Belcher. If it wasn't the correct one, he would have to ask directions. Matt turned into a gravel driveway that led over a creek to a small, white-framed house that was about a hundred feet off the road. The driveway pebbles made a crunching sound under the Explorer's tires. When he stopped in front of the house, two dogs—one a little, brown mutt and the other a big, black, short-hair mixed breed—came tearing from underneath the front porch barking at the Explorer. This wasn't going to be easy, Matt thought. He had handled a deadly rattlesnake today and lived to tell about it. Why should a couple of barking dogs frighten him?

Taking a deep breath, he opened the door and placed his left foot on the gray, igneous formed gravel. The dogs didn't charge toward him as he moved out of the car and stood beside its open door. The smaller, brown mutt with its high-pitched yelping came closer, while the bigger, black dog with its roaring bark moved a step away from Matt who watched the animals while thinking about survival of the fittest.

He took a cautious step closer to the house, about the time a young woman bound out the front door clapping her hands. "Shut-up, brown-dog. Hush, black-dog." The woman, maybe in her late teens or early twenties, continued moving forward and clapping her hands at the dogs. She stopped at the edge of porch and looked down its three steps at Matt as he stood close to the Explorer. The two mongrels put their tails between their back legs, lowered their heads, and relocated themselves halfway between the girl and Matt. Even though her chestnut-brown hair was thin and hanging limp to her shoulders, and her face was as pale as the house, she was attractive but homely. She stood facing them in an A-line, yellow dress covered with green and blue polka dots. With one hand resting on her hip, Matt could tell that the girl was very skinny under the dress that stopped at her knees.

Her facial features were sharp and engaging, but Matt detected tiredness beneath her emerald-green eyes.

She looked up from the dogs. "What you'ns want?"

When Matt looked behind the girl, he saw the face of an older man peeping around the unpainted door. The man looked as if he could be the girl's father, but Matt wondered why he had sent her out to confront them and not come himself. The man moved a little farther out of the doorway until Matt could see his attire of faded blue overalls over a green flannel shirt. The man looked dull-witted. His lower jaw dropped and his mouth hung open allowing saliva to drip freely on his bib. When the short man of about forty grinned, he showed a speckling of black, rotten teeth.

The girl finally noticed Matt glancing over her shoulder, so she turned and saw the man who now stood in the middle of the porch. She clapped her hands at him like she had at the dogs. "Get inside, John!" A frown replaced the old man's smile, his bottom lip poked out, but he obeyed the younger girl and puttered into the house.

When the girl turned back, Matt had decided it was time to ask the question. "I'm looking for the Belcher residence. Can you help me?"

"What for?" said the girl. "What you'ns want with them?"

"I just need to speak to Rebecca Belcher," he said, now knowing she knew them but wondering why she didn't tell him where they lived.

The girl inhaled deeply and glanced toward the Explorer. "What you'n want with her? Who are you?"

"I'm Matt Fagan, and I need to speak to Rebecca Belcher if you'll tell me where she lives."

"She use to live here," said the girl crossing her arms in front of her chest and shivering.

"Where is she now?"

"Dead," said the girl.

"Oh," Matt said, knowing now he was wasting their time. He had only decided to search for Rebecca because her name struck a note in his brain, and he thought she might know something about Mark Belcher, alias Emmanuel. It was time to get back to Chattanooga. Matt dropped his head and started to get in the Explorer.

"I'm her granddaughter," said the girl.

Matt's head shot up, and he moved toward the girl. "Then she once lived here?"

"Yes," said the girl. "She died right after Christmas. Cancer."

"I'm sorry to hear that," he said taking a step closer to the stairs where the girl now stood. Both dogs jumped to their feet. Brown dog growled. Matt stopped. "That man out here a few minutes ago, was that your father?"

"No," said the girl moving backwards to the bottom step. "That's my uncle...I watch after him. He's retarded."

"Where're your parents?"

"Dead," said the girl without showing emotions. "At least my mother's dead. I never knowed my father."

"Who watches after you?"

"Uncle Mark sends us money to live on."

"Mark Belcher?" Matt said. His heart slammed against his sternum. "The preacher?"

"Uh huh," said the girl.

"Why don't you live with him?"

"He don't want people knowing about his brother, John. I keep him here, and Uncle Mark sends us money to live on."

"Do you have any other family?"

"Why you asking all these question?" The girl steps backward and up one step to the top of the porch.

"Your uncle has inherited some money, and I was just trying to find him," Matt said.

"Really?" said the girl. She moved back down to the bottom step. "How much?"

"A lot," Matt said with a smile. He had planned to sneak the next question into the conversation as soon as possible. Now seemed like the best moment. "Do you know any Fagans that live around here?"

"I've heared the name, but I don't know any," said the girl. "Ain't that your name?"

"Yeah," Matt said. Her answer made him stop a moment and try to think of a way to get the conversation back on her family. "I take it that your mother was Emmanuel's sister?"

"Who's Emmanuel?" said the girl.

"I mean Mark Belcher was your mother's brother, right?"

"Of course," said the girl. "How much money you'n talking about?"

"I can only tell him how much he won. When did your mother die?"

"Last spring," said the girl. "Just after grandma died."

"Did your mother have cancer, too?"

"No," said the girl glancing down at her Nikes that had long since lost their whiteness. She dragged her right toe across the dirt. "Are you'ns the law?"

"No, why?"

"'Cause she did something illegal," said the girl.

Matt held his breath a moment, trying to appear calm. "Well, I'm not the law, and besides she's dead and they can't do anything to her now." Matt waited half a minute, then after no response from the girl he said, "What'd your mother do, honey?"

"I guess it don't matter none, then if you'ns wants to know," said the girl still staring at her Nikes. She continued making little circles with her right toe.

"That's right," Matt said staying still and trying to hide his impatience while waiting for her to tell how her mother died. At first, Matt really didn't care how the woman died, but after all of this he had to know.

The girl waited a long moment before answering him. "She was a handler and got bit."

"A what?" Matt said. "I'm sorry, I don't understand what you're talking about."

"She handled rattlers," said the girl, finally looking back up and directly into his eyes. "She got bit by a canebrake rattler on the neck. She died next day. It was awful. Shouldn't nobody die like that."

CHAPTER NINETEEN

Leaky zipped his olive-green lifejacket all the way up next to his throat, but it didn't make him feel any safer as he motored down the swiftest part of the Tennessee River. This was the part of the river called Suck Creek, and it lived up to its name. It was hard trying to steer Matt's fishing boat—the type often called a johnboat by the locals—in these choppy waters. Because it was only fifteen-feet long, and it had taken all of Leaky's strength to control its course since leaving the Marina, the possibility of drowning filled his thoughts.

Leaky kept telling himself that only a lamebrain idiot would be out in such a tiny boat with waves that were more like those found in the ocean than in a river. Every time the flat-bottom front end of the craft topped a three-foot wave, it immediately came crashing down the other side with a smack, sending a spray of mist over Leaky's face. He was glad the waves were coming at him head-on instead of from the side. He continually wiped fish-smelling water from his face with a wet hand.

Earlier, after Matt went to meet the Meehan woman, Leaky had tried to approach the compound in his car, but the law enforcement camped around the "Refuge" had kept him away. Matt had asked Leaky to find the way Emmanuel's people were getting in and out of the compound undetected. However, Leaky gave up trying the direct approach when most of the law enforcers he saw were out-of-town FBI agents and didn't know him. After much deliberation, he had no recourse but to attempt to reach the compound by water. If he could have found another way to get closer he would have, but he couldn't let Matt down.

Checking his watch, Leaky saw that it was five-ten. He had been on the water for almost an hour, now. Leaky's heart skipped several beats when the engine stuttered, then sputtered and acted like it wanted to stop but didn't. With his left hand, Leaky pulled back on the throttle handle, and the boat halted in the water, waves slamming into the bow with a smack. Standing in the rocking boat that bounced around like a cork proved most difficult for a land-lover like Leaky. He grasped for the dash, the seat, the console and anything available to keep his balance, and then crawled on his knees the few feet to the two gas cans in the stern.

He had failed to check the two five-gallon cans before leaving the dock, and now one gauge showed that the tank he was using was empty. He almost hated to look at the other one for fear of it being empty. He had mixed emotions when he saw that the other tank was half full. Quickly Leaky changed gas lines to the full tank, but the twenty-five horsepower engine he'd left running died before he finished. "Shit," he said aloud.

Before he could even turn back toward his seat to crank the engine, the boat had drifted sideways in the river. Each wave now hit it broadside with a loud bang. The craft rocked so high from port to starboard that Leaky had to crawl on his hands and knees back toward the steering wheel. With each blast of a wave, a spray of water showered into the boat. When Leaky finally pulled himself up and regained his place behind the controls, the boat came flying up to meet him slamming his ass into the driver's seat hard enough to jar his teeth together. He held tight to the steering wheel with one hand and twisted the key with the other.

The Mercury outboard engine hacked, spit, and gargled but didn't catch. About to go out of his mind with the fear of drowning, he twisted the key so hard it almost broke off in the switch. "Shit fire and save matches," Leaky said.

The motor's starter slowed and began to drag as the battery lost power. Realizing he couldn't lose the battery, Leaky released the key and tried to think of what he should do next to keep from dying.

"Shit." he screamed when a huge wave splashed over the side of the boat and soaked his already wet pants. Finally his panicked mind cleared, and he remembered he'd not pumped the priming bulb on the gas line.

"You dumb piece of monkey shit," he said scurrying back to the gas tank. Holding on to the side of the boat with his left hand, Leaky reached with his other one and squeezed the black, rubber ball until it tightened full of gas. Then, after nearly falling headfirst into the water, he regained his balance in time for his ass to slam back into the driver's seat.

Leaky said a quick prayer as he turned the key. With a spitting, spewing and sputtering the Mercury outboard turned over and started humming. It was sweeter than any music Leaky had ever heard. When he put it in gear the craft jerked forward with a jolt snapping Leaky's head back.

At first, Leaky didn't know his location, but after checking, he was able to swing the boat's flat nose around to face the oncoming waves. Finding himself blown into the middle of the two hundred-foot-wide river almost put Leaky into another state of panic. He knew better than to turn directly toward the bank, because that would place the craft broadside of the waves. He made a heading of about forty-five degrees toward the grassy shore to his left and pushed the throttle to three-quarter speed. Water built from the spray sloshed on his boots.

He managed to maneuver the boat to within twenty feet of the riverbank and turned back down stream. It was much colder here in the shade but safer. Finally, after another ten minutes, the wind stopped completely, and the waves diminished to nothing. The river that only a few minutes ago was terrifying had turned placid.

Leaky remembered that it was common this time of year for the wind to dwindle in the late afternoon when the sun dropped far into the western sky.

He pulled back on the throttle slowing the craft and permitting its nose to glide across the water that had now turned to glass. Leaky's major concern turned to his gas supply, and if he had enough of the precious fuel to get back to Matt's cruiser when he had to return. He glanced up at the trolling motor wondering if its battery was charged, but he realized that even if the battery was fully charged, the slow-going trolling motor couldn't get him back to Matt's dock alone.

The river, now as still as a polished mirror, would have been relaxing at any other time. A minute splash to Leaky's right caused him to turn his head. He saw circular ripples spreading across the water and figured a fish had jumped. Before Leaky could turn his eyes forward, a fish jumped only ten feet from his boat. He saw what he thought was a bass this time, and realized the fish were now feeding on shad along this section of the river. He'd love to have his fishing equipment.

While looking for more bass out in the river Leaky let the johnboat get too close to the left bank and almost ran into an anchored pontoon boat just ahead of him. With lightning reflexes, he turned away from the craft just before he missed ramming into its side. Fortunately, no one was on the boat or on the shore near it. All was quiet except for the chirping crickets and katydids that had recently started their nightly serenade. He felt sure this was the pontoon boat that had taken Crystal across the river earlier today.

He killed the johnboat's engine, hurried to the trolling motor in the front and slid its propeller into the water. When he pushed the "on" switch the johnboat jerked forward before settling out at two miles per hour.

As the johnboat skimmed behind the back of the pontoon boat, Leaky noticed that someone had tied it to the shore with a long rope that wrapped around a small oak sapling. He stood in the front of the johnboat to get a better look at the shore as he slid beyond the craft. Still, he saw no one.

After traveling at least a hundred feet past the pontoon boat, Leaky nosed his vessel toward the bank. At the last second, before hitting shore, he lifted the trolling motor out of the water so it didn't jam into the muddy bottom. He leaped onto the bank, grabbed the front-end of his boat, and pulled it half way out of the water. He got back into the craft, lifted the Mercury engine's shaft out of the water, and locked it in the up position. Taking several deep breaths, he got back out of the boat and, using every muscle fiber in his body, pulled the johnboat completely out of the water. He rested a few seconds before towing it an additional five feet onto shore under some low-growing brush.

With the johnboat safely out of sight, Leaky lay back, closed his eyes, and tried to catch his breath. The fishy odor of the river filled his nostrils. He thought about dry clothes. He thought about going home. He thought about dying and pulled himself to his feet. He took off his lifejacket, and then checked the beached johnboat. When everything looked secure, he struck out toward the pontoon boat. It took him almost five minutes to weave through the thick underbrush of vines and briers along the riverbank to the anchored craft. Still no one was there. His wet shirt and pants clung to his wrinkled skin as if glued. He felt plain miserable. Damn miserable. He felt like he'd donated his body to science before he had finished using it.

"Dammit," said Leaky, visually searching through the foliage that meandered up a worn trail in the direction of the compound. He stood looking up through the brush trying to decide what to do next. The sun had disappeared behind Raccoon Mountain and deep shadows cut through the forest floor. Turning, Leaky moved forward up the trail. He squinted his eyes, but it didn't help him see in the growing dimness.

After moving ten feet up the trail, something snapped in the woods ahead of Leaky. He fell to his knees on the sandy path and grabbed for the Smith and Wesson pistol he carried in a holster on his side. It wasn't there. He'd left it in the johnboat in a dry compartment under the seat. Another snap then a popping sound reached Leaky's ears a split second before he saw an acorn falling out of an oak tree. The oak seed, bouncing off several branches, sounded like a batter hitting a baseball with a wooden bat. Leaky looked up the oak and saw two gray squirrels chasing one another.

"You dumb piece of bovine fecal matter," Leaky said to himself while pushing his belly off the ground. He felt like a dog on his hands and knees. "If I was any more stupid, I'd have to be mowed once a damn week."

A different rustling sound accompanied by murmuring human voices caused Leaky to freeze in his crouched position on one knee. Whomever it was approaching came directly toward Leaky's location there in the path that led to the river and the pontoon boat. Leaky's heart jump-started, picked up speed, and raced in his chest. His brain screamed for him to hurry and get up, but he couldn't move. On they came. _Move your black ass_, his brain screamed.

Trying to keep from panicking, Leaky slipped back to his hands and knees and crawled into the underbrush of mountain laurel to his left, away from his johnboat, away from his pistol that he'd left in it. After he had crawled only a few feet into the evergreens, the people approaching were upon him. Trying to avoid making a sound in the leaves, Leaky lowered himself onto his belly. The scrapes on his legs burned. He knew if anyone glanced in his direction, they couldn't miss seeing a leg, an arm or some part of him. He concentrated on being very still and acting like a fallen log. The ground smelled of rotting vegetation. With his heart pounding like a bass drum, he continued to stay motionless and not breathe. He dug his fingers into the soil.

Someone in a deep male voice walked beside where Leaky hid and said, "I hope that piece of crap'll crank. I don't feel like swimming up river."

"We don't have to swim if it don't crank," said another man. Leaky glimpsed up and saw the barrel of a shotgun beside the man's leg.

"Yeah," said the first man. "And you going to tell Emmanuel we couldn't take care of everything like he ordered?"

Hearing the men step onto the pontoon boat, Leaky pulled his face off the ground and tried to determine the two men's location. He spied through the bottom of the underbrush but could only see as high as the floats of the boat that bobbed in the water.

"You're right," said the second man. "We got to get going."

"What we going to do ain't so little a job," said one. "If we get caught we're in big trouble."

The pontoon boat's engine sputtered and spewed but cranked in only a few seconds with coaxing and begging from the two men. Leaky watched one of the men leap off the boat's front, untie the rope from the oak and push the boat into the water before jumping back aboard. In seconds, they were churning on the pontoon boat out into the river.

Leaky eased back to his all fours, pushed a limb of mountain laurel to the side, and watched the pontoon boat turning away from the near bank. Once they got the boat turned, the men faced the river and away from Leaky. Brushing dead leaves off his wet clothes, Leaky got to his feet but stayed alert to dive back into the cover if one or both of the men should turn their heads toward him.

After several minutes the men landed on the far shore and got inside an older model, black GMC pick-up truck driven by a redheaded woman. In seconds, they rushed away down Suck Creek Road toward Chattanooga. Leaky wondered what had happened to the Suburban Matt had filled full of .45 caliber holes. It was gone.

Leaky thought about going back to the johnboat to get his pistol, but he was afraid the waning light would disappear before he found the way into the compound. He kicked himself for forgetting to bring a flashlight from Matt's place. This had definitely not been his day. He reminded himself to be careful until he got back to the dock.

Leaky turned away from the river and toward the mountain. He followed the dirt path for almost fifty yards up a steep incline toward Cash Canyon Road. Just before reaching the road, the trail ended as it entered a clump of low growing cedar trees. He thought his eyes were deceiving him in the near darkness. How could the path just disappear into a thicket like that?

Being very careful like he was defusing a bomb, Leaky pushed aside a limb of one of the cedars and peered behind it. At first, all he saw was blackness, but soon he realized that he was staring into a dark hole. A cave.

He moved past the cedars and into the mouth of the cave that was just tall enough for him to enter without bending at the waist. He halted because of the pitch-blackness ahead and told himself to get out of there because he had found the way Emmanuel's people were getting in and out of the compound. But he didn't follow his own advice. His curiosity made him take a tiny step deeper into the cave. His right foot hit something solid on the cave floor causing whatever he kicked to slide ahead of him a few inches. Bending over and groping with his hands in the darkness, Leaky felt a wooden box. It was about the size of a suitcase. He found a metal handle on its side and pulled it outside into the fading light.

When he raised the lid he found what he needed, for it contained four identical long black flashlights. He picked one out of the pile and turned it on. Its yellowish light showed only a few feet into the cave before it went out. Leaky tried another one, then another, until he found one that cast a white light deeper into the rocky shaft.

Pushing the box back inside, he took two steps forward then stopped and listened to the echo of his boot heels on the solid stone floor. A strong musty odor mixed with something that smelled like animal feces rushed past Leaky causing him to cringe and breathe only through his mouth. But he still detected the pungency of defecation.

Walking on his toes to eliminate the sound of his boot heels, Leaky crept deeper into the cave. It took several minutes to traverse about a hundred feet up a steady ten-degree incline and around a few stalagmites growing out of the ground. There he came to the opening of a larger room—a cavern in rock. Leaky knew these type caves were common in this part of the world with the famous Ruby Falls Cave less than ten miles from where he now stood.

After stepping into the room that was about fifty feet in diameter, he moved the cone of light along each wall and noticed three other openings leading into the cavern. Stalactites hung about thirty feet over his head. Someone had re-moved their matching stalagmites from the room's floor—a floor amply covered with bat shit. Leaky's olfactory nerves had fatigued to the point that he no longer smelled the sulfurous odor of feces. Shinning the light up and past the stalactites, Leaky saw that the ceiling was thick with the winged mammals that squirmed together like bubbling tar. Their glowing eyes looked eerie, reflecting light back at Leaky. When they screeched out with an ear-piercing call, Leaky cringed.

Quickly, Leaky checked each of the other three shafts leading out of the room and realized that only one had a smooth worn floor. It also was the only one that continued to stretch upward at the correct angle, and it was the only one that drew a slight wind into it created by the chimney effect. He knew for it to reach Emmanuel's compound, the shaft would have to continue rising. Without hesitation, Leaky moved into that shaft.

The sound of dripping water caught his attention soon after moving only thirty feet up the path. He paused and listened. Leaky's body quivered as he thought about the men from the pontoon boat coming up behind him with their shotguns. He didn't know if they had the weapons with them, but they most likely did. What would he do if they suddenly walked up behind him? *Run, but where?*

"Get your black ass out of here, now," he said to himself, and then listened to his own words reverberated back to his ringing ears.

Without warning, his flashlight went out. Pitch darkness enveloped him like a blanket.

"Sweet Mother of Jesus," he said frantically hitting the light's switch and beating the tube in his hand.

His light flickered on. It went off. He held the extinguished light to his face.

"Be cool," he told himself. The flashlight beam burst through the blackness striking him in the eyes. Again, he pointed it through the forbidding tunnel ahead. It flashed off, then on. He held it still, and the light stayed with him.

He took a deep sigh of relief, but before he could relax, he heard the creaking of a door opening somewhere ahead. Far ahead, someone moved down wooden steps. His feet felt like they were stuck in cement for he couldn't move them. Then, he heard human voices coming in his direction. He turned off his flashlight and darkness swallowed him again. He didn't know what to do. New fear electrified a million nerves in his brain when he saw a faint yellowish glow flashing far ahead from where the voices came. Their light grew brighter. He snatched for his Smith & Wesson, and then remembered where he'd left it.

CHAPTER TWENTY

At first glance she looked older than ninety-one, but if Matt's luck held she'd be sharp-witted enough to help him learn what he had to know.

Her companion, a short, round woman of about fifty, placed a hand on the woman's shoulder. When the old woman looked up, the granddaughter said loud enough to be heard across the street, "You've got company, Mamaw. This young man wants to visit with you a minute. Okay? You feel up to it?"

The old woman didn't answer her granddaughter but only turned her blue-gray eyes toward Matt. Her eyes, set deeply in a face of sagging wrinkled skin, were glistening and bright and had only a hint of cataracts. She sat in an uphol-stered, high-back chair; her shoulders stooped far forward. Her thin white hair dangled in scanty strands across large, drooping ears.

"One of your great-nephews, Carl Fagan, sent him over," said the grand-daughter. "Carl is Peter's boy. You remember Peter, don't you? He's your brother, Julian's boy." The granddaughter turned toward Matt and in a normal voice said, "She ought to know Carl since he's lived next door to her for sixty years, but sometimes she forgets."

"Lordy, lordy, of course I know Carl," said the old woman in a rasping but strong voice. "You think I'm a fool? I ain't dead yet, Wanda, darling. I know my own family. Most of 'em, anyway." She stared at Matt while squinting her eyes. "Lordy, lordy, how you'ns doing, Carl?"

"No, Mamaw," said the granddaughter. "This ain't Carl. This man went to see Carl wanting to know if he's kin to him. This nice looking man's name is Matt, and his last name is Fagan. Like Carl and Peter, and you, he's a Fagan."

"Oh," said the old woman, but she had a confused look on her face. "What's his name?"

"Matt Fagan," shouted the granddaughter throwing her hands up in frus-tration. "Let him tell you. I'm going back in here and talk to his wife." The granddaughter left the dim bedroom shaking her head and mumbling to herself. When she shut the door, the lone lamp on a bedside table next to the old woman gave yellowness to everything there.

Matt hadn't bothered telling the granddaughter who Medora Meehan was. He'd asked Medora to wait in the car, but she refused, failing to hide her anger with him for wasting their time and not going back to Chattanooga to find her daughter. At least Medora hadn't demanded to follow him into this room.

The old woman reached her shaking hands toward Matt. "Give me a hug." The loose skin quivered from her elbows up to where her arms entered a once green robe that had now faded to almost yellow.

Matt bent at the waist permitting the woman to place her arms around his neck. She had a different odor, a musty smell that he couldn't identify. Matt had not been around the elderly enough to recognize their scents.

Placing his hands around her back in the hug, Matt felt the woman's bones beneath the thin cotton. In fear of hurting her, his embrace stayed light. He tried to pull away, but her grip was strong. She held Matt next to her cheek an extra moment before releasing him.

After a few seconds, the old woman pulled her face away from him and said, "Now, tell me you'n name again."

"Matt Fagan."

She stared at him a long moment. "Sit there so I can see you." She pointed with a forehead nod toward a straight-back chair without arms. Its wicker seat was coming apart in several places. Matt moved the wooden chair so it faced the old woman.

"My name before I married was Fagan, too." started the old woman. Matt didn't yet know her first name. "I wedded when I was fourteen. My husband's name was Ferrol Fagan—a good man. My second cousin, too." She paused a long moment. Her eyes focused on a distant time. "Rattler got him, long time ago."

Matt's heart stopped, then started back with a jolt like an electric shock.

Squinting those blue-gray eyes almost shut, she stared at him. "Whose boy is you?"

"I don't know," he said. "I don't remember my parents. I was hoping you might could help."

"Lordy, lord, if you don't know, then I don't know. That's for sure."

"Are you related to the Belcher family?" Matt said not knowing exactly why he asked that question. Maybe he did it because of what Crystal had said this morning about Emmanuel looking like him. Matt guessed that's what started this useless trip. "The Belcher clan that lives around here—you kin to them."

A cold expression crossed the old woman's face. For a mini-second Matt saw anger and hate leak from her eyes as they narrowed. "No."

Feeling drained that he'd come this far for nothing, Matt dropped his head. Medora was right—he'd wasted their time and learned nothing.

"Not anymore," the old woman said.

His head shot up. "What you mean, not anymore?"

"My nephew's wife married that sorry Belcher man. She was expecting my nephew's child when she married that no-good Belcher man."

Matt didn't understand what the old woman meant. "Did your nephew die?"

"Of course," said the old lady.

Matt didn't know why, but he was afraid to ask how he died. "What was his name?"

"Steward," said the woman.

The name Steward Fagan didn't sound familiar to Matt.

"Steward Belcher," repeated the old woman.

Matt regrouped his thoughts. "I mean your nephew. What was his name?"

"Isaac Fagan."

Matt felt a familiarity with the name Isaac, but he couldn't think of where he knew it—maybe the Bible.

"Isaac had two sons," said the old woman.

Matt's heart emptied of blood. He wanted to know the sons' names but couldn't make himself ask. "What's your name?" Matt said instead. He could only whisper, now.

She looked up at him with a bewildered expression. "Mamaw."

"I mean the name your parents gave you."

"Lucinda May...Fagan," the woman said. "But when I was younger everybody called me Aunt Lucy."

Blood rushed back into his heart with a punch, shaking his chest like an earthquake and making his head dizzy. Matt could wait no longer. "Aunt Lucy... you said Isaac had two sons, right?"

"Yes."

"Was one of his sons named Mark?"

"Yes," said Aunt Lucy. "But his mother gave him the name Belcher. That wudn't right, you know? He was conceived a Fagan but born a Belcher."

Matt took a deep breath and leaned closer to Aunt Lucy. He had to close his eyes to talk. "The other son...what was his name?"

"That poor child," said Aunt Lucy. Her eyes, buried deep in sockets, started leaking tears. "It was so long ago. Lordy, lordy, I ain't seen that baby since he's about four or five. They gave him away. Sent him off like he's an animal they didn't want no more." The tears streamed down and across the deep wrinkles on her face. "That no-a-count Steward Belcher...Sorriest man God ever put a breath in...His mama was sorry, too, but Linda Pearl Belcher had the brains in the Belcher family and fixed everything up to get rid of that child. They're both burning in hell this very minute for what they did to that child."

Matt couldn't ask his name, so he said, "How'd they give him away?"

"They told us the government took that child...They said us Fagans weren't fit to take that boy and raise him, 'cause we let him handle snakes...His daddy, dying from a snakebite and everything was the final nail in the coffin." New tears tumbled from her eyes. "And then somebody—I know it was Steward's mother,

Linda Pearl Belcher who told the sheriff about that child handling a snake, and he come and took our baby away. And we'ns never seen Isaac's oldest son since."

Matt's body quivered. Another gush of electric current surged through his chest. "The boy handled poisonous snakes?"

"Only once," said Lucy, her voice hardly audible. She appeared to be weakening. Her eyes dropped. "But everybody knowed when that child grabbed that rattler by the tail and pulled it away from his stricken daddy, that he had the gift of the serpent. Not many have the gift to take up serpents and not get bit, but that child did. That monster rattler got so calm when that baby touched it. It almost went to sleep." Her eyes got a far away look again. Matt didn't want to disturb her. They sat in silence except for the constant ticking of an old pendulum clock hanging on the wall—a wall that had long ago lost its luster.

Sweat covered the palms of his hands. Matt opened his mouth to speak, but she spoke first.

"It's just as well that child didn't have to live in that house with his mama and her new husband. That mean, mean man, Steward Belcher." She paused. The clock ticked. "He beat Mark, the youngest son of Isaac's, all the time. Lordy, lordy I thought he'd killed that boy several times when he beat him in the face with his fist. That boy's eyes swoll shut for days. He abused that child 'cause he weren't his'n. We couldn't do nothing about it neither, 'cause we handled snakes, and the judge thought we evil people." The clock ticked. "Yeah, it's a good thing they didn't let the older one stay with his mama." Her last words were barely audible and Matt had to lean close to the old woman's face to hear what she said next. "I knows that Steward did something else real bad to that poor Mark. Something that should never happen to any child, boy or girl."

Matt didn't know what to say, but he understood the hidden meaning of her words, and thought he had a better understanding of Emmanuel's problems.

Finally, he looked into her face, a face that now looked every bit its age, and said, "The Belcher's, they had other children, didn't they?"

"Yeah," said Lucy with renewed vigor. Anger swelled in her eyes. "They had two more boys and one girl. All them Belcher children were what I'd call dull." The clock ticked, on and on. "But God cursed the last boy. He's touched in the head and just plain stupid like a dumb mule…No, a mule's got more brains than that poor child."

"Is that son called John?"

"Yeah. John," she said. "Lordy, lordy, I can't believe the way their mama named all them children. I believe that cursed them from the very start."

"What you mean? How'd she name them?"

"From the Bible. She named them after the first four books of the _New Testament_."

128

Matt tried to recall the first books of the <u>New Testament</u>. The old man that raised him had read the Bible to Matt, but now his mind locked down and wouldn't work. Before he could stop from learning what he was afraid of knowing, Matt asked the question he'd avoided for too long. "Their names are what?"

She looked at Matt with scorn on her face. "Get my Bible for me. It's over there on the table beside my bed."

The Bible, worn from years of use, weighed heavily as he brought it to her. She took it with shaking hands, then from her robe pocket; she pulled out a small magnifying glass. Starting near the end of the oversized book, she tediously thumbed forward through the crinkled pages searching for documentation of her statement. There was no doubt in his mind that she knew the answer herself. She had to let Matt see it with his eyes, because telling him the answer was not proof enough.

Matt remembered a few books of the Bible, but he didn't know which ones were in the <u>Old Testament</u> or which ones were in the <u>New</u>. Definitely, he didn't know their order.

She looked up at Matt. "Get over here beside me so you can see."

He slid beside her and dropped to one knee.

"This one," she said moving the magnifying glass to the title at the top of the page, "is <u>Acts</u>. It's the fifth book of the <u>New Testament</u>." She licked her shaking fingertips, placed them on the page and moved forward from back to front instead of from front to back. "Now, we're moving into <u>The Gospels</u>."

"What you mean by <u>Gospels</u>?"

"<u>The Gospels</u> tell about Jesus' life on earth," she said. "Each one tells the same story of Christ but in a different way and by different folks."

"Oh."

"This one," she said moving the glass to the title at the top of the page, "is <u>The Gospel According to JOHN</u>, and that's what Rebecca, the boy's mother, named her fourth son, after the fourth book. He and the third one were by Steward Belcher and weren't one of my blood kin."

"Okay," Matt said taking a deep breath and anticipating what the first child's name would be. Matt already thought he knew.

Like a movie in slow motion, she turned the pages. Then she stopped and pointed to the top of another page. "The third book and the third son of Rebecca's is Luke. He's the mean one…He's like his daddy, short and mean as the devil himself."

Somewhere deep in Matt's brain, he wondered if this could be his half-brother that she was describing. Did he really want to know the truth? Matt fought from rushing from the room, getting in the Explorer and racing back to the bowels of his boat on the Tennessee River. He had trouble getting a full breath.

"Here," she said pointing to the second book of The _New Testament_. "This is where Marcus, second and last son of my nephew Isaac, got his name."

Matt didn't see Marcus at the top of the page. He saw _The Gospel According to MARK_ printed there. Placing his finger at the title, Matt tried to ask her a question, but she answered him first.

"Marcus is another name for Mark, but the author's Hebrew name was John. It sounds confusing, doesn't it? Anyway, Rebecca named him Marcus and called him Mark. He's a preacher now himself, somewhere. I haven't heard anything about him in a long while. Bless his heart. That child went through hell on earth with that step-daddy of his'n."

With a determined expression, Lucy began to flip the thin pages—searching. Matt placed a hand on his chest and felt his heart racing out of control—too fast for a person his age. He concentrated on the clock's ticking.

There it was. Matt saw it at the top of the page. A gnarly finger almost a hundred years old moved to point out the words—_The Gospel According to MAT-THEW_—the namesake for Rebecca's oldest son.

Matt's head spun like something had just struck him. He tried breathing slowly.

"Matthew," said Lucy in a quiet, respectful voice. She looked like she was about to cry again but fought against it. "Lordy, lordy, that child had the most beautiful blue eyes. They were just like his daddy's." She stared up at Matt. "And just like your eyes."

"This nephew of yours that died," Matt started very carefully. "Tell me about Isaac's death, and did Matthew see his daddy die?"

"You should know."

Matt's vision blurred. "What do you mean, I should know?"

"The name Matt is short for Matthew. Ain't it?" Tears tumbled from her eyes and streamed down deep creases on her cheek.

"Yes, but there're a lot of Matthews in this world."

"Not many that have the last name Fagan."

He started to say that that didn't prove he was her great nephew, but she continued. She pointed to a closed door across the room. "One more thing, there's a beige hatbox in that closet. Get it out. Bring it to me."

Matt found the hatbox and hurried back to the old woman that now claimed to be his relative. He'd never had a relative except for his sons.

"Open the box. Look inside."

He did. The clock kept ticking. The odor of moth balls filled the room.

"Find a dark brown, wooden picture frame about this big," she said holding two crooked fingers about six inches apart. "You'll find a picture of a beautiful man in it."

Matt didn't move—couldn't move. The clock kept ticking.

"Hurry up," she said. "You've waited many years for this."

Searching through the box of old pictures of people he'd never seen, Matt found the one that fit her description. Afraid of looking directly at the picture, he handed it to her.

"Look at it," she said without taking the old frame from him. "What you see?"

Matt glanced down. He couldn't believe his eyes. There in the picture was a young man that looked very familiar to him—too familiar.

"Does he look like anybody you know?" she said in a whisper.

Matt forced himself to speak. "Me. He looks like me."

"Yes. He does, don't he, Whistle Britches? There's no doubt in my mind. That's your daddy. I took you to see him the night he died. Don't you remember?"

"Yes," he said. And Matt did. The clock kept ticking.

CHAPTER TWENTY-ONE

The yellow cone of light from the new arrivals' flashlights bounced off the rock walls and floor plotting its course in Leaky's direction. Could they have shotguns? Leaky wasn't sure, but he knew they were going to be unhappy finding him in their path. The modern South wasn't that modern when it came to encounters like this, and Leaky knew it.

When one of the rays of light slid within inches of Leaky's feet, he made himself move. Turning, he ran headlong into the darkness a few steps before turning on his flashlight. It flashed on and projected a guiding beam of light along the uneven cave floor. He winced, waiting on the shotgun blast, but it didn't come.

As soon as Leaky entered the large chamber, he had to stop. He couldn't remember which tunnel led to the outside. The sound of the pursuers' shoes slapping the floor as they rushed in his direction made Leaky's flesh grow millions of bumps.

"Which one," Leaky screamed in a panic, stumbling to the middle of the cavern. He glanced from one dark opening to another trying to decide which one led outside and to the river. The soles of his feet tingled.

"Halt!" yelled the pursuer only seconds away from entering the chamber.

Leaky picked one of the three openings and sprinted inside.

"Stop there," yelled the man now entering the shaft behind Leaky.

Leaky ran another twenty feet when his flashlight blinked off and darkness surrounded him.

BOOM—a shotgun blasted behind Leaky. Pellets ricocheted off the rock walls. The pursuer's flashlight chased after Leaky's heels causing him to sprint through the dark shaft with the extinguished flashlight in his hand.

When the cave floor disappeared from beneath Leaky's feet, air left his lungs in a scream of pure terror. Free falling, tumbling; someone had snatched the cave floor from beneath him. This was absurd, but a glowing flashlight spun out of control somewhere next to him. How did it come back on? He sucked in air and snatched at the light like it was a lifeline but missed.

He continued falling, then SMACK—again air rushed out of Leaky's lungs, pain shot across his back while a freezing liquid engulfed him. He tried to take in air and got only water. In horror, he pumped his legs like pistons. Grappling, he struggled toward the water's surface reaching his hands upward and through the never-ending black liquid with clawing fingers.

Shooting his head out of the water, Leaky filled his lungs with one huge gulp of air. He surfaced in total darkness with blackness sheathing him. Kicking his legs with animalistic determination, Leaky fought from letting his head slip back under the frigid water. Overhead, his right hand hit something slimy and he grabbed for it, but because of the strong current pushing him along, the slick fiber slipped from his grasp. Scratching and clawing upwards, he felt yet more stringy tentacles dangling above him. Leaky lunged blindly for them until he held fast to the object with both hands.

Giving one powerful jerk, Leaky pulled his shoulders out of the rushing stream of water that sucked at his body trying to pull him under. Blackness crushed against the backs of his eyes. The roar of rushing water filled the chasm and pounded against his eardrums.

In only seconds, his arms began to quiver and weaken as his hands lost hold on what felt like wet vines. The lower half of his body swayed in the current as he fought from falling back into the icy water. Pain radiated from his hands and along his arms as his muscles lost the ability to contract.

"Roots," he shouted above the roar when he realized what he held. "Help me, oh God."

His hands and fingers grew numb. Strength left them and his arms began to tremble. His chin slipped under the rushing current. He couldn't breathe.

He gave one jerk and his head surfaced. "Shit," Leaky said as the roots slipped out of his cramping hands. The water yanked him under.

His body shot through the water. Twisting, tumbling in the gloom of complete darkness, Leaky came up momentarily and filled his burning lungs with air. The current grew more powerful, and he almost stopped resisting. He came up again and something brushed against his face, pushing him down, keeping him from surfacing. *Oh God*, he realized the roof was dropping and the roots were now down in the water. Blindly, he reached up. His hands no longer felt air above. Only the rocky top of the roof pressed in on Leaky, until finally there was no space above the water's surface. No air to breathe. There was only black, icy water tugging him, hauling him down and away.

Matt's face appeared, clearly as if real and spun ahead of Leaky, calling his name. "Leaky, don't give up, damn you."

The current pulled, catapulted, and pushed Leaky forward like prey in the mouth of a predator. His lungs burned like fire. Death was at hand. There was no way out of this but to die.

Then the roar of the rushing water ceased. Quietness joined the darkness, and the two oozed through Leaky until he hung in emptiness. Floating. Serenity engrossed Leaky's being with a full measure of its tranquility. Surrendering, he searched out willingly for death.

"Kick, damn you," Matt said.

Leaky thought he felt his heavy feet kick, but then he drifted. Peace spread like a noiseless vapor through his body. He became aware of his arms expanding like a hovering angel, hanging in the water. His lungs were on fire.

"Move your black ass," he heard Matt shout.

Violently, Leaky kicked his legs until he shot through the surface of the water. He coughed and gagged until air rushed into his lungs causing him to cough out water. Light appeared. There was light, but it was so dim. He reached for the tree roots that were gone. Distant stars had taken their place. Taking in air with big gulps, Leaky looked around and realized that he was now outside the cave in the Tennessee River.

With only enough strength to keep his head above water, he paddled toward the near shore that was only a few feet away but looked like a mile. The shoreline continued to change as he glided along with the current of the river. After several minutes and many more kicks, he grabbed a young sapling that extended over the water's edge, and with great effort, pulled half his body out of the river.

With the side of his face pressed into the mud, Leaky closed his eyes and listened to his own labored breathing. He opened his eyes for a moment and rolled onto his back. There were no sounds of insects or birds or other living creatures. Only the quiet purr of the river reached Leaky's ears as it glided along toward the Gulf of Mexico still many hundreds of miles away. He closed his eyes, rested, and allowed his breathing to still.

Leaky wasn't sure if he passed out or went to sleep, but when he awoke, he was cold and shivering with his legs dangling in the water—water now warmer than the chilling air. Pulling himself to an upright position was most difficult, but Leaky knew he couldn't stay along the riverbank all night. He had to find the johnboat and get back to Matt's marina. Once on his feet, Leaky turned right hoping the johnboat was in that direction. He staggered along holding himself up by grabbing onto limbs, vines, and brush along the shore. He fell, got up, fell again. He crawled on hands and knees—mud oozed between his fingers. His joints ached. He turned and sat on his ass until he caught his breath. He closed his eyes, but after a long minute when he opened them, he saw the reflection of the moon off the silver of the johnboat. It rested in the bushes only ten feet away from him.

Leaky crawled to the johnboat, but now he lacked the strength to push it back into the river. He got inside the beached craft and opened the storage compartment under the middle seat. He remembered that Matt always kept dry clothes there in case he got wet while fishing. Leaky pulled out a navy blue, Russell sweat suit, took off his soaking clothes, and slipped into the soft, warm garments. He reached deep inside the compartment, grabbed his Smith and Wesson pistol, and laid it on the aluminum seat beside his leg. He wanted to sleep, needed to sleep, but he didn't have time. He wished he had dry shoes, but he couldn't have everything. He slumped on the metal seat.

"Get up," he said to himself. "You gotta get outta here."

He crawled over the side of the boat, and limped toward the back of the johnboat to have a look before pushing it into the river. Something moved on the water. A pontoon boat with only its red and green directional lights glowing skimmed along the water toward the near bank. It would land less than a hundred feet above where Leaky now stood.

"Catch this rope," said a man from the boat.

Through the dim light, Leaky saw someone toss a rope from the pontoon boat toward another person at the water's edge. The quiet hum of its motor turned to an accelerating shriek as the driver revved the engine and propelled the craft's nose upon the bank. Then, its motor died.

"Did you get it done?" said someone from shore.

"Yeah," said one of two men stepping off the boat. "There's gonna be a big explosion up river in a little while. I'd like to see it."

"When?" said someone.

"A little over an hour."

"Did anybody see you?"

"No, I don't think so."

"Where'd you put the bomb?"

"In the boat, dumb ass," said the man. "Where else would I put it?"

"Was anybody there?"

"Didn't see a soul," said the man. Their voices faded as they moved away from Leaky.

"Well, we did," said another man. "Somebody was in the cave, but..."

"We don't know if it was a person," interrupted a new voice that sounded like a woman. "It could have been some animal."

Leaky couldn't hear what they said next, because the group had moved too far from his present position. They had moved toward the cave entrance.

With renewed strength, Leaky pushed the johnboat into the river, stuck the trolling motor into the water, and turned its speed to high. Silently, he ran the boat out into the Tennessee River and turned it toward Brown's Ferry Marina. He needed to get farther away before cranking the big engine, but the trolling motor had difficulty moving the johnboat upstream against the current. Frustrated, Leaky realized the Nickajack dam below him was probably letting water out creating this stronger current.

Looking at his watch, Leaky saw that the time was seven-forty. He had to get back to warn Matt before the hour passed—no, he had less time than that now.

"To hell with being heard," he said. Leaky jerked the trolling motor out of the water and rushed back to the driver's seat. He turned the key in the boat's ignition and the outboard motor rumbled.

"Thank you, Jesus" he said, pushing the throttle forward as far as it would go. This jutted the front of the boat almost straight up in the water. Leaky kept his hand pressed against the throttle until the nose of the johnboat dropped. A steady cold wind rushed across Leaky's face. He thought about Matt being on the boat and the bomb.

CHAPTER TWENTY-TWO

Listening from the bedroom with Crystal beside her, Sarah heard everything Emmanuel and his followers said in the next room. No one had bothered to shut the door. What could the submissive Sarah do, anyway? She was useless to the group except as a baby-making machine and a sex object for Emmanuel. And Crystal, she had already learned that escape from them was impossible. By now Emmanuel and his chosen group of Luke, Irene, Myra, and Daniel Crider didn't care if Sarah and Crystal were listening in the adjoining room.

"Well," said Irene. "It don't look like the law's going away and leave us alone, now does it?"

"No," said Luke. "So what we gonna do?"

Sarah didn't hear anything for a long moment. She thought they were waiting on Emmanuel to answer them, but he didn't. Finally, Sarah heard him mumble something.

"What'd you say?" said Luke.

"What you think?" Emmanuel shouted, his tongue was thick with drugs, alcohol, or both. "I'm listening to see what y'all got to say, and then I'll let you know what's best."

"I could give myself up," said Irene. "I'm the one they came here to get in the first place, but now they want me and the dummy that shot at them this morning...That was one more stupid act. Who did that, anyway?"

"That don't matter," said Emmanuel. "What happened earlier don't matter. It's now that matters. What y'all think we need to do, now?"

"We could escape," said Luke. "We could go through the tunnel and get out of here. They'd never catch us."

"No. No. No," screamed Emmanuel. "We're not leaving all my people here alone."

No one talked for almost a minute. Sarah and Crystal sat very still, holding hands and listening.

Finally, Daniel Crider, who had been quiet the entire time spoke, "We could give out the weapons and fight our way out."

"Very interesting," said Emmanuel. "A lot of people might die on both sides. But that'd show 'em we mean business, wouldn't it?"

"Yeah," said Irene. No one else spoke for a long moment.

Emmanuel said, "Everyone in the world would know me then, wouldn't they? I'd be as famous as Jesus, wouldn't I?"

"Maybe," said Daniel Crider. "Are you ready to spend the rest of your life in jail?"

"You're right," said Emmanuel. "We got to think of something else."

"How about suicide?" asked Myra in a placid voice.

Sarah stared into Crystal's eyes that had suddenly widened.

"No," said Daniel Crider.

"Shut-up," said Emmanuel. Then, in a calm tone, "Go on Myra, tell us what you got in mind."

"We could use potassium cyanide," said Myra. "We got lots of that, don't we Irene?"

"I...I guess," said Irene. Her voice was shaky.

"How you use that stuff?" said Emmanuel. His speech was slurred.

"It's a quick killer," said Myra. "It's a white crystalline powder that'd be best put in something to drink. Of course it's got an odor of bitter almonds, so we'd be better off putting it in grape juice or something like that to disguise the taste."

"I don't know about all that," said Luke. "Suicide's pretty permanent. We're not gonna do that, are we?"

"Why not?" said Emmanuel.

"That's what Jim Jones did," said Luke. He couldn't hide fear in his tone. "And that guy in Waco, Texas, he did it...And Applewhite's people all committed suicide trying to get a ride on a comet...We don't wanna be like all of them, do we?"

"Luke, you big crybaby," said Emmanuel. "You got a better idea?"

"Give me a little time," said Luke. "There's gotta be something better than all us killing ourselves."

"Okay," said Emmanuel. "You got 'til tomorrow night at nine o'clock."

"What happens then?" said Luke.

"Myra," said Emmanuel. "You and Irene get those cyanide pills ready. And find the best way to give it to everybody, so we don't have mass panic on our hands. Tomorrow night is Sunday night, so after the prayer meeting we'll all do it. And I said all, unless Luke comes up with a better plan. But I don't think he'll do that. No, I don't, 'cause he ain't that smart. He's like his daddy—he's stupid."

Emmanuel started laughing and couldn't stop until he finally choked on his own saliva. Then he started coughing and couldn't stop.

Sarah's body began to tremble.

CHAPTER TWENTY-THREE

She had not asked a single question about the old lady. In fact, Medora had sat silently all the way back to Chattanooga from Dayton. She realized either Matt needed time to contemplate what he'd learned from all these strange people they'd met, or she was angry with him for going on the trip in the first place. Matt couldn't decide. He didn't care.

Driving and thinking, he'd not offered to talk with his client. Only for a moment had he wondered if the drive back had been uncomfortable for Medora, but it was only a fleeting thought. For most of the return trip, Matt tried to piece together his past life in a flustered and highly confused head. He now had parents, brothers—a past family. Past events when he was with a real mother and father were rising from deep inside his brain. Matt had someone other than the old man who had raised him on a farm in Cohutta, Georgia—someone other than the ladies from the Methodist Church that took Matt in when he was thirteen after the old man died—someone other than the teachers at Webb School in Bell Buckle, Tennessee, where the ladies had sent him—someone other than his army buddies in Vietnam—someone other than his cheating wife that had taken his sons away.

But Matt didn't feel good. In fact, he felt like crap. Matt felt like somebody had pulled his guts out, stomped on them and then put them back inside his viscera. That's when Matt decided to stop and buy a case of Budweiser Beer. He hadn't had any alcohol in twelve years but that was about to change. He'd been sober long enough. He'd always kept wine on the boat, but that had never been a temptation to him, because he couldn't stand the stuff. Matt kept it for any women that might come along, but that didn't happen often, either.

When Medora and Matt pulled into the Brown's Ferry Marina, he realized the lights were off to the marina's small sign out front. He thought that was odd, he'd never seen that before. Looking at the green lights of the Explorer's dash clock, Matt noticed the time to be eight-sixteen. He felt the pangs of hunger creep across his midsection. Matt would check on Leaky and the boat and then take everyone out to eat.

Matt stopped the Explorer in his usual parking spot facing the boat. "You hungry?" Before the words got out of his mouth, Matt realized the lights along the dock were off, too.

"Whatever," she said without looking at him.

Matt figured she was still pissed-off that he had taken her on such a long trip and not gone immediately to rescue her daughter. Matt hadn't determined how he was going to remind her of their agreement that he was going to find her daughter but not rescue her. Matt wanted to be just a fraction on the sober side of drunk before telling her he had no idea of how to get inside the compound. He opened the door and cold air filled the Explorer. Matt looked at her and said as indifferently as he could, "You thirsty?"

She didn't comment but sat silently staring out the front windshield.

Matt was tired and didn't feel like arguing with her. The beer would wait. He had to get rid of this bitch. "I'm going down to the boat for a second. Then, we'll go downtown and eat. You wait here 'till I get back."

"No," she said opening her door, stepping outside and standing before he did. "I need to use the bathroom. You do have one, don't you?"

This time, he didn't answer her. In a rush, she hurried down the wooden walkway to the docks and to his boat. Once there, she turned to wait on him with her fist clenched. She glared at him, miserably trying to hide the fact that she had a full bladder. Matt continued to stand beside his car and watch her bounce from one foot to another. The air was crisp, but it had a pleasant odor of burning firewood. He loved the smell of winter.

"Please," she said. "Hurry."

After Matt felt he'd irritated her long enough, he grabbed the beer, ambled down to the boat and opened the door. "I never lock it," he said to the back of her head as she disappeared down the narrow stairs. "It's in the front on the right," he yelled. Then he followed her down as far as the stateroom.

When he glanced around looking for Leaky, Matt noticed the red light flashing on the answering machine. The bulb blinked in short quick pulses so he realized that someone had left the message from inside without actually making a phone call to the machine. He mashed the button to hear the messages.

Leaky's voice spilled through the machine's tiny speakers, "Looks like you're gonna stay out long enough to kill the night, good buddy. Well anyway, I got Dusty, and we took off down river to find a way into that damn camp, or refuge, or whatever you call it. I should be back by nine, so wait on me. If you don't mind, that is." The answering machine made a clicking noise as it turned off and the tape started rewinding.

"Who was that?" said Medora from behind him.

"Leaky, he's my associate," Matt mumbled. "I sent him to find a way to get inside the compound where your daughter is."

"I didn't know about him," she said excitedly. Then her tone turned sarcastic. "I'm glad someone's doing something for my money. Who's Dusty?"

"That's my johnboat," Matt said trying to hold back his anger but finding it as difficult as trying to hold back the flowing Tennessee River under them.

"What's a johnboat?" She tried to smile but he could tell it was false.

"A johnboat is a small fishing boat I pull behind the _Desperado_ when I go out in the river. You can't just run this big cruiser upon the bank when you need to go ashore."

"Oh," she said moving to the sofa.

Thirst crept over Matt. "Can I get you a beer or some wine?" He said putting the beer into the small refrigerator. "That's all I got, unless you want water." He wasn't about to offer making coffee.

"You have a white wine?"

"Yeah," he said reaching for a bottle in the fridge. "I think I got some Chardonnay." He didn't offer to tell her the brand—_Fetzer_.

After half filling her wineglass with the beverage, Matt checked the time—Eight-twenty-two. He handed her the glass, opened a Budweiser, and drank from the can. The hunger pains subsided after his third gulp. He'd forgotten how good beer tasted. He checked around the cabinets for something to snack on but saw nothing but a stale donut. Before today, he'd not had a woman aboard this boat in a long, long time. Now, he'd had two in one day. It wasn't that great, especially this one that was over there staring at him from across the room like Matt was about to pull his pants down and moon her.

He took a long swallow of Budweiser. Then looked at her looking at him. "You mind waiting on Leaky?"

"Of course not," she said. "He's trying to help me get my daughter, isn't he?"

"He's trying to find me a way in so I might get to Crystal and your daughter." God, why did he say that? Was he losing my mind? He took a longer swig of Budweiser.

"Who and my daughter?"

"Remember me telling you about Crystal, the girl that told me about your daughter being there?"

"Oh, yes," said Medora using both hands to hold her empty wineglass. "You didn't tell me all she said, did you?"

"What do you mean?" he asked trying to conceal the fact that she was right.

"I just had a feeling you left something out today when you told your story about my daughter. Did you?"

"It's not that important." Matt had trouble lying and for that reason, he tried telling a small one. He reached for her glass and refilled it.

Matt took his time getting the wine, hoping she'd forget he hadn't answered her. When he got back she took the glass of wine from his hands and said, "I think I should be the judge of what's important and what's not. I'm paying you for information, remember, so I would appreciate hearing the entire story."

Matt opened another beer, knowing it had to be his last if he planned on driving later. Glancing at his Seiko and seeing the time to be eight-twenty-four,

Matt decided to give her a little more information about her daughter. "Crystal said your daughter Sarah had an affair with this Emmanuel fellow and he thinks her child—your grandchild—is his." Matt didn't want to tell her about the abuse, yet.

"I can't believe Sarah would have an affair. Of course her stupid husband isn't much of a man, but...never mind, I can't believe that of her." Medora paused a moment and glanced around the room. "Is that all?"

"I'll try and remember," Matt said taking a long drink of the beer.

She jumped when a mantle-clock he kept on a shelf behind her chimed the half-hour. Matt didn't bother telling her it ran five minutes fast.

"It may not be true," Matt said. He felt uncomfortable, and he wanted Leaky to hurry and get there, so he wouldn't have to tell this woman all he had heard. Matt took a sip of beer. She took a sip of wine. He said nothing. She stared at him—waiting.

After an awkward silence and killing his second Budweiser, Matt said, "Crystal just mentioned the affair being rumor. But things like that just happen sometimes, you know?"

"What, just happens?"

"Affairs," he almost screamed thinking about his own failed marriage. He reached for another beer.

"How'd that happen?" Medora said. "That scar." Then, a look crossed her face signaling she'd made a huge mistake. "Excuse me, I didn't mean to pry. Forgive me. It must be the wine."

"That's okay," Matt said. "I'm not ashamed of it anymore. I was defending our country. At least that's what they said I was doing—the army, that is. But everybody else said we were killers—baby killers."

"In Southeast Asia?" she said a little above a whisper. "How awful for you..."

"Awful," he interrupted. Matt gulped his beer and looked at the Seiko. Eight-twenty-eight. He'd let Leaky drive, if he ever got his ass back here. "Yes, it was pretty awful, but not for me. I was one of the lucky ones. I think, but maybe I wasn't. Who knows? I came back. Now, I've got memories to live with."

"I lost a brother over there," she said. Sadness engulfed her face. "It was horrible for my mother and father, the whole family...Bad...If they'd only found his body. He was a pilot, shot down—MIA." Matt noticed the tears forming in her eyes as she looked at the wall across from where she sat. But she wasn't seeing anything there; her mind had slipped into the past. Taking a long swig of beer his thoughts went back in time to that night long ago in Viet Nam. After a short pause, Medora's words brought Matt back to the present.

"I can understand," she continued "I can understand if you don't want to talk about it."

"Everything we did back then seems so stupid," he said feeling a little high. "I was stupid."

"Like how?" she said softly, like she treaded near a sensitive nerve.

"Slow," he said, closing his eyes and drifted on the three beers in his stomach. He popped his fourth. "I reacted too damn slow, and he died."

Matt's watch showed eight-twenty-nine.

"Who? Who died?"

"My best friend, Frank Waters. Leaky's daddy. In my arms."

He sat down. Eight-thirty. She only looked at him. In her eyes Matt saw compassion. Or was it pity? He hoped not. Matt took a long drink of beer. His body grew numb. They only watched each other; she waited, he waited. Her hands trembled as she poured another glass of wine. Watching, Matt whispered to no one. "It was all my fault...my fault he died."

CHAPTER TWENTY-FOUR

The johnboat churned through the dark water so close to the right bank that Leaky had to push away the overhanging limbs with his hand. He glanced at his Freestyle watch and saw that it was thirty-two minutes past eight o'clock. There was little time left before Matt's boat would explode. And to make things worse, Leaky still had a quarter of a mile to go before reaching the entrance to the cove leading into the marina. The gas gauge showed that his last tank was on empty, but for the moment his luck held, for the motor continued to hum.

Leaky kept glancing behind the johnboat into the black night expecting someone from the compound to pounce upon him at any second. The Smith and Wesson between his legs on the seat made him feel a little less apprehensive, but he would be glad when he could pull the johnboat next to Matt's _Desperado_ and get onto dry land. Then, and only then would he allow himself time to worry about the firebomb.

When he looked behind the johnboat for what felt like the hundredth time, the Mercury outboard motor coughed twice, then sputtered. The boat lurched forward several feet and died. Except for a few frogs chortling, silence prevailed. The boat came to a complete stop in the water. Before he could get to the front of the boat and drop the trolling motor off the bow, the johnboat started to turn with the swiftly flowing current of the Tennessee River. It moved in the opposite direction that he needed to go.

"Shit fire," he yelled when he couldn't get the small electric motor running by turning its throttle to full speed. "Piss, piss, piss!"

In the blackness encircling him, he ran his hand along the thick cable that extended from the trolling motor to the twelve-volt marine battery. There, he found his problem. One of the connecting clamps to the battery's post had been jarred loose severing the connection needed to power the motor. It took him almost a minute to replace the clamp. He was frustrated and just plain tired. When he jerked his body back through the darkness toward the throttle, his foot hit the cable knocking the connections free again. Because of the steady flow of the river the johnboat picked up speed as it drifted back down and further away from the shore. Leaky could feel the boat turning although he couldn't see in which direction the bow of the boat was heading.

It wasn't until Leaky finally got all the battery's connections back in place and the silent engine running at its full speed of three miles per hour that he noticed another craft moving quickly upon him from the rear.

"Hey, stop," yelled Leaky. He waved his arms over his head trying to stop the on-coming vessel from ramming him. He thought about his running lights that he had decided to forgo earlier and how stupid he'd been for failing to use them. But suddenly, he realized the boat about to hit him didn't have its light on, either.

He took one step toward the seat where his pistol lay when a bright search-light struck him in the eyes, blinding him. He wheeled to his right, slipped sideways, but just before falling into the water, he caught a firm hold on the john-boat's railing, saving himself from another drenching. If he had only known what the future would hold, Leaky would have gladly jumped into the icy water.

"Stop right there," a man said as the vessel bumped into the side of the johnboat but only hard enough to push it into another spin.

"Shit," said Leaky, holding tight to the rail and expecting to topple into the water at any moment. "You trying to kill me, or something."

"Yeah," said someone from the pontoon boat. "That may prove to be neces-sary. Keep your hands where I can see'em or I'll put some of this shotgun lead in your black ass."

Now, Leaky realized who these people were. He could see the silhouette of someone standing beside the spotlight on the pontoon boat. The figure had a shotgun trained down upon Leaky. Another person reached for the johnboat and pulled it along the side of the pontoon boat.

"This ain't your day is it, boy?" said the man holding the double-barreled weapon on him. "You're just in the wrong place at the wrong time. Ain't that right, colored boy?"

"You bloody fool, what you want with me?" said Leaky trying to sound like an English gentleman. "I have done nothing to you. I was just motoring along the river minding me own business, when I ran out of petrol."

"Oh!" said the man holding the johnboat next to the pontoon boat. "We got us a real smart colored here, Ralph."

"He's gonna be a dead colored boy in a minute if he don't shut up," said Ralph. "Get your sorry black ass up here, now. Move it!"

Leaky stood with caution before stepping up onto the side of the pontoon boat. Still aiming the shotgun at Leaky's face, Ralph stepped back into the dark-ness, allowing his hostage room to board and move to the middle of the craft.

"We finally caught the nigger in the woodshed," said the man pushing the johnboat away from the pontoon boat. "I guess you lose this time, boy."

Still using an English accent Leaky turned his head toward the gunman. "It doesn't matter if you win or lose, if you fight a skunk you're going to come out stinking."

The dark night turned into a salvo of dazzling fireworks when someone's boot came ripping into Leaky's groin. With an unbelievable detonation of pain that penetrated his lower torso like someone had stabbed him with a butcher's knife that ran from his testicles to his chest, he fell forward onto his knees. He curled into a fetal position on the carpeted floor. A sick feeling grabbed his stomach and spread up his esophagus toward his head. Without maintaining any control, vomit spewed from his mouth. Gasping, Leaky rolled over onto his side, fighting to regain his breath.

"Damn, boy" said someone just before kicking Leaky in the kidneys. "You got that puke on my feet."

Accompanied by new and excoriating pain, Leaky rolled onto his back and continued to gulp for needed oxygen that was out there somewhere; he just couldn't find it. After several long and anxious moments, air rushed back into his oxygen-starved lungs. He heard the pontoon boat's engine accelerate and felt his body shift as they made a turn down river toward the tunnel and the compound. Opening his eyes as wide as possible, he tried to adjust them to the almost total darkness. It took only a moment to determine the location of his two adversaries. One stood at the steering wheel while the other, still holding the shotgun, sat on a bench seat across from where Leaky sprawled.

The driver yelled at Leaky over the clamor of the boat's churning engine, "Why you messing around our cave, boy?"

Leaky didn't answer; he just stared out into the inky water gliding beside him, his brain racing on how he would get out of this mess and help his friend, Matt, before the explosion.

"Are you gonna answer me, boy?" said the driver. "What you doing in our tunnel?"

Leaky looked at the driver, then at Ralph who now had the shotgun resting across his lap. Leaky started talking slowly. "Well, boys, I ain't been doin' nothin' but ridin' around eatin' fried chicken and throwin' the bones out the winder."

The driver started laughing. And Ralph let out a fought-against chuckle.

"I know what you're trying to do, boy," said the driver to Leaky. "I know how you coloreds like white women. You trying to get laid, wudn't you boy?"'

"You good old boys," started Leaky, "don't mind if I get up off this wet carpet and in that there seat, do you?" He didn't wait for permission but slowly moved to the bench seat across from Ralph.

"Suit yourself," said Ralph pulling the shotgun closer to his chest.

"You ever did it with a white woman, boy?" said the driver.

When Leaky didn't answer the driver said, "That's what you colored boys dream about, ain't it? White pussy, that's y'all's main goal in life, ain't it?

Leaky turned a hard gaze toward the driver. "You know what you can do when you wanna get laid, don't you?"

"What?" said the driver. Ralph lit a cigarette.

"When you wanna get laid," said Leaky, "all you gotta do is crawl up a chicken's ass and wait."

Ralph laughed so hard he choked on the big swig of cigarette smoke he had just pulled into his lungs. The driver didn't laugh. He closed his eyes, and, for a second, his face screwed up like somebody that had just taken a bite of a green persimmon. He glared at Leaky. "You watch your smart ass mouth, boy. I don't care for no uppity coloreds, especially one been snooping around where he shouldn't. That's a good way to get yourself hung."

Leaky started to tell the man he was already hung but wisely had second thoughts and kept his mouth shut.

"Oscar," said Ralph to the driver. "Let me see this boy's gun."

"What gun?" said Oscar. "What gun you talking about?"

"The one in the seat," said Ralph. "The one I told you to get?"

"What you talking about," said Oscar. "I didn't see no gun. You didn't tell me to get no gun. Did you?"

"Dammit!" said Ralph. "I meant to. Can't you do nothing on your own? I thought you saw it there on the driver's seat, hell!"

"Well, I didn't," said Oscar. "I sure didn't see no gun. If I had, don't you think I'd a got it? And by the way, you better stop that cussing 'fore you slip up and do it in front of Emmanuel."

"Oscar," said Ralph as he flipped his cigarette into the water. "You just drive the damn boat and don't worry about what I say, 'cause I might just have to kick your sorry white ass."

When Oscar didn't reply, but only poked his bottom lip out, Leaky knew who the boss was—Ralph.

"Ralph," said Leaky. Ralph looked a little startled that this black man had used his name, but Ralph didn't say anything. "Who is this Emmanuel he's talking about? The only Emmanuel I've ever heard of was the Lord Above, God himself."

"This guy is a god," said Ralph "Emmanuel, he's Jesus come back to earth."

"Oh, man" said Leaky. "I got to meet Jesus."

Ralph leaned over with his face closer to Leaky. "That's gonna happen 'fore you realize it. And by the way, don't call him Jesus. His name is Emmanuel. And another thing, I don't know if he's gonna like you, the way you been snooping around trying to sneak in his place through the cave. And don't try to fool with me. I know you're that colored boy that was with Crystal and that other man." Ralph laughed aloud. "How'd you like our little snake in the car yesterday? We gotta lot more where he came from. You'll see soon enough, boy." Ralph smiled. "And that reminds me, are you the one that shot up our Suburban or was it that white man you run with?"

Leaky didn't answer; he just stared at Ralph trying to keep a neutral expression on his face even though he doubted that Ralph could see the sudden fear of snakes consume him. The semi-dark created by the red and green running lights on the front of the pontoon boat with their low-wattage bulbs gave a faint luminescence to this confined sector on the flat platform.

"Where'd that white friend of yours get that scar on his face?" said Ralph.

"Vietnam."

"Vietnam?" said Ralph. "Was he in Vietnam?"

Leaky wanted to say that Matt didn't go to Vietnam, he got the scar shipped over and it only cost $19.99, but he just nodded his head to indicate yes.

After Leaky's weak answer, Ralph asked another question. "Was he in the war?"

Leaky couldn't take any more of this man's stupid questions. He leaned over toward Ralph. "No, Matt was on vacation over there when he got it at the Redneck Tattoo Shop."

Leaky expected Ralph to hit him again, but the man only sat there with a puzzled look on his face.

Suddenly, a rumbling like distant thunder rolled past them and Oscar stopped the boat. When Leaky looked north toward the marina, he saw a red glow spread like it was a living creature. He knew what had happened. He thought about running headfirst into Ralph and knocking him into the river, but Ralph must have realized what his captive was thinking for he had the shotgun level on Leaky once again.

"I just hope," said Ralph between clinched teeth, "that your buddy with that ugly scar was there."

CHAPTER TWENTY-FIVE

Matt awoke to the smell of burning wood, rubber, and oil. He tried to swallow but his mouth felt like he'd stuffed it with toilet paper. He just couldn't figure out if it was clean toilet paper or not. Finally, opening his eyes, Matt wondered where Medora Meehan was; then, he realized she was asleep in his bed.

The pain shooting across his lower back screamed for him to get his ass off the sofa where he'd slept for what felt like ten minutes. With great difficulty Matt sat upright. His left foot tingled as blood flowed back into it. He lifted the numb appendage and twisted it in all directions, trying to speed up the process. The two empty wine bottles and thirteen empty beer cans strewn on the coffee table and in the floor reminded him why his mouth was as dry as desert sand. After the boat fire died last night, Matt had drunk way too much on an empty stomach. The snapping and gnawing in his midsection reminded him that he hadn't eaten yet. Matt checked his Seiko and saw it was almost eight o'clock in the morning. He'd only been asleep four hours.

With much self-prodding, Matt finally got to his feet and limped to the sink where he took a long drink of tasteless water. He opened the refrigerator and looked at the full Budweiser cans for a long moment thinking about how good one would be. "No, not now," he said and closed the door. He fumbled around the galley and got a fresh pot of coffee brewing.

It had all started last night about a quarter until nine when a firebomb detonated his neighbor's yacht, located in slip 19-A, ninety feet across from Matt's slip 19-B. Only hours later, after too many beers, did Matt comprehend that the bomb was probably meant for him. In fact, Medora had been the one to mention that detail about three this morning.

With the help of a few good neighbors and the quick response of the county fire department, only four boats had caught afire and only two of those a total loss. Matt knew it could have been much worse. Luckily, no one had been hurt, but that was because no one had been aboard the Edelstein's boat when it blew up. Matt's entire body quivered when he thought about what could have happened if the bomb had been on the _Desperado_.

In truth, Matt hadn't realized a bomb caused the fire until the fire inspector mentioned it while questioning him. The inspector told Matt he had found evidence of a timing device in the bottom of what remained of the Edelstein's yacht. Most large watercraft leaked and periodically had to use bilge pumps on timers to keep water out of their keelson. For some reason the Edelstein's pumps or timers had not been working efficiently, and too much water had collected along the yacht's centerboard. This had saved the bomb's timing device when it fell there. Matt had asked the fire inspector what type of device they found, but the man said he couldn't tell now.

The aroma of coffee slapped Matt across the face about the time he heard someone call him from outside the boat. Matt checked the surveillance camera's image of the rear of the boat on the little black-and-white TV next to the sink. He didn't see anything except someone's gray cat perched on a rail licking itself.

"Matt," yelled a man. "You in there?"

Matt lumbered up the steps to the pilothouse and said too loudly because it hurt his already throbbing head, "Yeah, I'm here. Who wants to know?" At first Matt didn't notice anyone until he glanced toward the open water in front of the boat and saw Detective Joe Johnson comically trying to get out of the Sheriff's pursuit boat and onto the dock without falling back into the green water. The last time he'd see Detective Joe Johnson was yesterday morning when someone at the compound had shot out Joe's windshield.

"Shit," said Joe Johnson to his young associate as he slapped the man's helping hand away. "I can get out by myself. You think I'm a damn old man, or something?"

"What's up, Joe?" Matt had already climbed down the ramp to meet the detective. "Don't fall in that water, we might not get your ass out."

"You can kiss my ass, too," said Johnson. Then he turned back toward his colleague. "And Dammit, don't you start laughing your ass off either. You just stay right there and wait on me." Joe walked past Matt toward the steps leading into the boat.

"Where?" was all Matt said before Johnson interrupted him.

"Dammit, I need a cup of coffee, so get your tight ass up here and fix me one."

Matt smiled as Detective Johnson, still wearing an orange life vest over his tan uniform, scurried up the back steps and disappeared into the pilothouse.

Matt followed him inside and discovered that Johnson had already gone down stairs, so he hurried after him, trusting Joe had not walked in on Medora.

"What you been doing?" Johnson said while pouring a cup of coffee. Matt was glad that Medora had not come out of the bedroom. "You had a hell of a barbecue here last night, didn't you? About burned the place down, didn't you?"

"Yeah," Matt said reaching for the pot to pour his own coffee. "Didn't have any marshmallows, though."

"Ten-four, on that," laughed Johnson. He ambled over to the sofa, flopped down, pushed away a bunch of empty beer cans and sat his steaming coffee where they'd been. Then, Johnson, using only a thumb and forefinger picked an empty wine bottle up by the neck and inspected it through the bottom of his bifocals. "You drank all this wine and all this beer by yourself?"

"Maybe."

Johnson with a smirk on his face sat the bottle down. "You got company, ain't you, boy? Who's in there?"

"What you want, Johnson?" Matt asked, trying to act serious and avert Joe's attention from such questions. Matt's act didn't help. Before he could finish his sentence, he heard the shower come on in the bedroom.

Detective Johnson didn't fight against the wide grin that crossed his chubby jowls. He encouraged it, then said, "No wonder you set the place on fire last night." Then his expression turned serious. "You been away from the world a long time, buddy. You needed to get out and live a little."

"It's not what you think," Matt said. "It's a client, and she stayed here because of all that happened last night...."

"What happened last night?" said Johnson. He was grinning now. "Can I guess?"

"Nothing," Matt said a little too loud. "She slept in there. And me, I slept on that sofa you got your fat ass parked on. What the hell you want, anyway, detective?"

"If that's the truth, then I can see why you're mad."

"I'm not mad, and what the hell you want, Johnson?"

Johnson grinned and rolled his eyes. "Ain't you got a johnboat named Dusty?"

"Yeah," Matt said. Fear replaced his agitation with the detective. After all the excitement of the fire, he'd forgotten about Leaky being out in the johnboat and not coming in last night. "What about it? Leaky was using it." Matt's heart picked up its pace when Joe Johnson's face turned to that of a suddenly worried man.

With great care, Detective Johnson reached into his inside pocket and pulled out a stainless steel Smith and Wesson .45 pistol. "Whose is this?"

Reaching for the weapon, Matt's legs felt so weak he thought they'd collapse before taking the two steps needed to reach Johnson's extended hand that held the pistol. "Leaky's. Where...what's...where'd you find this?"

"In your fishing boat," said a serious Johnson. "Didn't you notice it beside my boat a few minutes ago? We towed it in."

"No!" Matt wanted to move, go somewhere, and find Leaky, but he didn't know where to go or what to do. "Where did you find my boat? Where the hell's Leaky?"

"Calm down, good buddy," said Johnson.

"Where'd you find the boat?" Matt tried to appear composed but failed. His breathing increased to twice its normal rate, and he couldn't slow it down. Matt took a deep breath and turned toward the door. "Where's Leaky?"

155

"This gun was in the driver's seat of the johnboat," said Johnson while following Matt up the steps and outside. "There was no one in the boat. This guy named Kelsey—he and his family were out in their speedboat this morning—they found your empty boat lodged halfway under a fallen tree on Williams Island."

"Yeah," Matt said going down the outside platform steps two at a time.

Johnson, already gasping for air, hurried down the steps behind him and almost fell on his face. Matt heard Joe when he said, "They called us…and now that I ain't got my car till they get my windshield fixed…I went out with one of the water boys this morning." On the edge of the dock next to Matt, Johnson put his hand over his wide panting, life-vested chest. "Dammit, man, why don't you slow down 'fore I have a heart attack."

Matt only turned and looked at Johnson.

"Anyway, as I was saying," said Johnson. "Good thing I did go with the water boys, 'cause I knew whose boat that was, and all. If it wudn't for me they'd took several hours tracing down the serial number, and all. Well, anyway, we got it about fifteen minutes ago, and there it is."

"Any blood or sign of a struggle?" Matt said, then stopping his breathing until he had an answer.

Detective Johnson said toward the officer still in the sheriff's boat, "Swing that johnboat over here by the dock." Johnson wiggled his chubby finger back and forth while pointing at the boat then at the dock where he wanted the boat moved. "Hurry up, boy."

Before the man got the johnboat to the dock, Matt leaped into it and started inspecting everything. Heaped in the bottom of the boat were someone's clothes.

"You know who those belong to?" said Johnson.

"Yeah," Matt said, holding the wet material aloft and turning them in his hand. "They're Leaky's." Matt laid Leaky's garments down on the dock, opened the compartment under the seat, and felt a little relief, but not much. The extra clothes Matt keep there were gone. He pushed a tackle box aside in the compartment and pulled out one life jacket. "One's missing. Leaky must be wearing the other one."

"Then he ain't drowned," said Johnson.

"Not unless one of them big coal barges came along and run him over."

Leaky knows how to take care of himself," said Johnson. "He's either walking in, or he may be home. You called his house?"

"Now when do you think I had time to call his house? You been right here with me, Johnson." Matt checked the two gas cans. "They're empty."

"That may explain what happened," said Johnson. "You going to call him?"

"Yeah," Matt said, getting out of the johnboat and taking giant strides toward the steps leading back inside the _Desperado_. "But he could be on Williams Island."

Matt returned to stand beside Detective Johnson. He'd not received an answer at Leaky's apartment or his cell phone, and Leaky's grandmother had not seen him in several days.

Medora had gotten out of the shower but stayed locked inside the bedroom.

"How about it?" said Johnson.

"He's not home," Matt said, moving to the johnboat, tying it to the dock and removing the gas cans. "I'm going to Williams Island to look for him."

"You going in the johnboat?"

"No," Matt said carrying the empty cans up the ramp toward the gas pumps. "But I'm taking it with me."

"You taking the _Desperado_ out?" said Johnson. He tried to keep up with the fast pace Matt set and was panting like a spent dog in the process.

"Yeah," Matt said. "And I'm not coming back 'til I find Leaky."

CHAPTER TWENTY-SIX

The night had been another chapter in Sarah's permanent nightmare. At least Emmanuel had been too busy with these new events to come to his own bed where Sarah, Tommy, and Crystal had slept. When the guards brought the black man Crystal knew as Leaky into the apartment, Emmanuel went crazy trying to get the poor fellow to answer his questions. Sarah admired Leaky for being so brave and for refusing to give Emmanuel any information, but the unfortunate man had paid dearly when the torture started around midnight. Sarah and Crystal had not witnessed the actual beating, but they had heard it through the open door of the bedroom. It had been a frightful ordeal for Sarah, because having been through similar afflictions, she felt the man's pain.

Even now, in the big sanctuary where most of Emmanuel's followers waited on the completion of the morning service, Sarah failed to erase from her mind the man's tormented groans and the sound of a fist striking flesh. Sarah closed her eyes to keep from seeing the congregation staring up at her as she sat on the platform with Emmanuel and his chosen few. She hated being there.

Sarah checked to her right where Crystal sat next to her. Crystal had been so upset this morning, she had stopped talking to anyone, even to Sarah. Now, as Crystal's eyes stared at the back wall, Sarah wondered if this friend might blame her for all the problems as of late. She prayed to be wrong, because Crystal was the only friend Sarah had left on earth, other than maybe her own mother who started all of this when she had hired that detective. Sarah also wondered if Leaky could have died. If not, then he must be in deep pain and needing medical attention. Hate rose up through Sarah when she saw Emmanuel strut like a conquering general to the pulpit to begin his sermon.

"Brethren," Emmanuel almost whispered into the microphone. "My heart is troubled." He paused a long moment. "I have been betrayed as was our Lord and Savior, Jesus Christ, was betrayed two thousand years ago." He dropped his head.

"No!" some woman in the back screamed causing Sarah to jump.

"Yes," said Emmanuel, shaking his head and sounding like he was about to start crying. "I have been betrayed by one of our very own, here in this room."

Sarah shuddered for she knew he must have been talking about her. She wanted to drop her eyes without looking at the back of his head, but her entire body deadened in its present position with her sight locked there.

"Who?" yelled a man on the front row looking up at his messiah with eyes full of devotion.

"That's not important," said Emmanuel shaking an open palm at the man. "You will know soon enough. We have other things to take care of now. We have to decide what we are going to do about the devils at our gate who want to come in and destroy me. Maybe I should go with them and let them have me to crucify."

"No!" screamed half the crowd as they moved to a new frenzy.

"Never!" shouted the other half jumping to their feet.

Emmanuel raised both hands above his head to hush the crowd. In only a moment, all was silent. Their savior lowered his arms and raised his head slowly like its weight was more than he could bear. "There won't be a decision until tonight's service. Everyone must be here on time at seven o'clock. Until then, is there anyone willing to die for me?"

"Yes!" cried almost everyone.

Emmanuel turned toward his brother Luke. "Bring him here, now."

Luke walked to the back door. Sarah turned to watch. Once there, Luke slung open the door and grabbed the front of the shirt of a battered man who could hardly stand on his own feet. Two other men had each of this black man's arms holding him almost off the floor while they took him to stand before Emmanuel. The black man's right eye was swollen shut and the right side of his head and face appeared to be puffed up to twice its normal size. The crowd began to murmur. Sarah heard a growl radiate from deep inside Crystal's throat. Sarah seized Crystal's clenched hands and placed them in her lap. Then Sarah said a quick prayer that her friend wouldn't try something foolish and get them both killed.

"This man," Emmanuel screamed, "was caught breaking into the compound last night." Emmanuel held a shotgun aloft. "And he was carrying this to use on me."

The congregation began to rumble in hushed voices again. Sarah saw anger in everyone's eyes as they stared at the beaten man.

Crystal leaned close to Sarah's ear. "That shotgun's exactly like those carried by the compound guards."

"They want to kill me, assassinate me, crucify me." said Emmanuel, now hollering over the microphone. "That's why I've got armed guards." He handed the shotgun to Luke. "The devil is out to destroy me, and he's using these people at our gate. Beware! Satan may use some of our very own here to destroy us from within. Beware of Satan." He brought both hands up with the backs of them toward the crowd, his fingers in the shape of claws pointed inward. "The devil is a strong foe to fight. Listen to your neighbor, to your parents, to your children, to your husband or wife. Do they doubt me? If they do, it's the devil using them. The devil gets inside their minds. The devil!" He slowly squeezed his fingers together before his face until they formed a fist. "He gets inside their minds—the devil." His fist started to shake. "Yes, the devil does. If you even see the devil in your own mother tell one of my people, and we'll council them and get the devil out of them before it's too late, ah."

A quiver ran the length of Sarah's body. She touched her sore breast and felt the knot beneath her skin.

"The end is near," Emmanuel said returning to a normal voice. Everyone quieted, and all eyes locked onto their Christ. "When I sent word to the FBI out front that this building was wired with explosives, I don't think they cared." The crowd reacted—most of them moaned.

He raised his hand until all were quiet. "But it will never be the same. Those people at our gate will never go away until I'm dead. Tonight, tonight, some very important decisions will be made about our future, tonight. I want you to spend the day in prayer. Pray for me, that I'll do the right thing for you tonight. Yes, tonight...tonight."

Sarah thought of Emmanuel's recent discussion about poisoning everyone. She noticed Luke cut his worried eyes toward Irene who maintained an expression on her jowls as cold as graveyard stone.

"As for this man," said Emmanuel placing his hand on Leaky's shoulder. "Tonight we'll bring out the snakes." The crowd began to stir with excitement. "We'll let the snakes decide this man's fate. If the devil is in him, we'll know it. The rattlers will let us know. Harm will only come to those that are disloyal to God. So as poison only destroys the unbelievers, the bite of the serpent only destroys the heretics. Tonight, tonight. Praise God, it's tonight."

The crowd roared with everyone shouting, "Amen," and "Praise Emmanuel" as loud as they could scream. Some clapped their hands. Sarah, Crystal, and Leaky were the only quiet and still people in the building. Again, Emmanuel raised his hands over his head. But this time he started shaking them like they were on fire and he wanted to extinguish the blaze by his rapid wiggling from head to toe. Sarah lowered her head to pray that everyone might see the truth before it was too late.

CHAPTER TWENTY-SEVEN

It was almost noon before Matt got the _Desperado_ water-worthy and ready to pull out. When he eased both accelerator throttles forward, the twin 450 horsepower Chrysler engines came alive, creating a steady vibration beneath his feet. This gave Matt some solace, but the back of his neck and head still throbbed because the muscles along his spine tightened from too much stress for too long a time. He tried to will these aches and pains from his body but couldn't. His thoughts lingered on Leaky. Matt was about as worried as he'd ever been. Medora must have sensed his mood, for she had said very little since learning of the news about Leaky.

Matt had sent Medora to the Kroger store for a few groceries and supplies while he gassed up the johnboat, changed all the craft's electricity over to the generator and got the _Desperado_ ready for the river. He was surprised Medora hadn't minded picking up some buckshot for his twelve-gauge shotgun.

Matt sat on the edge of the captain's stool, neck craned, vigilantly analyzing his next actions in guiding the _Desperado_ safely out of its narrow slip. He had both arms about shoulder-width apart in front of him on each side of the pilot's steering wheel without touching it. He worked the throttle to the right engine in his right hand and the one to the left engine in his left. Medora stood behind Matt looking out the front windshield with her arms folded across her chest. She appeared snug in the cool air wearing Matt's flannel-lined denim jacket, which hung off her shoulders.

Easing forward, Matt finally slid the craft out of its slip and made a sharp right turn by using only the two throttles while never touching the craft's large steering wheel. The backend of the heavy boat slipped around as the craft's nose swung to the right and pointed toward the main river. The smell of burning gasoline replaced the odor of the river. Matt continued to push the throttles forward and backward piloting the cruiser between the narrow banks. After all these years, it still excited him. Several times, he had only five feet of deep water on each side of them in which to maneuver. Although he felt pressed to hurry and find Leaky, this was one job where Matt had to take his time, or they could tear a hole in the boat's bottom.

It took fifteen minutes of hard tacking before they churned into the choppy Tennessee River and turned left toward Williams Island and the encircled compound. Matt kept the _Desperado_ moving at ten knots and close to the left bank, so he could search for any signs of where Leaky may have beached. He prayed he'd see no lifeless body half exposed in the brush along the shore. Just off his left shoulder, Medora watched.

The north wind pushed three-foot waves toward the boat's bow causing it to half slice and half bounce forward in a spasmodic rocking motion. Medora stumbled and grabbed onto his shoulder to keep from falling backward. Her unexpected move caused Matt to flinch.

"Sorry," she said as though she really was.

"Kind of rough," he said. "The wind's against us."

"Seems like everybody is," she said releasing her hold on Matt and moving to the sofa.

"Yeah," he said continuing to feel her hand on his shoulder.

"The fire," she said changing the subject. "I still think it was intended for you."

"I know," Matt said, turning on the MK2 Furuno radar and tilting the glowing, yellowish-green screen forward. "At least that's what I think, too."

"This Emmanuel must be a crazy man."

"Yeah," he said, mashing a button with a negative (-) sign on the radar and watching the picture change to a closer view of the area 360° around them. He felt her move back behind him.

"What is that, radar?" she asked.

"Yeah, just got this one several months ago. Still learning how to use it."

"That the river?" she asked pointing her finger over his shoulder and brushing her forearm against him.

"Yeah," he said glancing to his left to search the riverbank visually. He mashed the positive (+) button several times, and the picture on the screen changed. It now looked like a smaller curved hose with a large area of black along its left side and a thin black line on its right. "This is the view of the area at sixteen nautical miles. That's as far as it'll go. I can reduce it to one-eighth of a mile and see a person or a stick floating in the water when it's not this choppy."

"What's that?" she asked pointing to the dark area on the left of the screen.

"Raccoon Mountain." He could smell her clean scent.

"And that?" she pointed to a large teardrop shaped mass where the river forked and moved around it before coming together again some distance higher on the edge of the screen.

"That's Williams Island," he said. "We'll be there in a few minutes." Medora's change to a calmer, more congenial attitude this morning caused his tense muscles to relax slightly.

Matt pointed on the screen where the river broke to the left of the island. "Here the river's called Jackson Bar." He slid his finger across the screen where the river broke to the right of the island. "And here it's called Burris Bar. The sandbar is about a mile long and about a quarter of a mile wide. See on the other side of the island, where the river comes together again?"

"Yes."

Matt pointed past the Island on the screen to the narrowest part of the Tennessee River. "Here, the river's called Suck Creek."

"Where did they find your jackboat, johnboat, whatever you call it?"

"Johnson said my johnboat was right here at the fork of the river along Jackson Bar. It had caught in some fallen trees. I don't think Leaky left my johnboat that way. He would've secured it. And he wouldn't have left his gun in the boat like that. But I'm going to check out the area in case he's on the island. I don't think he's there, though."

"Where do you think he is?"

"At the compound," Matt said. He almost said, *or dead,* but he caught himself first, and said, "Where your daughter is."

She went silent for a few minutes, and they continued to cut through the oncoming waves which pitched the bow of the *Desperado* up and down. Without talking, Matt looked from the radar screen to the riverbank where fallen leaves covered the water's edge. Usually at this time of year, the leaves covered a large part of the river, but today's wind and waves pushed them toward the calmer waters near the shore.

On the radar's screen, Williams Island grew nearer, and when he looked forward through the front of the *Desperado*'s windshield, he could actually see where the river separated and started its fork around the island.

"What's that?" asked Medora pointing to a huge black mass appearing on the right side of the radar screen. The mass on the screen extended along the far part of the river called Suck Creek.

"That's Signal Mountain, now on the right and Raccoon Mountain on our left."

"You have a lot of mountains around here," she said. The boat rocked hard to the side when they hit the swifter current of Jackson Bar. She placed her hand on his shoulder and spread her feet. "Where's the compound?" she said.

Pointing an index finger at the screen, Matt traced the mountain's image along the left side of Suck Creek. "Somewhere in here on Raccoon..." As he stared at the screen, Matt suddenly remembered something he hadn't thought of either yesterday or today.

"There're some caves all along this section of Raccoon Mountain. The most noted one's called Pitchfork Cave, but there're a few others without names in this area. They're everywhere along the base of this mountain."

"Why's that important?"

"I bet that's how some of those cult people are getting in and out of the compound. There's a cave somewhere they're using to get to the river without being seen. Yeah! But finding the cave, if that's truly what's happening, isn't gonna be easy."

"But you can, right?"

"Maybe we can," he said, staring at the screen and trying to remember where he and Leaky had seen Crystal and her abductors go into the woods after crossing Suck Creek in the pontoon boat.

Medora said, "We? I don't know about all this. I'm afraid that I'm not much of an outdoor person. There has got to be all kind of snakes in those woods and especially in a dark cave."

Matt didn't say much for a few seconds, having his mind suddenly shift to yesterday's ordeal with the rattler, and that she may be right about the snakes in the caves. He remembered what Crystal had said about the snakes.

After a long minute, he said, "Too cold for snakes."

"What?"

"Snakes don't like this cold weather. They're hibernating now." That was partially true, he knew.

"It is really cold up here," she said.

When he turned the wheel and changed their course from a north to a northwestward direction, following the bend in the river, the _Desperado_ swayed from side to side as the waves slammed into its starboard side.

"Un huh," he said without thinking while staring out the boat's windshield and moving the steering wheel back and forth between his thumb and index finger. "If the wind dies tonight, we may get our first frost."

"I didn't realize the hundred-and-twenty miles between Chattanooga and Atlanta could have such contrasting weather."

"Only about five degrees difference, on the average," he said.

"I really don't know much about such things."

Matt couldn't believe she was admitting a personal weakness. It struck him how relaxed she'd become since they had started this quest for her lost family. "When you live on a boat, you've got to watch the weather."

"The leaves on the trees are so much more colorful here than in Atlanta."

"Probably more deciduous trees here. More pines in Atlanta."

"Yes, but it's so lovely along your river now. I bet it was really something a couple of weeks ago. Atlanta comes alive in the spring when the dogwoods and azaleas bloom."

"Un huh," he said not listening now. They churned along in silence for several minutes before he said, "I certainly love the river, but I've developed respect for it. This one's claimed many lives in the past. A lot of ghosts hover above its surface; but, for me, it's worth the hazards to have such a beautiful place to live." He waited almost a minute while steering the boat, then said, "Most of the leaves left on the trees have lost their brilliant colors in the last few days."

Just a hundred yards ahead of the _Desperado_, the river separated and branched around Williams Island. Matt pulled both throttles back, slowing their movement to a crawl. The high waves dwindled to nothing.

"What happened?" asked Medora.

"The smooth water's only temporary, 'cause the island's blocking the north wind."

Matt inspected every detail along the sandy shoreline of the flat island. Only low growing trees and shrubs covered its surface. The dangling whip-like branches of the weeping willow protruded several feet over the riverbank brushing the surface of the water. There was no sign of Leaky. This didn't surprise Matt, because in his guts, he knew Leaky's location—The Refuge—with Emmanuel. Matt felt rage creep up his shoulders, reddening his throat and finally settling in a blood-filled face. He felt the hair on the back of his neck bristle.

Matt took the ship's black microphone in hand and brought it close to his mouth to speak. "Leaky...Leaky Waters." The sound of his voice was so strong it bounced off Raccoon Mountain to their left and echoed back through the glass windows of the _Desperado_ to reach Medora and Matt a second later. He opened the sliding windows on both sides of the boat. Medora stood behind him, out of his way, as cold air spilled inside.

"That sure is loud," Medora said.

"Gotta be," He said without seeing her. His mind was so filled with his own thoughts of what had to be done that Medora had almost cease to exist for Matt.

Turning the large, chrome steering wheel to the left caused the _Desperado_'s nose to pivot toward the left branch of the river. Creeping now, they slipped into the offshoot of this part of the river called Jackson Bar as it ran along the Westside of Williams Island that now glided past them on the right. A skinny crane that had been feeding along the island's shore flapped its snow-white wings. It gradually lifted into the flame-blue sky. When it got about ten feet high, the north wind shoved it south. Its sudden change in direction reminded Matt of a helicopter in flight and a long time ago in Vietnam.

"Leaky," he said again into the microphone. "Leaky, can you hear me?"

Matt listened but heard only the rhythmic breathing of Medora blending with the quiet rumble of the twin Chrysler engines.

On their left, opposite the island, a large cove that descended into the side of the mountain interrupted the river's bank. Matt visually searched the shaded inlet but saw no sign of his friend. They slid through the water until the river bent slightly to the right. Again, the waves increased, jostling the craft. The north wind sliced through the open windows, cutting through Matt's navy-blue flannel shirt.

"Leaky, Leaky Waters," Matt said over the microphone for the last time. Ahead the two branches of the river joined to form the main channel again. He

pushed the throttles forward, and their speed increased. As the _Desperado_ passed
the northern tip of Williams Island, Matt wondered if the law officers around
the compound less than half a mile to their left heard his call over the speakers.
Emmanuel was close, now, Matt felt him.

Medora said, "Are you going to land on the island to look for your
friend?"

"Nope, I don't think he's there." Matt pushed the throttles forward and increased their speed to ten knots. Ahead the river narrowed causing its current to
increase. In a little less than five minutes they entered the area of the river called
Suck Creek, and Matt pulled back on the throttles slowing the engines.

"Why the slowdown?" she asked.

"The folks living along that side of the river don't like the wake," he said
pointing to a few old homes scattered on the right bank of the river."

As they ebbed next to an old deteriorating barn, Matt saw a middle-aged
man wearing bib-overalls sitting in a lawn chair with a blue-steel rifle resting
across his lap. Under the overalls, the man wore a red flannel shirt that looked
like he'd had it on a week. On the man's head a bright orange hunting cap rode
so far down it spread the tops of his ears away from his head.

Medora moved to the right and looked out that window. "What's that man
doing?"

"He's making sure nobody goes too fast along his river and causes a
wake."

"With a gun?" she said.

"Yeah, and he isn't afraid to use it if we go too fast."

"What about the law?"

"He and the rest of his family, they are the law back here. It's too far out for
the sheriff's men to patrol. These people take care of their own and everybody
else that uses their river."

"Their river?"

"Yeah."

"And they're all related?"

"Yeah," Matt said. Suddenly he got an idea and turned the _Desperado_ back
toward the man. Continually, checking his depth finder so they didn't bottom-
out, Matt drove to within ten feet of the grassy shoreline, and as close as he could
to where the old man sat guarding the river. Matt pressed the black button on
the dash next to the radar screen and heard the splash of the front anchor hitting
the water. As expected, in less than two seconds he felt the anchor's thick rope
go from taut to loose, which indicated the anchor had struck the river's bottom.
The _Desperado_ drifted downstream about ten feet, then stopped when the anchor
caught on something beneath the water. Matt tapped the yellow button next
to the black one, reversing the anchor motor and carefully tightening its rope a

few feet. Because the dam was open thirty miles below them, the river's current pushed the craft's rear around 180 degrees until they faced upriver. The waves slapped the _Desperado_'s flat stern and made a popping sound.

When Matt felt the boat anchored, he walked outside the pilothouse to stand on a walkway only a foot wide that led to the front of the boat. Medora remained inside.

Without taking his eyes from Matt, the man lifted the rifle from his lap and allowed it to rest across his barrel chest. The man leaned over to his right while still watching Matt and expectorated a long stream of tobacco juice that splattered beside the lawn chair onto brown, stained grass.

"Howdy," Matt said. "You doing okay, today?"

"Course," said the man through dingy teeth and a bulging jaw. His beady eyes squinted at Matt. The man didn't look too excited about this encounter. "What you'ns want?"

Matt pushed his cowboy hat down in the front and said, "You noticed any strangers in a pontoon boat coming and going a lot on the other side of the river?"

"Show 'enough has," said the man. "Them crazy sumbitches making me madder'n hell. I don't care if they is rentin' Cousin Glenn's dock and totin' shotguns, I'm gonna fill they asses full of hot lead if'n they don't slow it down some and shows me some re'spect. You ain't the law, is you?"

"Nope," Matt said. "I think those people in the pontoon boat are the ones that set fire to a bunch of boats last night at the Brown's Ferry Marina."

"Holy shit!" said the man. He spat again.

"Is that silver pontoon boat all they're using on the water?"

"Yep, that's it."

"Have you seen where they go when they get off their boat and disappear into the woods?"

"Nope."

Matt's sudden optimism dwindled with the man's blunt negative answer. Matt waited a long moment and then said, "Thanks, anyway," and turned to reenter the pilothouse.

"Bobby," said the man, "he's seen 'em though."

Matt spun back to face the man. "Who's Bobby?"

"Bobby's my third cousin," said the man dropping his rifle back to his lap.

"What's Bobby seen?"

"He went there a while back and seen where they be going. Yep, him sure did."

Matt felt excitement replace worry in his shoulders. He took a deep breath, and then said, "Bobby followed them, huh?"

"Yep," said the man with a grin. Matt waited a long few seconds for the man to tell him what his cousin Bobby knew. After the man didn't answer, Matt opened his mouth to ask what Bobby had seen when the man finally spoke again. "They live in them caves back there. A whole lot of'em."

"A lot of caves?" Matt said. He couldn't take his eyes off the man's large ears that stuck out from under his cap.

"No, no, no," said the man shaking his head. "A lot of people fur one little cave."

"I'd pay good money if you or Bobby'd show me where that cave is."

"I don't know where it is."

"Where can I find your cousin, Bobby?"

"Right cheer," said the man with a smirk on his brown lips. "Come out cheer, Bobby. We'ns gonna get to ride on this man's big boat."

Between two broken boards on the side of the barn stepped a filthy-faced, blond boy of about ten. He was dressed in denim bib-overalls and a thin T-shirt that must have once been white. Grinning, the boy spat a long stream of tobacco juice on the ground.

CHAPTER TWENTY-EIGHT

"Who was that dirty man?" said Medora. She stood next to Matt with an expression on her face like somebody who had just gotten a whiff of dog shit.

"Herbert," Matt said pulling into Cousin Glenn's dock that was a little less than a mile farther down river from where they'd left the cousins. Since Matt figured it would take Herbert and Bobby ten additional minutes to walk to the docks, he needed to check for signs of the Suburban Leaky and he had chased yesterday.

After docking, Matt jumped off the _Desperado_ and tied it to stout posts on the landing then looked back up the grassy riverbank, where he saw Herbert and Bobby ambling along about halfway to them.

After securing the _Desperado_, Matt left Medora and walked up the bank looking for a sign of the Suburban. It didn't take long before he found a large spot of dying grass that still had the smell of antifreeze mixed with oil and gas on it. He visually checked through the woods toward Suck Creek Road—nothing there either.

Herbert was fifty yards away and closing when he placed a new wad of black tobacco in his mouth. "What you'n looking fur?"

Matt waited until they got closer before answering. "A white Suburban that was here earlier."

"Ain't seen it," said Herbert, spitting tobacco then looking at the little boy. "How 'bout you?"

Behind the dirty face, the boy had the bright eyes of a healthy child. Matt figured this boy was experienced beyond his years in the lifestyle along the river. His hair looked like dingy cotton and his bare feet were as dark as chunks of coal. He looked up at Matt, tilted his head to the side, and said, "Them took it away."

"Who?" Matt said.

"Who what?" said the boy.

"Who took the car away?" Matt said a little louder while trying to maintain patience.

"Don't know," said the boy, turning toward Matt's boat and walking away.

Herbert followed. Trying to communicate with these two was proving to be a challenge. Matt shook his head and followed the cousins.

As they approached the dock, Matt glanced across the river, and there in the shadows sat a silver pontoon boat tied to the bank. He had been too busy earlier to check that shoreline. That wasn't good—he needed to be more careful.

No one guarded the pontoon boat, or, at least, Matt had not noticed anybody on the opposite shore where the craft swayed in the choppy waves. Matt felt relieved that Emmanuel's people were so confident that they had failed to post lookouts along the river.

Herbert and Cousin Bobby stood on Cousin Glenn's dock and watched with slacked jaws as Matt untied the johnboat from the *Desperado*. He planned to cross the river on it and wasn't pleased knowing that he'd have to make two trips, but Medora insisted on going with them. The boat was too small, and Matt couldn't chance taking all of them across at the same time on such rough water.

When everything was ready, Matt raced inside the *Desperado* and grabbed his pistol, shotgun, and night goggles. Medora who had been downstairs changing into a pair of Asics running shoes came up from the stateroom.

"You ready to go?" Matt said

"Yes, of course," she answered and didn't wait on him but went out the pilothouse door.

"Wait," Matt said rushing out on the back landing. But she didn't wait. Medora, turned her backside to a big-eyed Herbert, grabbed the chrome railing, and went down the six-rung ladder with the swiftness of an experienced roofer. Matt noticed that Herbert's bottom jaw had dropped much lower and tobacco-drool dripped down his chin. The thought of Herbert being a product of incest crossed Matt's mind.

"Hello," Medora said to Herbert and Cousin Bobby, when she reached the dock and turned to face them.

"Howdy," said Cousin Bobby grinning. Herbert wiped his chin and nodded his head.

"I'm Medora, and you are?" she asked looking at the dirty-faced boy.

He didn't answer her question but only looked up at his Cousin Herbert for help.

Matt could tell they didn't understand that she was asking for their names so he said, "The little one's Bobby, and the big one's Herbert."

She said, "I'm glad to meet you."

Before going inside for his hat that he had forgotten, Matt checked once more across the river. When he saw a man and a woman boarding the pontoon boat, Matt's heart jumped and tried to come up his throat. He leaped off the back of the *Desperado*. Medora, Herbert, and Bobby flinched and stepped back from him as Matt started untying the johnboat from the boat landing.

"Get back aboard." Matt said trying to appear calm. Herbert, Bobby, and Medora just stood staring at him, so he screamed, "Dammit! Get in the *Desperado*, now!"

Medora and Bobby scurried up the ladder and into the pilothouse. Herbert saw them too and stood still as granite with squinting eyes watching the people across the river. He moved the rifle across his chest.

After getting the johnboat situated, Matt untied the _Desperado_ from the dock. Then, he turned to Herbert. "You going?"

"Nope! You'ns go on. I'm gonna wait cheer and have a word with them there sumbitches."

"You gonna tell those people that I'm looking for them?" Matt said while climbing the ladder to the cruiser's door.

"Nope, less you wants me to," said Herbert.

Matt stopped and glanced down at Herbert who continued to stare across the river as the pontoon boat backed into the river with the man and woman aboard. Two men with shotguns stood on the far shore watching the pontoon churn into the river. Matt looked back at Herbert. "They're going to ask you who I am."

"If'n they don't already know who you is, I'm gonna say you's my cousin, Billy Joe, from Knoxville."

"Thanks," Matt said entering the _Desperado_ and rushing over to its controls. When he turned the starboard's engine key it started immediately, but he had to hold the larboard's engine key in the crank position for almost ten seconds before it coughed, then started with a booming backfire. He pulled both throttles back causing the large cruiser to jolt backward away from the dock and into the choppy river.

About the time he visually found the oncoming pontoon boat bobbing halfway across the river, Matt heard the johnboat slam into the _Desperado_'s side. He squinted his eyes and thought about the possibility of the johnboat knocking a hole in the cruiser's wooden hull.

When Matt thought they were far enough out into the river, he started both the _Desperado's_ propellers churning forward and made a sharp turn with the wheel to place them facing back down river and away from the pontoon boat, which was presently passing within thirty yards from their stern.

For the first time since boarding the boat, Cousin Bobby spoke. "That be one ugly bitch."

Matt turned, wondering if the little boy was insulting Medora but quickly realized Cousin Bobby was talking about the woman on the pontoon boat. Medora and the boy stood side-by-side staring out of the back windows. Matt moved behind the boy to check the woman the boy called "one ugly bitch." Bobby was right. The woman's stringy brown hair whipped in the wind across a moon-shaped face. With her double chins hanging over the collar of a puffy red windbreaker, she reminded Matt of a pig in clothes. That's when he noticed she looked like Irene, the woman on the driver's licenses who used Sarah's name. The musty smell of Cousin Bobby assaulted Matt's nose, making him take a step back.

Before they moved up stream and around the next bend of the river, Matt checked the shore where the two men stood. They stood next to the water's edge and didn't appear to be in a hurry to go anywhere soon. They waited, watching both the pontoon boat and The _Desperado_ with their shotguns resting in the crooks of their arms.

"Cousin," Matt said to the boy. "The cave they use to get in and out of the compound, is it close to where those men are?"

"Aya," said Cousin Bobby who continued to watch the pontoon boat as it landed on Cousin Glenn's dock. Herbert, with his head going from side to side, was raising hell with them. A black Ford truck pulled up to the dock, and the fat woman, ignoring Herbert, pushed past him onto land. The man tied the pontoon boat to the dock as the ugly woman got into the truck driven by a redheaded woman. The man listened only seconds to Herbert's barking before getting in beside the two women. With Herbert left alone and screaming obscenities, the truck drove away.

Matt realized that fighting their way into the compound didn't seem to be the smart move at all now. He wasn't even sure if Leaky was there, but in his bones, Matt knew his best friend was there and in serious trouble. He slowed the _Desperado_ to almost a stop, took a deep breath of cool air, and tried to think of what he should do next.

"You'ns got anything to eat?" said Cousin Bobby.

"Sure," said Medora. "You want some soup?"

"Aya," said the boy. "What kind you got?"

"You want vegetable?"

"Aya."

"Come on," said Medora placing a cautious hand on the boy's dingy shirt and guiding him down the steps to the stateroom. "You need to wash up."

"Why?" asked Cousin Bobby.

After almost twenty minutes of creeping away from the men with shotguns, Matt still pondered their situation with no ideas of what to do next. All he could think about was the aroma of food drifting up from the galley. He had not eaten since yesterday's lunch at the Choo Choo. They had moved only a mile along the choppy river since losing sight of Cousin Glenn's dock. By the time Matt was sure his stomach was about to race up his throat to grab his tongue, Medora came up the steps carrying a tray with a steaming bowl of soup in its center. She'd placed crackers neatly around it on a plate.

"Great," Matt said reaching for the tray and placed it on the flat dashboard between the steering wheel and the windshield. "You make this?"

She grinned as though amused by his question. "Of course."

Matt couldn't figure this woman out. What had made her so happy? He took a spoonful of the soup and shoved it into his mouth. The heat set his tongue on fire. He blew air out between puckered lips trying to relieve the burning. "Hot, but good."

"Thank you," she said, still grinning. "I really didn't make the soup. I warmed it up from a can. The little boy ate one can by himself."

"What's he doing now?"

"He's still eating. I made him a peanut butter and jelly sandwich after he finished the soup."

Medora and Matt didn't talk until he had taken the last bite of soup. She stared out the window at the forested bank of the river. She was beginning to make Matt feel as leery about her in this good mood as she had when she was in a bad one. He waited for her attitude to change as if he were waiting on a stick of dynamite to explode.

"That was good," he finally said, setting the tray back on the dashboard.

"What are we going to do?" she said. "I mean, we're still going in there, and get my daughter, aren't we?"

Cousin Bobby lumbered up the steps and staggered over to the sofa holding both hands across his stomach. He had a contented, yet miserable look on his clean face.

After Matt failed to answer her question, Medora crossed her arms across her chest. "Well, are we going to find her, or what?"

"Yeah," he said without even glancing her way. The wick burned closer to the stick. Matt turned the _Desperado_ around, increased their speed, and started churning back toward Cousin Glenn's dock. "I have to decide how I'm gonna get in there, but I'm getting in there, if I have to. . ." he stopped in mid-sentence and gazed out the windshield at the long shadows being cast across the rough water. He didn't want to sound stupid, so he ate his next words.

"Have to what?" she said calmly.

He delayed several seconds as she continued to wait on his answer, her arms still folded across her chest. Now, he really felt stupid for failing to finish his sentence. He hated the way she could make him feel awkward. "I may have to shoot my way inside." There, he had said it, and it still sounded stupid.

"We," she said. "Not just you. I'm going, too."

Matt pushed both throttles forward. The Chrysler's engines roared as their speed jumped to full power. Twenty-two knots was the fastest he'd had the Trojan in years. As soon as they rounded the bend in the river, the dock came into sight, but so did the two men standing on the opposite shore.

Matt thought about Crystal. He thought about Leaky. He was getting mad. "They can't guard the cave forever. I'm not waiting forever. I'm gonna give them 'til nightfall, but after that I'm getting in there one way or another."

He heard Medora breathe what sounded like a sigh of relief. By driving very close to the right bank and the men with shotguns, Matt was able to look them in the eye as they passed. Matt thought he saw an expression of alarm flash across the shorter man's face. Matt slowed their speed and turned to watch the two men.

He stood by the window to give them a better look at his angry face. Matt was almost sure the short one recognized him. Matt wasn't sure what would happen next, but he thought that maybe the men would rush in to tell Emmanuel they had failed to destroy the boat or Matt.

Matt increased their speed to half, and they moved toward Williams Island, this time from the north. Matt reached in a cabinet next to the steering wheel and took out binoculars and handed them to Medora. "Watch 'em and see what happens."

"Who are they?" Medora said. She stood beside Matt watching the men as they peered back.

"Emmanuel's men," Matt said, pushing the throttles forward. Medora lost her balance and fell against the wall. Matt kept the nose of the craft pointed toward Jackson Bar on the right side of the island.

When he turned back to Medora, she stood with her legs spread to steady herself in the rocking boat while holding the binoculars to her eyes. Matt glanced over to see Cousin Bobby asleep on the sofa.

"One's leaving," said Medora still looking up river through the binoculars. "But the other one's still watching us."

"Let me see." Matt pulled the throttles back, took the binoculars from her hands, yanked his sunglasses off, and tossed them on the wooden dashboard. He saw one man still standing along the water's edge. He was leaning out over the bank to get a better view of them.

"Why'd you let him see your face?" said Medora.

"I thought I'd stir up a little action and see what'd happen next." Matt paused a long moment while his insides debated telling her his gut feeling. Then he brought his eyes down to her. "I really just wanted to make something happen, because I'm damn tired of waiting on a chance to get your daughter out, and save Leaky...Dammit, it's time I met that egotistical sonofabitch, Emmanuel." Matt jerked the binoculars back to his eyes.

"You talk as if you know him well."

"I feel like I do."

"How?"

"I can't explain it...It's not that important." Matt wanted to scream, "Because he's going to kill your daughter, Leaky, everybody." But he didn't.

She moved a step closer to Matt. "Does it have anything to do with you talking to the old lady yesterday?"

"No. Maybe...I'll tell you later...Dammit, only one of them has gone." Matt handed the binoculars to her. Then he went back to the steering wheel and pushed the throttles forward. they slid toward the middle of the river.

Very slowly, accenting each word she said, "What are you going to do?"

"It'll be dark soon." He paused. Silence. Matt felt her eyes cutting through him.

He continued, "We're going to a cove in Jackson Bar and anchor; then Cousin Bobby and I are going on the johnboat back up river to where their backdoor cave is."

"I'm going, too," she said, crossing her arms over her chest.

"But there's going to be trouble. There's no way around it...I don't like taking the boy, even if it is just to the cave entrance, but I've got no choice. I don't know where it is, and when I get inside the compound, I'm going to have to move fast. Emmanuel and his disciples are not going to just let me walk in there and get some of his people out without a fight. It could get bad, real bad."

"How are you going to do it?"

"I don't know," Matt said turning the craft into the shady cove with its surface as smooth as a tabletop. "This is not something you make a plan for. Especially when you don't know what you'll run into 'til you get there." The _Desperado_ sliced through the cove with a swishing sound as it cut the water out of its way. Matt pulled back on the throttles but not all the way.

"I'm going, too," she said. "I won't take no for an answer."

"Okay," Matt said. She was beginning to piss him off with her defiant attitude. He wanted to scream, so he did. "You're the most stubborn woman I've ever met, Medora Meehan."

"I'm a parent. Aren't you a parent?" she said with anger erupting from her voice.

He didn't answer her. Matt didn't feel like arguing any longer with such a persistent bitch. Finding they had moved to the middle of the cove, he turned the engines off and hit the button that dropped the _Desperado's_ anchor.

Without looking at her, Matt marched across the small room, opened a cabinet door next to the sofa, pulled out his black Stetson cowboy hat with its thin black band, and crammed it on his head with both hands. It rode too far down on his head, and the brim pushed the corner of his ears down. Then, from the same cabinet, Matt pulled out a leather shoulder holster and slung his arms through its narrow straps. He stomped back over to the dashboard, picked up the Smith and Wesson, and stuffed the 457 in its cowhide sheath under his left armpit.

Through squinting eyes, he looked up at Medora who, with a cautious expression on her face like he was a dangerous animal, pressed her back against the wall to get completely out of his way. Damn, he hated this headstrong woman, but somehow he couldn't help but admire her audacity.

Matt looked at his watch. "Thirty minutes till dark. WE'LL leave in fifteen...."

In the distance, a rapid sequence of gun shots exploded across the valley. Matt and Medora's eyes locked on one another's. Matt spoke first. "To hell with waiting! We're going in now."

CHAPTER TWENTY-NINE

The cold north wind knifing through Sarah's thin cotton dress caused her body to quiver. Or, was it from the fear of impending death? After morning services, about noon, Emmanuel had sent the congregation outside and instructed them to move to the entrance gate. There, they were organized into groups by Emmanuel's elite guard and placed on the ground in front of the gate and along the fence where they could watch the uniformed men and FBI agents stand behind cars watching the people who watched them. The entire situation was so ironic to Sarah, for freedom lay so close but yet out of reach.

For the first hour, most of the people with Sarah's group had stood directly in front of the main gate together. But now, after almost four hours, everyone was sitting or lying on the ground. Many of the smaller children, including Tommy, had cried themselves to sleep, awakened, cried for food, then fell asleep again. Trying to control her starving son and keep him warm had exhausted Sarah. Thank God, Crystal had been there to help. Sarah found a position on the asphalt and felt lucky. Some of the poor people now sat on damp fallen leaves or on the wet ground itself. Even a few of the adults had finally gone to sleep in the dwindling sunlight as the leafless limbs of oak and hickory trees cast long shadows down the hill in front of them.

Sarah was not sure who had fired the first shot that killed a government agent almost ten minutes ago. Sarah had just drifted off when a bullet struck a young man just outside the gate. Startled, breathless, she looked up in time to see the wounded man rocket backward across the hood of a black car. Before Sarah could turn her head away, she noticed that most of his head was missing. Blood and brain matter speckled the ground halfway to where she now lay as Emmanuel's men fired their shotguns spasmodically over her head at the law officers who were now hiding out of sight.

Most of the people on the ground with Sarah had stopped screaming and were now whimpering like a brood of pups away from their mother. The people cried as the headless man was removed from the hood by his brave friends. Sarah understood that some of her clan moaned for themselves. A few knew their own deaths were at hand. Sarah's swollen eyes stayed blurred from weeping continuously. They burned inside and outside.

"Mark Belcher," someone shouted over a loudspeaker. "Emmanuel." Sarah glanced up, blinking her eyes trying to get clearer vision. The crowd hushed. Sarah noticed a beige speaker atop one of the cars parked lengthwise just outside the compound's gate.

Crystal, lying next to Sarah, said, "Who's that talking?"

"Don't know," Sarah said. The taste of salt from tears slid down the back of her throat.

"Mark Belcher, Emmanuel," said a man's voice from the speaker. "Let your people come outside. We don't intend to harm anyone. We want to talk to you. We need to speak to you and..."

A series of shots erupted behind Sarah and struck the car holding the speaker with metallic thuds until one of the projectiles silenced the speaker by blowing it into infinite pieces.

It was only a short time after the firing stopped before his guards found Sarah. Strong hands jerked her to her feet with one quick movement. Tommy fell from her grasp onto the pavement. Crystal took him in her arms and wasted little time rocking him back and forth and humming a song in his ear as he cried and reached in desperation for his mother.

The guard called Ralph pulled Sarah hard by her left arm through the crowd. She tried to glance back toward her son but couldn't see over Ralph's shoulders. Her left arm soon went numb. She felt that if the man pulled just a little harder her arm would snap into. Her feet hardly touched the ground as he pushed her through the mass of people lying across the area and up the narrow path toward the sanctuary. Even with her tear filled nose, she could detect Ralph's musty body odor.

Once inside the sanctum, she saw Emmanuel glaring at her through his bloodshot eyes. Surrounded by six or seven guards, he slumped in his pulpit chair. His white shirt, filled with wrinkles, twisted on his torso. It hung out of his black pants on the right side. The other side of his shirt draped across his crotch. Emmanuel appeared worn, tired, and probably drunk. His silver-and-black stripped tie was half-undone and draped sideways from his neck. Hostility spilling from his face.

Ralph pushed, pulled, and then yanked Sarah toward this self-proclaimed Jesus. Once they reached the pulpit, Ralph pushed her to her knees in front of Emmanuel. Because Sarah's arm had no feeling, she was unable to break her fall. She landed on her shoulder, bumping her forehead on the pine floor. Still dazed, she worked her way to a sitting position and pulled her dress over her knees. Sitting with her legs tucked under her dress, she massaged her left arm as a tingling sensation spread to her fingertips and expanded toward a wrist that ached.

Softly Emmanuel said, "Sarah, Sarah, my troublesome Sarah." She could smell alcohol on his breath even from this distance. "What am I going to do with you? I think I'll give you the same treatment that snooping black detective's going to get." Emmanuel pointed over Sarah's left shoulder and off to his right. She turned her head in that direction.

With natural reflexes, Sarah's right hand shot to her mouth when she saw him. A sickness grabbed her stomach and squeezed. In a bloodstained T-shirt, the man called Leaky slumped backward over a pew with his arms tied behind his back. His legs sprawled, one foot protruded forward and the other angled backward under the pew. His black face showed bright-red bloody splotches over a right eye swollen shut. Blood streaked down the cheek below the left eye and to his lower lip that drooped. His head wobbled on a limber neck, and his left eye appeared dazed from the beatings. When Sarah started to turn away from Leaky Waters, the traces of a smile rushed across his mouth. She turned back to see that the grin had faded, and he had closed his eyes.

Emmanuel said in too calm a voice, "Sarah darling, one of my men saw your mother this afternoon."

"Oh! No!" said Sarah trying to stand, but Ralph shoved her back to her knees.

"Your mother was with that guy's partner," said Emmanuel pointing to Leaky. "Your mother and that man were down on the river. I suspect he'll try to get you out of here soon." Emmanuel, staring at Sarah as a teacher would at an unruly student, waited a long moment. "But I don't think he's superman, and I don't think he'll live 'till morning. There's going to be a lot of dying before the sun shines again on this mountain. You ready, Sarah?" He leaned his head forward waiting for her answer. None came.

As Emmanuel opened his mouth to speak, the front door to the sanctuary burst open, and in stomped Irene holding a black suitcase. All eyes, including Sarah's, moved to Irene as she approached the pulpit.

"You get it?" asked an excited Emmanuel.

"Yeah!" answered Irene setting her burden down beside Sarah. "It wasn't easy, but I was able to come up with enough, I think." Irene opened the suitcase and stepped back. Emmanuel approached. Sarah glanced over to see about 10 liter-size brown bottles with white labels across their front. And then Irene said, "Did you hear that scar-faced detective is alive and moving on the river?"

"No problem," said Emmanuel. He picked up one of the bottles, looked at the label and read, "Sodium Cyanide Capsule."

"Each tablet is enough for any human," said Irene

"Is it fast?" said Emmanuel putting it back in the suitcase.

"Very," said Irene. "Only seconds and it's over with."

"Just one capsule per person?"

"Yeah!"

Emmanuel returned to his chair. "Get everything ready for tonight."

Sarah scanned the sanctuary. Luke had an expression on his face of pure terror. He was unable to hide his fear. Most of the guards stared straight ahead, but she saw several glancing back and forth at one another.

"You," said Emmanuel pointing at his guards with a sweeping finger. "I don't want you men to take this stuff." Sarah saw a look of relief run across some of their faces. "I want you to make sure everyone, and I mean everyone," Emmanuel glared at his brother Luke, "takes this poison. If they don't swallow it, then kill'em with the shotguns. It's going to get rough, so you must be strong. I'm depending on all of you."

Ralph stepped away from Sarah and asked, "What do you want us to do after everyone's dead, kill ourselves?"

"No!" said Emmanuel. "You are to escape. Go to my sister's house in Dayton, Tennessee, and wait for me. I'll be there in three days."

Ralph screwed his face up in a puzzled expression. Sarah glanced at Luke who now ceased trying to hide his anger. Also, Irene had a look of bewilderment cross her face, that had grown red like she'd been in the sun all day.

"My children, you will be the witnesses to wonder. You will prepare the world for my rule."

Ralph said, "Where you gonna be for three days?"

"I will be dead," said Emmanuel. "But I won't stay dead. Like before, I'll arise, but this time I'll rule the world. Everyone will follow me."

"Oh!" said Ralph. A blank look of confusion dominated his face, and Emmanuel must have noticed it, too.

"If you doubt me, Ralph," said Emmanuel, "then you better think twice about it. I'll only trust the ones who believe in me. Everyone else will die, and non-believers will go straight to hell."

"What about me?" said Luke. His left hand rubbed the back of his right hand.

"Yes, yes, yes," said a smiling Emmanuel. "You are your daddy's son, brother Luke. I've got something special for you."

"What?" said Luke. He rubbed harder now.

Emmanuel crooked his finger toward Irene in a calling gesture. "Come here."

She went to Emmanuel's side and lowered her ear next to her savior's mouth. She grinned and moved to the suitcase.

"Luke," said Emmanuel. "I love you so much, I'm gonna let you go first."

"Go where?" said Luke. He couldn't take his eyes off Irene who opened a bottle of sodium cyanide and spilled a capsule in her hand. She hurried out the back door. Luke's face went ashen.

"Go to prepare a place for your brother," said Emmanuel. "Go see your mother. But you might go to hell and see that sorry-piece-a-shit daddy of yours. If you do, you may be really happy when he pulls his pants down. Of course, you never had to do that when you was little, did you?"

Irene rushed back through the door and up to Luke carrying a cup in one hand and the capsule in the other.

"Please, Brother!" said Luke. "I've been loyal to you, done everything you've asked. Please let me live! Please!"

Emmanuel walked over to his half-brother. "I'm doing this out of love. You will come back with me when I rise from the dead. Don't you believe?" Emmanuel placed a hand on his brother's trembling head. "You must believe in me, or you will burn in hell with your sorry-ass daddy. You don't want to go through the gates of hell with him, do you?"

"No." Tears rolled down Luke's face.

"Then do this, quickly," said Emmanuel, handing Luke the capsule and cup. Slowly, tenderly Emmanuel moving his hand across his brother's shoulder.

"Please," said Luke. "Please, let me go with you."

Emmanuel took the capsule from Luke's hand and gently placed it on Luke's lips. "You will go with me. Take it, now. It's about finished."

"What...What's about finished?"

"Life in that short fat body of yours." Emmanuel pushed the capsule into Luke's mouth.

Luke looked up with pleading eyes. "Swallow it now?"

"Yes," Emmanuel said softly.

To Sarah's astonishment, Luke's face transformed from a cry into a grin. "This is one of your tests, ain't it? You're trying to see if I believe in you, right?"

"Drink," said Emmanuel rubbing his brother's shoulder.

Luke swallowed, grabbed the cup, and gulped the liquid down his throat. Sarah held her breath.

For a moment, all was silent except the heavy, ecstatic breathing of Emmanuel as he continued to hold his brother's shoulder.

Luke's eyes shot wide open and rolled to the back of his head as he clutched at his throat with both hands. Emmanuel released his grip, held his hand up as if his sibling was dirty. Emmanuel watched his brother stagger backward, and fall off the pulpit onto the wooden floor with a thud. Luke's right leg kicked violently for several seconds before his entire body quivered so fast a rattling sound emanated from him. Luke's body went rigid, and then relaxed as air flowed from his lungs. He lay on his back staring at the ceiling with cloudy, lifeless eyes.

Emmanuel chuckled like a child that had just pulled a prank on someone.

Although Sarah had never liked Luke, she cried for him and said a quick prayer before his soul reached its destination. His problems were no more, but hers and all the others were just beginning.

CHAPTER THIRTY

"What's that?" asked Medora.

"A crossbow." Matt said. "A medieval weapon but still used by deer hunters today." He strapped it onto the backpack along with a dozen eighteen inch, stainless-steel arrows with barbed tips.

"But you can't use all those weapons, shotgun, pistol, crossbow."

"Not at the same time, true," he said, taking giant strides to the cabinet next to the sofa, pulling out a seven-inch hunting knife in a leather scabbard, and strapping it to his hips. "The crossbow is a silent weapon and I might need it, and I might not. I just got it. This isn't going to be easy, you know. Not going on a picnic. And we're not going to be able to come back and get what we need." He shoved a black flashlight into the backpack and stood, looking around the room trying to remember what he was forgetting. "You ready?"

"I guess," she said.

"Then, let's go," he said, moving past her and through the back door. The light of day had almost disappeared. An orange hue spread across the calm water. Matt knew the light they had now would be gone in a matter of minutes. The smell of burning wood from a distant fireplace laced the air—air that was turning cold. When Matt reached the boat's platform along the water's edge where he'd tied the johnboat, Matt looked back up at Medora who was already climbing down the ladder. "Be careful."

"Sure," she said sarcastically. Once she reached the platform, Medora extended a hand for the boy, who followed her down the latter.

"Get in the boat," Matt said. "Move to the front and let Cousin get in the middle. And put this on." Once she was aboard, Matt handed her an olive green lifejacket. He lifted Cousin under the armpits and swung him into the johnboat. That action caused the johnboat to rock from side to side, and Medora, in the process of placing the lifejacket on, had to hold to the sides of the boat with both hands until the rocking stopped. Working frantically, Matt tossed Cousin Bobby a child's orange lifejacket and commanded him to snap the front clasps together.

After handing the boy the backpack and Medora the shotgun, Matt untied the rope connecting the johnboat to the _Desperado_ and crawled into the middle driver's seat next to the boy. Sitting in the bow, Medora faced the back of the boat and Matt.

"Hand me the shotgun," Matt said, holding an impatient hand toward Medora.

"Yes sir," she said mockingly and shoved the heavy weapon his way.

Cousin Bobby stood, took the weapon from her, and turned toward Matt. "What kindda shotgun this be?"

"Remington, Model 870 Express," Matt answered, taking it from the boy, and then he turned the ignition key. The outboard engine cranked easily.

"Nice," said the boy. "It a twelve-gauge, pump, ain't it?" The boy acted proud to know that information.

"You got it," Matt said. Then he pulled back on the boat's lever next to the throttle. The transmission jumped into reverse causing the boat to glide backward away from the _Desperado_. Matt was glad the wind had finally died when night fell. After backing only ten feet away from the _Desperado_, Matt pushed a lever forward and the gears changed allowing the motor to propel them forward. Turning the steering wheel quickly to the left, they swung away from the big boat and toward the main river a hundred yards ahead. Matt ran at about ten percent power while making a visual check to see if his passengers were secure and ready to go faster.

"It loaded?" said the boy.

"No, dammit," Matt said just remembering what he'd failed to do. Matt pulled back on the throttle and they coasted in the water. He looked at Cousin. "Hand me the backpack."

"What kind bullets you'ns got?" said the boy reaching in the floor of the boat for the pack.

Matt was getting tired of the questions, so he didn't answer Cousin Bobby but dug into his pack and pulled out the green box of Remington shells Medora had bought for him earlier today.

What little light they had left was fading fast, so Matt flipped on the flashlight and, shinning it on the box, read aloud, "Premier copper solid SABOT slugs," with emphases on the word sabot. He'd never heard of this type ammunition. He turned the box around and continued to read, "On impact, the four precise nose cuts expand to over two times slug diameter, then break off to form additional wound channels. The slug base continues to penetrate with devastating effects." Matt made a whistling sound. "That's some bad ammunition."

"Bad?" said Medora.

"No, no," Matt said. "Bad means, good. I mean...Ah, to hell with it."

"Whatever you say, but you told me to get buckshot," said Medora. "And those had a picture of a buck deer on it."

"That's okay," said Matt as he placed five green shells in the shotgun. He had removed the standard plug, required by hunting laws, which had allowed the weapon to hold only three shells. Matt laid the shotgun in the floor of the boat. As He reached for the throttle, Matt thought he heard something coming over a loudspeaker and out of the woods somewhere toward the compound. He turned the key killing the johnboat's engine.

Silence engulfed them for a moment. Then, through the forest from the west, he heard, "Mark Belcher, Emmanuel, send your people outside. We don't intend to harm anyone. We want to speak to you. We need to speak to you and..." Matt flinched when the rapid firing of weapons interrupted the speaker. The distant blast continued for almost ten seconds, then stopped abruptly. The night fell silent again.

"What they do, over there?" said the boy. "Why we goin'?"

"They're some bad people over there, Cousin," Matt said placing a hand on the boy's shoulder. "They've got some people we love held captive. You know, against their wills and we gonna get 'em back."

"And you'ns needs to go through the cave?" said the boy.

"Yes," Matt said. After hearing no weapon's fire for several minutes, he cranked the motor, and running the engine at ten-percent speed, took them into the river that had calmed considerably from the time they'd been there almost thirty minutes ago. Total darkness swallowed them, but, fearing detection, Matt still kept the running lights off. He increased to twenty-five percent speed and watched the dark western shoreline to their left. He was able to see the shore's outline only because of the three-quarter waxing moon to their east. Riding in the shadows of tall leafless trees caused Matt to remain cautious.

Matt was trying to think of the best way to approach the men guarding the cave entrance when Cousin Bobby said, "You wantta go up the crick?"

"The what?" Matt said.

"The crick."

"You mean creek?"

"Aya!" said the boy. "The crick. You wantta go up the crick?"

"What crick, I mean creek?" Matt said. He felt he'd left something important back on the boat, but he couldn't remember what it could be.

"That one," said the boy, pointing into the dark toward the west bank.

Squinting his eyes in the dark didn't help for Matt still couldn't detect anything closely resembling a creek running into the river to their left. "I don't see a thing."

"There," said the boy. "Let me drive."

Reluctantly, and without slowing the boat, Matt moved from behind the steering wheel and the boy slid in under it. Cousin Bobby swung the nose of the johnboat toward the far west bank like a person who knew what he was doing.

"You sure..."

"Shhhhh," said the boy, yanking the throttle back and slowing them even more. "I hear the water running in the crick."

"You don't see it?"

"Not good. Shhhhh."

Matt clenched his teeth when they glided into the black shadows of the west riverbank and disappeared into the dark. He couldn't hear anything but the quiet hum of the outboard engine and the sporadic splashing of the bow slicing through the water.

"Watch you'ns heads," said the boy about the instant a limb struck Matt along his right cheek and knocked off his cowboy hat. Matt lowered his head, grabbed his hat, and placed his trust in the boy wonder.

"You want me to get the flashlight?" Matt said.

"Nah."

They twisted and turned as the boy maneuvered the aluminum craft ahead in the almost pitch black. Several times Matt felt and heard the johnboat's metal sides bumping the muddy creek bank. He thought about his motor's propeller hitting the bottom and sheering a pin. He had extra prop pins but didn't feel like trying to replace one in the dark.

"Watch you'ns ass," said the boy just before killing the engine. In only a moment the front end of the boat skimmed onto the bank halting them. The dusky dark was so quiet that not even an insect chirped.

"Where's the cave?" Matt whispered.

"Up yonder," said the boy.

Matt wondered how they were going to travel together in the woods without light. He knew they couldn't use his flashlight without the possibility of being detected by the guards, he said, "How far?"

"Not far. Come on," said the boy throwing his lifejacket in the floor and moving toward the front of the boat where Medora sat.

Matt grabbed the boy's overall straps. "Wait just a minute, Cousin. I can't see a damn thing."

"Why? I can," said Cousin Bobby.

"I can see a little," said Medora.

"Damn, I need to eat some carrots," Matt said. Then he remembered what he'd forgotten. The new infrared night vision glasses were still lying on the sofa in the *Desperado*.

Matt reached for his backpack when out of the corner of his eye, he noticed a light moving between trees off in the distance. It took him a few seconds to realize he was seeing a flashlight that was shinning far ahead in the forest. Without uttering a word or moving a muscle they watched it move in a zigzag pattern around trees toward them. Whoever held the light appeared to be searching, jerking the flashlight beam from one location to the next.

"Get in the bottom of the boat," Matt said pushing them in that direction. "He's coming this way. Where's my shotgun?"

"Here," said Medora. She hit Matt in the side with it. "What are you going to do?"

"Shhhh," Matt gestured taking the gun from her. "Just stay quiet." Blindly, Matt stepped off the front of the boat and felt some relief when he touched solid ground. Clutching the shotgun in his arms, Matt crept toward the oncoming beam of light for approximately ten feet until he reached the base of a large tree. He stopped behind it, went to one knee, and craned his neck to watch the searching light, which moved closer to them. Matt figured that a guard had heard the johnboat's motor and was coming to investigate.

When the individual holding the flashlight got to within twenty yards of the tree, Matt could hear the person's steps rustling the leaves, and he could see a person's outline behind the light. There was only one intruder; Matt felt almost positive about that. But Matt also saw that the man carried a rifle, or it could be a shotgun.

The prowler took one, two, three additional steps, stopped, and searched ahead with his flashlight beam. Watching with a racing heart, Matt kept breathing shallow so he couldn't be heard. Before he could get his head back, the light shown across Matt's face blinding him momentarily. Matt jerked his head back behind the tree.

"Who's there," yelled someone in a deep man's voice.

Matt didn't answer, but stayed still in the shadows behind the tree trunk and watched the light's cone shine on trees and shrubs close to the boat. Matt clutched the shotgun in hands drenched in sweat. He'd have to pump a shell into the chamber before firing, and this, Matt realized, would have to be done quickly before the man carrying the light could react. The light grew brighter as the man approached. When the light's beam reached the boat it stopped. Looking back, Matt couldn't see Medora or the boy, and he prayed the man didn't either. Matt realized that he could not stop what was about to happen any more than he could stop the moon from circling the earth. The leaves rustled. The light moved toward the boat. Matt took a deep breath of air. The cold burned his lungs.

Staying hidden behind the tree, Matt eased to his feet with his back pressed to the tree's trunk. When the man moved past him, Matt stopped as if frozen. The man's shotgun was halfway up and ready in one hand, as he pointed the flashlight at the boat with the other. He was so close Matt could smell the man's musty body odor.

"Hey." said Cousin Bobby, bounding to his feet.

The man flinched and started clumsily jerking the shotgun up to fire. The boy stood fixed in the light. In less than a flashing second, Medora leaped to her feet and shot her hands over her head. The man wasted a precious moment trying to hold the light on the two in the boat and aim his shotgun. Matt sprang forward and, with all his force, slammed the butt of the Remington down on the back of the man's neck just below the base of the skull. A sharp whacking and bone crunching sound resulted. Then with a thud the man crumbled to the leaf-covered earth. The flashlight rolled toward the boat then stopped against a crumpled fern with the light's cone skimming along the sandy dirt and reflecting an oval ring on the water's surface.

With his heart pounding a hole in his chest, Matt moved over the motionless man, pushed the man's shotgun away with his own foot, turned him face up, and knelt beside him. Matt groped in the faint light for the guy's pulse. All the while he tried to hold his shotgun to the man's head. To Matt's surprise, he could find no pulse in the carotid artery along the front of the man's neck. Medora picked up the flashlight and shone it on the man's ashen face. Matt thought he was one of the men they'd passed along the side of the river. It was hard to tell because his glassy eyes stared through half open eyelids. Matt laid his ear next the man's chest. Nothing. Matt tried to will his own racing heart to slow. No good.

"Is he dead?" said Medora in little more than a whisper. She squatted next to Matt and held the flashlight in a pair of quivering hands. Cousin stood behind her.

"I think so." Matt could only whisper. "Turn the light off a minute."

"Why?" she said, fumbling for the off switch for a moment. Then, failing to turn it off, she handed the glowing light to Matt. He pushed the switch and darkness swallowed them again.

"Be quiet a minute," Matt said, looking in the direction the guard had just come. "See another light or anybody coming?" Matt could hear Medora's rapid, but rhythmic breathing and smell her clean aroma.

After seeing no signs of another intruder, Matt turned the flashlight on again and handed it to Medora. "We gotta get this guy's clothes off." Matt began to unzip the front of the man's blue jump suit.

"Why?" said Medora.

"I'm going to put 'em on," Matt said, then jerked the limber man's arms free from the suit and yanked the jumpsuit down the guard's legs. "Oh, damn."

"What's wrong?" she said. "What's wrong, now?"

"I forgot to take his boots off. Now his pants won't come off."

"Relax," she said, handing Matt the flashlight and untying the man's boot laces. "I'll help."

Matt noticed that her hands now appeared steady as she took the man's boots off. Then she reached for the light and told Matt to finish what he had to do. In less than a minute Matt had removed his own jacket and put the blue coveralls on over his other clothes. Matt took a long breath to steady his nerves.

"Let's go." Matt said. Then he slung the backpack over his shoulders and picked up the Remington shotgun as he reached to take the flashlight from Medora.

She didn't hand it to Matt but moved the light's beam to the dead man's hairy legs. "What about him?"

"He's not going anywhere," Matt said taking the light out of Medora's hand, and moving in the direction the man had come. Matt stopped after only a few steps. He turned back toward Medora and the boy who were staying close behind me. "Cousin, is this the way to the cave?"

"Aya," said the boy.

"How far?"

"Not far."

"I'm gonna lead the way with the flashlight on," Matt said. Then he remembered something important. Matt felt in the dead man's jumpsuit pocket that he was wearing and found a thin billfold in its right rear pocket. After pulling the wallet out, opening it and shinning the light inside, Matt said, "Robert Daily."

"My name be Robert, too," said the boy.

"Oh, crap," Matt said.

"What's wrong?" asked Medora.

"I bet the man didn't go by the name, Robert," Matt said. "He could be a Bobby, like Cousin, or Bob, or Rob. Damn. Nothing I can do about it now, anyway! So, let's go. And stay about five feet behind me and out of sight until we get to the cave. Okay?"

Neither Medora nor Cousin said anything.

"That okay?" Matt said a little louder.

"Sure," said Medora. "Lead the way."

Cousin said, "How you gonna find the cave if'n I'm the one that knows?"

"Okay, okay," Matt said. "You stay right behind me and tell me which way to go. Understand?"

"Sure," said Cousin. "I be telling you to go gee or haw"?

"What the hell is gee and haw?" Matt said.

Medora said, "You don't have to curse."

Ignoring the woman, Matt knelt in front of the boy and asked in a calmer voice, "What's gee and haw mean?"

"Gee means go right. Haw means go left."

"Why?" Matt said with all the composure he could muster, but feeling like the top of his head was about to explode. It had been a long time since his body felt this juiced on adrenaline.

"Grandpaw say it to his mules when he want's 'em to go right and left."

Medora giggled.

"I'm a mule, huh?" Matt said.

"I just knows it best that way," said the boy.

"Again, which one means to go right?" Matt said.

"Gee," answered the boy in an impatient voice.

"Okay. We ready this time?" Matt said turning away. "I hope so, 'cause this cussing mule's getting the hell outta here, with, or without you."

CHAPTER THIRTY-ONE

Sarah jumped when a deep male's amplified voice boomed out from somewhere in the woods beyond the fence. "Emmanuel. Mark Belcher, you must give yourself up, now." The man sounded angry. "You are responsible for the death of a fine, decent man with a wife and two small children. Give yourself up before more people die and there is more blood on your hands."

In the sanctuary, Sarah had no trouble hearing what the man said, and neither did Emmanuel, sitting in his high-backed pulpit chair. Emmanuel's eyes narrowed and an internal fire illuminated his face. Everyone else in the room stood frozen, listening to the man's words and watching their leader for any sign of his coming intentions. Luke, whose skin had turned a bluish-gray, still lay on his back staring at, but not seeing the ceiling. Two guards stood next to him with no expression on their faces.

"Get him out of here," said Emmanuel between clinched teeth to the two guards. "He's the lucky one. It's all over for him." The men hauled Luke out the back door.

Emmanuel pointed a shaking finger at Leaky Water. "Get the private dick out of here, too. And one of you needs to stay back there and watch him." Otis and another guard grabbed Leaky under the arms and drug the half-conscious man out the back door.

The man talking over the loudspeaker waited almost a minute before speaking again. "Emmanuel, you might as well give up and come out. We'll never leave this mountain. We're going to stay here for however long it takes, until you give yourself up. We'll never leave this post. That is a promise."

One guard reentered the room after being gone only seconds. Otis stayed behind to guard Leaky.

The voice outside who had to be a government's representative paused for a long moment, then said, "Do you want the blood of all these people on your hands? Are more innocent people going to die before you're willing to give yourself up to us? I beg of you, come out yourself, or allow your people to come out. We will not harm them. We will feed them and shelter them from the cold."

Emmanuel shifted his eyes toward Irene. "Get me the microphone. Hook it up. And hurry."

Irene's bulk quivered as she took short quick steps to the back of the pulpit and slung open a cabinet door in the rear wall. With a steady hand she pulled out a black, wireless microphone and laid it on the floor beside her. Then, she flipped a switch and turned a dial on the large chrome amplifier. She picked up the microphone, pushed a tiny button on its side, and tapped its black, ball-shaped head with her finger. The thud of Irene's finger striking the microphone reverberated down the mountain.

Irene crossed the platform and handed the mechanism to her savior. Emmanuel took the microphone from Irene without looking at her and brought it to his lips. From across the room Sarah heard the magnified puffs of his breaths striking the sensitive microphone.

They sat there in relative silence for over a minute before the government agent from outside the compound spoke again. "Emmanuel, you need to…"

Before the man could finish his statement, Emmanuel screamed over the speaker, "That is who I am. You are talking to The Anointed One. Emmanuel, himself."

"Please, listen to me," said the government agent.

"No," screamed Emmanuel. "You will listen to me. If you interrupt me again this conversation is finished. First, the blood of no one is on my hands. I did not ask that poor man to come stand at our gate and not let me or my people pass in and out. His blood is on the hands of whoever sent him, not mine. He should have been home with his wife and children. It is not my fault. He should be alive now."

Emmanuel's paused a short moment to catch his breath, then spoke again in a low, calmer voice. "Before the sun comes back to this mountain tomorrow morning, you will see that me and my people will be free at last. Free from the bondage of a society like yours where people cannot follow their leader and believe in their God the way they please."

"Emmanuel," said the man outside the compound. "Think about all those lives you control. All those children."

"I am," Emmanuel said. "They are my children, and I love them very much. I am going to call them all inside with me, now. And don't think you government demons can come waltzing in here once they leave the gate and come inside. If you step one foot inside this compound, all will perish. You remember Waco, don't you? You remember how all those people perished in flames created by you, don't you? Their blood is on your hands. Don't cover your hands with the blood of my people, too."

"Don't do it, Emmanuel," said the man.

Without either man seeing the other, they continued to argue over the lives of hundreds of people, the very same people who silently listened to the battle erupting over their right to live, to see the morrow, to grow older by just one day.

"Go away, now," said Emmanuel, "and all will live. Stay and all will die. It is up to you."

"No," screamed the man. "You control their destiny. Only you and no one else."

"Are you going to leave this mountain?" said Emmanuel.

"Never," said the man.

"There is no need in us talking any longer."

"Wait," said the man. "Why?"

"My brothers and sisters," said Emmanuel in his calm voice. "Quickly, and quietly get up and come inside the sanctuary. We must be together, so hurry."

"Emmanuel," said the man over the microphone. "Talk to me. We can work everything out. We'll get you help. There's no sense in all those people dying. Please! Listen to me. Talk to me."

"Come inside, my people," said Emmanuel. "We must be together, now."

"Emmanuel, no!"

Without an accompanist, Emmanuel started to sing in his baritone voice over the microphone,

> "Precious Lord, take my hand,
> Lead me on, let me stand.
> I am tired. I am weak…"

Still sitting in a chair on the pulpit, Sarah jumped when the double doors to the sanctuary swung open and people with blank expressions started pouring inside. Without hesitation, the men started moving to the left section and the women to the right. A few of the older men hugged their wives. One couple kissed before separating as though they knew they would never be together again in this world.

> "When my life is almost gone
> Hear my cry, hear my call."

While continuing to sing Emmanuel moved to the edge of the pulpit and motioned with his hand for everyone to enter. He tuned the microphone off but continued to belt the song from deep in his lungs.

Sarah held her breath until she saw Crystal and Tommy entering the door. With a frightened expression on her face, Crystal hurried down the aisle, moved past Emmanuel and onto the pulpit next to Sarah. She handed Tommy to her and sat in the chair beside Sarah. The boy grabbed his mother and squeezed. Sarah lost control. Tears rolled down her face and onto the boy's arm—a tiny arm that clung to her neck.

Most of the people now sang along with Emmanuel and their solemn voices filled the room.

> "At the river I stand, guide my feet, hold my hand, take my hand precious Lord,
> lead me home."

CHAPTER THIRTY-TWO

Matt, Medora, and Cousin Bobby stopped in the woods when they heard the two men talking over the loudspeaker. When Emmanuel's amplified voice reached them at the base of the mountain, Matt felt something akin to ice water flowing down his spine.

Emmanuel started singing at the end of the two men's conversation, and Matt realized what was about to happen at the compound. He started walking so fast that Medora and Cousin had trouble staying close behind him. It wasn't long until the singing stopped, and all Matt heard was the government agent pleading with Emmanuel to come out or let his people come out. Matt knew Emmanuel would never give in to the agency's demands.

The three trudged through the thick undergrowth for a few additional minutes when, out of the forest ahead of them, a man yelled, "That you, Robert?"

Matt froze.

The man yelled again, "See anything?"

Not moving, Matt trying to establish the location of the man's voice and what, if anything, he should say to him.

"Did you?" said the man, turning on a flashlight and searching through the woods. His position was only twenty feet ahead of Matt, and it was only a matter of seconds before he found them with his light.

"No," Matt said and sprinted toward the light. Matt turned on his stolen flashlight, brought it up, and placed the beam in the person's eyes trying to blind the man.

"Slow down. Why you running?" said the blond man in a blue guard's jumpsuit like the one Matt now wore.

Closing to within a couple of feet from where the guard stood, Matt flipped off the flashlight, brought it up, then slammed it down across the top of the man's head with all the strength in his body.

With only a quick groan, the guard crumbled to the ground at Matt's feet. The man's flashlight rocked back and forth in the grass beside his head

With his own light off, Matt grabbed the flashlight from the ground and shone it into the man's face. Blood spewed from a flat, crushed nose as the unconscious man, trying to get air, choked on his own body fluids. Matt flipped him on his stomach, jumped on the man's shoulders, and jerked the guy's arms behind his back. Taking off his own backpack, Matt reached inside, pulled out a pack of twenty-inch, black plastic ties, and jerked one out of the pack. He laced it around the man's wrist, interlocked its clasp and pulled the end tight so that the guard's hands stayed securely locked together on his back. The man's choking sound stopped as his blood now flowed on the ground.

Standing behind Matt, Cousin Bobby said, "You see that damn face on that guy?"

"Yes," Medora said in a whisper.

"Cousin," Matt said, reaching in his backpack for the flashlight he had brought from the boat.

"Aya," said the boy.

"Hold this," Matt said, handing him the guard's glowing flashlight.

The boy did as ordered.

Turning on his own light, Matt got up. "Come on, Cousin, show me the cave. There's not much time left."

Walking beside Matt as he followed the boy, Medora said between breaths, "You think that Emmanuel's...going to kill everyone?"

"Yes," Matt said. "I can't lie to you anymore."

"What are we going to do?" she said now falling in behind Matt.

"Try and stop him, what else?"

"But how?" she said.

Matt didn't answer her. He had no idea what he was going to do when we got there. Without warning, Cousin slipped out of Matt's sight between two cedar trees.

"Where you going?" Matt almost screamed at him.

"In the cave," said the boy, pushing his head back through the tree limbs and glaring up at them.

"Okay, go," Matt said, turning Cousin around and pushing him back through the trees. Matt didn't have to check to see if Medora was keeping up. She bumped into his ass and held to the back of his jumpsuit.

"Here it is," said Cousin stopping just past the trees. In front of Matt was a black hole between two large rocks. He noticed the musty smell as a steady but light breeze sucked at his back and ran up the tunnel's shaft.

"Does this lead directly to the compound?" Matt said, shining the light deeper into the cavity.

"I don't know," said Cousin. "I never go in. They go in, they come out, here."

"All right," Matt said. "You can stay out here and wait on us, or you can go back to the boat and take it across to your cousin's dock. Whatever you want."

"I go with you," said Cousin.

"I don't think so."

"I go with you," said Cousin crossing his arms over his chest.

"Damn, damn, damn," Matt said, stepping past the boy and along the worn path. He didn't have time to argue. "Stay behind me, and be quiet."

They entered the cave and, after climbing a continuous incline up the narrow path for several minutes, they reached a larger hollowed-out cavern. In haste, Matt searched the large room with several other tunnels leading out of it. For a moment, Matt almost panicked, because he didn't know which one to take. Then he noticed that only one of them led upward at the same angle they'd been walking. With only a slight hesitation, Matt entered the dark shaft while his companions followed. The air sucking at his back made him feel more confidant that he'd made the correct choice.

The shaft's twisting path led steadily upward, and in only a short time they came to a small wooden footbridge leading across a deep chasm. This construction told Matt he'd picked the right tunnel. He pushed forward, and two hundred feet after crossing the bridge they came to a set of wooden, circular steps going straight up a shaft. Standing at the base of the steps, Matt shined the light up the steps but couldn't see beyond their first turn.

"Stay here," he said moving up two steps.

"In the dark" said Medora. "Are you crazy? I'm coming, too." She pulled Cousin up the staircase with her as they stayed on Matt's heels.

"Damn, damn, damn," Matt said under his breath.

"What's wrong?" she said.

"Nothing," he said and continued upward without turning back.

After climbing three turns on the creaking stairs, Matt came to a small four-foot square landing in front of a wooden door. When he stopped, Medora and the boy were moving so fast and staying so close behind him that they hit him in the back and knocked his face into the closed door. Grimacing at them, he shined the light back down the steps. he calculated that the stairs rose almost twenty-five feet above the cave floor, and that he'd already ascended a considerable distance since entering the cave.

Medora was the only one having trouble catching her breath as she panted with an open mouth. Matt turned back to the door and inspected its latch. He felt like jerking it open, but he hovered there trying to decide his next move. He knew somebody, maybe someone with a weapon, might be standing on the other side.

"What are you waiting on, go!" Medora half whispered. She reached for the door's lever-type latch.

"Hold on," Matt said jerking her hand away. He ran his left hand along the edges of the door. Air blew out through narrow cracks at its top and along its latch side. "Turn off your light, Cousin."

The boy did.

Matt wheeled to face Medora and the boy who were standing too close to him. "I'm gonna turn my flashlight off, so don't panic. Okay?"

Medora nodded her head, and Matt flipped off the light. Darkness enveloped them. Matt waited almost a minute trying to let his eyes adjust to the absence of light, then he tried to detect any sign of light coming through the cracks in the door by placing his eyes next to the air-sucking cracks along the seal. He saw nothing, no light.

"Stand back," he said still in total darkness. "I'm gonna try to open the door."

"I'm not moving," argued Medora too loud. "And don't you either, Cousin. We might just fall down that flight of stairs and break our necks."

Matt flipped on the flashlight, shined it in Medora's face, and screamed in a whisper, "Shut up, Miss Meehan, you're about to piss me off. I know you're not accustomed to taking orders, but you do exactly what I tell you, and don't even think about questioning what I say, or you won't have to worry about falling down those damn steps, 'cause I'll push you down 'em. I don't have time to explain to you every little thing I do. What I say goes, understand?"

"Sure," said Medora with an expression of what-did-I-do on her up-turned face. "Whatever you say."

"Okay," Matt said realizing if anyone was close to the other side of the door they could have heard him yelling and were probably waiting on them with a loaded shotgun.

"Why are you mad?" she said.

"I'm not mad, dammit," Matt said, turning off the flashlight, reaching for the door latch and compressing it. It made a clicking sound and he froze, waiting for someone to jerk the door open and start blasting away with a gun. Nothing happened. He counted to ten in his head, took a deep breath, and slowly pushed open the door.

Matt vaulted through the opening, holding the shotgun in one hand and the extinguished flashlight in the other, assumed a kneeling position and glanced around the room. He found himself in a dimly lit storage room about the size of a two-car garage. There were cardboard boxes and wooden crates against the wall and out on the floor. Faint light filtered through a dirty window situated next to a door directly across from where he knelt. Feeling relieved that no one was there, Matt stood and tiptoed to the center of the room.

"Psss," he hissed back toward the cave door. "Come on."

Without checking to see if they complied with his orders, Matt tiptoed to the window and peered through its lower right corner. But he stayed ready to pull his head back if anyone was there looking in. Searching the open area beyond the window, he saw nobody. At first, Matt only saw a lone security light, dangling from a creosote-covered utility pole. It cast a ghostly, yellowish radiance amid the leaves that were scattered across the ground. In only a moment his eyes adjusted, and he noticed a very large building halfway beyond the security light.

The white, wooden structure sat about two hundred feet away and slightly uphill from him. Matt realized he was probably seeing only the back of the building and part of one of its sides. In the back of it, he saw a ten-by-ten-foot uncovered deck leading up one step to a single door. Over the door, a light fixture gave off a minimal orange glow. It surprised Matt that he could detect no window either on the side or back of the building.

About the time he decided the large building beyond the light was the sanctuary where Emmanuel now held his people, a loud crashing noise erupted behind him.

He flinched, then whirled around to see Medora and Cousin moving away from a small wooden box that had hit the floor and now rested on its side. From the box radiated a steady clacking, rattling sound. Medora's piercing scream added to the chaos. Matt jumped across the room and clasped his hand hard across her mouth. She fought and tried to pull away from him, but, with one hand on the back of her neck and the other over her head, Matt squeezed so hard he thought he might break her neck. In seconds she gave in, stopped fighting, and stood trembling in his hands.

"Shhhh," he said next to her ear just like the old man did to him a long time ago when he awoke frightened from the nightmare. "You're gonna bring something deadlier than a rattlesnake in here if you scream again. Shhhh." With caution Matt removed his hand from her mouth but held it ready to use again if she yelled. He kept his other hand on the back of her neck for a long moment listening to her rapid breathing. Even the snake had stopped rattling and now lay quietly in its box. Cousin had moved back to the cave entrance door ready to bolt down the steps.

"Don't move, you two," he ordered, sliding back to the window to see if anyone heard Medora scream and was now approaching. At first, he didn't see anyone, but when he looked closer, he noticed that the back door to the building now stood open. In the dark shadows of the landing, he caught sight of the minute but bright red glow of a cigarette. When the person smoking brought the cigarette to his mouth and pulled in a puff, Matt saw that it was a man dressed in a jumpsuit—a jumpsuit exactly like the one he'd taken off the guard at the river and now wore.

"What is it?" said Medora, speaking directly over Matt's shoulder while trying to see out the window. "What about that snake?"

"I told you not to move," Matt said. "It's in a cage and not going to hurt anybody, so be quiet."

"But, but," she said. "What's that out there?"

"A man," Matt whispered. The door to the sanctuary rolled open and a bright, white light poured from its half-opened backdoor. Matt tried to see what was inside the building by squinting his eyes, but all he could see was a stack of portable water coolers in the floor.

When Matt saw another man walking around the side of the building toward the open backdoor, he moved back, bumping into Medora. A shotgun hung from the man's side. The man turned the corner and walked up to the open porch. The other man smoking in the shadows dropped his cigarette to the ground, stomped it out, and then reached down, got the cigarette butt, and placed it in his pocket.

Medora's warm breath struck the side of Matt's face. It irritated him, and he wanted to send her back through the cave and out of his sight. He didn't care if he ever laid eyes on her again.

At the sanctuary door the two men in matching jumpsuits stood talking for almost a minute when the one that had approached from the side turned away from the other and continued his march along the back of the long structure. Matt watched him until the man disappeared around the far corner. Matt figured that the walker was circling the building as a lookout. The cigarette-smoking guard reentered the back door and closed it behind him.

Matt turned around to face Medora. "That's where Sarah and Leaky are. I've got to get in there."

"But how?" Medora said. "What can you do with all those guards?"

Matt grabbed Cousin's overall straps and pulled him away from the window without answering Medora, because he didn't have a clue as what he should do.

Pulling away from Matt, the boy said, "Use the arrows."

"Do what?" Matt said.

"Shot 'em with the arrows," said the boy backing away from them.

"You mean the guards?" Matt said.

"Aye," said the boy still shuffling backwards.

"I'd thought of that," Matt said. But how to get inside the building and then save his friend had not come to him yet. Matt closed his eyes trying to think when Cousin accidentally stumbled into the wooden box on the floor, and started the snake rattling again. Medora grabbed onto Matt, but this time she held her scream. A second snake began its steady buzz and then a third, until their rattling vibrations filled the tiny room. Matt took off his backpack, unfastened the crossbow, and pulled out the arrows.

"You can't expect to do anything with that, can you?" Medora said with a nervous laugh. "Use your guns."

"I need to get rid of the guard walking around the building without anybody hearing me," Matt said, while assembling his crossbow and arranging the arrows. He didn't like to use the word "kill," but that's what he planned to do. "Then I've got to take care of the smoker when he comes out the backdoor. I hope he's the only one in the back 'cause when I take care of him I can get inside that way."

"What're you going to do when you get inside?"

Matt reached in his backpack, dug out a palm-size cell phone, and handed it to Medora. "If anything happens to me call 226-1111. That's the sheriff's office. If you can't remember that, dial 911. I don't know what they can do but...anyway here's a phone." Matt turned to go, then spun back. "While I'm gone, I want y'all to count the snakes and see how many we got in here."

"Why?"

"I got a plan."

"What? I don't like snakes."

"Me neither," said Cousin.

"You don't have to hold 'em, just count 'em," Matt said. With Medora hanging on his back and trying to ask another question, Matt walked through the shed door and outside. He was finally alone.

CHAPTER THIRTY-THREE

When Otis reentered the back room with the stench of cigarette smoke chasing after him, Leaky realized why the tobacco-addicted guard had left him alone in the back room for the last five minutes. The smell made Leaky want to vomit, but at least his headache had started to ease, and he had finally growing accustomed to the throbbing in his swollen eye although he still couldn't see clearly out of it.

Otis bent at the waist and leaned over Leaky. "What you looking at?"

Uncomfortable, in a wooden chair with his hands still tied helplessly behind his back, Leaky looked up at Otis with a grin. "Da man."

"You better believe, I'm the man," said Otis shaking his head like a fighting cock that had just spurred a foe.

Just before Otis had left to go for a smoke, and, while the people continued to sing, the fat woman called Irene and another woman, a redhead called Myra, had come in this backroom to fill coolers with water and divide the cyanide capsules into six separate bottles for the six women who would hand them out. All the while, Leaky pretended to sleep. After Irene and Myra reentered the sanctuary, Otis went out to smoke. That's when the singing in the sanctuary had stopped and Emmanuel started preaching and praying that everyone believe in him and follow his instructions.

Presently, while watching Otis shake his head up and down, Leaky wondered what would happen to him now, and how he could escape this hell he had discovered. His wrists continued to ache with the tight binding cutting into his skin. He had given up trying to free his hands and decided to try using his wit to see if he could talk his way out of bondage. "I like that hairdo your leader's got."

"Huh?"

"Great hairdo," said Leaky. "He's got enough grease in his hair to fry chicken."

"What you talking about?"

"Your leader," said Leaky. "He's your Jesus, ain't he? And he's going to kill everybody, ain't he?"

"He knows what he's doing," said Otis.

"Would you die for him?"

"I don't know," said Otis pacing the floor now. "I guess so. He probably ain't going to kill everybody. He likes to test us to see if we're loyal."

"Like he did his brother?" Leaky pointed with his head toward Luke who laid in the far corner with blank eyes staring at nothing.

"Huh?"

"Was he testing his brother's loyalty? You know, the brother over there deader that 4'o'clock. Did he pass Emmanuel's loyalty test?"

"He loved his brother," said Otis as though that were all he needed to say to prove a moot point. "We trust him."

"Yeah," said Leaky. "Trustin' him's like taking a crap with ya pants on."

"Huh? What you talking about, taking a crap with you pants on?"

"Yeah, do that, and you're going to get shit all over your ass."

"You shut it up, and I mean now! I ain't talking to you no more. You don't know nothing about trust, loyalty, or even love, so shut up!"

Thinking about a Country and Western song, Leaky asked, "You ever fried bacon naked, Otis?"

"What the hell you talking about? I don't go naked."

"Loving Emmanuel's like frying bacon necked. You gonna get your shitty ass burned."

"You want to die, nigger?" said Otis now back nose to nose with Leaky. "You ready to die, colored boy?"

"Wow, Otis," said Leaky mockingly. "I didn't mean to make you mad. Relax, now."

Slapping at one pocket then another, Otis reached inside his jumpsuit and yanked out a green-and-white pack of Kool cigarettes. He put one of the smokes in his mouth, then jerked it out. Panting like a hungry dog, he stared at Leaky with eyes as wide as quarters and all the time rolling a cigarette in his fingers.

Leaky frowned and said, "Emmanuel don't mind you smoking?"

"Shut the hell up."

"I sure would like one of them smokes," said Leaky. "You know, if I'm going to die, then I sure would like to have one last cigarette. I can taste it now. Um, um, good!"

"Gonna die, hell, you're already one dead nigger."

"Nigger ain't a nice word, Otis. Specially from a Christian man like you."

"Shut up! You're making me mad!"

"Calm down, now Otis, you're going to have a coronary."

"Huh!"

"I tell you what, Otis. Before you get too excited, let's go outside and have one last smoke. What do you say, Otis?"

"I don't know. I might get in trouble." Otis now paced faster back and forth before Leaky.

"You can take me outside and fire yourself one up and give me a puff or two. Okay, Otis? What do you say to a dying man? Okay?"

Otis stopped and looked down at Leaky. "But what if they ask me why I took you outside?"

"Tell 'em I got sick and you didn't want me to disturb the services in there." Leaky pointed toward the sanctuary with his head.

"I don't know."

"I know what we can do," said Leaky with enthusiasm. "Tell 'em I had to piss and you didn't want me to piss my pants. I know. I'll say I had to piss."

"You will?"

"Sure, Otis I'd do anything for a good old puff of one of those Kools going down in my lungs. Yes, sir. I can taste it now."

Otis licked his lips, looked at the closed door to the sanctuary and then to the door leading outside on the porch. "Okay, but if you give me any trouble you're a dead nig...dead colored boy."

"Don't you worry your head about that, Otis. I'll be the best man you ever killed."

"You promise?"

"Yes, sir," said Leaky, slowly getting to his feet. Otis opened the door leading outside, stepped back, and motioned Leaky to move toward it.

Somewhat light-headed from his previous beatings, Leaky stumbled a step, got his balance and took a deep breath of chilly air being sucked inside the room; air so cold it burned his throat. Then, he felt the steel of Otis' shotgun shoved against his back pushing him toward the open door.

CHAPTER THIRTY-FOUR

Matt took a deep breath and held the front sight of the taut crossbow on the person exiting the open backdoor of the sanctuary. He prepared to compress his right index finger, which would release the steel arrow into the person's chest. As Matt's finger tightened, he noticed another person still inside the building and directly behind the man. Because the light from inside the room was behind the two in the shadow of the door, they appeared as only dark silhouettes in his sights. Although Matt lay in the grass only twenty feet away from the porch, he couldn't see any of their personal features. Relaxing his index finger, Matt decided to hold his fire for the moment.

With his heart pounding and brain racing like someone on speed, Matt couldn't decide what to do next. Finally, he opted to act fast. He planned on shooting the lead person, grabbing his own knife and charging the other man before he could react. It would be a risky maneuver, but Matt didn't feel as though he had another choice. He couldn't use his Smith and Wesson without announcing to Emmanuel that an intruder had entered his camp.

Luckily, Matt continued to stay composed. He expected hand tremors to hit him much later, after everyone was safe—if that ever happened—if he didn't die first. But Matt couldn't think about that now. While watching the two men walk through the door, Matt tried forcing his brain to forget about dying or death, even after all the killing he'd done this day.

His latest kill, still warm, lay out of the light in the blackness directly behind him under some low growing laurel bushes. He'd just finished dragging the dead guard there. It seemed like an hour, but it'd only been five minutes since he'd stood on the other side of the building, hiding behind the trunk of a large oak tree, waiting on the man he'd seen earlier walk full circle around the building. When the man had gotten to within ten feet of Matt, he stepped out from behind the tree with his crossbow aimed at the man's breastbone. The surprised guard had stopped and started to bring his shotgun up when Matt pressed the crossbow's trigger. The arrow made a zinging noise as it sped the short distance before piercing the man's torso with a slicing thud. The guard staggered backward two steps, and then strength left his legs as they crumbled under him. By hitting the guard in the chest, Matt's arrow had knocked the wind out of the man on contact, preventing him from crying out. By the time the man got his wind back, his severed heart had ceased beating and he lay dead in the footpath. Matt was glad that it'd been a quick kill, and he'd not had to use his knife to slice the man's throat. Like Vietnam, like earlier tonight, that kill lay in Matt's past now. He couldn't go back. He had to forget about it and think about surviving.

Presently, lying on damp leaves, Matt kept the crossbow's sight on the lead man's chest as he walked into the faint glow of the light hanging over the door. Once they were through the door the man in the rear kicked the door shut and the brighter light from within vanished. When this happened, Matt could see both men's faces under the yellow light and Matt's heart turned over in his chest with a heavy thump. With a battered face and hands tied behind his back, Leaky turned and walked to the side of the building. All the while the guard held a shotgun to Leaky's back. Matt shivered realizing that only a moment ago He'd almost killed his best friend—maybe, his only friend.

Anger replaced Matt's shock when he looked closer at Leaky's swollen eye and realized he'd been beaten and beaten severely. Again, Matt brought the crossbow's sight to his eye.

Leaky and the guard moved off the landing and into the long shadows next to the wall. The guard placed a cigarette in his mouth. Matt took a deep breath, lined the sight on the man's upper torso, and curved his index finger around the trigger. Because the man's side faced him, Matt had to wait until the guard turned, so he could hit him full in the chest with the steel arrow.

The guard struck a match on the building's wall, and a flame ignited in his hand. He brought the fire to his cigarette, took a long drag, and smoke boiled from his mouth and nose.

Turn, damn you! Matt thought.

The guard stuck the lighted cigarette in Leaky's mouth. Matt watched while his friend took a long draw of smoke. This surprised Matt, because he knew that Leaky had stopped smoking long ago. Leaky coughed, but Matt could see him trying to hold it back. Something looked wrong with the scene before Matt, and that made him hesitate.

The guard took the cigarette away from Leaky and leaned against the wall with a shotgun relaxed in the crook of his right arm. His chest now faced Matt, perfectly. The guard placed his right foot against the back of the building for support and took another puff. With the thin sight aligned on the middle of the guard's chest, Matt took in a deep breath then held it to steady his hands. Matt placed his finger around the trigger.

When the backdoor burst open and light flooded the deck, Matt flinched. A fat woman wearing a white nurse's outfit stomped outside screaming, "Otis, where the devil are you?"

Matt relaxed his finger and exhaled. Behind this "lard ass" woman walked two men dressed in blue jumpsuits like the man with Leaky—like Matt. Through the open back door, Matt saw other men in blue jumpsuits picking up water coolers and taking them through a door that opened into the sanctuary. Matt wondered why they needed water coolers inside the sanctuary. Then it hit him like a jolt of electricity—the coolers had something to do with poisoning the people.

The fat nurse Matt thought might be Irene stopped at the edge of the porch, placed her hands on her hips, and spread her feet. "Otis, what in the world do you think you're doing out here with that nigger?"

"He got sick, I mean he had to piss, pee, yeah, he had to pee," said Otis.

"And you had to have a smoke," said the woman.

"Well, uh…he had to…"

She stomped her right foot and pointed a finger at Otis. "Shut up. I don't want to hear another excuse out of you. It's about to start. In half-an-hour we're giving out the pills and it'll be over for everybody, even you, Otis. So get that nigger up here, and y'all go inside, now."

That confirmed it, Matt knew the answer, people were about to die inside the sanctuary.

Otis grabbed Leaky and jerked him toward the porch. Leaky stumbled forward almost tripping as he stepped up on the landing. Anger boiled inside Matt with no safety valve for release. He pulled the Smith and Wesson from its holster and pointed it at Irenes but stopped before pulling the trigger. Matt's teeth ground together.

Irene grabbed Otis by the arm. "Wait."

"Yeah?" said Otis, seizing Leaky by the back of the collar.

"He wants a snake," said the woman. "So, go get one."

"Who?" said Otis. "Emmanuel?"

"Yeah, dumb-ass!" she said, spit flying from her machine-gun mouth. "Never mind, you ignoramus! Take the nigger inside, and Walter'll go get the snake." She shook her head in disgust and pushed Otis in the back. "Go, now, move it, you moron."

Otis slapped the back of Leaky's head, and then shoved him through the backdoor. Matt jerked the pistol up, leveled its sights on Otis's back, and almost came up off the ground. But he waited. Leaky and Otis disappeared inside.

"Walter," said Irene. She turned to the tall man behind her. The guard's body went erect as she turned to face him. "Go get the biggest rattler we got and bring it in. Hurry! Go!"

Walter only nodded. Then he turned with his shotgun in one hand and jumped off the porch.

"Wait," said Irene.

Walter stopped.

She said, "Bring it inside when you get it, but keep it at the back of the pulpit until he asks for it. Hurry!" She opened the door then turned back toward Walter. "And it better be a big one."

Walter jogged toward the shed where Medora and Cousin hid. Matt almost jumped up to catch Walter but waited. Matt shoved the pistol pack in its holster. Before the door completely closed behind Irene, he leaped to his feet, knife in one hand, taut crossbow in the other, and sprinted after Walter. When he reached the security light between the two structures, Matt saw that Walter had already entered the shed, and the door stood open.

Reacting with little regard for his own safety, Matt raced to the side of the shed and hid against the wall next to its open door. A light came on inside and its glow spilled at Matt's feet. He tensed, ready to jump inside and kill, expecting to hear Medora scream. However, her scream never came. No one yelled. No one spoke. Matt figured Medora and Cousin had seen the guard coming and rushed back through the cave door. Matt told his body to relax. It wouldn't. Matt placed himself in a position so that when Walter exited the shed he couldn't see him unless he backed out of the door.

With his ear to the wall, Matt heard someone moving wooden boxes and knew that Walter was looking for the biggest snake. Rattling erupted inside. Matt's heart pounded so hard and so fast he thought that Walter might hear it. Matt clutched the armed crossbow across his chest and held his breath. Matt sensed Walter approaching the door. Waiting to kill or be killed, Matt pressed his head and back hard against the wall. The shed's light went off.

Unaware of danger, Walter walked through the door facing forward with his back to Matt whose lungs burned, starving for air. Matt brought the crossbow up and sighted it between the man's shoulder blades. Matt didn't know why, but he couldn't shoot Walter in the back. He had a name, Walter. Unaware of Matt, Walter continued to walk toward the big building, away from Matt. The distance between them swelled.

Matt knew he had to stop this man or his plan wouldn't work, and everyone inside would die. _Do something_! Matt screamed in his head. Then, Matt yelled, "Hey!"

Thirty feet away, Walter froze, box in one hand shotgun in the other. Matt held the crossbow's sight as steady as he could, took a deep breath, held it, and waited. Walter turned his head without moving his body.

A danger signal flashed through Matt's racing brain. Walter dropped the box, brought the shotgun toward his shoulder while turning his body to face the shed where Matt stood. A rattling poured from the box on the ground at Walter's feet.

Matt knew he'd have only one chance. Failure meant death. His lungs burned. Why had he refused to shoot Walter in the back? As in a slow-motion scene from a movie, Walter's shotgun leveled onto Matt's chest. The rattlesnake buzzed louder. _How stupid_ was the last thought that raced through Matt's brain before squeezing the trigger and feeling the slight recoil of the crossbow.

CHAPTER THIRTY-FIVE

It could have been the dim light, or it could have been the stress of having a shotgun pointed at his chest that made Matt jerk the crossbow upward. But regardless, Matt missed his mark by almost a foot. It was not a clean, quick kill as before.

Instead of hitting Walter in the middle of the chest, as Matt had intended, the barbed arrow struck Walter less than an inch below the thyroid cartilage, the Adam's Apple. Its tip sliced through skin, muscle, and cartilage tissue, then through thousands of arteries and veins before lodging in one of the cervical vertebrae. It failed to sever his spinal cord like a bullet would have. On impact, Walter flopped to the ground like a puppet with its strings cut. Fighting for his life, Walter's hands clutched at the wound at his throat, and his legs shuddered, heels striking the ground. It reminded Matt of a person having an epileptic seizure except for one thing: Instead of foam coming out of Walter's mouth, out rolled blood.

Throwing his crossbow down, Matt pulled his knife out of its sheath and ran to stand over the floundering man ready to finish the kill. Walter's eyes, wide with terror, stared up at Matt. With each of Walter's heartbeats, dark blood pumped from between his fingers. A low gurgling sound boiled from the wound in the man's throat as blood bubbles formed there with each exhalation and then disappeared with each faltering inhalation. A constant rattling spilled from the wooden box lying next to the perishing man.

Matt wanted to bury his knife in the man's chest and end it all, yet he realized the guard had little blood left and little time remaining. Around Matt's feet, the ground grew dark with Walter's vital body fluid. Because of this, Matt stepped to the side, unable to stop watching as death spread over the man. Matt felt sorry for the guard called Walter, dying here with a stranger, his killer standing over him, watching him, the last thing Walter's eyes would ever see.

Matt flinched backward as all at once, the man's arms shot to his side, his palms slapped in the dead leaves and his legs jerked more violently. The gurgling sound intensified for several seconds, then Walter's eyes went glassy, and then, air oozed from his wound in a long steady stream. His body went limp as life released him.

"Matt," Medora said from several feet behind. "Is he dead?"

"Wow," said Cousin next to Medora. "Look at all that blood. He looks like one of grandpa's stuck pigs. Wow."

"I hope he's dead," Matt said. Then, thinking about Leaky and all those about to join Walter in death, Matt reached down, grabbed a handful of the man's pant leg, and pulled Walter behind the shed out of sight. Medora, with arms folded across her chest, stood next to Cousin and watched. Matt came back, picked up the snake in the crate, and tried kicking leaves over the bloody spot on the ground, but when that proved useless, He gave up.

"What's happening up there?" Medora asked, following Matt back toward the shadows of the shed.

"Nothing, yet," Matt said, not telling her about the poison. "Give me the phone."

She reached inside Matt's jacket she wore, got the palm-size cellular phone, and handed it to Matt. He started dialing a number.

She said, "Who you calling?"

Matt didn't answer her but said in the phone after a few seconds, "This is Matt Fagan and I'm in...."

"Hi, sugar," said a woman's voice over the phone. "I haven't heard your sexy voice in a long time, why don't you come in and see us anymore?"

"Is this Brenda?" Matt said.

"Why honey, it sure is," said the woman. "I'm impressed you remembered me. Why don't you...."

"Brenda," Matt interrupted. "I'd love to talk, but I'm in a jam."

"What you need, Matt?"

"I'm inside the compound that the authorities have surrounded out on Cash Canyon Road."

"You're what?" she said. "How? I mean, you're not inside are you?"

"Yes, inside, and I just had to kill somebody."

"Who?" she said. "Tell me about it."

"I'd love to Brenda, but I've got to talk to whoever's in charge out here at the compound." Matt wanted to reach inside the phone and shake Brenda to alert her of the danger they faced, but, instead, he fought to stay calm. "You know, I really need to talk with the FBI agent in charge out here, or anybody that's presently outside the fence, ASAP. That crazy sonofabitchin' preacher is about to kill everyone inside. We've got less than thirty minutes before hundreds of his people start to die."

"What?" said Medora who stood next to Matt. She started toward the sanctuary.

"Hold on," Matt said grabbing the back of her collar. She tried to pull away but couldn't.

"Let me go," she screamed.

"Wait a minute, Brenda," Matt said into the phone. He pulled Medora to his face. "Don't fuck it up. Do what I say or so help me…I'll…I'll tie you up and leave you in that cave. You understand?"

After a few more twist and turns, she stopped and glared hard into Matt's eyes, fear radiating from her stare like a captured animal. Matt wanted to strangle her until he saw tears forming in her eyes. One trickled down her cheek.

Matt couldn't explain why, but he felt so sorry for her. He spoke gently like he would if talking to a child. "Don't worry, Mrs. Meehan. If I have to run in there and kill that sonofabitch and all his cronies, I'm not gonna let 'em use that poison. Okay? I don't have much time; so stand here and let me get something done. I don't want my friend to die anymore than you want your daughter to die. So trust me."

She relaxed as additional tears spilled from her blue eyes. For some unknown, bizarre, mixed up reason, Matt wanted to hold her next to him. He did, and she hugged Matt back. Strangely, Matt didn't know if it was for her comfort or his. He patted her, then released his grasp and she stepped backward and turned her gaze to the sanctuary.

"Brenda," Matt said in the phone as I continuing watching Medora's back.

"No," said a deep male's voice. "This is Agent Adam Ware. I'm talking to you from outside the compound. They tell me you're a private detective, and you've found a way inside the compound, right?"

"Yeah," Matt said. "We came in through a cave…"

"A cave," interrupted Agent Ware. "Where's this cave? And who are we? Who's with you?"

"That doesn't matter, now," Matt said. "We don't have that much time, and you wouldn't have time to find the cave. Listen to me."

"How do I know you're on the level—that you're who you say you are?"

"Find Deputy Joe Johnson, or ask Brenda," Matt said. "Surely, she told you who this is. You're going to have to trust me, or lots of people, innocent people are going to die."

"Wait just a minute, you sure?" said Ware.

"Hell yes," Matt said controlling his frustration by biting his lower lip. "You're the one that talked to him tonight over the speaker. You know he's going to kill them. He told you."

"How's he going to kill them?"

"Listen, Agent Ware," Matt said bluntly. "We don't have much time. So, listen very carefully. I think he's going to give them poison."

"Not explosives?"

"What?" Matt said. "I didn't see any explosives. Where'd you get that idea?"

"They sent a nurse out, and she said the building was wired with explosives, and if we came in Emmanuel had given orders to detonate the sanctuary."

215

"I didn't see explosives, but I wasn't looking for any. I'll check it out, but I bet it's a bluff. I'm looking at it right now, and there aren't any wires, boxes—nothing.

"We can't bet on people's lives. We've got to be sure."

"Well, I am sure of one thing," Matt yelled. "He's going to give them poison in less than twenty minutes, now. I saw it, and they've already taken them inside. I heard the fat nurse tell a guard that it would be over, and they'd all be dead in thirty minutes, and that was ten minutes ago."

"A hefty, nurse that looked like a bulldog?"

"Yeah. More like a lard ass bulldog."

"Okay," said Ware. "What you need from us?"

"Can you arrange to have the electric power to this compound turned off?"

"Yeah, I'm sure we can. Why?"

"Can you do it in ten minutes?"

Matt waited for an answer but only heard Agent Ware talking to someone else. As hard as Matt tried, he couldn't hear what Ware was saying. In a long two minutes Agent Ware was back on the line with Matt. "Yes we can, but I've got to know why."

"What's your direct line number?"

"Why?"

"Dammit, I need it."

Matt heard Agent Ware asking someone else. "What's this number?" Matt could hear someone speaking but not what they said. Ware came back on phone with Matt. "This number is 543-6107. Got it, 543-6107."

Matt repeated the number in his mind several time—etching it there, and then said, "If you were waiting and ready, and I called you back, how long would it take before the blackout?"

Matt sensed Ware talking to someone near again. Matt waited, glanced at his watch and fidgeting. It took almost two full minutes again before Ware returned to the line. "About twenty or thirty seconds, why?"

"I'll call back in about ten minutes and say only one word, 'now.' Then you turn off the power. Got it? I'll say, 'now.'"

"You got to tell me why."

"I don't have time to explain, but I'll be inside the sanctuary, and it'll be a matter of hundreds of lives, including my own if you don't come through on your end. Can I trust you?"

"How are you..." started Ware, but he stopped in mid-sentence.

"Time's running out," Matt said. "Be ready in eight minutes, please. It's a matter of life or death. I can't explain any more, or wait any longer. People are about to die. Good bye." Matt hit the *END* button and disconnected them. Matt trusted they would respond when he called back.

Matt moved a few feet away from the shed into the faint light cast by the security light and punched in the number five. The green light of the cell phone came on and he moved back into the shadows and punched in 543-6107. Matt placed the cell phone in the breast pocket of the blue jumpsuit he still wore.

"What's happening?" asked Medora. Tears had drawn black mascara lines down her cheeks.

"In the shed, hurry," Matt said. "Both of you." He sprinted to the spot where Walter had died, picked up the box containing the rattlesnake, and raced into the shed.

Once inside Medora said, "Where'd you go?"

Ignoring her, Matt grabbed the boy. "Where's the flashlight?"

Cousin went to the cave door, reached inside the dark hole, and brought one out. He turned it on and the circular beam bounced off the boxes in the shed.

"Give me the light," Matt said. Cousin did. "Medora, watch the building and if you see anybody moving up there let me know, so I can turn off this light."

She moved toward the window without questioning him this time.

Using the light, Matt searched the room for any type of large bag. He saw boxes of toilet paper and other supplies neatly stacked on the shelves. After what felt like an hour but probably no more than a minute, he found a large box that read HEFTY 32-gallon trash bags. Rushing, Matt pulled one out of the box and shook it until it filled with air.

"Hold this," Matt said handing Cousin the flashlight. "Shine it on this bag."

"Okay," said Cousin.

Matt moved to the box with the large rattlesnake that Walter had tried to take earlier. Holding the black plastic bag in one hand, Matt opened the lid, which covered most of the top of the wooden box. This caused the rattler to buzz violently. Stepping back one step, Cousin continued holding his light on the box. Matt had no time or little choice of how to get the serpent out, so he reached inside the crate and felt the cool but dry body of the rattlesnake. It felt as big around as his forearm. With one quick, steady movement, he lifted the six-foot wiggling piece of pure muscle from the box and shoved it in the plastic bag. The old woman had been right, Matt had no fear of the snake.

"Damn," said Cousin. "Damn!"

Moving to the next wooden carton, Matt pulled out a four-foot rattler and put it with the first snake. The bag grew heavy in his hand. In less than another minute, Matt had placed five canebrake rattlesnakes in the bag, each at least four feet long, along with two small pigmy rattlers, and all this without being bitten. Cousin kept saying "Wow or Damn" every time Matt took a snake in his hand and stuffed it in the bag. Matt couldn't explain why he had no fear of these deadly snakes. Maybe the old woman, Aunt Lucy, was right; he had the gift of the serpent.

When he lifted the bag after placing the last rattlesnake inside, it felt so heavy Matt was afraid the plastic would rip. He took another bag out of the box and double-bagged the snakes.

Hurrying over next to Medora who still stared out the window, Matt said, "Seen anything?"

"No."

"Okay," Matt said turning to Cousin who was staring. "You go back through the cave. It's going to get dangerous for little boys, I mean little men around here and besides, I can't be watching out for you and do all I've got to do." Matt patted Cousin on the head and handed him five folded twenty-dollar bills. Cousin didn't argue about staying this time. The young boy stuffed the bills in his pocket, took his flashlight, and moved through the cave door into the darkness.

"Okay," Matt said turning to Medora. "I'm going in the back door of the sanctuary. You staying or going?"

"I'm going," she answered. "I've got to find Sarah and my grandson."

"Whatever you say. Let's go," Matt said, lifting the heavy sack of squirming serpents and turning to make sure Cousin had left. "You're on your own once everything goes down, but try and stay close to me after finding your daughter. I'll try and keep an eye on you, but that's going to be hard to do. You got it?"

"Fair enough," she said following him out the door. "Don't worry about me."

They ran the rest of the way to the back porch without saying another word; she carrying his shotgun and Matt the snakes. Matt's boots made a thumping noise when he stepped upon the wooden decking and moved toward the closed door.

"All right," Matt said, between labored breaths. The snakes felt heavier than he had imagined. "Give me the shotgun." He put the bag down and took the weapon from her hands. "Stand back." Matt pumped the Remington, placing a round in the firing chamber.

Bending at the waist, Matt turned the doorknob and pulled the door open a crack. He heard a man, probably Emmanuel, talking, from an adjoining room, but Matt couldn't understand what he said. In one movement he swung open the door. Pointing the weapon in four directions at once, he bounced into the small room praying no one would be there. Emmanuel's rasping voice leaked through the wall.

Matt jumped after seeing something that looked like a person lying in the back corner of the small room. He swung the end of the Remington toward it and tensed his finger around the trigger. There lay a man—a very, very still man. Matt relaxed his grip and tiptoed toward him. It didn't take but an instant for Matt to realize his condition.

"He's dead?" said Medora in a whispered but startling Matt. He'd expected her to wait outside.

"Yeah," Matt said, retrieving the bag of snakes and sliding to the door leading into the sanctuary. Checking the wall beside the door, Matt noticed a single light switch and turned it off. Everything went dark. In a few seconds, he caught faint rays of light seeping under the sanctuary door. Matt reached for the doorknob, then remembered something. "Medora."

"Yeah," she whispered so close to his cheek he could feel the warm air from her breath.

"I'm gonna open this door a little bit. Then I'm going to try and see what and where everything is in there. Okay?"

"Sure."

"Then, when I move back, you take a look and find your daughter. Okay?"

"Yes."

One of the snakes rattled slightly, and it sounded very loud in the confined room. Matt froze until its buzzing died.

After taking a quick breath, Matt turned the knob and pulled the door toward him. Emmanuel's strong electrified voice soared inside the tiny room. "...and Jesus Himself ridiculed Caesar, the government of His time..."

When Matt had a crack of about a quarter-of-an-inch, he bent at the waist and peered inside. There stood Emmanuel, fifteen feet away with his back to Matt.

"...And Jesus followed God's signs, which He gave to His people, praise the Lord!"

Arranged in two rows of chairs, in a V shape, behind and on each side of Emmanuel sat about ten people. It didn't take long to find Leaky sitting beside Irene who wore the nurse's uniform. On the other side of Leaky, Matt saw the side of Crystal and beside Crystal sat a young blond mother holding a sleeping child of about two. In only a second, the mother turned her head slightly, and Matt saw enough of her face to confirm his hunch. Even with her puffy eye, Matt knew that Medora's daughter was beautiful.

Guards, in blue uniforms, stood with their shotguns around all three walls of the sanctuary. Five or six women in white nurse's uniforms poured Dixie Cups full of liquid from the coolers and put them on trays.

Emmanuel continued to preach, "And these signs shall follow them that believe."

Matt pulled his eye from the crack, turned to Medora and whispered next to her ear, "Good, your daughter is on the stage and so is Leaky. We'll have a better chance to get them out of here. It looks like Sarah has a black eye, so don't panic. Take a quick look and be careful."

Medora's eye went to the crack in the door.

Emmanuel continued, "They shall take up serpents; and if they drink any deadly thing, it shall not hurt them."

Medora pulled away and in the ray of light passing through the crack in the door, Matt saw her eyes had formed new tears.

Matt reached for the cell phone, lifted Medora's chin, and looked into her eyes. "I'm gonna call Agent Ware, now, and hopefully, he'll get the power cut off. When the lights go out, I expect we won't have much time before Emmanuel's people get some type of emergency lighting in there, because they probably have generators of their own. We've got to act fast, understand?"

She shook her head. "No. What are we going to do? What am I supposed to do?"

"You go to your daughter and get her and her son out this door and back to the shed. Crystal, the black girl next to Sarah, may go with you, or she may wait. Whatever, I'll meet you there with Leaky if everything goes as planned. If for some reason you know we're not going to get there, go on through the tunnel without us. There's a flashlight in my backpack beside the cave door. Give us a chance, though. Wait as long as possible before leaving us here. Okay?"

She nodded.

Matt went back to peep through the crack again. Irene stared at the door with an angry expression on her jowls. Matt didn't know if she saw him, or if she was upset that Walter and the snake had not returned. Nurses continued handing out the poison.

Emmanuel said, "One among you will take up a serpent—yes, a big, poisonous rattlesnake. Then, after that we'll all drink the 'salvation cocktail' that the nurses will pass among you. You must be a believer. You must trust God. You must trust me, or you will perish."

That statement made Matt move. He pressed the SND button on the cell phone and listened to the first ring, then a second ring. When no one answered on the third ring, his heart stopped. On the forth ring Agent Ward answered, "Yes! Hello!"

Taking a deep breath, Matt said, "Now. Turn the power off, now." After Matt pressed the END button, placed the phone back in his pocket, picked up the Remington with his right hand and a bag of rattlesnakes in the other, he kicked open the sanctuary door and, suppressing his fear, stormed inside the sanctuary ready to do battle with a self proclaimed Jesus. Or was it the devil?

CHAPTER THIRTY-SIX

Since the group's move to Raccoon Mountain, Sarah had always wondered if Emmanuel was insane, but now she had no doubts. Watching Emmanuel, Sarah leaned her mouth close to Crystal's ear. "You think he's insane?"

Crystal's eyebrows arched, she turned her head half way around to Sarah and whispered, "He's off the charts, madder than a hatter. He's traveling in another realm of absurdness without the slightest idea of what's real and what's not, and he really believes he's Jesus Christ. He's a schizophrenic if I ever saw one."

Sarah smiled, almost laughed, although she knew they were about to die. With Tommy asleep lying across her shoulder, she rocked him gently and watched this madman before her ranting and raving about the evils that lurked nearby. Her eyes burned with no more tears to keep them moist. Her arms ached with the weight of her life's blood sleeping there. Tommy's warming breath felt comforting against Sarah's neck. She gave him a squeeze and kissed him on his cheek. A cheek turned red and warm.

Sarah glanced at the young black man Emmanuel's guards had abducted and felt remorse for him and the rest of them. With a blank expression on his battered face, this innocent man watched the nurses, some holding bottles full of poison and others filling the cups with water. She wanted to weep, but she couldn't cry any more.

Turning her gaze forward to the upturned faces of a somber crowd listening to their Lord and Savior, Sarah felt compassion and deep sympathy for them. Blindly, many of them would eagerly die trying to prove their devotion to this demonic personage. No matter how hard she tried, Sarah couldn't understand why they failed to see the truth. And even if some of them suddenly realized the danger, and refused to follow him to death, the guards would butcher them like cattle in a slaughterhouse.

Emmanuel had prepared them for this day for so long with all of his loyalty tests and fake suicides. Most didn't understand their hopeless situation. The few who did probably denied it. Sarah saw the anguish in several of the guards' eyes. It's over, Sarah told herself.

"And in the book of Mark," preached Emmanuel. The pompadour of his black hair bounced with each accented word he spat out. Huge beads of perspiration squirted from a face turned crimson. The color of his skin showed through the white, sweat-filled shirt that clung to his shoulders and back like cellophane stretched over raw meat. Emmanuel grabbed his leather-covered Bible and started thumbing frantically through its pages. "It's here in the Gospels, in the book of Mark that reports the words of Christ before His ascension into the heavens." One page ripped in his hand, but he kept digging, searching. Frustrated, he slammed the open Bible on the podium, traced his fingers along its pages, and began to read with his nose in the Bible. "'And these signs shall follow them that believe; in my name shall they cast out devils; they shall speak with new tongues. They shall take up serpents and if they drink any deadly thing, it shall not hurt them; they shall lay hands on the sick and they shall recover.'"

Old man Burgess, without a tooth in his head, slapped a thick hand on his thigh and said, "Bless him, Lord." Then he clapped his hands together. "Praise God!"

"And in Luke," shouted Emmanuel, thumbing through the Bible with added fervor. "Yes...Here it is in Luke ten, nineteen. 'Behold, I give unto you power to tread on serpents and scorpions and over the power of the enemy: and nothing by any means shall hurt you.'"

Mr. Burgess was rocking back and forth in his seat with his head wobbling like it was on a loose spring. "Hallelujah, precious Jesus!"

Emmanuel seized his Bible, held it over his head, and said in a rasping voice, "One among you will take up a serpent with me—yes a big, poisonous rattlesnake." He shot a stern look at Irene.

"Me," shouted Mr. Burgess, leaping to his doddering feet and toppling backwards.

Another old man, Philip Lowe, put out a hand to steady Burgess and said, "Please Jesus, let it be me." A murmur spread like molten lava through the crowd until most chattered with their neighbors.

Sarah noticed that Irene stared hard at the backdoor, the door behind Sarah where they had kept the black man.

Emmanuel cleared his throat, paused, and looked at the floor. Finally, a hush fell over the group as all eyes locked upon him. His gaze shot up to meet his people. Although Sarah couldn't see his eyes, she could picture them in her mind's eye pleading. "Then, after the handling of the snakes we'll all take the 'pills of eternal life' that the nurses will now start passing among you. Don't drop them ladies. Don't waste a pill. Swallow them down, brothers and sisters. But wait until I tell you to. The nurses have prepared shots for the little ones that they'll start giving as soon as they've finished distributing the capsules and water."

The crowd began to moan, and some began to cry. Now, many more knew their fate.

"Calm down," Emmanuel said in a pleading voice. "God wants this. Trust me. I'll not lead you astray."

The women, the mothers, moaned the cry of death as women had done for thousands of years.

Emmanuel turned to Irene and put his hand over the microphone. "Where's that slimy-ass snake."

CRACK! The door shattered open behind Sarah. She turned, and there marched a guard carrying a shotgun in one hand and a black garbage bag in the other. As he moved toward the front where Emmanuel now stood with his open mouth, Sarah realized something didn't look right about this guard. It took only a moment for her to realize she had never seen him before, and, unlike the other guards, he wore a cowboy hat. By the time he reached Emmanuel, Sarah saw a scar on the right side of his face that agreed with the serious look in his eyes

Sarah didn't see the person moving behind the strange guard until the woman turned to face her. The woman opened her arms and said, "Oh, Sarah,"

Tears flooded Sarah's eyes. She stood, Tommy in her arms. "Mother!"

CHAPTER THIRTY-SEVEN

At first Emmanuel had a puzzled look in his eyes; that shocked look Matt had seen a few times from wild animals caught at night in the glare of a car's headlights. Emmanuel, Mark, Matt's brother, or whatever, didn't look as Matt had anticipated. In truth, Matt didn't know what he'd expected from a sibling he'd never known, met or even seen. Emmanuel looked much older and much more drawn than he'd foreseen. But his eyes, those ice-blue eyes made Matt's skin feel like ants were crawling all over it.

Dashing toward the front, Matt forced his eyes from this man and surveyed the room for a guard shouldering a weapon or rushing forward, but they only leaned forward staring up as though bored. Out of the corner of his eye, Matt saw the man next to Leaky rise, a relaxed shotgun across his chest. Matt realized the guard had not yet realized what had happened. Leaky stared up with a blank expression on his face, evidently not yet recognizing Matt.

Stopping before an opened-mouth Emmanuel and laying the squirming bag at his feet, Matt noticed puzzlement embedded on the perspiring face of his brother.

Matt had counted to five, and then six in his head, praying that soon the power would go off darkening the room.

With his senses powered by huge doses of adrenaline, Matt heard the click, an unmistakable gun-cocking sound coming from near by, but he couldn't locate it. Trying to stay calm, his eyes scanned the crowd. More chemical stimuli filled his blood stream, his heart thudding in his chest.

"Watch out!" shouted Leaky.

Matt stepped beside Emmanuel, brought his Remington up, wheeled back toward Leaky who sat only ten feet away and saw the standing guard with his 12-gauge shotgun in a firing position on his shoulder. For an instant, Matt looked down the dark barrel of the shotgun. The guard, who had been outside smoking with Leaky earlier, hesitated only the slightest moment, probably because his god, Emmanuel, stood too close to this intruder. It didn't matter why, he wavered and that cost him.

Matt squeezed the Remington's trigger. A deafening blast erupted and the wooden stock recoiled violently against his upper right arm as the end of the barrel jerked upward. Matt didn't notice the gun's kick or the pain when it slammed into his biceps, because he had fired before getting the weapon secured against his shoulder.

The Remington's Sabot Slug, the slug designed to expand and break apart on impact, did its job a millisecond after passing through the soft tissue of the guard's nose and entering his nasal cavity at the speed of 1500 feet per second. There, it struck the nasal, lacrimal and ethmoid bones and broke into five fragmented pieces. The main slug continued straightforward and detonated through the sinuses. Then, it dug its way through his soft, blood-filled brain and erupted with a large portion of that brain tissue out the back of Otis' head creating a momentary hole in his occipital bone big enough to put a man's fist through. As intended by its inventor, the other four pieces burst apart like a skyrocket forming their own wound channels that ran and twisted in all directions until Otis' head blew apart like someone striking a ripe watermelon with a sledgehammer. Blood, brain and bone shot in every direction, bathing all nearby with a red and pink colloidal substance.

Headless, except for his lower jaw, Otis crumbled backward to the already blood-sticky floor like a dropped bath towel. His body jerked and undulated spasmodically several times before relaxing in death.

Matt whirled, aiming the Remington at guards along the outer wall, daring someone else to make a move or raise their weapons. Stunned expressions radiated from all the guards' faces. Matt heard air rushing back into Emmanuel's lung, or was it his own? Babies began to cry, and a lone woman somewhere screamed a shrieking scream of terror. Still shouldering the shotgun, Matt swung back toward the headless corpse to see Irene, face contorted in personal agony, pulling pieces of Otis' brains and skull off her heavy chest. A skinny red-haired nurse stood beside the fat one with a gapping mouth stuck in a silent scream like a painting Matt had seen somewhere a long time ago. Leaky stared up at him. The redheaded woman spewed vomit onto the bloody floor.

Somewhere, Matt had lost track of counting the seconds. A guard ran out the front door. Two others started to move. Without aiming, Matt fired a room-shattering round from the Remington at one of the escaping guards and blew a sizeable chunk of plaster off the wall near the guy's head. The two guards stopped in mid-step as if they were in a video suddenly placed on pause.

Matt shoved the end of the Remington's warm barrel into Emmanuel's face and screamed at the congregation, "Freeze! Every one of you, stand still. If anybody even thinks about moving again, I'll blow this man's head off. Lay your shotguns down on the floor, now!"

Mothers holding their children tried to hush them by rocking back and forth, while others placed quivering hands over their child's mouth.

"Jesus. God." Emmanuel whispered to no one, anyone, himself, but maybe really to God.

Hearing a commotion near the stage, Matt tightened his finger on the trigger and turned his head. Matt relaxed when he saw Medora, Crystal, and the young blond, Sarah, carrying a child pushing their way through several stunned people toward the back door.

Thirty! Thirty-one! Still light, why? Agent Ware had not cooperated as promised.

"Who are you?" said Emmanuel after looking into Matt's face—a face that looked like the one staring at Matt. "My God!"

"No," Matt said. "I'm not God. I'm the brother that comes straight from hell, and Daddy said to tell you hello."

"Daddy?"

"Our real daddy, Isaac," Matt said. "And he sent you some of the family pets." Matt pointed at the black bag beside his feet.

Suddenly, all the lights went off and darkness swallowed them. A woman screamed, then another. Adults started to cry along with their babies.

"Shut up!" Matt yelled. He'd never experienced such blackness. "Everybody stay seated and be quiet. Shut up! Stop those children from crying. Now, dammit!" In only a second all hushed, except for a few whimpers that Matt heard in the blackness. Working quickly but carefully in the dark, Matt propped the Remington against the podium and grabbed the plastic bag at his feet. Matt turned the bag upside-down and heard the snakes thump as they tumbled out of the plastic and onto the wooden floor with a flop. One began to rattle its tail, and then another and another until their harmonious symphony filled the room.

"Don't move, or you'll die, brother." Matt said to Emmanuel while groping for the Remington in the dark. Almost instantly Matt's hand touched the hot metal of its barrel. "Daddy's pets have got a hell of a bite, so don't move a muscle."

"Matt," said Leaky now moving closer. "What's happening?"

"Stay back, Leaky," Matt said.

"What's going on?" Leaky approached, cautiously.

"Just stay back," Matt said forcefully to his friend. "Stand still, and I'll get to you in a minute. I'll explain later."

"You de man," said Leaky.

"Who are you?" asked Emmanuel, no longer in panic, but Matt could still feel the fear in his voice.

The snakes' buzzing began to dwindle. In only a moment, the last rattling died and the snakes grew quiet.

Speaking low so only Emmanuel could hear him, Matt said, "I'm your oldest brother, Matthew Fagan." Matt felt the heavy weight of something crawling, slithering across his boot. He remained still. "Your full-bloodied brother. Not half brother like Luke and poor, retarded John."

"Who says?" said Emmanuel in a quivering voice.

"I do." Matt said. "Your brother says so."

"How do I know you're my brother?" said Emmanuel.

"We are the children of Rebecca and Isaac Fagan. Did no one ever tell you about me, your older brother?"

"Maybe. Who knows?"

"Don't give me that," Matt said. "Somebody told you about me, so cut the crap."

"Yes, someone told me about an older brother once, but I didn't believe her."

"Was it Mother?" Matt said feeling so strange saying the word, mother.

"No."

"The old woman, then?" Matt said. "Our father's aunt, Lucy Fagan told you?"

"Mother said Lucy was crazy," said Emmanuel.

Matt heard the soft click of a door opening behind him.

"I got a deal for you, brother," Matt said. "Tell everyone to go outside and through the gates to the authorities before..."

"Never," he interrupted.

"I'll get you help. You need to see a doctor."

"Shut up. I need no one, especially a brother."

"I don't want to see all these people die," Matt said. "And I'm not going to let that happen."

"How many rattlesnakes are in the floor?" said Emmanuel changing the subject.

"Daddy's pets," Matt said. "Some are rattlesnakes, but one's a cockatrice."

"A what?"

With a flash, the lights came back on and their brilliance flooded the room, hurting Matt's eyes.

"The generator," whispered Emmanuel to himself, but Matt heard and understood that one of Emmanuel's men—maybe the one that slipped out—had turned the lights back on.

"Stay still," Matt yelled out into the crowd, blinking to clear his vision after being in the dark so long. Something wasn't right. Matt glanced to each wall. Only two guards remained in the room still full of people. At least ten guards had slipped outside in the darkness. Matt looked for Irene. She too had slipped out, along with the red-haired one. Worry temporarily slipped over Matt like a shroud when he thought about Medora getting her people into the tunnel.

"You," Matt said pointing at one of the guards along the wall. "Shut the front door. And you." Matt pointed to the other guard. "Shut the back door." Matt checked for windows and saw none.

"Leaky," Matt said throwing the hunting knife at his friend's feet. One of the rattlers nearby started its monotonous song. Matt pointed the shotgun at one of the nurses. "Cut my friend loose. Hurry."

"Snakes!" screamed a woman near the stage. The gathering began to murmur as they, too, noticed the serpents. The crowd noise intensified. They began to stir. Some of the people in the front pew shrank back trying to hide behind one another. Sleeping babies awoke and started their wailing again.

"Shut up! And sit still!" Matt yelled.

Again, mothers clasped their hands over screaming children's mouths muffling their cries.

"That's better," Matt said, placing the gun again to Emmanuel's head and looking down at the floor. Most of the rattlesnakes slithered around their feet. A couple, including the biggest canebrake rattler, had coiled and appeared ready to strike at the first object that moved.

"Swallow your 'pills of life,'" screamed Emmanuel over the microphone surprising Matt. "It's time to go on our trip and. . ."

Emmanuel couldn't complete his sentence for Matt jerked the wireless microphone out of Emmanuel's hand and yelled over it, "Hold on a minute. No! Wait!" With horror, Matt saw eight or nine people's hands go to their mouths and then turn the paper cups to their lips and drink.

"You can't stop them." Emmanuel smiled confidently, then laughed a surly laugh.

"Noooooo!" Matt screamed to the congregation over the microphone. "We'll let the snakes decide. Wait. . .God wants you to wait." In a calmer, but more urgent tone, Matt continued to talk to Emmanuel's people. "We will let the snakes decide our fate. Your leader, Emmanuel, and I will take up these serpents, and if God wants you to die he'll send us a sign."

"Swallow them, now!" screamed Emmanuel with his naked voice.

"Hold on, brothers and sisters," Matt said over the speaker. The people sat without moving. Matt took the microphone from his mouth and looked at Emmanuel. "Surly, you're not afraid to do what the Bible says, are you?"

"What do you mean?" said Emmanuel. "You're nothing but a layman. You don't know anything about being a God."

Matt flinched when one of the women who had taken the poison a few seconds previously stood with a surprised look on her face. She flopped sideways onto another person beside her. Realization hit Matt that the woman had just died. He glanced around and saw several other people slide sideways or forward as they slipped from this world. Anger erupted in Matt's bowels, but he knew he had to control his reactions before others perished.

Ignoring Emmanuel's last words, Matt tossed the Remington to Leaky who stood behind them and said only to him, "Watch the doors and don't hesitate to use this if one of those guards tries to come in."

Leaky said, "Let's get the hell out of here. To hell with these. . ."

"Be quiet," Matt said to his friend. "I'm sorry, but I have do this, so just do as I say."

Matt turned back to the crowd and put the microphone to his mouth. "This man you call Emmanuel is my brother, Mark Belcher. He was born Mark Fagan and I'm his older brother Matthew Fagan. Our father died while Mark, Emmanuel, as you call him, was still in our mother's womb."

"Don't listen to him," screamed Emmanuel.

"Shut up and wait your turn," Matt said to Emmanuel in a tone he'd use with a child. Then, Matt turned back to the people. "Did Brother Emmanuel not just read to you from the Bible the words of Jesus Christ about the signs that will follow the believers? Did Jesus not say that His followers shall take up serpents and drink deadly things and it not hurt them? That's what I heard when Emmanuel was reading out of The Good Book."

"Then swallow the..." started Emmanuel just before Matt grabbed him by the throat, shutting off his words.

"Wait your turn," Matt said. "Next time you tell them to take the pills I'll rip your throat out."

Matt released his hold on Emmanuel who watched with wide eyes, and then Matt lifted the microphone back to his mouth. "I want you to turn in your Bibles to Acts twenty-eight: three through six." Matt paused a few seconds and watched the people quickly thumb through their Bibles. The old woman, Lucy, had given Matt these verses before he'd left her yesterday. He had looked them up and tried to memorize them last night after the fire and before he'd gotten too drunk. Now he couldn't remember the exact words; so, he decided to paraphrase the verses, hoping that to be good enough. "When you read it, does it not say that Paul shook off a viper that was fastened on his hand without suffering any ill effects?"

"My point, indeed," said Emmanuel to Matt. "Do you want to swallow the poison?"

"In time," Matt whispered for only Emmanuel to hear. "But first, we'll play my game. You're not afraid to handle a rattlesnake, are you?"

"No," said Emmanuel. "God will protect the righteous one...You pick one up first."

"We'll do it together," Matt said, then turned back to the people who now watched him with up-turned faces.

Matt stared out at the congregation and said, "In Exodus four: two through four you'll find more." Frantically, most of Emmanuel's followers flipped to the front of their Bibles. Matt waited what felt like an hour but at most a minute watching them read. The steadfast hum of the rattlers vibrated around his feet. Matt could tell that Emmanuel feared to move. Matt glanced back at the people who now looked at him. "Does that passage not tell us that God commanded

Moses to change his staff into a serpent, and after he did, didn't Moses reach down and pick it up by its tail?"

"Amen, Brother Matthew," said an old toothless man in the front row. "Pick up them snakes, boys."

"Soon, we will," Matt said. "First, I want all of you to turn in your Bibles to the book of Jeremiah, the eighth chapter, verse seventeen and read it silently to yourselves." In a frenzied state, fingers tore through thin white pages, as though racing to get there before the words disappeared.

For a long moment silence reigned over the people as they read.

Matt's confidence elevated as he talked to this large gathering—something he'd never done. "Emmanuel and I will handle each of these dangerous rattle-snakes. We will let God decide who lives and who dies."

"Praise God!" yelled the toothless old man. "Pick 'em up, brother."

Matt turned to his brother whose face showed just a hint of fear and said, "You want to start with a big one or a little one?"

"Shut up," Emmanuel said. "You first."

"Yes," Matt said. "I'll get one for you."

Emmanuel's breathing increased and Matt thought he saw him waver slightly.

Surprised with his on audacity, Matt took a step toward the big canebrake rattler that had taken a position near the front edge of the stage. He had to stride over one of the pigmy rattlers that coiled and shook its tail violently as he passed. Matt bent at the waist and reached his hand for the huge serpent. Its head rocked back across its coiled body as its tail sent out a wild clatter of warning.

"Are you the cockatrice?" Matt asked while gradually reaching his hand for the yellowish-brown body of the rattlesnake—a body as big around as his fore-arm. Its eyes, greenish-yellow and vertically elliptical, glimmered in the lights. The buzz of the rattler grew louder as its pair of heat-seeking pits below its eyes and above its nostrils detected something huge and warm approaching its head. Matt took a deep breath and grabbed its thick body in his right hand.

CHAPTER THIRTY-EIGHT

Sarah couldn't hear what her mother and Crystal had said as they rushed out the backdoor of the sanctuary. The blast from the shotgun still rang in her ears, and Tommy had started crying again.

Now, in the faint light outside the backdoor, Medora put her arms around both Sarah and Tommy and lavished them both with wet, tear-filled kisses. Her mother's sweet aroma comforted Sarah, and she relaxed in Medora's embrace. Crystal stood nearby watching and waiting.

"Come," said Medora pulling them off the deck and down toward a lone security light. "We've got to get to the cave."

"What cave?" said Sarah, but her mother didn't take time to answer.

"Go to the shed, hurry," said Medora, holding Sarah's arm, pushing them, prodding them down the slight grade toward the little storehouse. Sarah wondered why her mother took them toward the shed, but she didn't have time to ask. This wasn't real. She and Tommy remained alive, and there stood her precious mother. For a horrified moment, Sarah thought she might awake from this dream.

They passed under the security light and walked halfway to the shed when all lights went out and darkness covered them like a cloak.

"Mother," Sarah said reaching out. They stopped jogging, but Medora continued walking them, while leading them in the direction of the outbuilding. Sarah could not see a thing and wondered how her mother knew where to go.

"Sarah," said Crystal somewhere behind them. "Where are you?"

"Come here, child," said Medora toward Crystal while continuing to hold Sarah's arm in a vise grip. "Walk to my voice. We're waiting here for you."

"Okay," said Crystal walking blindly into Sarah's side. Crystal grabbed Sarah by the arm and said, "Let's go."

Even in the dark, Sarah began to see shadows as her night vision improved under the faint light of the moon.

Medora said, "Matt had the lights turned off, so I was expecting this."

"Who?" said Sarah.

Crystal interrupted, "Was that Matt?"

"Yes," said Medora. She continued moving them toward the dark silhouette of the shed only ten feet away. "I hope he doesn't take long. We're supposed to wait on him for awhile. God! I hope he hurries."

"Who's Matt?" Sarah almost yelled.

"I told you about him," said Crystal. "He's the man I met on the outside the other day."

"The one that looked like Emmanuel," said Sarah.

"Yeah," said Crystal. Then she turned toward Medora. "What's he going to do?"

"I don't know," said Medora as they reached the door to the shed and started through. "He's got to get his friend out and probably he'll try to save everybody. I don't know what he'll do."

"Let's go back, then. We have to help him," said Crystal, stopping just inside the door.

"No!" said Medora reaching for Crystal's arm. "He knows what he's doing, and this is what he told me to do. And, one thing I've learned, he's usually right when it comes to his line of work. Okay? Now, get in here."

"What was in the black bag he was carrying?" said Crystal following them inside. Sarah had forgotten about the plastic bag.

Before answering Crystal's question, Medora closed the shed door. Suddenly, from the back of the dark room, something clicked and the beam of a flashlight filled their eyes. Sarah's heart jumped into her throat and a warm liquid trickled down the insides of her thighs. Medora screamed but not as loud as she could have. Waiting to die, Sarah squeezed Tommy causing him to start crying again.

From behind the beam of light came a strange feminine voice, "Matt got snakes in that black bag. Big, bad, rattlesnakes."

"Dammit, Cousin," said Medora pointing her finger at the person behind the light. "You scared the hell out of me. And get that light out of my eye."

Confused, Sarah's heart continued to race.

"Sorry," said the individual moving the light out of their eyes.

Then Sarah realized a young boy stood behind the light, not a woman.

"Cousin," said Medora between breaths. "Why didn't you leave? You were supposed to go back home."

Crystal took Medora's arm. "Who is that?"

The boy answered before Medora who was still breathing rapidly could respond. "I's Bobby. I's a friend of Matt, and I's cousin to Herbert. I's also Glenn's cousin. You'ns know, the one that owns the dock."

"Oh," said Crystal who didn't want to know any of this.

Medora, getting new wind, took over the conversation. "Cousin's a good boy. He showed us how to get here through the cave." Medora grabbed the boy by his overall straps. "Why didn't you leave?"

The boy giggled. "I's havin' too much fun to go back, 'sides that cave dark, got spooks in it...or snakes."

"Where's the other flashlight?" said Medora gently shaking the boy by his shoulder.

Cousin pointed his light through the cave door onto a backpack. "Right there." Then he shinned the beam on something in his other hand. "And the crossbow's right here." He held something Sarah had never seen before. It looked like a regular little bow fastened onto a stock of a gun. The shaft of an arrow protruded from it. "I's got it loaded, too."

"Be careful before..." was all Medora got out of her mouth when she heard people talking outside the sanctuary. The beams of many flashlights crisscrossed as they cut through the blackness on the hill next to the sanctuary.

"Shhhh," said Crystal who heard and saw it too.

Tommy whimpered and Sarah cupped her hand over his mouth. He started kicking and squirming, but she held him tightly, almost cutting off his breath. Medora snatched Cousin's flashlight out of his hands and turned it off. Sarah's arms ached as Tommy continued to wiggle, so she kept her hand over his mouth.

Then the security light flickered and came back on to illuminate the area. The small light behind the sanctuary radiated a dull orange glow over a group of about ten people talking on the back deck.

Sarah's already racing heart skipped a full beat when she recognized Irene giving orders to a group of guards, each holding a flashlight and a shotgun. Beside the fat witch, stood red-haired Myra with her flashlight still shinning. After getting Irene's orders, three guards moved to the front of the sanctuary while two others took off toward the front gate of the compound where the FBI waited.

After the guards left, Irene, Myra, and three other guards started walking toward the storage shed where Sarah and her group stood hiding just inside the window. Sarah's heart turned completely over in her chest and her eyes went blurry at the thought of what might happen to them if found by Irene. And now added to her troubles, Sarah worried about her mother, a mother who had come this far and done so much, even risking her own life for a daughter that had abandoned her.

"Dammit," said Crystal through gritting teeth. "I'm not going back without a fight."

"In the cave," said the boy, pulling on Medora's jacket tail. "Come on, come on. Now!"

"Okay," said Medora pushing Sarah, Tommy, and Crystal toward the back-door. "Cousin, what about Matt? He's going to need a flashlight to get out of here."

"Later, go now," said Cousin pointing to the back door.

Medora grabbed the backpack beside the door and said at the same time, "Matt's going to be mad as hell."

"I bring it back later," said Cousin. He yanked at Medora who guided the rest through the door. "Come on!"

After Medora led Sarah and Crystal through the door to the narrow landing she said, "Follow Cousin, I'll stay in the back."

Sarah looked down steps that disappeared into the darkness below. Somewhat apprehensive about entering this dark, musty smelling cavity, but having no choice, Sarah followed the boy's light down the shaft. Going back meant sure death for them all. Squeezing Tommy across her shoulder, she flinched when she heard her mother close the door behind them. The stairs creaked even under lightly placed steps. The yellow cone of Cousin's flashlight gave little illumination to those following as they circled and scurried down to the solid rock floor.

Cousin stopped at the bottom, held the flashlight steady, and waited on everyone to reach the cave floor. When Medora stepped onto the rock, Cousin turned and took off into the blackness—blackness that moved down into the earth. No longer crying, Tommy squirmed restlessly in Sarah's arms—arms that grew weaker and weaker.

Crystal, walking ahead of Sarah, turned to her and said, "Give me Tommy." Without waiting for a reply from Sarah, Crystal took the child out of his mother's arms. Sarah didn't protest. Her arms had long since lost feeling.

They had moved only a short distance through the shaft of the cave when they heard the door behind them open and people's footsteps descending the noisy stairs. Sarah, feeling the hair on her arms prickling, tried to look back, but Medora pushed her onward and downward into the unknown.

Cousin increased their speed until they reached a narrow wooden bridge leading across a bottomless black pit where they stopped. Sarah peered down into the dark and shivered, thinking about tumbling into the chasm.

Turning, Cousin whispered, "We got to be quiet. Walk on tiptoes." With light in one hand and crossbow in the other, the boy led the way across the footbridge. Crystal, carrying Tommy, followed the boy, while Sarah and Medora fell in behind her.

Sarah heard Irene and her crew moving somewhere behind them—closing quickly. Sarah feared the gap between them would not last much longer. She took deep breaths trying to quiet her thumping heart for fear they might even hear it.

When they entered a large, empty cavern with a high, dark ceiling, they didn't pause. Cousin led them through another tunnel opening directly across the room. Moving always downward into the earth gave Sarah a feeling of being trapped with no way out and no time to ask her mother or the boy what lay ahead. Cousin's light moved ahead leaving the floor in darkness where Sarah stepped. She had no choice but to follow Crystal and pray they stayed on their feet.

Twisting, turning, dodging stalagmites, they plummeted through the dark shaft. Sarah lost track of their location and direction, except she knew they traveled downward into the earth. She wondered why they moved deeper into the earth and not toward the river.

Sarah heard Irene's voice closing in behind them, but Sarah refused to let herself turn. She wanted to run but could only follow, watching and chasing the dark silhouette of Crystal, the athlete, striding smoothly ahead of her carrying Tommy with such ease and grace, downward.

The voices behind them moved closer.

"Faster," Sarah whispered although she knew no one heard her words. She cringed, expecting to trip over a loose stone or a jagged protrusion in the granite floor, but they kept moving, downward—always downward into the black void ahead of the boy's amber cone of light. Irene's strong, almost masculine voice loomed behind them like a dreadful troll in search of a new sacrifice.

"Run," said Sarah, louder this time, but the boy stopped and turned the weakening light back toward them.

"Shhhh. Follow me," said the boy leading them. He turned, grabbed Crystal's free hand, and they disappeared between a curtain of black. The cave went dark.

"Wait," said Sarah, stopping momentarily, but her mother shoved her in the back, pushing her through the limbs of a snagging tree and out into the cold moonlit night.

"Hurry," said Cousin turning away from them. He did not follow the trail leading toward the river but veered to the right and into the thick underbrush growing under towering oak trees.

Medora nudged her daughter, hurrying her. Sarah followed Crystal and Tommy as they chased after the boy's light.

Thorny vines and shrub limbs clawed at Sarah's naked legs, but she didn't notice the pain, only their discomforting pricks ripping at her flesh. The hem of her cotton dress caught briefly on a prickly barb, but she pushed forward tearing the fabric along with her skin.

They had moved less than a minute through the brush when the boy stopped, and turned off his flashlight. "Everybody, down."

Sarah fell onto her knees in the semi-darkness. The ground felt damp and cool to her bare skin.

"Mama," Tommy said just before Crystal cupped her hand over his mouth.

"What?" said Sarah reaching for her son.

"Shhhh," said Crystal and her mother at the same time.

Flashlight beams belched from between the two cedar trees fifty yards behind Sarah. Still on her knees Sarah turned toward the cave entrance and heard the harshness of Irene's voice giving orders. "Spread out and find the bitches. They've got to be close. I smell them. They couldn't a gone very far, so find 'them and bring them to me. I'm going to finish this once and for all with that high-and-mighty whore. Hurry up! Move it!"

Before she could finish barking her orders, the flashlights with shadowy forms behind them had already started drifting away from one another in four directions, slicing their way through the darkness.

Sarah, throat tightening in horror, couldn't get a good breath as she saw one of their pursuers striding toward her with a shotgun in his hand.

CHAPTER THIRTY-NINE

The people in the sanctuary had become so quiet Matt could actually hear the snake's vascular organ thumping like a sewing machine in its body of pure muscle. Its diamond-shaped head undulated rhythmically, swaying from side to side and watching, not its holder, but the man before him, Emmanuel, the brother.

Matt took a deep breath then asked Emmanuel, "Is this the cockatrice I hold before you?"

Emmanuel didn't answer. Matt didn't think this madman had ever heard of a cockatrice.

Matt said to him—screamed to him, "Are you ready to take up this serpent and hold it as God commanded?"

Emmanuel surprised Matt by taking a step to the side of the huge rattler and placing both of his hands around its massive trunk. Matt released his hold on the reptile and noticed the surprise on Emmanuel's face when he caught all the weight of the creature in his hands.

The people made a sound of awe as though their savior had just performed a miracle. The rattler's tongue surveyed the room as it flicked it in and out. Its head revolved in a mystical circle, up and down, then side to side, always rolling around and around as Emmanuel held its body motionless in steady hands. A grin started to form on Emmanuel's lips and spread until it filled his entire face.

"Amen," said the old man in the front row. "Get you another one, boys."

"Praise God!" said the congregation in unison. "Blessed Savior."

Matt had not expected Emmanuel to handle the snakes. His mind raced, thinking of what to do next. He'd planned to shame his mad brother in front of his followers, causing them to see Emmanuel's distortion and turn away from him.

Matt glanced down seeing a gray pigmy rattler at his feet. He reached down, lifted its almost weightless body in his hands, and looked into its sliced eyes. The rattler's slender body looked out of proportion when compared to its large arrow-shaped head. A glistening black tongue flipped in and out of a closed mouth. Cautiously, Matt placed the small rattler on his head. The broad smile on Emmanuel's face vanished as quickly as it had appeared only moments ago.

"Amen, amen, amen!" said the old man, rising to his feet and clapping his hands.

"Praise God!" said the crowd again. Many stood applauding in frenzy.

Holding his neck stiffly so his head stayed straight, Matt brought the microphone to his mouth. "Everyone needs to remain seated. Please, sit down."

Strangely, they obeyed him without question as would students in a first grade class obey their teacher. Mothers quieted restless children.

Matt felt the snake move into a coiled position on his head. Its miniature rattler started buzzing. Matt let the microphone fall to his side and turned to Emmanuel. "Don't you need a crown like mine?"

"Huh?"

"Maybe, you need a necklace," Matt said. "I'll get you one."

Still keeping his neck and head straight, Matt bent at the knees and lowered his body to a squatting position. Before him, about two feet away coiled a large, yellowish, burnt-orange canebrake rattlesnake buzzing his tail with the ferocity of a revving engine. His flesh-colored eyes watched Matt's hand. Its yellow, almost white calcified tail that lifted up in an erection did not vibrate but stood as an admonition.

Matt reached a cupped hand out toward the poisonous monster and asked, "Are you the cockatrice?" Matt's hand inched closer—halfway there. The rattler's tail began to clank slowly at first, then faster until the sound mixed with the serpent riding Matt's head. Its head drew back and rose until it towered over Matt's outstretched hand. "I won't look into your eyes, for I fear you are the cockatrice." Matt spoke over the microphone for all to hear. "Are you the serpent hatched from the egg of a cock, having the power to kill by a single look? The One God talks about you in the Book of Jeremiah. Are you the one that God says will not be charmed? The one He sends to bite even the true believers?"

Its rattling grew quicker and louder. Matt prayed the seed of doubt would enter Emmanuel's head.

"Bullshit," said Emmanuel, bending over and laying the huge rattler he had handled on the floor. It slithered lazily away and hid under the podium. Emmanuel picked up a pigmy rattler about twelve inches long and carefully placed it on his head. Matt stood and felt a little light headed as blood rushed back into his brain.

"Amen," said the old man. The crowd applauded and stomped their feet.

Emmanuel, now with a stiff neck because of the snake on his head, turned and grinned at Matt. "You don't know who you've challenged; I'm Lord over all serpents. My powers range near and far. Pick up that rattlesnake you call the cockatrice and give it to me, if you're not afraid, that is. I'm not afraid to play your game. I'll wear it for a necklace if you'll give it to me." Emmanuel laughed deeply.

Matt stooped again before the coiled rattler, and the crowd grew quiet. Coiled before him, the creature's tail began its singing. Its head, still high above its body, stood over his outreaching fingers. Slowly, Matt inched his right hand toward the snake's thick body.

When his outstretched fingers reached the cool, scaly skin of the serpent, it struck. Like a taut spring, it drove at the back of Matt's hand faster than anyone could see. The blow from its massive head slammed into Matt's knuckles, knocking the palm of his hand to the floor with a smack before he could yank it out of harm's way. Almost unnoticed the pigmy rattler on Matt's head fell to the floor and slithered under a chair.

A woman in the congregation screamed, and the people began frantically babbling to one another.

Pain radiated down Matt's fingers and spread into the bones of his wrist. The rattlesnake's fangs had hit his carpal bones near his knuckles with the force of a blow from a hammer. Blood trickled down the back of Matt's hand, as it started to tremble. He felt dazed already. He thought about the valley of death and feared it.

Laughing, Emmanuel said so only Matt could hear, "Tough shit, my brother."

Leaky, running toward the stage, yelled, "Matt, Jesus Christ move back. I'll blow that sonofabitch to pieces."

"No!" Matt screamed holding up his stricken hand to stop his friend. "Watch the doors. Go!"

They stood staring at one another a long moment. Worry radiated from Leaky's face. Unwillingly, Leaky turned and ambled away, shotgun across his chest.

Matt glanced at the stab wound on his hand, checking for swelling. Nothing yet, only blood. For the third time, He knelt before the rattler. Matt noticed that the snake appeared addled and confused, probably because it jarred its brain when it slammed its open mouth into the bones of Matt's hand. The rattler's tail had dropped and his head searched weakly along the wooden floor in a random spasmodic fashion.

Moving much faster this time, Matt grabbed the thickest part of the rattler's body with his left hand. Lifting it to his chest, Matt took a deep breath. He couldn't believe its weight. It didn't strike but tried to squirm from his hand with a drooping head that pointed toward the floor.

"Oooooh," the people said in unison. Matt thought their crooning sounded like hundreds of mourning doves.

Matt allowed the dry creature to slide from his left hand to his aching right and then again and again as it crawled across his palms going nowhere. The dull ache spread to Matt's right wrist, but stopped there.

Matt looked into the no-longer-smiling face of Emmanuel who still had the little rattler coiled in his black hair and said, "This cockatrice was sent by God. You want it? Are you afraid?"

Sliding in Matt's fingers, the rattler lifted its head. So, Matt felt it would be only moments before the creature would recover completely and realized it was in trouble and strike out.

"I'm afraid of nothing," mocked the religious leader. "God protects me. Give me that cockatrice, I want to look into his wicked eyes for I am his Lord."

"Take it," Matt said handing the creature to Emmanuel. Matt's right hand ached with renewed pain. The shadow of the valley of death again crept into his thoughts.

Emmanuel took the dazed serpent, held it up before his people in both hands and said loudly, "See! Nothing harms me. I am God, the Jehovah. Get ready to swallow your poison brothers and sisters." He laughed in a deep sonorous tone.

Emmanuel brought the rattler's face toward his own nose until only inches separated them. The serpent drew back its head until its neck formed the shape of an S. The man and beast glared into each other's eyes. The self-proclaimed God, head bent forward, smiled. "You're the cockatrice, right? Well, you look like the biggest cock I ever seen."

Chuckling like an incubus attempting to defile a sleeping virgin, Emmanuel slung the canebrake rattlesnake around his neck and wore it like a necklace. He turned to face his people, holding his arms straight out, parallel to the floor. He turned his palms up in a jester of conquest like a triumphant hero seeking approval. With a pigmy rattler coiled in his hair and a monstrous serpent about his neck, Emmanuel struck an autocratic pose of corruption and evil. A smirk of victory crossed his face,

Feeling lower than at any point in his life, Matt knew he'd lost the battle with this man, and that the people would soon take their poison and die. Depression engulfed him. Matt glanced at Leaky who stood midway down the center aisle and stared with venomous eyes of hatred at Emmanuel. As Matt watched Leaky, his friend's noxious expression suddenly transformed into a look of surprise.

Matt turned toward Emmanuel and saw the snake around the leader's shoulders draw his massive head back and up until in stood on the same plane with Emmanuel's ear. As though preparing to take a bite from an apple the snake opened his mouth almost inside out. Then, it lunged forward, and clamped down on Emmanuel's neck several inches below his ear. Eyes wide, Emmanuel sucked in air. The serpent worked its head from side to side sinking its fangs deeper into the man's muscle. The pigmy rattler on Emmanuel's head worked its fangs into Emmanuel's forehead.

Except for Emmanuel's low moans of pain, silence surrounded the room until the pigmy rattler turned loose and slipped onto the floor with a thud.

Emmanuel's mouth shot open but no sound came from him. With the rat-tlesnake still clinging to his neck, working its poison deeper, Emmanuel turned toward Matt, with a horrified yet strangely astonished expression on a chalky face.

As devious as a deceitful child, the snake pulled away. Matt could almost hear the suckling sound it made, reminding him of a baby unwillingly releas-ing its mother's breast. Only two small specks of bright red blood appeared on Emmanuel's neck. At last, after flipping its black tongue at the stunned audience, the serpent slithered down Emmanuel's limp arm and flopped onto the floor.

"You looked into her eyes," Matt said softly. "You should never look into the eyes of a cockatrice. God has sent us a sign. Now, we'll see who dies first." Terror sprang from Emmanuel's eyes.

Emmanuel turned to his people and, in a loud voice said, "God will protect me. Don't worry, that snake can't hurt me. Watch." He raised his arms over his head and turned in a complete circle. A feeble smile formed on his face.

"Praise God," said a woman in the rear, then most everyone said, "Amen," but with weak responses.

Emmanuel grabbed each side of the rostrum with his hands and leaned forward. "Swallow your poison, now. God will protect us."

"Wait!" Matt screamed over the microphone. To his surprise, no one took their poison.

"My people," said Emmanuel in a gruff but disintegrating voice. Matt no-ticed beads of sweat springing from Emmanuel's forehead along with the two drops of blood. Some of the perspiration had already carved glistening streaks down his cheeks. "I feel tired...Pray for me...I will never...die."

The room grew so quiet that Matt wondered if everyone had ceased breathing.

The rear door burst open. Matt jumped. Before he could turn toward it, a blast of a shotgun exploded in the room. An instant later the thick thud of a heavy object slammed against a solid surface. When Matt turned toward the door, he saw a wounded guard skimming down the wall leaving behind a wide smeared streak of crimson blood. Leaky pumped the smoking Remington put-ting another round into its firing chamber.

Babies began to cry, and it sounded like whining cats filled the room.

Matt ran the ten feet to the open door and looked into an empty storage room. He slammed the door closed and locked its sliding clasp. Matt grabbed the dead guard's shotgun and carried it back to the front next to the podium that Emmanuel now used to support a pair of legs that had started to crumble.

"Oh...God...help me," said Emmanuel, head bowed.

BOOM! A shotgun blast erupted in the front of the sanctuary near the open double doors. When Matt looked up two men from the congregation had wrestled a guard to the floor. Above them plaster and wood sprinkled from a large hole in the ceiling. Leaky raced toward the men now brawling on the floor. He aimed the Remington in their direction but held his fire.

"Leaky, the door," Matt screamed when he saw another guard stepping into the light with his shotgun aimed at the men on the floor.

BOOM! Leaky's blast from the Remington blew the guard out of the door and out of sight into the dark. Leaky slammed the double doors shut. The two men from the congregation held the guard's back to the floor.

Leaky picked up the guard's shotgun and used the weapon to point at one of the back pews. "Ooh, what a big one you boys caught. Move him over there and keep him company, and if he tries anything kick the living shit out of him."

"Burn this place down," said someone over the loudspeaker. Matt looked up to see that Emmanuel had found the microphone and held it to his lips. "Be quick...Hurry up...Burn..."

Matt raced forward, grabbed the microphone from Emmanuel's hand, and screamed into it, "No!"

Unable to stay on his feet a second longer, Emmanuel fell to his hands and knees like a dog, then opened his mouth grossly wide and spewed vomit across the floor. The last visible snake crawled under a chair on the platform.

"No fires," Matt yelled over the speaker. The congregation stood and hysteria erupted with their panicked screams.

Emmanuel fell to his side into his own black bile. His eyes rolled to the back of his head as he fought to get air into his lungs. A rasping sound emanated from deep within his tightening esophagus.

Suddenly the lights went out and the room turned pitch black. Matt tried to shout over the microphone, but it, too, had lost power. Growing terror swept the room and the people's screams grew louder as they ran blindly into each other. Matt tried to get the congregation's attention but they grew louder with their shrieking.

Matt smelled the smoke moments before he saw the first red flames licking up one corner of the sanctuary.

CHAPTER FORTY

When the light struck Sarah's eyes, she froze for just a moment, and then she fell on her knees, too terrified even to scream.

The guard shined the flashlight in Sarah's face. He yelled, "Here they..." And that was all he got out before his words stopped in mid-sentence as the arrow found its mark. His shotgun boomed, sending buckshot into the ground five feet in front of Sarah. Dirt sprayed over her. Tommy started crying, but Crystal silenced him by covering his mouth.

Mesmerized, Sarah watched as the guard staggered in a circle for a few steps before he fell to the ground with a thump. There, on his back, he squealed like a wounded animal trying to get air into his blood-filled lungs.

"Ralph!" screamed Irene still standing near the cedar trees that covered the entrance to the cave. She and Myra didn't wait for an answer but pushed through the thicket in the direction of the guard's shrieks. "Answer me, did you shoot somebody or not?" The two women kept moving toward the downed guard. "What's wrong with you? Speak up."

Still watching on her knees, Sarah saw Irene's light moving toward the fallen Ralph who had rolled over onto his own flashlight making the area around him dark. Ralph continued to emit low groans of pain and to kick his feet spasmodically against the ground.

Beside Sarah, Cousin grunted and pulled back on the crossbow's powerful cord trying desperately to get it cocked.

Irene shined her light on Ralph's prone body and then looked back toward the cave and hollered, "Boys, get over here, now. Hurry up." Instead of coming closer to the dropped guard with an arrow through his throat, Irene and Myra ran back toward the cave entrance.

"I got it," whispered Cousin putting another arrow into the grove on the crossbow's stock. He stood. "Come on, let's go."

"Hurry up," said Medora jerking Sarah to her feet. "Back to the boat. Go, Cousin, hurry up."

"But we can't see," whispered Sarah getting to her feet.

"Black girl," said Medora. "Hold on to Cousin's overall straps. Sarah, you hold to the black girl's jacket."

"I'm Crystal."

"Okay," said Medora. "Crystal, just hurry up and do as I say. Let's go."

Behind Sarah she saw the other two guards' lights converging toward Irene now back at the cave's entrance. Irene barked out instructions. The guard with an arrow in his throat lay motionless.

Medora grabbed Sarah by the arm and called toward the boy, "Move it, Cousin, hurry up."

"Mama," cried Tommy. "Mama."

"Shhhh," said Crystal, but Tommy wouldn't hush.

"Give him to me," said Sarah.

In seconds, Sarah had him in her arms. Tommy clutched his arms around his mother and buried his head in the curve of her neck and shoulder. She stumbled through the darkness behind Crystal.

"How you know where you're going?" said Crystal to the boy leading them.

"I see's good in the dark," said Cousin. They moved between trees that Sarah only noticed at the last second. They zigzagged onward, moving deeper into the forest. Sarah's left arm that held Tommy grew weaker while numbness crept into her hand, wrist and forearm. She wanted to change arms, but fear kept her clinging to Crystal's blouse.

Sarah almost screamed when the beam of several flashlights started bouncing around in the undergrowth near them. She heard the footfalls of guards moving closer and making up ground between them. Cousin didn't slow but continued to drag them through the woods.

Sarah's left shoulder began to ache. She worried about falling. Then, a shining light struck them from behind.

"There they are," yelled a man.

"Shoot 'em," said Irene.

BOOM! For only an instant a flash from the shotgun cut a path through the dark and illuminated the night under the canopy of trees. Medora slammed into Sarah's back, knocking her into Crystal so hard it brought all five of their group to the ground like stacked dominoes.

"I got one," yelled a guard closing in on his prey.

"Don't shoot Sarah," said Irene. "She's mine."

Tommy bellowed.

The dead weight of Medora lay across Sarah's legs pinning them down. Dazed, Sarah grabbed for her son, but Crystal snatched him from her grasp. Sarah heard what sounded like herds of people running through the woods toward them. Trapped. Sarah tried again to kick her legs free but couldn't.

"Mother," Sarah said. "Get off me." Medora didn't move.

Heavy footsteps rustling leaves, and snapping tiny sticks were heard as they closed in on the fallen group.

"Bobby!" someone yelled.

"Here!" screamed Cousin. "Over here!"

"Lay flat on the ground, Bobby," someone yelled. "And stay there."

"Okay," screamed Bobby. "We're on the ground."

Sarah tried to grab for Cousin and shut him up, but she couldn't move.

BOOM! A gun flashed and lit the night. Sarah closed her eyes and waited on the bullets to enter her body, but nothing happened.

BOOM! BOOM! BOOM! Flames from weapons erupted all around them. Tree limbs and wooden splinters rained everywhere as bullets zinged over their heads. The noise grew deafening.

BOOM! BOOM! BOOM!

Tommy cried frantically, but Sarah could hardly hear him over the firearms exploding all round.

"Stop, hold your fire!" someone screamed and as quickly as the shooting started, it stopped. "Them boys gone. Stop shootin' them damn rifles."

The firing ended, and flashlights surrounded the group on the ground. Sarah, expecting to die any second, looked up from the ground to see strange men in denim overalls like Cousin wore standing over them. They shined lights from one fallen person to the next until they saw the boy.

"Bobby," said one of the men "You okay?"

"Cousin Glenn," said Cousin. "That you?"

"Yeah," said the man. "It's me, Cousin Herbert, Cousin Squirrel and your daddy."

Cousin dropped his crossbow and ran to one of the men who picked the boy up in his arms as though he weighed nothing at all.

"Worried about you," said the large man squeezing the boy. "I 'bout kicked Cousin Herbert's ass fur lettin' you run off with them folks."

"We found 'em," said a man spitting tobacco on the ground. "So you don't have to be talkin' 'bout kickin' nobody's ass."

When Sarah finally glanced down at her mother still lying across her legs, a scream caught in her throat. Blood trickled across Medora's forehead coming from somewhere in her bloody hair. Her mother's eyes stayed closed.

"Mother." said Sarah reaching for and shaking Medora. "Oh, God."

A tiny moan escaped through Medora's lips. Her eyes blinked open.

"Mother," Sarah said.

"Let me see," said Crystal pulling Medora off Sarah's legs.

Standing above Sarah, Cousin's daddy said, "Herbert, check and see if we'ns got any of them boys." One of the men in denim overalls started trekking through the dead leaves with his flashlight in one hand and a rifle in the other.

Weakly, Medora said, "What happened?"

"She's okay," said Crystal using her own blouse tail to wipe blood off Medora's head. "She must have been nicked by a shotgun pellet or a limb or hit in the head with something, but it's just a little cut. She might need some stitches. There's also a big bump on the back of her head."

Trying to sit up, Medora whispered, "How about my babies?"

"Right here, Mama," said Sarah moving over Medora.

"And Tommy?"

"Tommy's here too, Mama."

Medora reached up and took the sobbing boy in her arms. Then she squeezed him and started to cry. Relieved, Sarah started crying, too.

Cousin Herbert stomped back inside the gathering and walked over to Cousin's daddy. "Three of 'em deader than four o'clock up there 'bout thirty feet. And guess what?"

"What?" said Cousin's daddy.

"One's a woman," said Herbert. "A skinny red-headed woman with a bullet hole in her chest."

"Only one woman?" said Sarah.

"Yep," said Herbert.

"We best get out of here," said Cousin Glenn walking back into the group from the other direction. Sarah hadn't noticed him leaving earlier. "The law's gonna be here any minute. They 'bout half-a-mile up there coming in this direction."

"Yep," said the daddy, putting Cousin on the ground and walking over to the women. "The law's going to be here in about five or ten minutes. Keep your flashlights on. We'ns got to go. You'ns don't have to tell 'em who we is, now. Tell 'em you'ns didn't see who shot them people. Okay?" He handed Sarah his flashlight.

"Okay," said Sarah. "Whatever you say. You have nothing to fear from us. You saved our lives."

Crystal said, "How can we ever thank you?"

"No need," said the daddy. "You'ns took care of my boy."

Cousin picked up the loaded crossbow and handed it to Sarah. "This thing is loaded and ready to shoot. All you got to do is pull the trigger." He pointed to the trigger, then he turned, and in only seconds the women found themselves alone in the woods.

With one lone flashlight burning under the trees that draped over them like a black tarpaulin, the women and one baby huddled together waiting for help.

"You bitch," said Irene stumbling into the circle of light holding a shotgun feebly in her hands. Blood oozed from a deep reddish-black hole in her left forearm. "You didn't think I'd ever let you get away from me, did you?"

"Damn you, Irene!" screamed Crystal getting to her feet.

Smiling, Irene brought the shotgun up to her shoulder taking her time to point it at Crystal. Irene started to laugh as if she loved what she was about to do.

Sarah, still holding the crossbow, brought the crude weapon to her shoulder and pointed it between Irene's breasts. Her right index finger searched frantically for the trigger mechanism that the boy had showed her while she tried to keep the sight on Irene's torso.

Crystal took a step backward.

Watching only Crystal, Irene grinned as she laid her cheek onto the shotgun's stock and closed one eye.

Sarah's right finger pulled back on what she prayed was the trigger. The crossbow pushed lightly against Sarah's shoulder and a swishing sound sped only a few feet into the night.

BOOM! Irene's shotgun exploded and she staggered backward into the trunk of a large oak tree. Broken limbs from the blast and a few remaining dead leaves rained down upon the three women. Crystal fell to her knees unharmed but stunned.

When Sarah looked up, Irene stared at her with a pair of unbelieving eyes. Blood trickled from the corner of the fat woman's mouth. The end of the arrow stood halfway out of her chest between her breasts. Gradually, as though being lowered by someone else, Irene slipped down the tree trunk until she sat on the ground.

For what felt like a very long time Sarah and Irene stared at each other. Irene fought no longer against anyone but for only each breath she was able to suck into her starving lungs. Tommy whimpered in his grandmother's arms. Finally, Irene's chest grew still and her eyes grew glassy.

Crystal felt for a pulse in the carotid artery of Irene's neck.

"Is she dead?" Sarah whispered.

"Yes," said Crystal.

"I hope God will forgive me," said Sarah fighting against the tears that formed.

"He ought to give you a medal," said Crystal.

From out of the darkness a man screamed, "Put your weapon's down. Don't move a muscle." The man ran into the circle of dim light, fell to one knee and pointed a pistol in an outstretched hand at the women. He wore a blue vest and a matching baseball cap that had FBI printed across its front. He wore night vision goggles over his eyes.

"Hands on your head," said a woman running into the light with a revolver in her hand. Her outfit looked exactly like the man's. "Don't move! We're the FBI."

CHAPTER FORTY-ONE

The smell of burning wood and paint grew stronger by the second and Matt knew they had little time to get everyone outside before the noxious fumes would overcome them, trapping all inside the inferno.

Faint light trickled into the dark sanctuary through the open double doors in the front of the building. When the mass of panicking humanity started pushing in that direction, Matt thought he heard Leaky shouting and trying to direct everybody outside through the main entrance.

Just as soon as the first group reached the open doors, a series of shotgun blasts exploded sending shotgun pellets inside. The congregation screamed in renewed hysteria and fled back into the building. Matt could hardly see a thing, but he could tell that some people had fallen and now lay in the doorway. With horror, he realized the guards now kept everyone inside, trapped within the burning building.

Matt turned and took several steps toward the backdoor when shotguns erupted in that direction. A few of the church members stumbled back inside from there. Now everybody pinned in the sanctuary had to decide their manner of dying—a flesh-ripping bullet or burning to death.

With fumbling fingers, Matt reached inside his breast pocket and grabbed the cell phone. In the dark, he frantically hunted for the send button with his finger.

When he touched the phone's face, its green light appeared showing Matt its symbols. He pressed SND, placed the phone to his ear, and started counting the rings.

On the fifth ring, his head almost ready to explode from anger, someone answered, "Agent Ward here."

"This is Matt Fagan," Matt yelled into the phone.

"What the hell's going on in there?"

"Where the hell are you? You've got to come in here now, and…turn the damn electricity back on, and."

"Calm down, Mister Fagan we'll…."

"Listen to me Agent Ward," Matt screamed. "We don't have any time. We're trapped in the sanctuary and it's on fire. They won't let the people out and…"

"Where's the sanctuary?"

"Dammit, man!" Matt screamed. "Find the building on fire. The one the guards have surrounded. Dammit man, they're shooting through the doors. Agent

Ware, get in here now, or hundreds are going to be cooked on national TV. The building's on fuckin' fire!"

The line went dead. The smell of smoke grew overpowering. The left side of the room turned red from the flames fighting their way through the wall from the outside.

Matt hit the SND button on the cell phone. On the third ring the lights overhead flickered. Just as he looked up at them they turned bright burning his eyes. On the seventh ring, Matt dropped the phone.

People, young and old, male and female huddled together on the floor waiting to die. As sheep led to slaughter, they accepted their fate, their death, without a fight. At least five people lay in the front double doors bleeding. One woman moaned faintly while the others lay there motionless.

The white surging smoke filling the rafters of the building looked like boiling fog.

Emmanuel, his eyes closed, groaned and made a rasping noise as he gasped for air. His neck, swollen as large as his head, had turned a bluish-green. The huge rattlesnake that had bitten Emmanuel coiled next to the man's leg protecting its prize.

Searching the room for Leaky, Matt found his friend only five feet away crouching just below the platform with the Remington in his hand. The lights went out but the light from the fire now filled the room with a red glow.

A crackling, popping sound erupted from the smoldering wall. Flames jumped inside and leaped to the top of the open ceiling with a roaring noise. People finally began to stir. Some stood.

Matt cupped his hands around his mouth like a megaphone and bellowed, "Stay calm, help's on the way. Stay calm." Matt coughed. The smoke moved down from the ceiling.

Through the crackling of fire and the screams of people, Matt detected the sounds of weapons firing outside the building.

"Come on, Leaky," he said, grabbing the shotgun he'd propped against the podium and jumping off the stage toward the double doors.

"Wait," said Leaky over the roar of flames.

As Matt raced to the front doors, someone hit him in his lower back, wrapped their arms around his waist and wrestled him to the floor.

"What're you doing?" Matt yelled when he rolled over to see Leaky holding him down.

"Get those overalls off," said Leaky. "You look like one of those guards. And get rid of that shotgun before we go out there."

Matt understood. When the FBI saw him charging through the doors dressed like a guard and carrying a weapon, they'd fire at him without asking questions.

Many of the people started coughing. Matt's eyes and lungs burned from the smoke that had dropped from the rafters and started covering the room.

Matt started jerking the blue coverall off with Leaky's help but panicked when they wouldn't go over his boots.

"Sit down," said Leaky.

Matt fell on his back and Leaky yanked one of his boots off, then the other. Matt kicked out of the coveralls.

"Come on!" Matt screamed at the people. "Let's go!"

Through the thickening, boiling smoke Matt saw that they didn't move but stayed huddled together on the floor.

"Come on," Matt screamed again and pointed toward the exit.

Nobody moved, they just stared at him with blank eyes. Matt raced blindly through the thick haze toward the stage. There he found the microphone and prayed the power would stay on.

"Everyone," he said between short breaths. "Follow me out...Get up and get out...It's safe, the FBI..." he couldn't finish because smoke instead of oxygen had filled his lungs. Matt started coughing. Dizziness quickly overcame him, and he fell sideways off the stage onto the wooden floor. He fought for clean air, but his lungs felt full of smoke.

Matt's legs went numb, and with horror he realized he couldn't save himself. He fought to stay conscious. Matt felt someone grab him by the arm and started pulling him toward the door.

"Help me!" screamed Leaky dragging Matt through the choking fumes.

As Matt grew weaker, another person grabbed his other arm and they continued pulling him toward the door, until a mass of hands lifted Matt from the floor. In seconds, they poured outside into the cool night air.

That's when Matt slipped into a deep murkiness. His body drifted into darkness.

"Matt," someone sounding like Leaky said from the depths of Matt's mind forcing him back. Somewhere he heard Leaky beckoning his return. Dim lights like stars spun overhead and warmth enveloped Matt. He relaxed. He just wanted to sleep. The darkness returned.

"Dammit, Matt," said Leaky slapping Matt's face. "Breathe, I don't wantta have to do this."

Warm air filled Matt's lungs. Bright lights formed before his eyes. Again, warm air filled his lungs. With heavy lids, Matt forced his eyes to open slightly. Over him, Matt saw a black shadow.

Matt coughed. His lungs burned like they, too, had caught fire. He sucked in cold air and his coughing started again.

"There you go," said Leaky, holding Matt's nose clamped shut with his fingers. Leaky then bent over Matt and started to place his lips across his mouth again, but Matt weakly pushed him away.

"What are…" Matt started to say before he started coughing again. When Matt finally stopped hacking, he looked at a smiling Leaky and realized what his friend had just done for him.

"You're going to be okay," said Leaky grinning.

"The others?" Matt whispered. A huge red fire burned close to them. He could feel its warmth and see its giant red glow squirming in the trees overhead.

"They came out," said Leaky. "They came out carrying you."

Matt glanced behind them. Hordes of people, the congregation, stood staring at him with wide eyes—eyes that showed affection, love. Matt turned to Leaky. "Emmanuel?"

"No. I don't think he got out."

A young man dressed in a navy-blue vest and matching cap with FBI embroidered in yellow across its front knelt next to Leaky and Matt. "Either one of you know a Matt Fagan?"

"Yeah," said Leaky pointing at Matt. "This ugly guy right here's him."

The man stood and yelled, "Agent Ward. Agent Ward, here he is!"

With Leaky's assistance, Matt rose to a sitting position in the damp leaves. His head spun like he'd drunk too many beers. A middle-aged black man dressed the same as the younger FBI agent trotted toward them.

"You Matt Fagan?" said the man as he approached.

"Yes sir, Agent Ward," Matt said recognizing the man's voice. "Where the hell have you been?"

"It good to see you, too," said Ward, squeezing Matt's hand and shaking it long and hard. He grinned. "I don't know how we'll ever repay you."

"Not to worry," Matt said.

"By the way," said Ward, "there's some women over here we found next to the river who've been asking about you."

"They okay?" Matt asked.

"Yeah," said Ward. "The older one's got a little cut on her head, but she won't let them take her to the hospital until she sees that you're all right. She's really worried about you. That your wife or something."

"No, no," Matt said.

"I don't know what you got," said Ward, "but there's a young white girl and a beautiful Afro-American woman wanting to see you, too."

Matt looked up at Leaky, smiled and held out his right hand—a hand not swollen nor in pain because the bones of his knuckles had prevented the snake's fangs from penetrating enough to release the venom. "Help me off my ass. This old man ain't lost his charm yet."

"You better hurry before you do," said Leaky, laughing and pulling Matt to his feet.

"Never."

ABOUT THE AUTHOR

David Cady grew up in Northeast Georgia not far from the Tennessee River and Raccoon Mountain where this story *The Handler* is set. He earned his undergraduate degree from Middle Tennessee State University and his master's degree from the University of Georgia in Athens. He lives with his wife, Cindy, in Dalton Georgia. He is the author of one other novel and many short stories.

2553891

Made in the USA